Light in a Dark Place

Laura HERVEY

Alabaster Box Press

Text copyright © 2019 by Laura Hervey
Alabaster Box Press
Akron, New York

Cover design and title page designed by Paper and Sage Design

ISBN 978-1-7325187-7-3 Trade
ISBN 978-1-7325187-6-6 POD
ISBN 978-1-7325187-5-9 e-book
Library of Congress Control Number: 2019913767

Printed in the United States of America

Dedication

To every person who has ever struggled with addiction and to those who love them.

Acknowledgements

Without the expertise and encouragement of my faithful critique partners, Gloria Clover and Linda Turner, this book might never have been completed. To both, I owe a debt of gratitude. Special thanks goes to my four beta readers, Valerie Ramos, Jeanne Fuller, Sarah Rizzo, and Pat Means.

CHAPTER ONE

Abby Collins piled wet clothes directly from the washer into the dryer, draped her mother's blue cashmere sweater over the empty laundry basket, and tossed in the last of the delicate load. Then she dumped the basket of darks into the washer and started the "permanent press" cycle. She should spread the sweater over a clean towel on the laundry room table, but her boyfriend had been texting her for hours, distracting her from her chores and her homework. Good thing her parents both worked full-time. Neither of them had time to check parent portal. They had no idea she was failing Physics and Economics. *That* worry was a minor issue though. If she buckled down, she could bring her grades up before report cards came out in a month. She'd done it before. If only Luke would give her a minute to breathe. If only she could muster up enough energy to do more than the minimum required each day.

In her jeans' pocket, her phone vibrated for the third time in five minutes. Abby shoved her hand in and easily retrieved her cell. How had she lost so much weight that her favorite jeans were sliding down her hips? Had she remembered to eat today? She'd overslept, dashing out of the house without making a lunch or even grabbing a banana. The cafeteria food turned her stomach. Lately. Today, she'd almost had to cover her nose while her friends, Lisa and Megan, enjoyed taco-in-a-bag, one of Abby's favorites. She'd ignored Lisa's suspicious look and steered the conversation to tomorrow's Economics test.

Feeling lightheaded, Abby headed up the carpeted basement stairs and into the spotless kitchen. The clock on the stove read 7:35—ten minutes later than the actual time, which was her mother's strategy to ensure that every member of the Collins family was infallibly punctual. It worked for Mom, but the rest of them remembered to subtract ten minutes or to ignore the kitchen clocks altogether. Since Mom invariably left the house long before anyone else, she never suspected that her fool proof plan failed miserably. Abby and Sam complied with Dad's strict orders not to tell Mom that he drove Sam to school at least once every other week. In some ways, Dad was much easier to please than Mom, but both of them freaked out whenever Luke's name came up. Abby didn't like lying to her parents, but she disliked conflict even more. So she let them believe what they wanted to believe—that she'd broken up with Luke at the end of the summer.

This wasn't the senior year she'd imagined for herself. She was almost as disappointed in Luke as his parents were, though she would never let him know that. Not when her faith in him could help him get out of the mess he was in.

Hungry at last, she lifted the lid on the slow cooker. Mom's simmering chili wafted to Abby's nose. Her hand flew to her mouth, her fingers blocking out the nasty smell. Abby frowned, instantly replacing the lid, slamming shut *that* door. She grabbed an apple from the fruit bowl on the spotless counter, took a bite, put in her password, and opened Luke's latest message. "Where are you? I need you now."

Ugh! He expected her to drop everything, get in her silver Mustang, and drive across town to his dingy, upper level apartment that always reeked of weed and spoiled food. If her boyfriend or his roommate ever cleaned, Abby had never seen the evidence. Cleaning up after two sloppy guys was *not* part of her definition of a good girlfriend. She shook her head. When was the last time Luke gave any thought to being a good boyfriend? A second glance at his demanding message irked her even more.

"Can't," she texted back. "Babysitting my brother." She set her phone down, rinsed the bowl Sam had left in the sink, added it to the dirty dishes in the dishwasher, and started the "pots and pans" cycle. At least he had eaten. Neglecting her little brother was high on Dad's "you're-grounded list." Luke would flip if Abby got grounded.

Her phone vibrated on the marble countertop, signaling another text. "Leave him. You'll be back before your parents get home."

Bile surged up her throat and into her mouth. She tossed the half-eaten apple into the trash. How could Luke expect her to leave her eight-year-old brother alone? Her boyfriend was high. Or worse coming down and craving another fix. She'd seen that hunted, haunted look in his eyes for the past year, ever since his doctor had refused to give him another script for the oxy he'd been taking since he'd blown his meniscus in the Homecoming game his senior year. His promises to get clean meant nothing. She rubbed her hand over her flat stomach and released a whoosh of air. Heading up to her room, she keyed in one word. "No."

Seconds later, her phone rang. Luke's smiling face appeared on her screen. Abby might as well get it over with.

He wouldn't stop until she picked up. She was in no mood to fight with him tonight. Not after the test. Suddenly finding it hard to draw in enough air, she swiped the green icon, connecting the call. "I can't leave Sam." The words tumbled from her trembling lips. "He's only eight. He wouldn't know what to do in an emergency."

"Abby, honey, I wouldn't ask unless—"

"I can't come over there. I won't." Dreading what would come next, she froze at the top of the stairs, gripped the railing, then forced her feet to move across the hardwood floor of the hall.

"Babe, I just need a little money."

A quiet desperation laced his plea, one she'd heard too often. Last week, he'd been fired again, this time from his job as a stock-person at Wegmans. She cringed, knowing what he'd say before he even asked.

"Whatever you can get from the ATM."

She'd already depleted her college fund by over a thousand dollars. If she withdrew anymore, someone was bound to notice. "You promised." Abby hated the whine in her plea. Why should she beg as if she were asking *him* to do something unreasonable? Tears pricked her eyes, then streaked her cheeks. "I love you, Luke. But I can't do this anymore."

"Then get in your car and come over. We'll have the apartment to ourselves."

Longing, resentment, and grief warred in her heart. The words she needed to say clogged her throat, cutting off her oxygen. Her knees buckled. Was she going to faint? Right here in the upstairs hallway with Sam doing his homework in his bedroom two doors down the hall? "Until you're clean, please don't call me anymore."

A nervous laugh was his first reply. "Babe, you've said

that before. More times than I can count. We're meant to be together. The minute I bumped into you outside Chem lab I knew you were the only girl for me."

The image of that day was permanently imprinted in Abby's mind. Luke Bradford's mesmerizing eyes, blue with flecks of silvery gray, had captivated her even before he flashed his flawless smile and lifted a lock of her poker-straight, brown hair over her shoulder. Heat flooded her face, and she willed herself not to tremble as shivers of awareness skittered through her. His first touch, tender and possessive, suspended every thought but one. Easton's gorgeous quarterback was talking to her, the girl most likely to *not* get invited to the prom. Or anywhere else for that matter.

From that day, they'd been inseparable, though she'd been only a sophomore. Until Luke's graduation when he'd met Cole Marchman.

Abby swiped at her tears, nearly dropping her phone. *God, give me courage.* "It's over, Luke. Getting high means more to you than I do."

"How can you say that?"

The hurt in his voice pulled her into the circle of his dark world, a world in which her love was the only light.

"Abby, are you still there?"

"I'm here, but I—"

"You know I love you, babe. I've never loved anyone the way I love you."

She heard what he didn't say—that his parents didn't love him enough to stick with him. He expected—no needed her—to be different from them. Abby slid to the floor and hugged her knees to her chest. The paneled wall was solid behind her. At least she wouldn't faint. "I used to believe you. That you'd never lie to me, Luke."

"I didn't lie. When I say I'm going to quit, I mean it."

She squelched the urge to hurl her phone into the wall. He was lying now. To himself and to her. With every fiber of her being, she wanted to be wrong. "You don't see yourself the way I see you. Nothing matters to you anymore."

"You're not serious." He laughed, but she heard his fear.

"I've never been more serious in my entire life. If you ever loved me at all, if you remember how we used to be, please don't call me or try to see me." Each word felt like she was ripping her heart out with her own hands.

She disconnected the call before he could reply. Before she could change her mind. She'd said what needed to be said. His answer didn't matter. It would take more than empty words to convince her to give him another chance. They were done.

Now all she had to do was figure out how she was going to tell her parents she was carrying Luke's baby.

She was still crying when her brother's small hand gripped her shoulder. Why hadn't she had the sense to get up, go to her room, and shut the door? At least then she'd have had thirty seconds to compose herself before her nosy brother turned into Sherlock Holmes.

"What's wrong with you? I've been talking to you, and you didn't answer."

Abby scooted away from Sam's touch, pressed her fingertips against her eyes, then dragged her fingers over her face to erase the tears. Forcing a smile, she met his probing gaze with what she hoped was a confident look. "I didn't hear you. I was on the phone."

Sam towered over her, his expression of disbelief reminding her of Dad's annoying ability to read her when she most wanted to hide her thoughts. It didn't help that Sam looked exactly like Dad had at that age. Abby stifled a groan. Sitting on the floor put her at a disadvantage. She stood, hoping to remind him that she was the big sister, the one who was supposed to take care of him, not the other way around.

Her brother made a face like he'd eaten a bad strawberry. "You were talking to Luke."

She was tempted to lie. He was just a kid. He wouldn't understand, and even if he could, what was happening with Luke was nobody's business but theirs. And nobody could help because Luke didn't want help.

Sam reached for her arm and patted her as if she were the younger sibling. So much for standing up tall.

"If he makes you cry, why don't you break up with him?"

Narrowing her eyes, she stared at him like he was crazy. "What are you talking about? Luke and I broke up two months ago." The lie pinched her conscience. Was God mad at her for lying about breaking up with Luke? For sleeping with him? After that first time, Luke had convinced her that it didn't matter because they were going to get married after college anyway. Clearly, it did matter, because now, she was pregnant and unmarried. "It's none of your business anyway, Sam."

Hurt followed by steely determination erased the boyish gleam in her brother's green eyes. "I see things, Abby. I hear things, too. Luke never used to make you cry. Not when he was home with his parents."

That was true. But Sam couldn't possibly know why. Unless … unless kids at school were talking. Luke's brother, Joe, was two years older than Sam. Surely, Joe didn't know his brother was …. Abby pressed her lips tightly together. What could she say to get out of this conversation? She and Luke might not be together anymore, but she wouldn't betray him. "Do you need help with your homework?"

"My homework's done. We're not talking about me. Ever

since Luke moved out, he makes you sad. Mom and Dad might not know what's going on, but I do."

She shook her head, then tried for a quizzical expression that said she had no idea what he was talking about.

"I hear you crying in your room."

Arguing with Sam would only convince him he was right. "Are you sure you finished all of your homework? There's still some chocolate peanut butter pie in the fridge if you're hungry."

"Yeah. I checked my agenda. Everything's done, and I even put the clothes in the dryer for Mom."

"You didn't. When? How long ago?"

Sam scrunched his eyebrows together. "Um. Ten minutes ago. Why?"

Abby whirled in the direction of the laundry room.

As she barreled down the stairs, Sam called out, "Can I still have pie?"

"Get it yourself."

Praying Mom's sweater wasn't ruined, Abby flung open the dryer door. She'd been doing the laundry for the past two years. She knew what couldn't go in the dryer. Sam definitely did not know. Why was he helping with the laundry anyway? Frantic, she tossed shirts, pants, and socks out of the hot drum without caring whether the clothes ended up in the basket or on the floor. Finally, her hand closed around the soft, damp cashmere. She held the blue v-neck up to the light. Were the sleeves shorter? Maybe a little gentle stretching would repair the damage caused by the dryer's heat. Mom could replace the sweater, but Grandma had brought this one back from Scotland on her last trip, two months before she'd died of breast cancer. If the sweater was ruined, Mom would be heartbroken. Abby couldn't let that happen.

She spent the next fifteen minutes blocking out the sweater the way Grandma had taught her. Then Abby held it against her body, examining the length and width. She adjusted both sleeves, too. She and Mom wore the same size. Satisfied that she'd avoided disaster, Abby gently placed the sweater back on the towel and went upstairs to study for her Economics test.

By ten o'clock, she was fighting sleep, reading the same paragraphs over three or four times, and jerking her head up so often her neck hurt. What was Luke doing? Had he found somebody to give him some money? Hopefully not. Then maybe he really would quit. She took one last look at her phone. Luke had sent three new texts. She couldn't bear to open them. Not tonight. She turned back the covers, lay down without getting out of her clothes or brushing her teeth, and cried herself to sleep.

*

Abby frowned at Luke and reached for their baby girl, intending to lift the whimpering infant from Luke's arms into her own. But Luke spun 180 degrees and strode off in the direction of his apartment building.

"Wait! Wait for me." She couldn't let him take their daughter into that smoke-infested apartment. Babies could get high off second-hand smoke, couldn't they?

Panic surged in her veins. Abby sat bolt upright, her eyes struggling to focus in the dim morning light of her bedroom. Rain pattered on the roof and pelted the windows.

She wrapped her arms around her barely rounded stomach in a belated attempt to protect her child. "It was only a dream."

Not a dream. A nightmare. What a way to start the weekend.

She retrieved her phone from the nightstand, put in her

code, and checked her text messages. Two from Lisa, one from Megan, and five more from Luke. She missed him. Not answering his texts for the past three days was only postponing the inevitable. She had to tell him in person about the baby.

Today.

Hiding the truth from everyone was exhausting. Being pregnant and what it would mean for her future was all she thought about. Focusing on her schoolwork was a joke. If she hadn't taken pictures of Lisa's notes, she'd have failed at least two quizzes this week.

She missed Luke. Cuddling in his arms. Losing herself in his eyes. Forgetting everything but being together. If only she could turn back the clock. Could she have done something to keep him from playing in that game? Definitely not. No one could have predicted the horrible accident that changed their lives forever.

She wanted to be with Luke. Even now. Especially now that she was having his baby. Before the two blue lines confirmed her pregnancy, she had imagined them getting married after college. They'd have three, maybe four kids, a Labrador retriever, and a pretty house in the country. But that wasn't going to happen. Luke hadn't officially dropped out of college, but UB took academic probation seriously, didn't they? Maybe if his parents intervened. The Bradfords were proud alums, and their substantial financial contributions to the University of Buffalo certainly should give Luke some special treatment, but did those privileges include an extension on a well-deserved academic probation? Luke had failed three classes his first semester and one his second semester. How many was he failing now? She wanted to shake some sense into him. Hopefully, her news about the baby would do just that.

*

A knock startled Luke awake. He stumbled out of bed, his right leg tangling in the blankets he'd piled on his bed to keep warm. The late October night had dipped below 30° F—too cold to do without heat, but Cole insisted they leave the furnace off until the end of the month. Money was tight, and since the gas bill was in Cole's name, Luke complied. But not without regular surges of resentment, sometimes against his parents, often against Cole.

Luke shivered into the hoodie he'd tossed on the chair yesterday and made his way to the door. Trained to screen for unwelcome "visitors," he peered through the hole in the door. Abby? His heart sped up.

He hadn't expected to see her so soon. She usually punished him for four, sometimes five days before she would come around. Her cutting disappointment in him echoed in his brain, but he ran his fingers through his hair in an attempt to look somewhat presentable. Then he pasted on a welcoming smile. Maybe they could pretend everything was okay with them. If he could get her into his bedroom, she'd soon forget about breaking up with him. He'd never had any complaints in that department. Except ... no, that was just a fluke. He'd been too high. That was all.

He swung open the door, intending to pull her into a hug, but her tear-streaked, red-splotched face turned his arms to lead hanging limply at his sides. Her lips were pressed tight together, but the lower one trembled the way it always did when she was trying not to cry. Asking her what was wrong was sure to open the floodgates. Prickles of anxiety snaked up his spine. He had a couple of oxies in his pants pocket. Too late to take one now. Abby would flip.

He brushed a kiss across her lips. She stiffened. Not a good sign. "Good morning."

She didn't respond. Apparently, she hadn't forgiven him yet.

Her eyes were red, her pupils constricted to pinpoints. "I hate you." She gulped back a sob. "For what you're doing to us."

His fingers grazed her cheek in a feeble attempt to brush away the tears that began again in full force. "Don't cry, babe. I promised you I'd quit everything, and I will, soon. I've got another job interview Monday morning after Math class."

The bleak expression in her eyes accused him of lying. He couldn't blame her. Skipping work and classes had become his MO, but he had no intention of messing up this job like he'd messed up the last two. "Mom set up an interview at Abercrombie. They're hiring Christmas help."

Abby fished in her jacket pocket, pulled out a clump of folded tissues, and blew her nose. "You look like an Abercrombie model. Or at least you did. Before."

He wanted to argue that point, but fighting with her wouldn't accomplish his purpose. He took her hand and led her into the kitchen. The smell of burned coffee assaulted his nose, and he poured the thickened brew over the mound of dirty dishes, hoping the drain wasn't clogged again. "I'll make a fresh pot."

Abby didn't reply. Ignoring the tension between them, Luke stuffed a coffee filter into the basket, dumped in the last of the ground coffee, added water to the chamber, and started the brew cycle. Her continued silence rankled him. Why couldn't she make it easier on him?

"I'm sorry about the other night," he said with his back to her. He put two slices of wheat bread in the toaster and waited until the coils glowed red to make sure it was working before turning to see Abby slumped over the kitchen table, her head in her hands. He folded his body over her rounded back and kissed her cheek. "I love you, babe." He cupped her chin so that she had to look at him. "Please don't cry anymore. You know I can't stand to see you hurt like this."

Abby squeezed her eyes shut, then opened them, her accusing gaze boring into him. Her lower lip trembled again. "I'm ... I ... I'm pregnant, Luke."

Shock coursed through him like a toxic hit of bad junk. Hadn't they been careful?

Every single time.

Except that night she'd gotten the news about her grandmother. They'd been safe the first time but not the second. When he'd awakened to her cold tears against his chest, her soft sobs tore at his heart. Comforting her was all that mattered.

Obviously, he'd been wrong. His mind scrambled for an easy way out of this disaster. Abby was pro-life. She'd never consider having an abortion. She'd hate him if he even said the word. Getting married wasn't an option. He couldn't even support himself.

Or his habit. Self-loathing short-circuited his thoughts, and he fingered the oxies in his pocket. Abby was the planner in their relationship. But they hadn't planned for this. And she certainly hadn't planned for him to be MIA every time she needed him.

"What do you want to do?"

"What do *I* want to do?" Her eyes shot daggers at him. "This is *our* problem, Luke Bradford. Yours and mine."

He squelched the urge to get defensive. "I only meant ... you know what I meant." His fingers closed around the plastic zip bag of pills in his sweat pants pocket. Could he swallow a couple without her noticing? Probably not.

The toast popped up. He spread peanut butter on both slices, watched it melt, and added a squirt of honey to each piece. Stalling, he swirled the honey until it blended into a glistening, sticky layer. Then, as an afterthought, he grabbed a second paper towel and sat across from Abby. He slid a piece of toast to her. "Are you hungry?"

*

Luke was trying. He'd been trying, or so he'd claimed for over a year.

And now she was pregnant.

It wasn't altogether his fault. Abby had known they were taking a huge risk having sex that night. Ever since she'd made up her mind to be with Luke, she'd kept track of her cycles. She didn't want to take the pill, and he was conscientious. Except the night her grandmother died. Abby had dismissed the nagging thought that she'd ovulated a few days before. She'd give anything to go back and redo that night. If only she'd gone home after the first time instead of falling asleep with his arm tucked around her, his heart beating a steady assurance in her ear that she would get through the grief of losing the one person Abby could talk to about anything. Now the grief of losing her future threatened to drown her. She wanted, no needed, Luke to be strong for her. A tight pain in her chest screamed he would fail her again. She clenched her hands together in her lap, staring vacantly at the coffee mug near to overflowing, and refused to meet his eyes.

"Are you going to eat that?" he asked his tone devoid of emotion.

Frustrated that she couldn't read him, she slid the toast back to him. "I haven't been hungry." Almost on signal, a wave of nausea rumbled in her gut. "Do you have any crackers?"

He shook his head. He'd eaten all of the crackers last night to ease his stomach cramps until Cole got home with a new supply. "I'll make you some dry toast."

She swallowed hard. "Okay."

He smiled, but nothing was okay.

His own food forgotten, he hurried to do this small thing for her. What had she expected him to say? She'd had 24 hours to wrap her head around the reality of her pregnancy. The test had been positive almost instantly. All three times. She'd wanted the first test to be wrong, and even dared to hope that the second test was defective, but the third test confirmed what she'd known for the last three weeks. She and Luke were going to have a baby, and there'd be no turning back the clock for either of them.

He handed her the browned toast, and she bit off a corner and forced herself to chew.

"Have you told your parents?"

Abby swallowed past the cardboard lump of toast lodged in her throat. She choked once, praying she wouldn't be sick. She sipped her coffee until she could speak, but she suddenly had no idea what to say. This was a nightmare she'd brought on herself, and her parents would be … horrified? Horribly disappointed? Ashamed of her? Angry enough to …. She shuddered, not wanting to speculate another second.

She shook her head and took a tiny bite of the toast.

Luke downed the rest of his coffee, waiting for her, expecting to follow her lead.

But she had no idea what to do. If her grandmother were still alive, Abby would have confided her suspicions even before the drugstore test confirmed her pregnancy. If Grandma were here, Abby wouldn't be going through this alone.

Talking to her other grandparents was impossible and foolish. Grandma and Grandpa Collins would betray her confidence within a day. Their loyalty was not to their granddaughter but to their son.

Luke reached for her hand. She flinched and pulled away, but not before his fingers grazed hers, reminding her of how much she missed him. But that didn't matter. The sweetness of being together couldn't possibly staunch the apprehension pulsing through her veins now that she had finally said the words, "I'm pregnant," out loud.

"Do you want me to go with you when you tell your mom and dad?"

Did she? If he were clean, his reassuring presence would bolster her courage. As it was, Luke was the last person her parents would expect to see in their house. Seeing her boyfriend would set her father's teeth on edge, and she needed Dad on her side. "That's not a good idea."

Luke frowned, his brows knitting together. "Are you sure?"

She resisted the urge to squirm, to avoid his questioning eyes. Why hadn't she told him before that she'd been lying to her parents? "They think we broke up Labor Day weekend."

He blinked twice, his grip so tight on the coffee mug that the veins on the back of his hands swelled into blue ridges. "You were ashamed of me." His voice was flat, emotionless.

But the hurt and anger in his eyes were unmistakable.

This time she reached for him, but he jerked away. "Try to understand, Luke. When your parents kicked you out, your mom called mine that same day. Dad forbade me to see you. He ..." She hesitated. How would Luke react if she told him everything? Would he hate her dad?

"He what, Abby?"

"He said he wouldn't stand for his daughter dating a drug addict. He wouldn't help me pay for college unless I promised to stop seeing you."

"What else?"

"He was going to sell my car. I would have had no way to see you." Abby's stomach clenched with nausea. "It was easier to let them believe that we'd already split up after our fight at the barbecue. Everyone heard us screaming at each other."

Luke raked his hand through his hair and chewed his lower lip. "So you told them it was already over." A sad expression stole the light from his eyes, then the anger returned. "Couples fight, Abby. That doesn't mean they're going to split up."

She refrained from telling him that sometimes it meant they should move on. She was tired of lying to Luke and to her parents. "I planned to break up with you, but you changed my mind." Heat flooded her cheeks, and she cursed her pale complexion.

Luke grinned. "I remember."

She remembered, too, though admitting it now would take this discussion in an entirely different direction. Luke's eyes held the promise of passion and comfort. But the anguish in her heart couldn't be eased by spending the morning in his arms. "I'm going to tell my parents next weekend. Probably Saturday. You'll want to tell your parents at the same time, unless you want them to hear it from Mom."

Luke exhaled. "They're not taking my calls."

Abby's stomach clenched in frustration. Surprisingly, she hadn't had to run to the bathroom. "Then go see them."

He shoved back from the table, the chair scraping against the dirty linoleum floor. He lurched to his feet, poured himself a second cup of coffee, and reached into his pocket. He swallowed one pill—she had no idea what—right in front of her. She wanted to shove his hand away from his mouth, slap his face, pound his chest, kick his shins. She did none of those things.

She buried her face in her hands and sobbed. Her baby's daddy was an addict, and she would have to raise their child alone. Unless she could bring herself to give the baby up. A closed adoption would mean never seeing her child after its birth. An open adoption would be worse, would lacerate her heart beyond repair.

Luke's hand on her shoulders repulsed her even as her senses awakened to him. His fingers moved down the length of her arms to her trembling hands. He pulled her to her feet and into his arms. She buried her face against his chest, ignoring the smell of weed that clung to his clothes.

"You're not alone, Abby." He cupped her chin until she met his gaze. "I'm not going to let you face your parents by yourself. Tell them whatever you want. That we're back together. That I'm in rehab. Whatever. Just so long as they don't kick me out of your house. I *am* going to be sitting right next to you when you tell them we're pregnant."

Oh, how she wanted her and Luke to be a "we." But it was her body that would swell beyond recognition. Her life that was going to change completely.

She wasn't even sure Luke would be able to change the one thing in his life that would convince her parents to let him anywhere near her. Or their baby.

CHAPTER TWO

An hour later, Abby was leaving without letting him make love to her, not that Luke hadn't tried. She wouldn't stop crying, so he'd finally resigned himself, disappointed that he had no comfort to give her. Instead, they'd sat together on the couch, her head on his shoulder and his hand stroking her silky hair until she dozed off. He'd lifted her in his arms, carried her to his bed, and covered her with several blankets. She looked so helpless, curled into the fetal position, her folded hands resting against her perfect mouth. The memory of their first kiss came like the arm rush of cocaine skittering just under his skin. Resisting the urge to crawl in bed beside her, if only to hold her in his arms, he'd headed back to the kitchen to wash the dishes and finish his online psychology homework.

Staring out the window as Abby backed her silver Mustang out of his driveway, Luke fought the panic crawling along his limbs. What had they done? She'd never be free of him now. And he was no good for her. The truth rocked him off the precarious precipice he'd teetered on for months. He wasn't going to become the man she deserved. If only he'd let her go that first time she caught him shooting up. He'd ignored the disdain followed by despair that dimmed the light in her beautiful blue eyes. Worse, he'd lied and said it was the only time he'd ever done heroin. She had believed him, and God help him, Luke needed her to keep believing him. Because he had already lost faith in himself. And maybe, in God, too.

Abby was right. He cared more about getting high than he did about making her happy. He had all but given up on making her proud of him. Their dreams for the future were a thin vapor dissipating in a stagnant fog of getting high and looking for ways to get up and stay up.

And now she was pregnant. Abby's sense of honor would prevent her from ever shutting him out of their child's life, but Luke had nothing of value to offer her or their baby.

Not unless he could free himself from his addiction. But what was he addicted to? Heroin? Oxies? Valium? Pot? The truth burned a path in his brain. He would never get clean without help, and as soon as she told her parents about the baby, Abby's dad would do anything and everything to ensure that Luke never got within 50 feet of Raymond Collins' only daughter.

Despair pounded in his ears. Loser. Junkie. She's better off without you. She'll meet someone else. A better man. One she can count on. One who would put her and the baby first.

But the thought of another guy raising his kid sucked the air from his lungs. Another guy would hold Abby in his arms and wake up to her smile. Luke couldn't let that happen.

He slammed his fist on the table, sending his laptop careening to the floor. He caught it inches from disaster, his shaky hands yanking the computer into his lap. He cursed. Abby would be better off without him, but he would *not* be better off without her.

He would change. He could do it for her. He had to.

He opened the laptop, navigated to the web browser, and typed "drug rehab" into the search bar. Over four million options popped up in less than ten seconds. He added the words "in western New York" and hit "search" again. Luke drew in a sharp breath. Still millions of results. How was that possible? He scrolled down until he found webpages that offered lists of under thirty local rehab programs. He had no idea there were so many rehabs in the Buffalo area. He opened a few websites, but none of them provided more than basic information. The longer he searched, the more the descriptions blurred together. The only distinguishing factor was whether the program was inpatient or outpatient. No way was he signing up for an inpatient program. Even if it was voluntary. The restrictions would suffocate him, which would make him need his drugs more.

Besides, he needed to be available for Abby. And he couldn't do that if he was stuck in some 30-day, 24-7 detox facility.

Did he really need something that structured? Maybe he could attend a few Narcotics Anonymous meetings, go someplace where no one knew him, where he could sit in, listen, and absorb a few tricks that would help him clean up his life enough to satisfy Ray Collins. Abby's dad was no slouch when it came to his only daughter's well-being, but surely he wouldn't go to all of the trouble of checking up on Luke's attendance at NA.

Luke spent the next thirty minutes exploring their website. The group operated much like AA. He scribbled down the addresses and meeting times for several nearby groups.

To reassure Abby that he meant his promise to quit, Luke would go to as many NA meetings as it took. As it took to what? Persuade her that he was on the right track? Fear snaked viselike around his lungs. What if he couldn't quit? He wanted to try. He had to try for her. If he could swallow the sob stories and all of the drugs-will-ruin-your-life rhetoric, maybe he could attend regular meetings. Did NA have sponsors like AA? Luke cringed at the thought of another guy knowing his personal business.

Maybe Abby would want to come to a meeting with him. He couldn't even imagine exposing her to all those seamy details. His face burned with the shame of it all. No. Abby didn't need to know.

Luke clenched and unclenched his fist to steady his jumpy nerves. He was fooling himself. He'd been trapped since that first rush of heroin zinged through his veins. The completely irrational thought that nothing bad had happened or could happen to him seemed not only reasonable but a deeply hidden truth he had only grasped with the help of the drug. Sure, he'd wanted to play quarterback in college, but he'd never been pro material. Not really. So it didn't matter that he'd screwed up his knee. He wasn't going to make a living as an athlete. That had never been the plan.

But what was the plan? Luke couldn't dredge up even a hint of a memory of a single goal beyond the basics. Food, shelter, Abby, drugs. He didn't want to think about what he would put first if he had to choose. She'd said he cared more about using than loving her. Was it true? It couldn't be.

The front door slammed, penetrating Luke's muddy thoughts. Cole was back.

"Hey, man, where are you?" his roommate hollered from the front room. The soft sound of feminine laughter drifted through the apartment.

Great. Not happening. Cole was always trying to hook Luke up with some girl. His roommate had no respect for

Abby. Luke knew that. Did she? Maybe that was why she couldn't stand Cole. The guy treated her like she was invisible because she refused every drug he'd ever offered her. Abby's answer was always the same. "I'm the designated driver."

"Yeah, right, you're more worried about your car than you are about Luke," Cole had spouted just last week. Luke had wanted to pound the guy, and he would have if Abby hadn't smiled and sloughed it off as if no one could possibly be that rude.

If he had somewhere else to live, he would have ditched Cole long ago.

Luke closed his math book and dropped the notebook and textbook into his backpack. The timer on his phone went off. Why had he set it? Brain fog eclipsed the answer. He dragged his hands through his hair, kneaded his temples, and ignored the queasy feeling roiling in his gut.

Cole grinned, his six-foot, four-inch frame filling the doorway. "I brought you a surprise."

Two giggles, followed by a low, "Shh!" penetrated Luke's confusion. It was Saturday. He didn't need to go to class. He was free for the rest of the day. Free to enjoy whatever Cole had brought home, as long as it didn't come with strings, strings that would break Abby's heart if she found out. Even if she didn't find out, Luke couldn't bear adding to the shame he already felt when their gazes locked. All of his secrets felt bare and open when his girl peered into his soul.

"Did you hear what I said, man?"

Luke shook his head, his eyes scanning the room, looking everywhere but at the two blondes peeking from behind Cole.

The twins, Jenna and Elena, slipped past his roommate, but he encircled each girl, tucking one under each arm. "The girls and me ..." Cole hesitated, his bright eyes measuring

Luke. "We made a little deal," he announced, obviously pleased with himself. He kissed first Jenna, then Elena. Just light pecks on their cheeks. Reminders that Cole intended to collect on their debts.

Luke glared at his roommate. "No offense, girls, but I'm not available."

The panic settling in their eyes made Luke flinch, but he couldn't back down.

Cole dropped a packet of white powder on the kitchen table. Luke's best friend and his worst enemy. The stuff was pure, purer than the brown they'd had earlier in the week, but Luke wasn't up for the kind of party Cole wanted. The girls didn't owe Luke anything. He averted his eyes, ignored the clenching cramp in his gut, and willed his feet to move, to take him out of the apartment and far away from the siren encased in a plastic zip bag.

*

Laden down with two bags of oversized tops and three pairs of jeans in a size larger than she normally wore, Abby slipped into the house and up the stairs without anyone accosting her. Because Mom had been out of town at some educator's conference, Abby had succeeded in avoiding her mother for over a week. Ever since she'd buried the positive test sticks at the bottom of the bathroom garbage bag, tied it, dropped it into a second bag, double knotted that, and carried her secret out to the trash can just before Sam hauled the garbage and recycling out to the street for pickup, Abby feared her secret was tattooed on her forehead. At mealtimes, she'd been unusually quiet, and when she had dared to meet her father's eyes, his expectant expression whispered that he knew something was wrong. She almost missed the all-day nausea. Her constant hunger was packing on pounds.

Terrified and relieved that the day had finally come

when she'd tell her parents the truth, she shifted her packages to her left arm and turned the knob of her bedroom door. The brass felt oddly warm, as if someone else ... Abby blinked, barely suppressing a gasp. Her mom squatted in front of the dresser, unloading a basket of folded laundry.

"Mom? What are you doing? I was going to take care of my clothes as soon as I got back from the mall." Hopefully, she didn't sound as frantic as she felt.

Breathe, Abby. Don't blow it.

Her mother didn't look up from the shirts, pajamas, and socks she was carefully stacking in Abby's drawers. Abby seized the opportunity to deposit her purchases in her closet. Mom was used to Abby's shopping habit, so she probably wouldn't ask any questions, but she might want Abby to model her new outfits. That wasn't happening. Even though big tops were trendy this season, she refused to give her mother a chance to guess her secret. Telling her parents together at four thirty, right before dinner, was still the best plan. Luke promised to be here by four fifteen, just so she wouldn't get nervous about him being late.

About him being too high to remember at all. An image of him passed out on the couch, the television blaring in his dingy apartment, chipped away at her faltering faith in her baby's daddy.

God, I need him here. He promised.

Abby stowed her bags out of sight, slid the door of her walk-in closet closed, then turned to her mom. "You didn't have to do that, but thanks."

Mom nodded. No smile. No reply. Her violet eyes measured Abby. "I went on parent portal this morning."

So that was it. Mom knew about her failing Physics and Economics. Abby wanted to sigh with relief. Instead, she manufactured what she hoped was a concerned, but apologetic demeanor. She let her chin drop, shook her head, sank to her bed, and without meeting her mother's gaze, said, "I'm so sorry, Mom. I messed up."

Her mother gripped her shoulders, her manicured fingernails exerting just enough pressure to send a clear message. Mom was seriously frustrated. How dare her straight-A daughter allow her grades to dip below the passing mark? "How did you let this happen? You're not still seeing Luke, are you? Even his parents aren't speaking to him."

Abby heard the unspoken, neither should you, loud and clear. She kept her face averted from her mother's scrutiny. Four thirty couldn't get here fast enough. Tears pricked against her eyelids. A cauldron of emotions threatened to spill over and ruin everything. She shook her head. She'd already accomplished that. After today, nothing in her life would ever be the same.

Absolutely nothing.

"No you're not seeing Luke?"

Had Abby said that? Oh. Yeah, she'd shaken her head, making her mother draw the wrong conclusion.

"Abigail Marie Collins, I asked you two questions."

Her mom's firm, but gentle tone magnified Abby's guilt. She swiped at the trails of moisture on her cheeks and raised her face to her mom. "I ... I wanted to get my grades back up. I missed two labs." She tucked her knees to her chest to hide her rounded stomach. "Mom, Economics is so boring. The textbook puts me to sleep."

Her normally composed mother bit her lower lip. "That's no excuse. You can't expect to like all of your classes. It's not realistic."

How was she supposed to reply to that? Abby would say practically anything to get her mother to leave her alone.

Texting Luke to make sure he was on his way was her top priority right now. "I'll stay after to make up my labs next week, and I'll ask Mr. Davies if I can do some extra credit for Econ."

Mom smoothed a strand of frosted hair that had escaped her signature French braid. "I can't promise you that your father won't ground you."

Abby almost laughed. Considering what she had to tell them today, being grounded seemed trivial. She had no idea how her parents were going to respond to her being pregnant. But she would not panic. They'd never reject her the way Luke's parents had him.

"Abby, what is wrong with you?"

She clenched her teeth together, then immediately relaxed her jaw, and forced herself to make eye contact. "Mom, will Dad be home by four?"

Suspicion flickered in her mom's eyes.

Abby rushed ahead, preventing any questions. "I need to talk to you both. Together. At four thirty. Before dinner. While Sam's still next door playing with Trey."

Mom nodded.

Satisfied that she'd concealed her fear, Abby added, "I want to talk about my plans for next year without Sam interrupting." That part, at least, was true. She definitely didn't want her brother in the room when she broke her parents' hearts.

*

Luke had tried to plan his day to keep just enough drugs in his system to stave off the panic that crashed through him every time he imagined her parents' reaction to Abby's pregnancy. The controlled rage he envisioned on Ray Collins' face convinced Luke to swallow the last oxycodone. He'd taken one this morning, but the effects were wearing off way too early. The steady calm he'd maintained up until lunch had disappeared as the numbers on his digital clock approached the time he would need to leave.

He cursed his own foolishness. He could have prevented this disaster. Should have. He had no one to blame but himself. Abby had been overwhelmed with grief over losing her grandma. He should have kept his head. If only they could turn back the clock. How far back would he go?

That was easy.

He'd say no when Dr. Mallory told him he was prescribing oxycodone for Luke's post-surgery pain. Everyone knew that stuff was highly addictive. Why on earth did doctors prescribe narcotics at all? It was Dr. Mallory's fault that ....

"NO!" The sound of himself shrieking like a girl rattled Luke. He stared at his reflection in the mirror on the far wall. His eyes looked too bright, a dead giveaway that he was using. Even if Abby's parents didn't catch on, she would know.

And be hurt.

Without even knocking, Cole thrust his head, shoulders, and upper body into Luke's room. "What's wrong with you, man? You need a hit of something to keep you steady?"

Did he? Probably not. "That's not a good idea."

"Why not? No sense of feeling bad when you could feel amazing." Cole held out his hand. Laying in his palm was a small packet of white powder and a rolled dollar bill. "Snow's exactly what you need to face your girlfriend's parents."

Luke scratched his arms. The itching was making him crazy. "How'd you know about that?"

Cole guffawed. "The walls in this apartment are thin as paper." Cole set the roll and the coke on Luke's desk. "I had my share. The rest is for you."

Luke raked his hands through his hair and tried to shake the desperation threatening to swallow up every sane thought in his head. He sucked in a slow, deep breath, and struggled to force a denial past his chapped lips. No words. Not a single "no" escaped.

Cole locked eyes with him.

Luke's fingers flinched.

His roommate wore a smug, satisfied expression. "That's what I thought," he declared and closed the door behind him.

Luke stared at the coke. Maybe it would help. Keep him alert. Zoning out driving over there, or worse during their conversation with her parents, would be a disaster.

Two straight lines later and his confidence soared. In a couple of hours, the dreaded conversation would be over. Of course, her parents would be hurt and angry. They'd probably insist she stop seeing him, but fathers had rights. They couldn't keep him away from his kid. Or Abby. Yeah, he had rights.

And responsibilities.

Responsibilities? Ticking off a mental list of all the baby would need, Luke stuffed his arms into his jacket. The sheer cost would have vaporized any hope he had of measuring up as a dad, if not for the sweet combination of oxy and coke keeping him on an even keel. Like always, Cole seemed to know exactly what Luke needed. All he had to do was cover his share of the rent each month, and his roommate kept Luke supplied with an assortment of drugs to supplement his prescription. At least, his doctor kept renewing the oxy script. The way Luke figured it, as long as he didn't blow through more pills than Dr. Mallory expected him to take, the man wouldn't suspect a thing. Abby would be furious if she found out Luke had been lying about the script. He hadn't planned to lie to her, but when she'd walked in on him shooting up, there'd been no other way to explain his using heroin.

He was rationalizing. He'd read enough about the thought patterns of addicts to know that much. But it didn't matter because he was going to get clean soon.

For sure before the baby came.

When was the baby due? Abby hadn't seen a doctor yet. That's why he didn't know the due date. He'd never forget something that important. Would he?

He reached into his jacket pocket for his gloves. A white index card fluttered to the floor. The times and locations of local NA meetings stared up at him. He hadn't gone to a single one. Who was he kidding? Going to NA would mean no more using. No drugs of any kind. Just the thought threatened to split his head wide open.

He resisted the urge to slam the apartment door. That couldn't have been very pure cocaine if it was wearing off already.

*

Abby stared at the digital clock on her nightstand. "4:25" glowed with mocking certainty. Luke wasn't coming. How could he do this to her? The boy she fell in love with would never have let her down. He'd changed into a self-centered, selfish addict. One who only *talked* about getting help. And she'd given him money, countless times, to pay for his drugs. She was an enabler, just like they'd learned in health class sophomore year. How on earth had she sunk so low?

No more. Her baby was her first priority. She couldn't help Luke. God knows, she'd tried, and look where that had gotten them. Nowhere good. That's for sure.

She sank to her knees beside her bed, willing herself not to cry. *God, help me tell my parents about the baby. Don't let them freak out on me. I don't think I could handle that.*

The sound of the doorbell pealed through the house, interrupting Abby's prayer. Luke! She had to get downstairs before Mom or Dad sent Luke away. Abby flung open her bedroom door and raced down the stairs in time to see Sam ushering her boyfriend inside.

"You hurt my sister, and I'm gonna hurt you." For eight, her brother sounded fiercely protective. Abby groaned at the ludicrousness of his threat.

Luke mumbled a reply that she couldn't catch.

"Just so we're clear," Sam warned, placing his small hands on Luke's chest and shoving him so hard he stumbled backward.

The startled look in Luke's eyes would have made her laugh if she weren't struggling so hard to keep from crying. Why hadn't Sam gone to Trey's? Mom knew that was the plan.

With pang of remorse, Abby acknowledged the truth. No matter how she tried to keep him out of things, her little brother was going to get drawn into the mess she'd made of her life. Nothing she could do would change that. Her mistake was going to affect every person she loved. Maybe, it was good that Grandma was gone. Abby swallowed the sob building in her throat and prayed for courage. Hesitating halfway down the stairs, she gripped the railing and offered Luke a tremulous smile.

"I'm sorry I'm late." His eyes met hers, pleading for her understanding. And shimmering with unnatural brilliance. He was on something.

Of course he was high. Did she actually think he could make it through this conversation without chemical assistance? His smile was too broad and altogether inappropriate given their situation.

She squelched her frustration. At least, he was here.

"That's okay. You aren't really late." She glanced at the designer watch on her wrist, the one her dad had given her when she'd aced the college entrance exams. 4:29. One minute until her life would blow up in her face. "I told Mom I wanted to talk at 4:30."

"Oh, yeah, you wanted me to get here early so you wouldn't have to worry about me ditching you."

He said it matter-of-factly, as though he'd gotten used to disappointing her, but she couldn't think about that now. His anxious expression raised her blood pressure. Maybe, she shouldn't have let him come. Her dad was going to be furious, angry that she'd defied him and continued to see Luke after his parents kicked him out. Angry that his baby girl was unmarried and pregnant.

How had she let this happen? All of her plans for attending college, becoming a teacher, and making a difference seemed impossible now. She was going to have a baby. No amount of wishing would make this pregnancy go away. There was only one way, and she wouldn't even consider that.

She needed a few minutes alone with Luke, needed for him to hold her so she didn't feel so alone. His gaze locked with hers, he reached for her, and she fell into his arms, breathing in his spicy cologne. "Thank you for coming, Luke. I—"

"I know, babe," he whispered in her ear, his warm breath stirring her hair and her senses.

Every part of her—heart, soul, mind, and body—responded to his nearness. It had been so long since she'd lain in his arms, lost in the wonder of their love. But that's what had gotten them into this mess in the first place. Her head knew the truth, but her heart and her body said they belonged together. She brushed a kiss across his lips then reluctantly wriggled out of his embrace. Her eyes narrowed in a weak rebuke, but he ignored her and pivoted to wink at her brother, who had remained in the foyer, his arms crossed over his chest and his feet spread wide in a stance that would have been funny had he not been so somber.

Her little brother had appointed himself her bodyguard. It was sweet, but entirely unnecessary. Disconcerted that she'd been totally oblivious to Sam's presence, Abby groused, "I thought you were going to Trey's."

Sam nodded, and for the first time, she noticed her brother wore his jacket.

"I was on my way out when the doorbell rang. Lucky for you and Luke that Dad didn't get to the door first."

Tempted to tell her brother to mind his own business, she thanked him instead, and Sam held his back a little straighter. "Happy to help."

After he left, Abby slipped her arm around Luke's waist. His ribcage poked against her hand. He'd gotten so thin, but she couldn't think about that now. "I didn't tell my parents you were coming."

Luke frowned, and his brow furrowed the way it always did when he didn't know what to expect.

At least his emotions hadn't flat-lined on her.

"Are you sure that was a good idea?" Luke's gaze shifted around the room.

Scoping out quick exit routes? *Oh, no, you don't, Luke Bradford.*

To ease both their tension, she kneaded his abs in a half tickle, half caress. He stepped out of her reach then immediately pulled her in for another hug. He cupped her chin, his eyes locking with hers, drawing her, making her almost forget what they had to do. His mouth covered hers, and she responded, reluctantly at first, then giving herself to a wave of gentle passion that eclipsed her panic, if only for a moment.

She pulled away first. It wouldn't help their case for either of her parents to find them making out in the hall. "Trust me, I know my dad. He'll hear us out at least."

"What are you going to tell them about your plans?" Alarm laced Luke's words and etched deep lines across his brow.

He looked older. Why hadn't she noticed what the drugs were doing to his face? Had she been deliberately blind, not wanting to believe there were any long-term effects? "Only that I'm determined to carry this baby. I don't know how, but I want to finish school on time, too."

Luke raked his left hand through his sandy brown hair—another sign that he was as nervous as she was. Putting his hands on her shoulders, he said, "Whatever you decide, I'll support you."

His words sounded definitive, but a shadow of shame revealed how unsure he felt. He was probably wondering if he could make good on his promise to be there for her.

Abby steeled herself against a wave of sympathy. She couldn't help Luke get well. Not until he admitted he needed help. She reached for him and laced her fingers with his to reassure herself as much as him and to show her parents that she and Luke were together. A united front, hand in hand, they approached the broad archway of the living room. Her parents sat on the matching recliners that flanked the oversized sofa facing the fireplace. A crackling fire cast a soft glow over their profiles, but they weren't as relaxed as the ambience suggested.

Instinctively, Abby backed a few steps into the foyer. Luke squeezed her hand.

"What's going on?" her dad asked her mom.

"She probably wants to talk to you about her grades."

If only that were it. Abby tugged Luke's hand, leading him into the room. She had to get this over with.

"Abby, honey." Her mother's mouth gaped.

Both of her parents were on their feet in seconds.

Luke stiffened. All of Abby's attempts to bolster her courage dwindled to shaky bravado at her father's first sharp look of disapproval.

"I thought I made myself clear." His caustic tone dared her or Luke to disagree. "You, young man, are not welcome in my house." He pointed toward the front door.

Abby tightened her grip on Luke's hand and moved closer to him so that their arms pressed together. "Daddy, please sit down." She looked to her mother for support, but Mom shook her head, the gesture so slight Abby nearly missed the message. "Dad, I have something to tell you. Something that concerns all four of us."

Her mother's face bleached white, and her hand flew to her mouth. "Please, tell me you're not—"

"Sit down, Stephanie. I want to hear it out of her own mouth." Her dad's scowl took them all in, commanding them to be seated. "Abby, Luke."

He could barely say her boyfriend's name. A sob built in Abby's throat. If only her grandmother were here. She glanced at Luke, hoping to reassure him but knowing instantly that was impossible. He recognized what they were up against as well as she did. This was not going to go well.

For a split second, the thought of how much easier it would be to just have an abortion and keep her parents completely in the dark flitted through her muddled thoughts. Horror flooded her mind. *Lord, help me. I didn't mean that. It's not the baby's fault. The baby doesn't deserve to be punished for my mistakes. Having sex with Luke makes me feel like we're married, but I know we're not, and we may never be. God, we should've waited. Forgive me.*

"We're waiting, Abigail."

Everyone was staring at her. Dad didn't use her given name often. She was his Abby-girl, his ray of sunshine. Her lip trembled slightly. She wasn't her daddy's little girl anymore.

"Abby's pregnant." Her boyfriend's announcement sucked all of the oxygen from the room. A dark look crossed her father's face, but Luke must not have noticed. "The baby's mine, and I—"

Abby crossed the room, dropped to her knees in front of her father. "Dad, I'm so sorry. I should never have let this happen."

Her father swore. He never swore.

Her mother wept softly. "What do you want to do about the baby?"

"I'm not sure. But I am *not* having an abortion."

"Whatever Abby decides, whether she wants to keep the baby or give it up for adoption, I'm going to do everything I can to make things as easy as possible for her."

Ignoring Abby, Dad marched over to Luke. "That's just fine, Bradford. It's a little late to be thinking about what's best for my daughter."

Luke's hands were shaking, but he didn't break eye contact with her father.

Lord, please. Help him hold it together.

Only God knew what her dad would do if he realized how strung out Luke was. She had to do something, say something to deflect her father's anger. She grasped his arm, pulling him away from Luke.

Dad whirled, his face filled with fury. "Let go of me."

"Dad, please, it takes two people to get pregnant." Hot

embarrassment flooded her cheeks and neck. "This is my fault as much as it is Luke's. We were careless. It happened the night Grandma died."

"Oh, Abby," Mom cried from behind her. She grasped Abby's shoulders and pulled her away from her father and into a comforting embrace. Abby wanted to cry in her mother's arms, but that would leave Luke entirely at Dad's mercy, which was practically nonexistent right now.

"I'm okay, Mom." Abby eased back so she could look into her mother's eyes. "We'll figure something out. I just need you and Dad to ..." What did she want them to do? "Keep loving me, no matter what."

"Of course we love you." Mom slipped her arm around Dad's waist. "Right, Ray?"

"This isn't about whether or not we love you, Abby. We need a plan."

She cast a glance at Luke. His shuttered expression meant he couldn't handle much more of this conversation. "Can we talk about that later, please? Luke promised to take me out to eat."

Her father opened his mouth to argue, but one look from her mother silenced him.

"I can't tell you both how sorry I am," Luke said. "For what it's worth, I love your daughter, Mr. Collins."

Abby suspected that in her dad's mind, Luke's love for her wasn't worth much.

Not unless he could get clean and stay clean.

CHAPTER THREE

On Wednesday morning, Lisa was waiting next to Abby's locker. "Is it true?" she demanded, readjusting her floral print backpack.

Her best friend's look of shocked betrayal increased Abby's guilt. And she did not want to feel guilty. At least, not any more than she already did. She had never deliberately hurt anyone, but every time she turned around, she was confronted with someone else whom she had unintentionally hurt by her actions. Lisa was disappointed and probably sad that Abby hadn't confided in her, but at this moment, she couldn't even think about helping Lisa feel better. Abby needed all of her willpower to corral her own emotions and to get through another school day.

Turning to her locker and presenting her back to her best friend, she sucked in a calming breath and turned the lock to her combination numbers. Her fingers trembled, and she messed up the sequence. She tried again. Lisa leaned close and whispered against Abby's ear, "*Are* you pregnant?"

This day had to come eventually, but Abby had wanted to prolong it for as long as possible. For another month at least. She was only twelve weeks along and barely showing.

Why hadn't people assumed she'd simply gained weight? Probably because she'd gone from no appetite to non-stop carb cravings. Maybe because buying pants a size bigger than she usually wore didn't conceal her rounded belly. Gym class was the worst. She should have bought a pair of sweatpants, though she hated that sloppy look. Yoga pants highlighted every extra pound she'd gained in the last two weeks. If Lisa knew the truth, others did, too. A wave of shame mingled with nausea slammed into Abby. How she wished she could escape and run away where no one would know her, where no one would see her as the valedictorian who had screwed up her life by getting pregnant at seventeen.

God, where are you? I can't face this alone.

Students were talking up and down the hall, the same as they did every morning before homeroom, but today they were whispering about her. Hey, did you hear Abby Collins is pregnant? Who's the father? Luke Bradford, who else? They used to be the perfect couple. Prom King and Queen. Most likely to succeed. Even after Luke destroyed his knee. Did you know he's a heroin addict now? I feel so sorry for her.

Slain by her own imagination, Abby slumped against her locker. Lisa's hands caught her in her armpits. "Do you need to go to the nurse?"

Wouldn't that give everyone something to talk about?

"No, I was dizzy for a minute. I'm all right now."

The expression in her friend's eyes had changed from hurt to sympathy. "So, it is true?"

Abby nodded, willing the tears pressing at the corners of her eyes not to fall. "It's true."

"Does Luke know?"

A short laugh erupted from her tight throat. "Of course he knows. And my parents."

The warning bell blared. Abby bent down and grabbed her Economics and Physics textbooks and binders then closed her locker. Needing, but not wanting, to know, she faced her friend again. "Who told you?"

"A couple of kids were talking about you on the bus this morning." Lisa ran her hand down Abby's arm. "I'm sorry, Abby."

She was sorry, too, because before the day ended, the whole school would be talking about how she was pregnant and her baby's daddy was a heroin addict with no future. If only she could go home, climb back into bed, and sleep all day. But that would just postpone the inevitable. "Please don't say anything to Meg."

They'd been like the three musketeers since kindergarten. But what did they have in common now? A month ago, they were composing college application essays and taking aptitude/interest tests to discover what careers they'd be good at. Today, she was trying to figure out how she could still graduate in June with the rest of her class.

"Abby, she's going to hear it from somebody, if she hasn't already."

"I want to tell her myself." She and Megan had Physics Lab second period, which was less than an hour away. Still, the odds weren't good. "Just don't say anything."

"Not even if she asks me flat-out? You know what a terrible liar I am."

Abby smiled. *She'd* been an Oscar worthy liar. "Do your best."

Lisa started to hug her then apparently thought better of announcing to everyone nearby that Abby needed consoling. "It's going to be all right."

Abby didn't see how. "Thanks, Lis. See you at lunch." Dread tightened the muscles in her shoulders. The cafeteria would be another reckoning. All eyes would be on her. Except the ones who wouldn't look at her at all. "If I don't head up to the library."

Lisa nodded, understanding softening her features. "Text me if you need anything."

Abby shook her head. There was nothing anyone could do. Except maybe not treat her like a pariah or look at her with pity. She squared her shoulders and navigated the crowded halls with more enthusiasm in her steps than she felt.

*

Seconds after the last homeroom bell, she slipped into her third row seat. From directly behind her, Jack Rogers tapped her shoulder with a pen. "Are you all right?" he whispered, his deep voice resonating with concern.

Shifting in her chair, she dared a glance at Jack's face. He knew. His eyes warned her not to lie. Not to him.

"Is it true?"

She was beginning to hate that question. "Why are you asking me?" She struggled to keep her tone even. "When you already know the answer."

She and Jack had been friends since the sixth grade. In fact, her parents considered him stellar boyfriend material. But she didn't feel that way about Jack. Sure, he was handsome, in a rugged, I-intend-to-steal-your-heart way, and he didn't make her crazy like Luke did, but Jack didn't stir her emotions either. She'd have to be blind not to know that *he* felt more for her than she did for him, but they'd settled into an unspoken agreement to keep entirely silent on that subject.

For the sake of their friendship. Which neither of them would willingly jeopardize.

He reached for her, and then quickly withdrew his hand

as if he realized he was about to cross a line they had established immediately after she'd started dating Luke. "Abby, how can I help?"

His offer soothed her shattered nerves. She managed a smile. How sweet he was. If she were honest, just the sound of his deep voice soothed her.

How much better would it have been for her if she *had* fallen in love with Jack? But she would never know the answer to that question because no matter what Luke did or didn't do, she couldn't stop loving *him*, hoping that by some miracle her love and their baby would be enough to save him from himself.

Jack, always the pragmatic one, was gazing at her expectantly, patiently waiting for her reply. He wanted, maybe even needed, a task. "What can I do?"

"Be my friend."

"I am, and I always will be." The look in his hazel eyes was pure, unselfish love. This guy would move mountains for her.

And Luke would move mountains for his drugs.

For a nanosecond, she wished this baby was Jack's, and as if he'd read her thoughts, a hope that had not been there a moment before illuminated his handsome face. His eyes held her captive, as if they were the only people in the room. Luke used to look at her like that, too, before his knee surgery, before the drugs clouded his vision.

With *his* heart in his eyes, Jack smiled, and she smiled back. The niggling thought that she was cheating on Luke shattered her moment of peace, but she needed the momentary security Jack offered, so she dismissed the irrational guilt.

"Stand for the pledge." Mr. Davies firm voice silenced the hum of morning conversation, and Abby turned her back to

Jack, relieved at the interruption.

Ashamed of her traitorous thoughts, she tried to picture Luke by her side, in the delivery room and after the baby's birth, but she couldn't. Not in the hospital, and not at home helping with their baby. Why couldn't she envision him in her future?

Dread snaked around her heart and squeezed. Every month the local papers reported more deaths from heroin overdoses. Didn't Luke realize it could happen to him? Luke wasn't immune. Surely, his knee injury should have proven to him that he wasn't invincible.

God, please.

Two words. Not much of a prayer considering her life had blown up in her face. And it wasn't going to get any better in the immediate future. Especially if something happened to Luke. Her baby needed a father. Unless ... unless she gave it up. Not "it." Him or her.

Abby's hands trembled. Her thoughts were spiraling out of control, and she had an entire school day to get through. *God, help Luke because I can't. I've tried. But nothing has worked.*

Mr. Davies opened up his presentation on the interactive board, and immediately, Jack tapped her elbow, urging her to focus. Abby should thank him for looking out for her. She forced herself to copy down the boring notes on economic and political conditions that typically resulted in a recession. She'd failed the last two quizzes. She needed to get at least an 85% on Friday's unit test. She smothered a scoff. What did it matter? The district might not even allow her to finish out the school year. Even so, she didn't want her teachers to start judging her, labeling her as *that* girl who cared about her grades until she got pregnant. She wasn't one of those girls. But now that she *was* pregnant, she wondered if any girls were actually like that. Why were people so quick to condemn others when they had no idea what was really going on?

The way Luke's parents had him.

She, too, had looked down on him, believing that somehow, he should have been able to overcome his addiction. If only he had tried harder. If he were determined enough, strong-willed enough, wouldn't he have quit six months ago, when his parents first threatened to kick him out?

What if he couldn't quit, even now that she'd told him she was pregnant? That was her biggest fear—that when she needed to lean on his strength, Luke would leave her alone to face everything without him. Jack would never do that.

Her cell phone vibrated against her leg, and she sneaked it out of her pocket to peek at the message. Luke's text said he couldn't pick her up after school. He had to work at Abercrombie's at four o'clock. He hadn't mentioned that when they'd talked last night. Had he picked up an extra shift? Or was he lying, making up an excuse? Was he nodding off already? It was barely nine o'clock. An overwhelming urge to get in her car, march into his house, and punch him in the face played in fast forward in her head. Good thing her car was at the dealership. Pregnancy hormones were definitely messing with her mind.

Pull yourself together, Abigail Marie Collins.

Abby refocused her attention on the teacher. He was saying something about a study session.

When the bell rang, she trudged up to his desk. "Excuse me, Mr. Davies?"

He looked up from the stacks of papers he was sorting into two piles. "Yes, Abby."

"I missed what you said. When is the study session?"

Mr. Davies raised one eyebrow, his subtle way of expressing his astonishment or disapproval. In her case, probably a mixture of both. "Tomorrow, ninth period. Sign up on the clipboard next to the door. For those who attend, I'll drop the lowest homework grade."

"Thank you. I'll be there." She considered telling him what had been going on with her but decided against it. She didn't really want any special favors. Her pregnancy was none of his business.

To her surprise, Jack was waiting for her outside the classroom door. "You didn't answer my question about what I could do to help."

Impulsively, she leaned close so that the students at their lockers couldn't hear her. "Luke can't pick me up today, and my car is in the shop. Could you give me a ride home after school?"

Jack didn't smile. He was reading between the lines, guessing at what she wasn't saying. "Of course. And I'll help you study for the econ test."

"When?"

"This afternoon if you want and tomorrow, too."

"Today I can do, but not tomorrow."

Jack shook his head.

Was he suggesting she should spend every spare moment preparing for the test? She pursed her lips in frustration. Tomorrow, she had her first doctor's appointment, but telling Jack would be awkward. "I wish I could, but I have somewhere that I need to be."

His eyes widened. "Is your mom going with you?"

Her cheeks burned. Was he a mind-reader or something? "I'll meet you by the south exit after the last bell."

Jack smiled and held up his hand in surrender, apparently getting her message that what she was doing tomorrow afternoon was none of his business.

They headed off in opposite directions, she to Physics lab and he to P.E.

Abby followed three feet behind Ian Bradford the whole length of the hall to the Physics room. Luke's cousin wasn't one of her favorite people. He and Luke had been inseparable, until Luke's parents kicked him out. Ian's parents were no better. They'd ordered Ian to stay away from his older cousin. In their defense, they probably feared that Luke would be a bad influence on their son. Abby understood. She felt the same way about Cole's influence on Luke.

Ian stopped directly in front of her, his linebacker shoulders blocking her way into the Physics room.

She nearly stumbled into him. "Excuse me."

Her barely veiled irritation earned her a scathing look. Without a word, he stepped aside, and she slipped past him, surprised that he hadn't had the courtesy to acknowledge her. What was up with him? Luke wouldn't have told his cousin that she was pregnant. He had taken Ian's defection hard. They'd been more like brothers than cousins, maybe because Ian was an only child. After the Labor Day weekend fiasco, Ian had come to her for news about Luke. And now he couldn't even say hello to her?

There was only one explanation. Everyone knew. This day was getting better by the minute. She'd gone from being one of the popular kids to an outsider. Pregnancy wasn't contagious, but people stared as if she were wearing a scarlet letter. Not an "A" like Hester Prynne had been forced to sew onto her clothes, but a "P" that identified her as one of those girls—pregnant and pitiful. Too stupid to use birth control. Too dumb to dump her loser boyfriend.

Abby couldn't stand people feeling sorry for her. Her

situation was challenging but not impossible. Her family would help her, one step at a time. First, finish high school. Then, have this baby and figure out how she'd manage college. Her internal pep talk lifted her mood a bit. If only she could ignore the rumors flying like a hurricane through school.

"Abby," Megan called out from the lab table in the far corner of the room. "Come help me understand this problem."

Ian muttered something to one of his buddies, but thankfully, Abby couldn't make out the words. Her heart pounded as adrenaline raced through her system. The urge to run out of the building into the freezing rain erupted then evaporated as quickly as it had come.

Ignore them. She could almost hear her grandmother's sage advice. But Grandma was tougher. Had been tough every day of her life. Abby envied her grandmother's unflagging self-confidence and determination. What others said about her hadn't mattered. But Abby cared about her reputation. She wanted people to respect and admire her. She was a leader.

Correction, you were a leader.

She suppressed a groan. She wouldn't make it through the day, let alone the rest of her senior year if she couldn't stop imagining that everybody was talking trash about her. She strode past her classmates, catching snatches of ordinary conversations about how kids had spent their weekend.

Just breathe. Not everyone is talking about you. This will blow over eventually. As soon as someone else does something to stir the gossip mill.

Megan grabbed her arm, pulling Abby over to their lab table. Their lab partners, Mandy and Ryan, hadn't made it to class yet.

"Are you all right?" Meg asked, soft enough that no one

could possibly hear. "What are you going to do?"

Her second question said it all. Meg already knew about the baby.

Abby raised her face until their eyes met. "Try to get my grades up before the marking period ends." *Try to finish high school before the baby comes.*

Her friend tucked her shoulder-length brown hair into a barrette. "Well, yeah, of course. That's what I meant."

Even more than Lisa, Meg could read Abby. Her friend understood that now was not the time to talk.

"I'll call you after school," Meg promised.

Abby half wished she wouldn't. Meg would try to say something, anything to make it better. Empathy and compassion would morph to pity as soon as her friends realized they could do nothing that would make a bit of difference.

By the end of Physics lab, Abby decided she'd made a mistake coming to school today. She hadn't carried her weight in lab, letting the others take all of the measurements and recording the data into her own copy of the report without even trying to analyze the information. She was physically present, but her mind was not at Easton High.

Her thoughts bounced like ping pong balls. How she would manage school once her pregnancy was obvious to everyone? When was the baby due? She guessed mid-May, but she wanted to be wrong. If the baby came before finals, when would she find the time to study? How were Grandma and Grandpa Collins going to handle the news? What was Luke doing? Was he going to his classes or sitting home getting high until he fell asleep? Would he go to work? Could he keep this job? And if he did, was he going to earn enough to help her with the baby? Anxious questions whirled like a vortex until she wanted to scream for someone, anyone to help her.

Up until a few months ago, her life had been on a straight-line path. High school, college, career, family. In that order. What had she done? She'd learned too late that every action has a consequence, some more far-reaching than she had ever imagined.

Meg's hand resting on her shoulder brought Abby back to the classroom. "Don't worry. We can write this up in study hall next period."

Mandy kept her eyes on her report, but Ryan glared at Abby.

Message received. She was a slacker. Great. Another label she didn't deserve. Everyone had an off-day occasionally. She would be having more than a few off-days in the coming months.

"Thanks for double-checking our measurements, Ryan," Meg said, clearly trying to placate him. "You're always so precise."

Ryan's mouth twitched, then he gave in to a smile that revealed his dimples. A slight blush rose in his cheeks.

Ryan interested in Meg? How had Abby not noticed? And more importantly, did her friend share his feelings?

Abby had been preoccupied with her fear that she was pregnant. Now that her suspicions were confirmed, she actually had some space in her brain to think about something and someone else. That was a good sign, wasn't it?

Focusing on something other than Luke's addiction or her pregnancy, if only for a brief moment, felt like a cool breeze on a scorching summer day. She liked to think of herself as a caring person, one who wasn't guilty of being self-absorbed. Seeing glimpses of her old self meant she would get through this.

The bell rang. Had Ryan responded to Megan's

compliment? Abby hadn't been paying attention. She shook off her distraction and headed out of the lab with Meg.

For the remainder of the morning, neither of her friends said anything about Abby being pregnant, but she could see the questions in their eyes. The only answer Abby had was that she was going through with this pregnancy. No matter how many times the thought popped into her head that having an abortion would be easier she didn't believe the lie. Her baby was a person, one who needed her protection. It wasn't the baby's fault that Abby had gotten pregnant at seventeen. She'd been raised to accept the consequences of her actions, and this situation was no different.

Still, knowing her life was never going to be the same weighed heavily on her heart and mind. Her whole identity had changed. She was that pregnant girl. Everything else that she used to be faded into the long shadow cast by that irrevocable truth.

*

Luke stared at the email from his father.

"Meet me for coffee at the Tim Horton's near my office at 1:00 today."

The words shocked his system, momentarily halting all thoughts but one. Panic. How on earth had his father known when Luke would be free? Sweat formed on his upper lip and palms. Abby was right. He should have told his parents about the baby right after they'd told her parents. In his defense, it had only been four days. He wasn't trying to keep Abby's pregnancy a secret, but he wasn't ready for the inquisition either. The truth was he'd never be ready. Now, his father would have the upper hand because the meeting would be on his terms. Luke bit the inside of his lower lip.

Could he pretend he hadn't seen the email? Probably. But that would only postpone the inevitable. If he failed to show up, his father would come looking for him. It didn't help that they hadn't been in the same room since Dad had calmly ordered Luke to pack his belongings and find somewhere else to live.

Tamping down his resentment, he rummaged in his nightstand drawer for the packet of coke he'd stuffed between copies of his most recent paystubs. His fingers closed around the plastic zip bag. Immediately, the tension in his neck and shoulders eased. He opened his wallet, pulled out a crisp bill, rolled it tight, and tore off a tiny piece of tape to hold the tube together. He poured a small amount of coke onto the desk and used his school ID to form two thin, soothing lines. With a sigh of relief, he inhaled the fine, white powder. He could face his dad now.

Luke opened his laptop, typed the final revisions of his paper on *Hamlet*, printed two copies, and attached the file to an email to his professor, then clicked send. It wasn't Luke's best work, but at least he had managed to submit it before the deadline. He couldn't afford to lose any points, not on this assignment or any other, according to his advisor, who consistently reminded Luke that academic probation was a big deal. He shrugged. As long as he did the work, his grades would rebound.

He couldn't say the same about his relationship with his dad. Richard Bradford cared about image and the family name. One time all-star quarterback, Luke had fumbled the proverbial ball in the final seconds. He'd screwed up his senior year, first by getting injured and finally by committing what his father considered the unpardonable sin. Bradfords were never weak. Bradfords relied on their strength of character to meet every challenge. Luke found his strength in a bottle of oxycodone, and that his father couldn't tolerate. Dad still hadn't forgiven Mom for allowing Dr. Mallory to write the script in the first place. Luke cursed under his breath. If his father had cut short his business trip to New York, *he* could have discussed pain management options with the doctor. Instead, he left the responsibility to his wife, and then blamed and belittled her when she didn't handle it the way he would have. Typical Richard, king of the castle, but absent whenever important decisions needed to be made.

Luke checked the time on the stove clock. 12:10. No wonder his stomach clenched with hunger. He opened the refrigerator door, knowing that he wouldn't find much. Eggs, butter, milk, assorted condiments. He scrambled three eggs, piled them between two pieces of wheat toast, and washed it down with a glass of water. 12:32. He needed to leave, immediately. Arriving late would only increase his father's disdain. Luke, the irresponsible son, the disappointment with a capital "D."

At precisely one o'clock, Luke marched into the Tim Horton's. He squared his shoulders. He wasn't nearly high enough for this conversation, but at least he would be able to keep a clear head. Show no weakness was the first line of defense according to the Richard Bradford code of conduct.

The moment Luke entered the coffee shop, his father stood, his eyes boring through Luke. Why had he thought he could hide anything from his father? The man's unparalleled ability to read others was what made him a successful real estate investor. Or so he had told his son numerous times.

But it didn't matter if Dad knew what Luke was thinking. Nothing could improve this situation. He was in no position to negotiate any terms at all. This would go down exactly the way his father planned.

Palm up, his father gestured to the seat opposite him. Luke took in the two coffees in porcelain mugs. No paper cups for his father.

"You still take yours with one cream and one sugar, I presume."

"Yep." Luke sat in the wood chair and resisted the urge to slouch. Posture communicated more than most people realized. He straightened his spine and met his father's appraising look with a steady gaze. After a moment, he reached for his mug and swallowed a fortifying swig of the hot brew. "I was surprised to hear from you."

One gray eyebrow shot up—his dad's single display of emotion. Luke's voice sounded calmer than he felt, but his dad clearly wasn't fooled.

"Ray Collins and I had dinner last night."

Wow. This was worse than Luke had imagined. "So, you know." What else was there to say? Abby was pregnant. She wouldn't consider an abortion. Her parents barely tolerated Luke's minimal presence in their daughter's life, but Luke was determined not to be shut out.

His father's stare bored through Luke. The protracted silence unnerved him, and he wiped his palms on his jeans, waiting for the boom to fall.

"I know I messed up."

His father's only response was to fold his hands and rest them on the table.

"We were careful, except that one time."

"The day Elise died." Dad leaned back in his chair, waiting, drawing out information with a magnetic force that Luke was powerless to resist.

"Abby doesn't want an abortion."

The slight twitch at the left corner of his father's mouth revealed his tightly controlled anger. Did Dad actually think that Luke would try to talk Abby into killing their child? His own life may be in the gutter, but he would never pressure her into violating her convictions.

"She's considering keeping this child, but if she decides to give it up, your mother and I will petition the court for custody."

Luke's eyebrows arched. Wouldn't that be weird? His son would become his brother.

"Abby will never sign her parental rights over to you."

"Ray and I have discussed the alternatives."

"*I* won't sign my rights over to you."

His father laughed. "That's what I told him you'd say."

Luke was a fish on a deceptively loose line. "What do you want from me? This baby was an accident. Abby and I are still figuring out what will be best for our kid."

The twitch was back. "Considering your present circumstances, I have no confidence in your ability to discern what's best for anyone."

Leaping to his feet, Luke said, "I don't have to sit here and—"

"Sit down," Dad commanded, his voice low. "You will check into a 90-day rehab. At the end of the ninety days, I will deposit fifty thousand dollars into an account for Abby to help her pay for whatever the baby needs, including child care until she finishes her education."

"Until she graduates in June?"

Dad shook his head. "Until she finishes college and gets a full-time job."

"Fifty thousand dollars isn't going to last that long." They were deleting Luke from the equation, as if his role as a father didn't matter at all.

"I expect *you* to pay me back." His father finished the last of his coffee. "And just so we're clear, if you decide rehab isn't working for you, I will not give your girlfriend so much as a penny of my money."

Luke's throat constricted, cutting off the oxygen flow to

his lungs. "That's blackmail."

"I prefer to think of it as an incentive."

His mind scrambled for a way to maintain his freedom, but the hook was set. Any attempt at intimidating his father was futile. Luke leaned across the table, desperate to extricate himself. "That's not exactly fair to Abby. Why should she and the baby suffer just because I can't ..." Shame burned his face and neck. "Or won't stop using?"

His father released a long breath and rested his hand gently, but firmly on Luke's forearm. "That's exactly what Ray and I are trying to prevent."

CHAPTER FOUR

Abby's alarm clock blared for the third time. The harmony of birds singing and water lapping against rocks, clearly orchestrated to make waking up easier, only served to annoy her, probably because she'd come to associate it with the nausea that had assailed her every morning for weeks. Today, her body felt super-glued to the mattress. She reached across the nightstand and tapped the base of the lamp until the bright light illuminated her bedroom. Squinting, she dragged her hands over her face, sat up against the headboard, and hugged her knees to her chest while she nibbled three saltines, just to be safe. She was pregnant. Between two and three months. It was a stark truth that smacked her in the head and stomach the moment her brain formed a single conscious thought. Each and every morning since she'd finally mustered up the courage to take the home pregnancy test, she berated herself for her carelessness.

One careless, terrifying mistake that changed her life forever.

When would the shock of it wear off? Maybe after her doctor's appointment this afternoon, she could finally accept reality. She was going to have a baby. More than likely before graduation and before exams.

If only she could go back to the days when all she had to worry about was whether or not Luke would ever get clean.

No. That wouldn't be far enough. She'd go back to before she and Luke first had sex. Before she'd rationalized going against everything her parents taught her about the importance of waiting until after marriage.

What Mom hadn't told her was how hard it would be to say no. Over the course of several months, kissing had led to so much more. Eventually, Abby hadn't wanted to say no. She had actually wanted Luke as much as he'd wanted her. And now she was pregnant. A brand new person was growing inside of her. A child who deserved a loving home and a secure future.

With two parents.

Abby shuddered, her shoulders lurching upward, tightening the knots that never seemed to loosen. Could she provide for her baby without Luke's help? Even before she acknowledged her pregnancy, her dreams for them had begun to crumble. Each time she saw him high or suffering from withdrawal, not because he wanted to quit but because he couldn't get the drugs his mind and body craved, the happy future she had envisioned seemed more unlikely.

How had this nightmare happened to them? Opioid abuse was a recognized, national epidemic, but she'd never imagined it would touch her life. Or Luke's.

God, I'm so selfish. The baby and I are healthy. But Luke is slowly killing himself. Help him, please. I ... I love him. Our baby needs her daddy or his daddy, if it's a boy.

As tears pooled in her eyes, she squeezed her lids tight against the tide of grief and hugged her knees to her chest. Unable to hold back the sobs, Abby swiped at the tears coursing down her cheeks and sliding down her neck, chilling her inside and out.

Surely, Luke would try to get clean so that his father would give her and the baby fifty thousand dollars. Luke would want her to have that money. He would do whatever his father asked for her sake, wouldn't he? But would he ever be completely free of his addiction so they could build a life together? Or would she and the baby have to shut their hearts against him the way his parents had?

A knock on her bedroom door made her leap from her bed. "I'm up."

"Just checking." Mom sounded tired and discouraged.

Abby had done that to her. And so soon after Grandma's death. "Every choice you make affects someone else," Grandma had told Abby more than once. She hadn't wanted to believe it, but now she saw the truth of her grandmother's words. Luke's choices affected Abby. Her choices affected her family. She'd messed up, and there was absolutely no way to fix any of it.

But she was determined that her baby wouldn't suffer for his—or her—parents' mistakes. But exactly how was she going to accomplish that?

She wasn't even passing Physics or Economics. Hopefully, her two-hour study session with Jack yesterday afternoon would help her pass the next test. She needed to get her grades back up. She couldn't take care of her baby if she didn't graduate on time. That wasn't an option. She was going to walk across the stage with the rest of her class. Unless she missed too much school or couldn't take her exams.

Abby drew in a ragged breath and released it with a whoosh. She had to stop borrowing trouble so she could get through today. By this time tomorrow, she would have seen the tiny infant, a shape on her sonogram that would confirm how far along she was. She would know her exact due date. Then she could start making plans. Plans she should be making with Luke.

He should be with her, sharing this unforgettable moment. A fierce hatred boiled inside her. Hatred for the drugs that were stealing Luke away from her and from their child. Rage surged through her. She wanted to slam her fist into something. No, into someone. Cole Marchman. The man deserved to rot in prison for turning Luke on to heroin.

It was his choice.

That one, quiet, undeniable truth deflated her anger for the moment. She knelt beside her bed. "God, help them both." She didn't want to pray for Cole, but she did. She had no business judging anyone. She was pregnant at seventeen. It didn't get much worse than that, at least not in her parents' eyes. They hadn't said much, but she knew they were disappointed in her. The only way to prove herself was to do the best thing for her baby. Tears welled in her eyes. "Lord, I'm sorry for letting everyone down, for letting You down by having sex with Luke before we were married."

She'd asked for forgiveness before and believed God forgave her, but knowing she was forgiven and feeling forgiven didn't always coincide. How long before she stopped beating herself up with regrets? She opened her Bible to look for comfort and strength. Ten minutes later, she'd read three chapters in the Psalms and composed herself enough to face her day.

The sound of the water running in the shower greeted her the moment she entered the hall. "That's just great," she muttered. Sam would use up all of the hot water. She banged on the bathroom door. "Hurry up!"

"Five more minutes," Sam shouted.

"If you use all the hot water, I'll—"

Her mother's hand on her back stopped her. "You can use my shower this morning. Your dad's already left."

"Mom, I …."

"I know, honey."

Abby wasn't sure what her mother thought she knew, but at this point, it didn't matter. "Thank you for changing your schedule so you could come with me today."

Mom smiled and opened her arms. Abby hadn't felt more in need of a hug in her entire life. Pregnancy hormones were morphing her emotions into a never-ending roller coaster ride. Wrapped in Mom's warm embrace, she quieted, the smell of her mother's lavender perfume soothing and restoring her equilibrium, if only for a moment.

All too soon her mother released her. "I'll pick you up at one o'clock. Your note for early dismissal is on the counter next to the coffeemaker. I've got to head into the office to take care of a few things, so I need to dash off." Mom paused, scrutinizing Abby's face. "Are you sure you'll be all right going to school? You can stay home if you want. Dad and I talked over several options for you last night, and we don't want you to be uncomfortable, what with the way teenagers gossip."

Hot shame stained Abby's cheeks. "They already are."

Her mother blinked, then her mouth set in the hard line that meant she was ready to do battle for her daughter.

That look warmed Abby's heart, until reality set in again. "There's nothing you can do, Mom."

"But your father and I—"

"I'll just ride it out. Eventually, my story will be old news." Even as she said the words, Abby didn't believe it. She would be in the spotlight for the rest of the year. She'd overheard a few girls arguing yesterday about whether Abby was really pro-life or simply keeping her baby because her parents were pressuring her.

"Dad and I talked about hiring a tutor for you. Home instruction would be better for you and the baby."

Abby couldn't reply. She wasn't ready to give up her senior year entirely. If only people would mind their own business.

"We'll talk about this more this weekend." Mom's tone broached no argument.

Abby shrugged and trudged to the end of the hall to the master bedroom suite. Her parents' queen-sized bed was already made. Early morning light filtered through the open blinds, highlighting the fact that every flat surface in her parents' room was clutter- and dust-free. Not a single thing was out of place. Impressive. Exhausting. Impossible. How did her mother manage teaching graduate and undergraduate classes, burning the candle at both ends? Working and taking care of a family suddenly seemed like a herculean task.

Could Abby manage as well as her mother?

*

Luke heard a distant voice, but his fuzzy brain couldn't connect it to anyone he knew. He shivered, his body convulsing against bitter cold. Cold that penetrated his bones and seared his lungs. He reached for a blanket, tugged it to his chin, and was rewarded with a piercing pain in his neck. An IV catheter? *You've got to be kidding.*

A wave of intestinal cramps demanded instant release. Luke struggled to sit up. He leaned his head over the edge of the bed and vomited onto the white tile floor.

When the retching finally ended, he wiped his mouth with his left hand and scanned the stark surroundings. A hospital room. He'd overdosed. Cole must have called 911. Otherwise, Luke would be dead.

"Abby." His voice sounded like a whimpering kid.

Fear morphed into gargantuan panic. He couldn't do this to her. What if he'd been alone when he'd shot up last night? He'd be dead. No more chances. Nothing. No chance to ever hold his baby.

"I don't want to die." The words bounced against the walls of the lonely room. No one heard. No one cared.

Abby cares.

It was true. Abby did care. She threatened to leave him, but she always came back.

Luke rubbed his fists against his eyes and cried. He was trapped. Every warning he had ever heard about heroin echoed in his brain. H is evil, man. That stuff will kill you. It's worse than prison. Every heroin addict ends up dead. Eventually. Quit if you can, but you're better off never touching the stuff. You're going to die. You'll stop breathing, and you won't even know it.

He wanted to bang his head against the wall to make the thoughts stop. He needed something to bring him down. Maybe buprenorphine. He'd heard that bupe helped with withdrawal. Luke found the call button, pressed it a couple of times, then steeled himself against another wave of abdominal cramps.

Holding onto the railing, he swung one leg, then the other over the bed. He gripped the cold, stainless steel bar and stood up, slow, like he'd never walked before. His legs ached, his vision blurred, all the while his stomach continued to spasm. He'd experienced withdrawal a time or two, but nothing like this.

A nurse in bright purple scrubs flung open the door. Her startled eyes took him in as he shouted, "Bathroom."

With her arm around him keeping him upright, they stumbled into the facilities. He tried to push her away, but her strong grip held him, helping him onto the toilet just in time. He cursed at her, demanding privacy.

Until a wave of vomit rose up into his throat and filled his mouth.

Instantly, she positioned a pan in front of his face. With her free hand, she kneaded his shoulder with gentle fingers. "It'll be all right. I promise. You can do this. We'll help you. I'll help you."

*

Abby had never heard anything more amazing in her entire life than the sound of her baby's heart beating. "Is it a boy or a girl?"

The ultrasound technician stifled a laugh. "It's too early to tell. But in another four weeks ..." She glanced from Abby to her mother. "Are you planning—"

"I'm keeping my baby," Abby said, cutting off the older woman's words. She couldn't bear to hear anyone even suggest the *possibility* of her having an abortion. With a jolt, she realized that was why she hadn't been willing to tell anyone sooner. For weeks, she had wanted to believe she couldn't possibly be pregnant. Once she'd taken the test, she had decided. She wouldn't, couldn't consider ending her baby's life to make her own simpler.

"My daughter will carry this baby to term." Her mother's tone was matter-of-fact, though Abby could only imagine what it cost her. "Can you estimate her due date?

"According to my measurements of the fetus, I'd say mid-May."

So much for her remaining in school. But she could still attend the graduation ceremony, couldn't she? Abby stared at the monitor. Her baby's arms and legs were clearly visible. One hand was clenched into a tiny fist pressed against the infant's mouth. "Are you sure?"

The technician studied her with sympathetic eyes. "Your baby could come a bit earlier or later. When was your last period?"

"I can't remember. I'm not always regular, so sometimes I don't bother to mark it down." But she did know the exact date she'd conceived. The date of her grandmother's death. August 23rd. She shot her mother an apologetic look. "I think I conceived sometime during the third week of August."

Mom pressed her fingers to the corners of her eyes to discreetly conceal her tears. "Can you calculate a due date based on the possible conception date?"

The technician nodded.

"August 23rd," her mother whispered.

If Abby had not wanted to justify her carelessness, Mom might never have known that the baby had been conceived the day Grandma died. If Abby had only kept her mouth shut, Mom wouldn't have to connect the baby with Gram's death. But it was too late to worry about that now. Abby certainly had plenty of other things to fret about. She eyed the technician. For one irrational second, she entertained the fantasy that the woman's calculations were off by a month.

A moment later, the technician plugged the information into an app on her phone. "May 15th," she announced. "Give or take a few days."

Abby sighed. She hadn't wanted to do the math herself, irrationally wishing her baby would wait until after finals. This was definitely not the senior year she'd planned for herself. Luke's senior year had ended his dreams of a football scholarship, and now she wouldn't be going away to college either.

She probably wouldn't have left Luke anyway. There were plenty of local colleges in the Buffalo area. She could still go. Maybe just a little later than she had planned. Her parents, and possibly even Luke's parents, would help her. But she didn't want to think about the deal Richard Bradford had made with his son, because it probably wouldn't work out.

Shifting her attention off herself and her concerns for Luke, Abby asked the most important question. "Everything's okay with the baby, right?"

The technician smiled. "Your sonogram looks exactly like we expect at about 13 weeks. Give me a minute to find the nurse, and we'll get you settled into an examining room to wait for Dr. Morris."

"Morris?" her mother said, surprise evident in her startled tone. "Dr. Robert Morris or Dr. Liselle Morris?"

Abby shot her mother a questioning look. Five obstetricians worked in this clinic, and Abby didn't see how it mattered which doctor she saw today. She would meet them all before the baby came anyway.

"Dr. Liselle. Dr. Bob is at the hospital delivering triplets as we speak. But you'll like his wife. She's amazing."

The instant the technician left the room, Abby reached for her mother's hand. "What's wrong? Isn't Dr. Liselle a good doctor? Should we reschedule? Go to a different clinic?"

Mom covered their hands with her free hand. "Liselle and I went to undergraduate school together at UB." She averted her face momentarily, then gazed steadily into Abby's eyes. "She and your father dated briefly during their freshmen year. Before he and I met."

Determination laced her last remark, almost as if Mom were trying to reassure herself that Dad had been completely over the other woman long before he'd fallen in love with her.

Her parents' marriage was solid. As far as Abby knew, her father had never given her mother any reason to doubt him. So, why did the mention of an old girlfriend rattle her?

"Mom, if you're uncomfortable, we can go somewhere else."

She shook her head. "Don't be ridiculous. And don't let your imagination run away with you. I simply forgot that when Dr. Bob bought out the practice this past spring that his wife joined the team to replace Dr. O'Reilly."

Abby relaxed. She didn't want to get used to new doctors. Still, if this Dr. Liselle ended up delivering the baby, it might be awkward. "Okay, we'll stay here then."

Mom reached into the outside pocket of her designer purse, pulled out her phone and frowned at the screen. The hand holding her phone trembled, and the cell clattered to the tile floor. She looked up, her face completely ashen.

Abby slid off the examining table and bent down to retrieve the vibrating phone. Caroline Bradford's name filled the screen. "Mom, why is Luke's mother calling now? Did you tell her about my appointment?"

Mom started to open her mouth to speak, but a gentle knock interrupted them. A nurse in pale green scrubs cracked the door. "The doctor is ready for you. Please follow me to examining room three."

Instinctively, Abby reached for her mother's hand. It was ice cold. Abby squeezed gently to let her mom know she didn't really mind Mrs. Bradford knowing about her appointment.

"I'll be right back," Mom said, avoiding eye contact. "I need to use the rest room."

Alone in exam room three, Abby smoothed the hospital gown over her legs, and taking several deep breaths, tried unsuccessfully to quiet her anxieties. The baby was fine. In spite of their disappointment, her parents, both pro-life, supported her decision to keep her baby. But did Luke's mother prefer …. No, Abby couldn't, wouldn't worry about what Caroline Bradford wanted.

*

Thirty minutes later, relieved by the doctor's confirmation that her pregnancy was progressing normally, but fighting exhaustion, Abby handed the keys to her Mustang to her mother. "Would you mind driving?"

Mom shook her head. "Let's walk a few minutes."

Abby frowned, shivering in her wool jacket. Her mother's voice sounded nervous, maybe even scared, but the temperature had dropped ten degrees since they'd arrived at the clinic. "We can't walk now. You need to get to campus, and I need to get home. Sam will be getting off the bus in twenty minutes."

She had no time to ponder why she needed to point out the obvious. The stricken look on her mother's face erased every thought but one.

Luke.

Abby grasped her mother's coat sleeve. "Mrs. Bradford wasn't calling about me or the baby, was she?"

"No, honey."

Tears filled Abby's eyes as she fought mounting panic. "Where is he?"

"ICU at ECMC."

"Mom, can you …? What about Sam? I don't think I can drive." Her mind racing, Abby stared at her shaking hands, frantic to get to Luke, but not trusting herself behind the wheel. Her scattered thoughts made little sense. Even to her.

"Trey's mom will get Sam off the bus, I'll drive you to the hospital, and Dad will meet us and stay with you while I go teach my seminar."

Abby tried to process her mother's words, but darkness was closing in fast. Struggling to breathe, she shut her eyes tight, then forced herself to focus on her mother's face. "He's still alive?"

Her voice sounded strange, the calm, almost flat tone revealing none of the tumult raging in her heart and mind. Even her body rebelled against the possibility that Luke could be …. "Tell me he's okay."

Mom gripped her shoulders, her face inches from Abby. "He overdosed, but he's alive."

Abby closed her eyes and whispered, "Thank You, God." Unzipping her purse, she double-checked to make sure the sonogram pictures of the baby were tucked next to her wallet. Hopefully, seeing his child would finally give Luke the courage he needed to stop using.

*

Luke curled into a fetal position, his hands gripping his restless legs. Why wasn't the bupe working? He could just rip out the IV and walk out. Cole would fix him up soon enough.

Ride it out, man. Get clean for Abby.

He'd let her down over and over again. What if she left him for good? Would she let him see the baby? She might want to, but Ray Collins would hire the best lawyer, spend any amount of money to ensure that Luke didn't get within ten feet of his kid.

That wasn't fair.

The image of himself overdosing again, a needle stuck in his arm, his baby crying out for food and attention, while Luke slowly stopped breathing, exploded like a bad acid trip in his brain.

Just as quickly, the idea of deliberately injecting a fatal hit of heroin overtook him with magnetic force, drawing him unwillingly to the only solution.

Kill yourself. Everyone will be better off without you.

You're worthless. You'll never be anything but a junkie.

You're better off dead.

Dead. Dead. Dead.

The word hammered with relentless repetition.

Luke gripped his hair, his fisted hands yanking, desperate to shut up the voices in his head. "God! Where are You?"

Luke ground his teeth until his jaw ached. He reached for the nurse's call button. Where was the nurse? Dying would be easier than this pain, his body and his mind screaming for the sweet euphoric calm that would settle his world.

A nurse pulled back the curtain, a sympathetic, pitying smile pasted on her flawless face. "How can I help?"

"Give me something. Anything. Now."

The nurse nodded, her gaze glued to his chart.

What was wrong with her? Couldn't she see he was desperate? Stupid woman. "Didn't you hear what I just said? I need something for the pain. Now. Not in four hours or two hours. Right now."

His rage didn't seem to affect her. Her features masked any reaction. Maybe if he pleaded. He touched her arm. "Please, help me. I can't take this another minute."

"I'll be right back."

Minutes stretched into eternity. Every nerve demanding heroin, Luke tore off the tape covering the IV catheter. His fingers shook as he tried to grasp the needle.

"What are you doing?" the nurse demanded. She had a syringe in her right hand.

Luke dragged in a raspy breath and sank back on the bed. Her question didn't require an answer. She knew. If she'd returned a minute later, he'd have been on his feet, yanking on his clothes.

He forced himself to relax as the buprenorphine took

effect. Must have been he'd needed more than the doctor had prescribed. Or maybe more time had passed than he realized. Luke closed his eyes and hoped for sleep.

CHAPTER FIVE

Soft lips kissing his forehead stirred Luke to wakefulness. Silky hair splayed across his face. A floral scent filled his nostrils. Abby. His Abby. To make sure that his senses had not betrayed him, he opened his eyes, and there she was. "You came."

"Of course I came."

He raised his arms, but she stood just out of reach. The fear in her eyes condemned him. Her eyes screamed what her words would not—you almost died. You almost left me. How could you do that?

"Babe, come here. Please."

She inched closer.

He sat up, pulled her onto the bed, and hugged her close. Her body was stiff at first, almost as if she thought she might hurt him. He rubbed his hand over her back, urging her to relax in his embrace. "It's all right. I'm okay."

She snuggled into his neck, then lifted her face to his. She'd been crying, maybe for hours. Her red-rimmed eyes and splotchy face gave her away. It always did. Tears spilled from her eyes. When was the last time he'd made her smile?

He couldn't remember. That fact was a painful reminder

of how much heroin had stolen from him and from her, too.

She wiped the moisture from her cheeks with the back of her hand. She stared at him as if she had no idea what to say. He almost wished she would yell at him. He certainly deserved it.

"I'm sorry, babe." He brushed his lips over hers, fully aware that no kiss could make up for what he'd done. "I messed up. I didn't know the stuff was that strong."

"You did," she insisted. She bit down to stop her lower lip from trembling. "Don't lie to me." Shoving against his shoulders, she moved out of his reach. "Don't lie to yourself. You just wanted a better high."

A painful knot twisted in his gut. Nothing he could say would erase the pain he'd caused her. "You deserve better. Our baby deserves better."

Her stricken expression lanced his heart. Wasn't Abby going to disagree with him, tell him she still believed in him? Even if no one else did?

She retrieved her purse from the chair and stuck her hand inside the leather bag. Probably to search for a tissue. Seconds later, she pulled out a manila envelope. "I brought this for you … to … to encourage you to get clean." She sobbed, and ignoring her tears, leveled him with that penetrating gaze that made him feel like she could see into his soul. "Stay clean for good this time, Luke. Please."

Almost afraid to discover its contents, he took the envelope from her outstretched hand. Had she written him a letter? Perhaps, her conditions for continuing their relationship or for allowing him to be part of their baby's life. He could never live up to her expectations and restrictions. Not with heroin as his slave driver. But he couldn't live without her or the baby either.

"Aren't you going to open it?"

No matter how much he might dread what was inside, her desperate plea compelled him to reach for the envelope. He opened the prongs and pulled out three photographs. They were a bit blurry and hard to make out, but he instantly recognized the tiny form in the photos. Their baby. With arms and legs and fingers and toes. A real, living part of him and Abby.

Tears stung his eyes, but he smiled. They were really going to have this baby.

"Promise me you'll be clean before our baby is born."

There it was. Her demand. Reasonable, sensible, but was it possible?

"I ... I don't know if I—"

"No excuses, Luke. We're past that."

He opened his mouth to respond, but she leaned close and placed her finger over his lips to silence him.

"I want you to check yourself into rehab. I don't care how many times you have to try. You can't be part of our baby's life until you're clean."

What could he say to that? She was right. The anguish in her eyes was more than he could bear. Utterly exhausted, he lay back against the pillow and turned away from her. The bed moved with her weight. Her body pressed against him. She kissed the back of his neck, and he shivered and rolled toward her. She kissed him, devouring his mouth.

She tasted like cinnamon. Her lips demanded his response, but he broke away. "What are you doing?"

"I'm showing you what you're missing." She grabbed his hand and placed it over her rounded stomach. "Soon, our baby will be moving. If you want to feel it—ever, if you want to share this miracle with me, you've got to stop using because I am never going to tell our child that his daddy died of a heroin overdose. You will not do that to us."

"It's a boy?"

She shook her head. "It's too soon to tell the sex. We'll know in four weeks. If you're clean, you can come to the appointment with me and find out. If you're not, then ... well, my mother will call your mom."

Her words shredded his last hope. If he lost Abby and the baby, he'd have nothing. Nothing but using and trying to get money to score his next hit. He grasped her hand. "I can't lose you."

Pity and compassion warred in her eyes.

"I need you. You're the only—"

"I love you, Luke." She touched his cheek. "I'll always love you. But I won't help you kill yourself. Not anymore."

His gut clenched at the guilt in her tone. He reached for her, cupping her chin in his unsteady hand. "It's not your fault. I ... I manipulated you." The truth tasted like bile.

She pulled away. He swallowed hard.

"I let you do it. I've lost count of how many times you said it was going to be the last time. I was a fool to believe you. I should have been stronger. For both of us."

She wasn't the fool. He'd destroyed his life with a spoon and needle. How stupid he was to think everything he'd heard about how addictive heroin was wouldn't apply to him. He'd be the one in millions who could use and walk away anytime he wanted. The joke was on him.

But he had no intention of becoming a statistic, just another one of the 150 or so thousand who died every year from a fatal heroin overdose. He wanted to get clean, needed to get clean, but he couldn't do it alone. Not without Abby in his corner.

"Can I call you?"

Ray Collins appeared behind his daughter. Obviously, he felt no need to knock before coming in. The controlled rage smoldering in the older man's eyes withered Luke's flagging confidence.

"Mr. Collins, hello."

"Luke."

The man couldn't even say hello? Luke weighed his options. Ignoring the tension crackling in the room, he met the man's scrutiny without flinching. "Could you give us a few minutes, sir?"

Ray exchanged a look with his daughter and started toward the door. "Five minutes. Not a second more."

"We're almost done, Dad. I'll meet you downstairs in the lobby."

Done? Abby wouldn't give up on him, would she? Even if she refused to let him see the baby, she wouldn't cut him out of her life entirely. She said she would always love him.

"I'll write to you from rehab." He stared at her, memorizing every feature of her pretty face. Ninety days seemed like forever. Forever to be without his drugs. And forever to be without Abby. "If they let me."

"I'll pray for you every day, Luke." She spoke with conviction, as if she were absolutely certain prayer could change things, could change him. "God wants to help you. If you'll let Him."

Luke felt a tug at his heart. Could he yield his life to God? His own faith probably wouldn't keep him clean a single day. Not living with Cole and not on the streets. That was certain. When Luke's strength tanked, he would need Abby's prayers. Especially if he grew too weak to resist heroin's siren song. Which would probably happen more than once. Didn't most addicts relapse several times before getting clean? And staying clean? One of his nurses had said that it would be a life-long battle.

What had he done to himself? To his family? And to

Abby?

"I love you, babe."

"I love you, too." She leaned over the bed, wrapped her arms around his back, and held him as if her life depended on it. Maybe it did. Maybe it didn't. His certainly did.

*

On Sunday morning, Abby sat between her parents in their usual church pew, but there was nothing usual about today. The tightness in her shoulders shot a current of tension down her spine. Her thoughts focused entirely on Luke. Had she been too hard on him? Didn't he have a right to be present when she found out the sex of their baby? Depending on when he entered rehab, he might not be able to come anyway. Should she tell him she'd changed her mind? She didn't want to discourage him, or worse, make him feel desperate. She didn't want to think about what he might do if he felt desperate.

But, maybe, he needed to hit the bottom before he could change. Surely, almost dying qualified as slamming head first into rock bottom. Abby bit down on her lip and released an audible sigh. *Oh, God, what can I do? How can I help him?*

The sudden weight of her mother's hand on Abby's thigh startled her. Mom squeezed once—her way of drawing her children's attentions back to the service. Abby shifted her gaze from a blank stare at the open Bible in her lap to focused attention on the sermon outline projected on the white wall behind the pulpit. The title, "Deliverance," popped in royal blue, bold letters.

Would Pastor Schwartz say something that would give her clear direction? Because, obviously, *she* didn't have a clue how to help Luke. Two sure things settled in her heart. She wasn't giving him any more money. And she had to put her baby's safety first. She could do this. She had to do this. She would not put her baby at risk. No matter how much she loved Luke.

Abby studied the pastor, trying to pick up the thread of his message.

"Everyone—his family, his friends, his neighbors—had tried everything they could think of to help this tormented man. But he had stopped caring about them. He spent all of his time alone in the cemetery. Sometimes, he even cut himself with sharp rocks, inflicting physical pain, probably to block out his mental torment. From what we read in Luke, it sure looks like everyone had given up on this tortured man. They tried restraining him, but he broke the chains every time. He was a danger to himself, and very possibly, a menace to the community. His family had probably begged him countless times to get a hold of himself. The Bible doesn't tell us about all of their sacrifices, but we can only imagine what they were willing to give up trying to help him."

Abby's mind drifted to her own sacrifices—the money she'd taken out of her bank account, the times she'd ignored her responsibilities to be with Luke whenever he needed her. But her biggest sacrifice was her integrity. For months, she had lied to her parents to protect Luke. But that wasn't the real reason. She hadn't been willing to give him up, and she hadn't wanted to go to war with her parents about continuing to see him.

Lord, forgive me. I shouldn't have lied to Mom and Dad. I'm not making excuses, but I love Luke. And I don't know what would have happened to him if I'd abandoned him after his parents kicked him out.

An image of him laid out in a casket flashed like a nightmare in her mind. She shuddered then wrapped her arms protectively over her stomach. She couldn't lose Luke, especially now that they were having a child together. *God, please.*

Pastor Schwartz looked right at Abby. "Sometimes, we have to step aside and let God do His job."

She squirmed beneath his scrutiny. Had she tried to do God's job? Probably. Yes, many times.

"We cannot deliver someone from the devil's clutches any more than we can save them."

The pastor's brown eyes softened as his gaze returned to Abby. "But don't get discouraged. God sees what is going on."

Abby looked down at her stomach. Did everyone know? Surely not. But they would soon. She forced herself to pay attention to the pastor's words, words that seemed to be meant just for her.

"God knows better than you do how desperately your loved ones need His help. And He hears your prayers." Pastor Schwartz closed his Bible. "Let's pray. Each one of you, for the people you know who are struggling, bound in Satan's traps set to destroy not the only the captive, but his or her family, too. Don't despair." He held up his Bible like a banner high above his head. "Our God is mighty to deliver. Shut yourself in with the LORD as Marlene plays "Jesus Breaks Every Fetter" on the piano."

Abby leaned forward, elbows pressed against her thighs, her forehead resting against her interlocked hands. *Father, please don't let Luke die. Help him stop using drugs. Take away the craving. Walk with him. Be with him, especially when he's all alone.*

What else should she ask for? Recalling the verse in Romans about the Holy Spirit praying for believers when they couldn't find the words, Abby released a soft sob. Tears spilled over her hands and slid down her arms.

Then she felt her mother's arm around her shoulder, pulling her close. Mom pressed a kiss to Abby's temple. The sweet citrusy scent of Mom's shampoo lifted Abby's spirit.

"It's going to be all right," her dad whispered in her ear.

Shifting to face him, Abby gave him a smile. She wasn't alone. Not like Luke was. So grateful, she whispered, "I love you, Dad."

His steady gaze conveyed a strength she could lean on, no matter what the future held.

Even if the worst happened. Fear momentarily gripped her heart. A cold sweat left her trembling in its clammy wake. How could she go on without Luke? How could she raise their baby in a world without his father?

"Never give up hope." Her dad's words were firm, but loud enough for her ears alone. He clasped her hand and bowed his head.

Was it possible that her dad didn't hate Luke?

"Lord, we need you," the pastor said.

Abby hadn't been praying or paying attention. What had she missed? Hopefully, nothing meant specifically for her.

"Watch over us and our loved ones in the coming week," Pastor Schwartz continued. "May we remember the words of Christ when He said He would never leave us or forsake us. Go before us and make our paths plain, Father. We need Your guidance, because our thoughts are not Your thoughts. And all God's children said, amen."

A chorus of "amens" surrounded Abby. Hope beckoned, a warm, steady light in her heart, urging her to trust God, to rely on His guidance, to believe that Luke would recover. A weight lifted from her shoulders. She could do this. With God's help, she would not give way to fear. She would have faith, faith to believe for a good future, for herself, for Luke, and for their child.

*

Luke hadn't known what to expect when his mom dropped him off at the Robert Ellis Rehabilitation Center. After his initial session with a counselor, Luke had been in meetings and so-called positive activities straight through until dinner, with the exception of twenty minutes for lunch. Even then, staff mingled among the residents, chatting and monitoring as if the dining area were a school cafeteria. At least the staff was easy to spot in their royal blue T-shirts with Ellis Rehab in bold gold letters across the back and first names just below the right shoulder on the front of their shirts. Even the doctors were Dr. Ryan and Dr. Lisa. Apparently, someone had decided that first names created a welcoming atmosphere, but the rigid schedule made Luke feel like a caged animal under observation. Ellis Rehab obviously considered free time the addict's enemy, and Luke supposed it was.

How had he ended up here?

The obvious answer was his father had connections, connections that assured that his son would comply with his expectations. "You will check into a 90-day rehab," his dad had said. Ninety days seemed like forever.

When exactly had Luke given up control of his life? The first time he'd shot up? Or when he'd kept taking oxy even after the pain from his knee surgery had subsided to a dull ache that he could have and should have easily ignored.

He had never thought of himself as weak. Obviously, he'd been wrong.

Like a swarm of hornets, cravings plagued him all day, distracting him from whatever discussion or activity the staff had planned. He wanted to trust that these people knew what they were doing. They claimed to have a 65% success rate, which seemed overly optimistic. Still, Luke certainly didn't know how to free himself from heroin's clutches. If he were honest, most times, he didn't even want to try. That was the look he had seen in Abby's eyes when she'd made her ultimatum. She knew he was lying.

Being an addict turned even the most honest person into a consummate liar. Stuck in here for ninety days would make getting clean inevitable. But staying clean was never a done deal. Freed from the constant surveillance, so many addicts relapsed as soon as they got out of rehab.

What made him think he would be any different than thousands of others who had gone through more than one rehab program and still couldn't get the proverbial monkey off their scrawny backs?

Killing yourself is the only way out.

The seductive words lured him in. He followed his breath in and out, felt his chest rise and fall, but couldn't stop his heart from racing, pounding a panicky, staccato rhythm. Was it true? Was suicide the only way out?

Killing himself would end his shame and frustration and, most of all, the all-consuming drive for the next high. A high that would only last a couple of hours before he'd need something else to keep him functioning.

Analyzing the logistics, he could make an overdose look like an accident. That would be easier on Abby and his mom. They would have less guilt because they wouldn't have to wonder if they could have done something.

He let the fantasy play out in his head, taking a perverse comfort. Until he envisioned Abby weeping over his dead body, the needle still stuck in his arm. And his parents having to tell his little brother. Suicide was a nightmare from hell.

He could not do that to them. They didn't deserve that. Not after everything he'd already put them through.

But he could let Abby go, sign off on his parental rights, set her free to love and be loved by somebody else. A man who would put her and the baby first. Because Luke didn't know if he could ever do that. His promises had meant nothing up to now. Heroin had turned him into a liar and a thief. And that wasn't the worst of it. Disgusted, he chewed on his lower lip, straining against an iron cage of his own making. He had no one to blame but himself. Not even Cole.

Abby blamed Cole, but Luke knew the truth. He had run out of oxy, and heroin was cheaper. In the beginning. Until his using had escalated into a $50 a day habit. Then he'd gone back to oxy, popping just enough pills to keep going, and restricting his heroin use to late nights and weekends.

If a man could die from self-loathing, he'd already be dead. Which would be better for everyone, wouldn't it?

What about Joe?

Luke's little brother idolized him. That was the reason Dad gave for insisting Luke have zero contact with Joe. No visits, no phone calls, no skyping, no texts. Nada. Luke had dared to send a birthday card in early September, but his mother had intercepted it, marking the envelope, "return to sender" in her flowing handwriting. At the time, he had wondered if she felt bad doing that, if she were only following his father's orders. It didn't matter either way. The end result was the same. Luke got the message. Absolutely no contact.

Did Joe think about him? Of course, he did. Joe probably hated him. After countless shared hours tossing a football back and forth or shooting hoops in the driveway, the kid probably felt abandoned. Luke had screwed up his relationship with his little brother. Maybe forever.

He couldn't blame that on his father any more than he could blame his heroin addiction on Cole. The blame rested squarely on Luke's shoulders. But what could he do about any of it? Heroin was a noose around his neck.

Maybe suicide was the answer.

Suicide's the coward's way out. Luke remembered his grandfather's words after finding out an old Army buddy had shot himself in front of his wife and twelve-year-old son. *Suicide's the most selfish act anyone can commit. You leave your family and friends to deal with what you did for the rest of their lives.* Gramps had been angry, but there was a lot of truth to his words. Luke raked his hand through his hair, hoping against hope that no matter what he was, he wasn't a coward.

"Hey."

Luke glanced up from his untouched plate of lumpy mashed potatoes, turkey, and gravy into the eyes of a guy not much older than him. His cheeks were hollowed, acne covered his sallow skin, and if it weren't for the eyebrow piercing, Luke could've been recoiling from a mirror image of himself.

"First time?"

Luke nodded. "How'd you know?"

"You have the look."

He raised his eyebrows, not sure he wanted to know what look the six-foot, 130-lb guy was talking about.

"My name's Dustin. Mind if I sit down?"

Luke gestured to the three empty chairs at the square table, and Dustin sat across from Luke. They picked at their food in silence for several minutes before Dustin pushed his tray aside. "I don't have much appetite. You?"

Luke shook his head. He was pretty sure a toddler could've done better with his plate than he had. He dunked a hunk of turkey in the mashed potatoes and forked it into his mouth. He forced himself to chew then swallowed. If he could get his hands on some weed, the food would taste better. He ate another bite, then covered his plate with his napkin.

"Suicide's not the answer, man."

Startled, Luke made eye contact with the guy. "I don't know what you're talking about. You don't even know me."

Dustin pushed his chair away from the table, leaned back, and crossed his arms, attempting a relaxed posture that didn't fit his lined face or the intensity burning in his dark eyes. "You got that haunted, vacant look, and your brows are knit so tight together you could hold a needle between them."

Luke laughed at the ridiculous sight he'd make trying to hold a loaded syringe between his eyebrows. Impossible. And stupid.

Dustin's tense features relaxed into an easy smile. "We've all thought about it. More than once. Don't get me wrong. Getting clean will be the hardest thing you've ever done, but I promise you it'll be worth the pain."

Even if he could manage the physical and mental agony, Luke doubted anything could replace heroin's euphoric buzz. His brain needed the feeling of every trouble slipping away like snow sliding off a warm metal roof on a sunny spring day. Yeah, it was that good. Why would anyone want to give it up? He studied the other man a moment. "You don't look like you've been clean long."

"About a week this time. I slipped up. But before that I'd been clean six months, three days, and fourteen hours."

The guy's tone was proud—pride marred by shame. Addiction was the ultimate oxymoronic situation. Oxycodone. Oxymoron. Moron. Luke suppressed a disgusted laugh, directed more at himself than at the other man.

Discouragement clawed its way to the front of his head. If this guy could start using again after six months, why bother trying?

Because you don't want to die.

He didn't. Not really. He just didn't know how much longer he could live like this—every waking moment using, nodding off, then coming around, and trying to figure out where to get more drugs. He'd only stolen money from his parents once—a thousand dollars in cash out of his father's desk drawer. It hadn't even been locked. Dad had made it so easy, almost as if he'd wanted to catch Luke. His father had kicked him out that same day. But not until he'd humiliated him by forcing him to take a drug test first. Hot color rose in his cheeks. The shame of seeing his mom's shocked face when his dad tossed the stick on the dining room table was a knife in Luke's heart even now.

Dustin's gaze bored straight through Luke. "I know what you're thinking. It's a life-long battle, man. Some people want to help you, but most of your so-called friends want to drag you back into their hell. I forgot that. But I won't forget again. Take it from someone who's learned the hard way— more than once. You have to cut off every user you know, even if the guy's your own brother. Don't put yourself in a place where you'll be tempted to use. Because you won't be able to resist."

"I appreciate the advice, but—"

"Come to the Bible study after dinner," Dustin said, his tone a mix of earnest plea and command. "You won't be sorry."

Luke considered the alternative. A movie in the entertainment lounge. *Remember the Titans*—for most people an inspirational, feel-good movie. But not for him. Watching the black players and white players come together to form a unified, unstoppable football team would only remind him of all he'd lost. "Okay. How long is it?"

"An hour. Sometimes, an hour and a half, depending on how many people want to share or ask questions."

Luke's spine stiffened. No way was he sharing anything about his life. Any questions he had, he'd save for tomorrow's private counseling session.

"I already know what you're thinking." Dustin put his elbows on the table, clasped his hands, and leaned forward, his body language not quite in Luke's face.

He wanted to dislike the guy. His forwardness was downright irritating, but in the end, Luke followed Dustin and a half dozen or so others upstairs to the hall of meeting rooms.

The minute Luke entered the pale blue conference room where the Bible study would be held, he regretted his decision. Comfortable couches and chairs in navy and smoky gray circled the perimeter of the 20-by-50-foot room. The close quarters pretty much nixed his plan to retreat to a back corner where he could slouch down in a chair and pretend to pay attention. No way was he joining in on an intimate circle of junkies and Christian do-gooders who believed they had *all* of the answers.

But if they didn't, who did?

God Himself? Well, yeah. Sure.

The trouble was Luke and God weren't on speaking terms. Not since the accident that had destroyed Luke's dreams. If he wasn't going to be an NFL quarterback, then he was nothing. God knew everything, right? So He knew that, too. He knew what the injury would do to Luke's plans. God could have prevented the whole thing, but instead He had stood by and let that defensive end slam Luke so hard he'd somersaulted a disastrous 400 degrees. Luke had crumpled like the spider he'd smacked with the plastic fly swatter Mom kept under the kitchen sink. That spider had hobbled off on five of its eight legs then fallen over in defeat. Roused by pity, Luke had slammed the critter a second time, effectively ending his misery.

God had not done the same for Luke.

He hated his life. Hated what he'd become. Hated the fact that he'd lost more than his opportunity to play football.

The door opened and closed behind a man in his mid-thirties, carrying a guitar and a knapsack. A young woman with straight, dark hair tied in a ponytail with a leather strap accompanied him. She smiled brightly as she greeted several people by name. When she stopped in front of Dustin, her smile faded.

"Hi, Leah."

She rested her hand on his forearm and blinked away the sheen of moisture from her blue-gray eyes. "It's good to see you, Dustin."

Luke heard the lie. She didn't want to see him back here again. No more than he wanted to be here.

She pulled Dustin into a quick hug, whispering in his ear.

Luke heard her soft words. "You'll make it this time, Dustin. I pray for you every day."

Dustin smiled. "You know I need all of the prayers I can get." He gestured to Luke. "This is Luke. Luke, Leah. Leah, Luke. It's his first day. First rehab."

This guy didn't understand the concept of TMI, too much information. Luke shrugged.

Leah clasped Luke's hand in a firm grip, giving it a reassuring shake. "Welcome to Ellis Rehab. I'll keep you in my prayers." The warmth in her eyes mirrored the sincerity of her words.

"Thanks." *I think.*

Leah nodded as another girl drew her aside. Before they

were even out of earshot, the young teen starting talking about what God had done for her that week.

Yep, prayer just might be the only thing that *could* help Luke. Abby had promised to pray for him, but she loved him. To Leah, he was a total stranger. A total stranger who was even now celebrating some small victory with a girl half her age who'd probably done stuff Leah had never even imagined.

As she moved to stand beside the guy with the guitar, Luke asked Dustin, "Is she for real? She just met me, and she's promising to pray for me?"

Dustin's easy expression morphed to grave intensity. "She knows, man. This plan saved her life. She's been clean six years."

"No way. She was a junkie?"

"Yeah. She ODed twice before she checked in here. It took her four tries to get clean. She understands what we're going through."

Leah didn't fit the profile in Luke's head, but neither did he. Heroin? A sweet girl like her? Apparently, no one was immune to opiates' clutches. A clammy hopelessness seeped into Luke's body. His shoulders slumped in despair.

The man with Leah called the room to attention and introduced himself as simply Jake. No last name. No reverend. No pastor. Just plain Jake.

"If you're new to Ellis, welcome. You're in a good place."

Several people called greetings to Jake.

When he opened the Bible study in prayer, there was nothing extraordinary about his simple words, but Luke felt as if he were eavesdropping on one side of a conversation between best friends.

Strange. He had never felt that way about God. Not even before the accident.

Curious, he opened his eyes and scanned the room to discover that nearly every person sat with their heads bowed. Luke bristled at the prick of shame that had become his almost constant companion. The only thing that banished the uncomfortable truth that he was ultimately responsible for his actions was the first sweet rush of heroin blooming in his brain. Could he get along without that incomparable relief?

What about the joy of holding your child?

Guilt slammed into his chest, and Luke put his hands over his ears in a feeble attempt to shut out the voice, the one that asked hard questions that dug deep into his soul.

"Are you all right, man?" Dustin asked.

To his horror, Luke realized people were staring at him. The prayer was over, and Luke's fear was center stage. Too bad. Hadn't they all been exactly where he was right now? At this moment, when he was facing the toughest choice in his life? The choice between the people he loved and the drugs he couldn't live without.

Leah caught his gaze, her eyes gentle and encouraging. Jake strummed his guitar, and she began to sing a haunting song about bringing everything to the table. What table was she talking about? The next words—that God already knew all about it anyway—rang with an irrefutable truth that burned to the depth of Luke's dark soul.

His muscles itched to race from this suffocating room filled with people softly singing out to God. God who had seen all of the ugly, vile things Luke had done. God who couldn't possibly stand to look at him or hear his feeble prayers. The urge to escape, to sprint down the stairs and out into the night where the darkness could hide him, exploded in Luke's brain with a drive more powerful than any he'd ever known. Trying unsuccessfully to suppress his agitation, he tapped his feet repeatedly, the sound drowned out by the music. He started to stand. But a greater fear gripped him.

If he left, could he come back to the program? Or would the doors be locked to him?

Look around you.

Ignoring the urge to run, Luke lowered himself back into his chair and allowed his attention to rest for a split second on each person in the circle. Expectation and, what was more amazing, hope shined on faces ravaged by addiction. Some of them looked near death, and yet they were smiling and singing about God's love for them. Could Luke dare to believe that he could know God as Jake and Leah and even Dustin did?

Hope was a dangerous thing, wasn't it? It could lead to crushing disappointments and defeat.

Leah was singing the chorus again. Bring it all to the table because God already knows. Like sunlight after an endless, dreary winter, hope drew him with cords of love. Hope could change everything if he gave himself over to its gentle persuasion.

Did God actually care?

LORD, I don't deserve anything good, but if you don't help me, I'm gonna die. Please, help me. Not for me. For Abby and the baby. For my family.

Luke buried his face in his palms. A moment later, he felt the weight of a strong hand on his shoulder.

Then the man began to pray in words so soft Luke barely heard them. "Save my brother, LORD. Deliver him from drugs. Set him free. Give him the abundant life Jesus promised us."

Abundant life? Luke had no idea what that would look like. Who could ever trust any addict? Could he trust himself to stay clean?

Would Abby ever trust him alone with their child?

CHAPTER SIX

Abby stepped on the scale. Five pounds heavier! That had to be wrong.

But apparently the clinic's scale was accurate to the tenth of a pound. What was done was done. She couldn't very well go on a diet while she was pregnant, could she? With a surge of maternal instinct, she placed her hands protectively over her obvious baby bump.

Frowning, the nurse directed Abby to sit in the nearby chair, then positioned the blood pressure cuff on her right arm. Trying to ignore the building pressure, she glanced at the nurse's nametag. Myra was droning on about how Abby's baby hadn't gained more than a half of a pound at most and how Abby herself was gaining far too much weight at this point in her pregnancy. Should she defend herself? After dealing with morning sickness and having almost no appetite for three months, she actually enjoyed eating again.

"You're blood pressure is up, too." Myra scowled, then schooled her lined features, clearly swallowing any further critical remarks.

Abby's mother should have been here to defend her. Something as inconsequential as giving a final exam should *not* come before finding out the sex of her first grandchild. Frustrated with herself, Abby fought the urge to burst into tears. She was seventeen. She could handle a simple doctor's visit without her mother holding her hand.

Or Luke.

She missed his touch, his smile, his arms drawing her close. Thinking about him not being here with her would make her cry.

Think about something else.

Her weight. Five extra pounds. How had she let that happen?

Maybe she *had* overindulged a bit. No more weekly trips to the Cheesecake Factory, even if she did crave chocolate cheesecake. Chocolate with raspberry, chocolate with peanut butter, chocolate with caramel. Chocolate reduced the sadness to a bearable level. As long as she didn't let her imagination drift to what it would be like after the baby came if Luke couldn't stay clean, she could get through a day without crying. Ellis Rehab was the best place for him now, even though they couldn't be together. She reminded herself of that fact every single day.

How she had wanted him to be here today, to hear the technician say, "You have a son," or "You have a daughter." It was wrong that Luke wasn't here to share this with her. Her life wasn't turning out like anything she had ever imagined. Before she could subdue her emotions, tears streamed down her cheeks. She swiped her face with the back of her hand. This crying was getting ridiculous. She couldn't control what was happening with Luke, and she couldn't even control her own emotions.

"What's wrong, Abby?" The nurse's soothing concern suggested that she actually wanted to know.

"I miss Luke." There. She'd said it out loud. For the first

time. Because she knew her parents didn't want to talk about him.

"Your baby's daddy?"

She gulped back a sob and nodded. She dismissed the familiar embarrassment, but the disappointment was harder to shake. She and Luke had been a golden couple. This wasn't how life was supposed to turn out. Not for them. They'd both grown up with all of the advantages two-income, upper middle class families could afford. They'd had their futures mapped out—college, career, marriage, children.

Nowhere in that perfect picture had she envisioned Luke addicted to drugs or herself pregnant before she'd graduated from high school.

Myra patted Abby's arm. "Let's go see if the technician can get a good picture of your baby."

Moments later, ignoring the slight discomfort of the procedure, Abby squinted eagerly at the computer screen. She studied the image, but her baby tumbled around like a future gymnastics champion.

After what seemed like forever, the technician announced, "You're having a baby girl."

Abby beamed, joy tingling from her fingers to her toes. A little girl. She was going to have a daughter. A daughter to love and adore and cherish.

Would Luke be happy? Or had he been hoping for a boy?

Raising a daughter by herself would be easier than raising a son alone.

Instantly, she dismissed that traitorous thought. She refused to let her mind go in that direction. She could not stop hoping. Hope fueled her prayers, and Luke needed prayer. That was one thing she was absolutely sure about.

*

Luke used his thumb to open the thick, off-white

envelope. The faint smell of Abby's floral perfume clinging to the paper stirred memories that he didn't dare dwell on and distracted him momentarily from the contents of the letter. Eager to learn how things were going this week, he unfolded the lined paper, and two items drifted to his lap. He picked up the pink postcard and a black and white photo of their baby. The pink caught his attention. A ribbon banner across the top of the card declared, "It's a girl!" in embossed silver letters.

So they were having a daughter.

He allowed himself several seconds to let that sink in. No matter how hard he tried, he couldn't picture being a father to a little girl. What he could he possibly teach her? Don't ever go out with a guy like me because addicts will never care about you as much as they care about their drugs? Abby would teach her that, and even if she never said a negative thing about him, more than one of their daughter's grandparents would, without exaggeration or embellishment because the truth was vile enough.

Fresh shame washed over Luke as he saw himself through his unborn daughter's eyes. He punched his pillow and wedged it between his back and the cold wall. December winds howled, rattling old windows that allowed frigid air to leach into the room. He stretched his legs out on his bed, grateful that the restless leg syndrome had eased off. This time. Unless he started all over again. He'd been here four and a half weeks, and he'd seen several people leave only to return within the week. Quitting was easy. Hadn't they all quit countless times only to reach for their drug of choice before the day ended? Despair pressed on his chest, sucking the oxygen from his system.

The irony was heroin could banish his depression. H would give him the temporary feeling that all was right with his world. That was the great temptation, the steel trap that cut his legs out from under him every time he thought of quitting for good. The solution was the problem, and the problem was the solution.

Agitated, he raked his hands through his hair, pulling and tugging until the pain interrupted his cyclical thoughts, allowing him a single lucid moment.

A possible turning point blazed like a light in a dark place.

He should pray. Every day, in this place, someone told him that God cared, that He'd sent His only Son, Jesus, to die for the whole world. Even for junkies.

Luke closed his eyes. What should he say? Jake urged them all to be honest with God, because like the song said, He already knows everything anyway. Luke could lie and hide from himself, but no one could hide from God. He had seen Adam and Eve in the bushes, and He had seen every evil thing Luke had ever done.

God, I want to be clean for Abby and for our daughter. I owe them that much. Even if I can't ever be the man they deserve. I'm not asking for myself. I ...

He was about say he deserved to be sent to hell, but wasn't his life already hell on earth? Instinctively, he knew the real hell was infinitely more terrible. A verse from last night's Bible study tickled the edges of his brain. Something about God's grace being enough. Luke hoped it was true. Even for him.

Because if it wasn't, he was a dead man.

"God, please don't leave me like this," he whispered then reached for the baby's picture and Abby's letter.

He stared at the sonogram photo of his daughter for several moments, then unfolded the lavender pages .

Dear Luke,

Honey, we're having a baby girl. She's a little gymnast. She was wiggling around so much I couldn't tell whether she was a boy or a girl. Not at first. The only thing I could see was arms and legs moving, filling the screen, and then her little face with a smile like yours.

I hope you're not disappointed that she's not a boy. We never talked about that. But won't it be nice to have a daddy's girl who will adore you?

The joy in Abby's words released a floodgate of gut-wrenching sobs. He wept for her, for his mother, for his little brother. He even cried for his dad. Drowning in grief and remorse, Luke reached for the only light. He needed to pray.

For what? Healing? Freedom from the desire to use? "God, make me willing to give it all up. For good."

Exhausted, he stretched out on his bed and drifted into a sleep fraught with nightmares.

*

When he awoke, he read Abby's four-page letter through three times. She said she was doing okay, but he could hear what she wasn't saying. School was hard, especially now that her teachers couldn't help noticing her pregnancy. Kids were talking about her, looking down their self-righteous noses at her, as if they were superior, morally and intellectually, because Abby had gotten pregnant, while they had been smart enough to prevent pregnancy or to avoid the risk altogether. He could only imagine how it hurt Abby to lose her place as a leader others looked up to. Kids who had cultivated her friendship now avoided her and talked trash about her behind her back, sometimes not even caring if she could hear their cruel, mocking words. He had done that to her. Getting her pregnant was totally his fault. He should have been the one to say no. Now, she was paying the price for his selfishness, for his utter inability to see beyond the moment.

God, forgive me.

Luke reached for the Bible on his nightstand and opened it to a random place toward the end of the book. The last verses in Matthew chapter eleven caught his attention. "Take my yoke upon you and learn of me." Learn? This book that was over a thousand years old could teach him how to conquer his addiction? Had people in Biblical times poisoned their lives with chemicals that destroyed their bodies and took over their minds? Opium had been available for a long time. Maybe, they had.

Luke read about the life of Jesus for an hour, until Dustin knocked on his door, announcing, "It's time for dinner, man."

Looking forward to the evening Bible study, Luke refolded Abby's letter and slipped it and the baby's picture into the nightstand drawer. "I'm right behind you."

*

Reclining on the living room couch with her laptop open to a blank document, Abby reread the selection of possible questions for her paper on *The Great Gatsby*. Why hadn't she dropped AP Lit when she found out she was pregnant? That would have been the smart thing to do. Her parents would have been totally onboard. Given Abby's constant exhaustion, her mother had suggested Abby continue with only classes necessary for graduation. Even her dad was willing to give her an easy out, but the pity in their eyes roused her determination to carry on with her senior year as planned.

Abby saw now what a joke that was. While her friends were enjoying their Christmas break, she was completing make-up work to finish her first-semester coursework. She sighed. The effort to complete the current assignments, let alone the overdue ones, required more energy than she could muster. What was worse, her heart wasn't in it anymore. The baby growing inside her and her worry over Luke consumed her. Like a pendulum, or riding a bungee cord, her thoughts of Luke swung her between hope and despair.

Laughter drifted from the kitchen. Sam and Mom were marathon baking several varieties of Christmas cookies. From the sweet aroma of cinnamon, Abby concluded that they had started with Snickerdoodles, her personal favorite. By the end of the day, numerous plastic containers and holiday tins filled with cookies carefully layered between sheets of parchment paper would be stacked like colorful towers along every square inch of the marble countertops. Mom always insisted they bring an artfully arranged platter to every party and event they would attend throughout the season. Abby usually looked forward to cookie baking day simply because it was one of the few times that their mother wasn't distracted by work and social responsibilities. To say that Stephanie Collins was a busy woman was an understatement, and Abby often wondered how Dad put up with Mom's neglect. Then again, he was frequently out of town looking at houses to buy and flip, but when they were together, they acted like lovesick teenagers. It was downright embarrassing.

Suppressing a groan, Abby opened Pandora on her phone and started her favorite holiday station. The house phone rang, and she ignored it. Anyone who wanted to talk to her would call her cell, and these days, she only heard from Lisa, Megan, or Jack. Talking to him was increasingly uncomfortable. He wanted more than friendship from her. She could see it in his eyes whenever Luke's name came up. Jack thought she should dump Luke for good. The fact that he was her baby's father didn't seem to matter to Jack.

Unless Luke totally turned his life around, he would never be a good dad, and he would definitely *not* be good enough for Abby.

Of course, Jack never said any of those things. He wouldn't want to annoy her. She was Luke's girl, not only because they were having a baby together, but because she loved him.

Enough to let him go?

Shaking her head, Abby dismissed that thought. God couldn't possibly expect that from her, and it certainly wouldn't be her choice, not as long as she could still work at repairing the vision of her ideal future.

Determined to crank out her paper by dinnertime, she spent the next half hour skimming *The Great Gatsby* for quotes to support her thesis that Daisy Buchannan was incapable of loving anyone. Satisfied that she'd gathered enough evidence to prove that Daisy was a selfish woman whose self-serving actions led indirectly to Jay Gatsby's murder, Abby composed her rough draft with her usual ease. After editing that draft in hard copy and incorporating the changes into her electronic document, she emailed the finished paper to Ms. Rosario. A quick glance at the corner of her computer screen declared the time to be five-thirty. The sun had long since gone down, and the living room was dark, except for the end table lamp, which Abby didn't even remember having turned on. Her stomach stirred in protest at the tantalizing aroma emanating from the kitchen. When had she last eaten?

"Mom, did you order the pizza yet?" Abby called out.

Not expecting or receiving any reply, she closed her laptop and wandered into the kitchen turned cookie factory. Cookies in various stages of preparation covered every flat surface in the room. She lifted a warm date pinwheel from a cookie sheet, bit into, and burned her tongue. She rushed to the cupboard nearest the sink, filled a glass with filtered water, and drank until her mouth stopped stinging. She didn't bother to ask why neither her brother nor her mother informed her that those cookies had just come from the oven. Focused on rolling out chocolate dough for cut-outs, Mom was completely oblivious.

Sam looked up from the chocolate cut-outs he was frosting. "Order a sheet pizza and a double order of medium chicken wings, will ya, Abby? I'm starved."

He was starved? Knowing her brother, he'd probably scarfed down a dozen cookies since they'd starting baking at noon. As if to confirm her greater need, her stomach growled loud enough to gain her mother's attention. "It's number five on my speed dial. And could you please check to see if that last text I got was from your dad?"

Abby scanned the crowded surfaces but couldn't spot her mother's cell anywhere. "Mom, where is your phone?"

She chuckled then retrieved it from her apron pocket.

Using a dishtowel, Abby wiped the sticky flour off the screen and keyed in her mother's password. Samabby2. The woman had no imagination or possibly no free brain space for storing and recalling passwords. Abby ordered the food, which unfortunately would arrive in approximately seventy-five minutes. She'd be starving by then, and eating a handful of cookies wouldn't help. She grabbed a blueberry protein yogurt from the fridge. Tearing off the foil cover, she announced, "The pizza won't be here until seven." Her words were meant to reproach them for not having called the order in earlier, but the shocked expressions of both her brother and her mother declared that her subtle criticism had missed the mark entirely.

"Good, your dad should be home by then." Mom slid the

tray of cut-out bells, trees, and stars into the oven then returned to the table to roll out more dough.

"There's no text from Dad, Mom." Abby watched for a reaction, which came in a nearly imperceptible raise of her eyebrows. "It was from Luke's mother. She wants you to call her when you get a chance."

Abby breathed deeply to quiet her agitation. No rush. That meant nothing was wrong with Luke.

But what could Caroline Bradford want? Maybe she wanted to go with Abby the next time she had a sonogram. That was probably it. Grandmas made a big deal out of such things. Abby should be grateful that she wanted to be part of her granddaughter's life. Maybe it was her way of doing what Luke couldn't, making it up to Abby.

"Abby?"

Mom leveled her with a scrutinizing expression. How long had Abby zoned out? "Did you say something?"

"Yes. I asked you what you did with my phone, and if you wanted to finish rolling and cutting out this dough so I could call your father."

Mom was irritated, but not with her.

"I'll find your phone." It didn't have legs, and she'd had it in her hand less than five minutes ago. She opened the fridge for two more yogurts, one for her mother and the other for her brother. That's where she found her mother's cell. Seriously? Where was her head? Maybe, she should take a nap until the food arrived. Laughing at herself, she handed the phone and a yogurt to her mother then tossed one to Sam, who caught it with a triumphant grin.

Her mother smiled with amusement and kissed Abby's cheek. "You look tired. Why don't you take a nap until the pizza gets here?"

"My plan exactly. But, Mom, can you do me a favor?"

"Of course, honey."

"Please ask Mrs. Bradford if she got a letter from Luke this week. I haven't heard from him since I sent him the baby's picture."

Sam dumped his empty yogurt container in the trash. "You're better off without him."

Mom scowled. "Samuel David Collins, mind your own business. And take that container out of the trash and wash it. You know we recycle plastic."

Sam obeyed, washing all of their empty containers and depositing them in the recycle bin under the sink. "I'm just saying what you and Dad said."

Mouth agape, Abby burst into tears. Wasn't that what everybody was saying? Never in her life had she felt more alone. Everybody believed she shouldn't have any contact with Luke. But they didn't understand how much he needed her. Or how much she needed him.

Mom placed her hands on Sam's shoulders, turned him around, and marched him to the door. "That's just about enough. Go to your room until dinner. And when your father gets home, we need to have a long talk."

As soon as Sam was out of earshot, Mom said, "It's not true. What your brother heard was a small part of a lengthy conversation. He took what we said out of context." She pulled a tissue from the pretty Christmas box and offered it to Abby to dry her tears. "Dad and I know how much you love Luke and how important it is to you that he make a full recovery. It's only natural. He's your baby's father, and you want him to be part of your lives, but, honey—"

"Please don't say it, Mom. I have to believe that Luke's going to be okay. God wouldn't leave him like that."

As soon as the words left her mouth, Abby wondered why some addicts recovered and others died. Surely, they all wanted to be free.

*

Luke enjoyed the Christmas Eve service, especially the short Nativity play. The young couple playing Mary and Joseph brought their two-month-old baby boy to play baby Jesus. Miraculously, the baby slept through the entire service, including the caroling. Now, a few of the residents were taking turns holding the smiling child who cooed and giggled with obvious delight over so much attention.

Luke couldn't bring himself to greet the parents, let alone hold their baby. Their happiness pierced his heart with shame and remorse. It had been almost two weeks since Abby had sent the sonogram picture. He'd tried writing to her, every day that first week, and then every other day. He would compose a page, read it over, then crumple it into a ball, and toss it in the trash. The words on the page could not express what was in his heart. He had to show her. He longed to see her, but she would not visit him without her parents' permission.

Jake rested his hand on Luke's shoulder. "Is something wrong?"

Luke met the other man's sympathetic gaze with what he hoped was a veiled expression. "You mean other than the fact that it's Christmas Eve, and I have no idea when I'm going to see my family again?" Hopefully, Jake would think Luke referred only to his brother and his parents. Talking about Abby was pointless.

"It can be a real downer if you let it," Jake said, lowering himself onto the couch and settling in for a talk. The guy's radar was uncanny.

"Enough to make a man—"

"On the other hand," Jake cut in, effectively shutting down Luke's rant, "some people don't have any family left.

What about *you*, Luke? Who are you missing tonight?"

Before he could stop himself, Luke blurted out, "My girlfriend, Abby."

Jake fixed Luke with a knowing look.

He had already said more than he'd intended. He might as well go for broke. "She's having my baby." To his shock, tears threatened. When had he lost all self-control? He clenched his fists in frustration and disgust. "And I'm stuck in here while she's going through this all alone."

Jake gripped Luke's shoulder. "That has to be hard. For both of you."

The guy's compassionate tone suggested he understood. He couldn't possibly. He and Leah were together.

Luke lurched to his feet. "I gotta get out of here."

"Luke, wait!" Jake called out.

But Luke pushed past people talking and laughing.

"Hey, man, where are you going?" Dustin shouted above the conversations and Christmas music.

Ignoring them both, Luke twisted the door handle and escaped, intending to bolt to the front door. Stopping at his room to collect his stuff would give someone a chance to stop him. He could not let that happen. His sneakered feet hit the stairs at a run.

But he had barely reached the landing when a strong hand caught his upper arm in a vise grip. Jake's face loomed inches from Luke. "What do you think you're doing? You're going to be no good to them, racing out of here in an adrenaline rush, thinking you can solve every problem. You know where you're really going."

"She needs me." Luke shuddered.

The desperation in his voice and the look on Jake's face said it all. Luke couldn't possibly handle the pressure of being outside these walls. Not yet. Not even for Abby.

Defeated, he slid down the wall, slammed his tailbone against the hardwood baseboard, and welcomed the pain. Tears fell in torrents.

A black cloud of self-loathing sucked every drop of hope from his heart. What was the use of trying so hard every single day if he was going to screw it up anyway?

"I'd be better off dead. She'd be better off if I were dead. My dad would make sure she had everything she and the baby would ever need. And *her* parents would always be there for her. I can never do that for her. She can't trust me. I can't even trust myself."

"You're wrong." Jake seized Luke's shoulders. "God has a good plan for you, for Abby, for your baby. Don't give up."

For several seconds, Luke searched the other man's eyes. How he wanted to believe. Fighting the magnetic pull of the other man's words, Luke muttered, "I know exactly how much I need to shoot up to end this all. So let me go."

"I can't do that, Luke."

Fury surged through his veins. "Why the hell not?"

"Because five years ago, I was exactly where you are now."

The world stopped while Luke gauged the sincerity of the older man's words. "You're lying."

"I'm telling you the truth. Ask Leah." Jake waited for Luke to process what he was saying. "We were having a baby. I was stuck in here, and after the baby came, I couldn't stand it. Like you, I bolted. I wanted to believe I was strong enough, that I was ready to conquer the world for them. I really wanted to be that man." He shook his head. "All I did was drag her into my addiction. Thank goodness her parents were able to care for our little girl, or we might have lost Lily forever."

Don't listen to him. Kill yourself. It's the only way.

Tormented, Luke lurched free of Jake's grip then banged his head three times, hard against the concrete block wall. The pain bursting in his brain erased the agony of failure and defeat. Pain so intense that it shut down all thought.

Until Jake restrained him in a straightjacket hold and began to pray, quietly asking God for mercy.

Luke tried to grasp the man's words, but hope flickered out like a candle in the wind, and darkness rushed in.

When he came to, four staff members were carrying Luke to his room. They laid him on his bed and held him down while the resident nurse injected him with a drug that erased the panic that threatened to shatter his sanity forever. Luke welcomed the prick of the needle as much as the drug's effects, though he felt a brief disappointment at not experiencing his beloved euphoria before drifting off to sleep.

*

He awoke several hours later. His first thought—that last night's episode was quite a setback—plagued him with cloying hopelessness. He reached for his Bible on the nightstand and read in the Psalms until the first light of Christmas morning spilled with fresh promise through his small window. He could not go on like this much longer. If he were ever able to leave rehab and return to any sort of reasonable life outside these brick walls, he would have to cast himself entirely on God. Last night had convinced Luke of that. His mind and body betrayed him at every turn. Happiness and sorrow alike roused his need for drugs. He simply couldn't function properly without chemical assistance of some kind. What was normal anymore? Dogged by cravings and thoughts of suicide, lasting peace seemed impossible.

Except when he was reading the book in his lap.

Was God really speaking to him? If God could do anything, the way Abby said, then God could give Luke back his life. Jake believed it. The man lived it. One day at a time. Apparently, so did Leah.

Luke found Jake in the kitchen with his wife, the two of them cleaning up after breakfast. Jake whispered something in her ear, and Leah giggled.

"Hey," Luke said.

Leah, face flushed, looked up from the pot she'd been scrubbing. "Are you hungry? I'd be happy to make you an omelet or oatmeal. Maybe some toast? Whatever you want. There's coffee left."

Luke's hunger went deeper than his stomach. He met Jake's questioning expression with one of his own. "Do you have a few minutes to talk? Maybe we could go into the chapel, if no one's there."

Jake nodded, tucked a loose strand of Leah's hair behind her ear, and brushed a kiss across her cheek. "We'll be back soon. Pray."

This last was a bare whisper, but Luke heard, glad that Leah would be praying, too. Because one thing was perfectly clear. Prayer was the only thing that could save Luke from himself.

CHAPTER SEVEN

Abby couldn't shake the feeling that Luke was in trouble. This was more than her usual fear that he would relapse. What could be wrong? He was still at Ellis. Mrs. Bradford definitely would have called to warn them if he'd checked himself out of rehab. If only Abby could see him, see for herself that he was okay, then she could dismiss her panicky feelings as hormones or stress-induced fear.

A fluttering response in her abdomen momentarily distracted her. Had that been the baby moving? She patted her stomach to encourage more movement, but her daughter wouldn't cooperate. Fear for Luke rushed back, supplanting the joy she'd felt a moment before. Willing herself to be calm, she finished her last bite of quiche, washed it down with the rest of her milk, and excused herself from her family's traditional Christmas brunch without her usual second slice of warm Christmas bread.

Her mother shot her a questioning look but didn't comment on how little she'd eaten.

Abby averted her eyes to the sideboard upon which their annual sumptuous feast had been artfully displayed, almost as if her mother were trying to make up for the countless meals she had missed since she'd accepted the position of department head last spring. Unfortunately, Abby didn't have the appetite to do her mother's efforts justice. Whatever was going on with Luke concerned Abby far more than her mother's hurt feelings.

With a glance at the antique clock, its hands positioned at half past ten, her father said, "Don't be too long. Your grandparents are expecting us promptly at two thirty."

"I just need a few minutes."

Looking seriously put out, Sam leaned across the table and glared at her. "She can't disappear now. We have to open presents right after breakfast. I've been waiting for hours."

Abby understood. It hadn't been that long since she'd leaped out of bed, eager to open her gifts. Now, the only present she wanted was Luke, whole and well and completely drug-free. "Don't worry, Sam. I'll be down before you've finished helping Mom clean up."

"But that's your job." His pout morphed into a scowl.

"Today, you'll do your sister's chores." Dad poured himself a second cup of coffee and added peppermint mocha creamer. "With a smile on your face. Is that clear, young man?"

Grateful for her dad's support, Abby mouthed a second "thanks" and exited the dining room. The heady scent of the seven-foot Douglas fir centered in front of the picture window, together with the pine garland encircling the stairs railing, roused both sweet memories of the past and tentative hopes for the future, all contrasting sharply with her uncertain present. Before Luke's accident, she had never imagined life could be so hard, and for a moment, she understood his urge to escape. If only they could turn back the clock. If only they'd known how highly addictive oxycodone was. Why hadn't the doctor prescribed something else? Surely, *he* knew the risks. Comprehensive, definitive information about the connections between oxies and heroin was all over the internet.

Anger rose from the pit of her stomach, up her throat, then burst in her brain, followed by a sense of powerless more debilitating than she had ever known. She'd never felt such complete helplessness. Not when her grandmother died. Not when she'd stood at the bathroom sink staring at the two blue lines on the pregnancy test stick, willing the second line to disappear, to be only a figment of her fears.

What was happening with Luke? She couldn't stand another minute of not knowing.

At the top of the stairs, an image of that first day she had noticed the needle marks on Luke's arms slithered into her mind. She shuddered. For weeks afterward, she had tried to convince herself she'd been mistaken. Luke would never do something so stupid.

But he had.

God, I can't do this. Being there for Luke is the hardest thing I've ever done. "I don't want to let him down, but …"

He's let you down. Over and over. Forget him.

Abby recognized the voice of her enemy. The devil wanted to destroy Luke, but she refused to be a part of his evil schemes. She would not turn her back on Luke. Not when her love could help save him.

Taking sanctuary in her room, Abby knelt on the shag rug beside her bed. She needed to pray, but she had no idea what to ask for, beyond pleading with God to protect Luke. From himself most of all. Her shoulders rose and fell with several deep breaths as she struggled to focus her thoughts. She said everything she believed God wanted to hear. She begged Him to forgive her for all of her sins, because maybe some of what was happening to Luke was her fault. And even if it wasn't, didn't she need a clean slate with God so that He would hear and answer her prayers? Satisfied that she'd owned up to everything she consciously knew to be wrong, she tried to bargain with God, promising to do everything in the future exactly the way He wanted. At least to the degree that she understood His will. Again, she asked Him to forgive her for having sex with Luke before they were married because even now she still wanted to be with him like a wife.

Finally, emptied of all reasoning, she sobbed until her throat ached and her tears were spent.

"Jesus died for him, Father. Please help Luke see that." After a pause, she added, "And please forgive me for trying to bargain with You."

What more could she say? Grandma always said, "God already knows. You don't need to worry."

Needing comfort, Abby snagged a pillow to kneel on, rested her head on her hands on the edge of the bed, and settled in to wait.

She expected an answer—some form of reassurance— perhaps God quietly speaking to her heart, but her cramped legs drove her to her feet before peace could erase her concerns. Resolute, she marched to her dresser and gazed at herself intently in the mirror. Shocked by the sight of her pupils constricted to pinpoints of fear, she sank onto the end of the bed, then scooted back toward the headboard. She hugged her knees to her chest and concentrated on slowing her breaths. She needed to calm herself. She had no more grounds for anxiety today than on any other day.

She didn't want to ruin Christmas for her family, and she definitely didn't want her parents or her grandparents to dog her with questions. And if they didn't, at least one of her aunts, uncles, or cousins would. Luke's problems were none of their business. It was bad enough that most of them would discover *her* problem just by looking at her rounded belly. At nineteen weeks, nothing she wore could conceal her pregnancy. She rubbed her belly and her daughter responded with a kick, or was it a punch? Abby smiled. "I can't wait to meet you, little one."

The baby responded with another kick, and Abby closed her eyes to pray some more. "Lord, You know how much I love Luke. The baby and I need him to get well."

Little by little, her perspective shifted and grew into a determination to ignore her feelings and trust the truth. "God, I know You love Luke more than I do. I trust You to take care of him."

Suddenly, worrying made no sense. But the fear remained. If she lost Luke forever, if he never came back to her, how could she go on? Could she really raise their baby alone?

Was it fair to ask her child to grow up without a father to love her?

Abby wanted to keep her baby, but adoption—her heart clenched painfully—wasn't that a reasonable option? She covered her hands protectively over her baby bump. No, she couldn't do that. If she gave her baby up, she would regret it for the rest of her life. And she would blame Luke. Hatred surged through her at the thought of his addiction causing her to lose her child.

She drew in a deep breath, tamping down her anger. This was her choice. Whatever Luke did or did not do, Abby would keep their baby. She wasn't alone. Her parents, and even Luke's parents, would help her. They would all help her financially until she could support herself and the baby.

A knock sounded on her door. Three firm raps. Not gentle, like her mother's, or insistent like Sam's. Abby opened the door reluctantly.

Her dad waited in the hallway. He'd changed into a white buttoned down shirt, black pants, and his traditional Christmas tie that played "Silent Night" and "O Little Town of Bethlehem." It was the first gift she had ever bought him with her own money. She'd been ten that year. She reached out and pressed the spot at the top of the manger scene that started the music. She closed her eyes, and for just a moment, she was a little girl again. A little girl without a care in the world. A little girl whose daddy was a superhero who could make everything just right for her.

Only he'd lost his superpowers. Even so, she wanted him to hold her in his arms, to stroke her hair, and to tell her that everything was going to be all right.

Always patient in a crisis, Dad smiled. "Do you want to talk about what happened downstairs?"

Did she? She pulled the door open wide and gestured for him to enter.

He clasped her hand, his grip strong and reassuring. For several minutes, they sat together in the window seat, her favorite spot to read in the late afternoon when the sun spilled across the pages. The sky outside her window now was white with dancing snow flurries. It was a pretty day, with enough snow to make kids happy without making parents anxious over treacherous driving conditions.

"Something's wrong," Dad insisted. "One minute we were all enjoying breakfast, listening to Christmas music, and looking forward to a relaxing day." He framed her face with his large hands, tenderly, the way he'd always done when she was in trouble. His eyes locked with hers, pouring his strength into her heart. "The next minute, your face was white as a sheet." He sat back against the cushions, urging her to open up.

She didn't know where to begin.

"Did you get a text message from Luke?"

She shook her head. "They can't have cell phones, Dad."

"Right. So what happened to shake you up?"

"I don't know. I can't explain it." Tears welled in her eyes, her mind flooded with images of Luke struggling in agony, desperate for a way—any way out of his addiction. "I ... I think Luke is ... thinking about suicide."

"Oh, Abby, what makes you think *that*?"

Saying the word put a name to her anxiety. For an agonizing moment, this new fear threatened to shatter her reason, then crystallized into an image of Luke knotting his bed sheets into a rope. "Sometimes, when addicts stop using, they try to kill themselves. They think there's no other escape."

"Luke would never do that. Not to you. Not to his family."

Her father spoke with a conviction Abby didn't feel. "I want," she choked the words past the sobs rising in her throat, "to believe that, to believe Luke loves us enough to never give up."

Dad pulled her into a hug, patted her back, and let her cry. "It's going to be all right, sweetheart. It's hard now. For both of you. But God hasn't forgotten Luke. Or you."

She wept until her tears soaked her father's shirt. Suddenly aware of the cold fabric against her skin, she raised her face to his. "Oh, Dad, we've made such a horrible mess. If I could go back—"

"You can't change the past, baby girl. You only have right now, this moment, to make the right choice. That's what makes a good life, making the right choice and not letting the past defeat or define you."

His words fanned the hope burning like embers in her heart. She nodded, relieved that her panic had receded to reasonable concern. Her father was a wise man. Maybe, both of her parents should have been professors. Her dad could have taught philosophy. He had a lot to teach people about how to live.

If only she had listened to him and broken up with Luke. No. That hadn't been an option. She could no more abandon Luke than she could stop breathing.

"I love you, Dad."

"Me, too, kiddo." He kissed her forehead then held out his hand to help her to her feet. "Are you ready to open presents? Sam can't wait much longer."

Smiling, she took her father's hand. Maybe someday, with God's help, Luke would be as good a father as her dad.

He held the door open for her. "After we've opened presents, I'll take you to visit Luke."

"Seriously? But Grandma and Grandpa are expecting us." The last thing Abby wanted to do was to disappoint her grandparents. Even though Dad had told them about her pregnancy weeks ago, Abby hadn't seen them since she started to show.

"No problem. We'll meet Sam and your mom at your grandparents. Grandma will understand if we're a little late. You need to see for yourself how much progress Luke's made in the last month."

She stood on his toes and kissed his cheek. "Thank you, Dad." She really did have the most amazing father in the world.

*

"You have a visitor."

Dustin's tone—happiness and barely disguised jealousy—arrested Luke's attention. He blinked. Had he heard correctly? "You must have me confused with some other guy. No one is coming to see me today."

His parents wouldn't interrupt their Christmas plans. Lunch with his mom's family. Dinner with his dad's. Then dessert at home in front of the television watching *It's a Wonderful Life.*

Some life.

Theirs *had* been pretty good until their oldest son was stupid enough to get addicted to heroin. His father wasn't likely to forgive him anytime soon. And his mother? Luke had broken her heart when he'd stolen his great-grandmother's pearl necklace and ruby pin. Dad had talked to every pawnbroker in a 50-mile radius, but by the time he'd uncovered the right shop, the jewelry had been sold. With 44 days of sobriety under his belt, the memory of his mom's face when she had learned he'd stolen and sold her great-grandmother's jewelry made Luke want to vomit. At the time, because he needed to score, he hadn't given his mother's feelings any thought at all. Now, he hated himself for stealing something she could never replace.

No, his parents wouldn't be coming to visit him anytime soon. Not until they were 100% certain their son wouldn't relapse, and from everything Luke had learned at Ellis, 100% recovery and heroin addiction never fully aligned. Even those who'd been clean for decades could still fall back into the same bondage. Heroin's sweet buzz called to them all. Learning not to respond—that was the key. That and learning to recognize the dead end.

Dustin cleared his throat. He stood in the doorway, waiting for Luke to follow him downstairs. With a shrug, Luke refocused his attention on the crossword puzzle he'd begun after breakfast. Ordinarily, they didn't interest him, but with all the free time today, he needed something to occupy his mind. Whenever he had too much time to think, self-pity led to bitterness, or worse, fantasies about leaving and nodding off, shutting out the self-hatred and the memories of the many reasons his family should despise him. His mind teetered between desperate longing and total revulsion. Heroin defined him, would continue to define him for the rest of his life.

Ending it was the only guaranteed escape. But he couldn't do that to Abby, to his family.

"Stop feeling sorry for yourself," Dustin scolded.

The guy was a mind reader. Sometimes, having someone understand how he felt comforted Luke. Today wasn't one of those days. "Look, man, I just want to be alone a while."

Dustin's eyebrows lowered. "Get downstairs, Bradford. You're baby mama is waiting."

Anger flared at his friend's choice of words. Abby didn't deserve that label. Which was just one more injustice Luke had inflicted on her. He'd made her the object of ugly gossip at school, and now some junkie who had never even met her was looking down his nose at her. That was harsh. Dustin wasn't some junkie. He was a good friend. Sucking in a slow breath, Luke considered the possibility that Abby's parents had actually allowed her to visit him. "Abby's here?"

"Tall, 5'6" or 7", dark hair, blue eyes, sweet smile?"

Joy coursed through his veins. "That's her." He rushed for the door and stopped. He didn't have anything to give her.

"Don't worry about it, man. She didn't come for that."

"What?"

"A present. She didn't come for a present. She came to see you."

Luke forced himself to descend the stairs at a normal pace. The second he entered the common room, he spotted her. She was a vision, a miracle he didn't deserve.

And she had never looked more beautiful. Or vulnerable.

Sitting in an arm chair with her feet crossed at her

ankles, she tapped her fingers together, the sparkly red polish glittering in the light from a reading lamp on the end table to her right, a magazine open on her lap. Looking up, she caught him watching her. His eyes drifted to her belly, visibly round in spite of the loosely-fitted green sweater she wore over black leggings paired with fur-lined suede boots. Drinking in the sight of her, he smiled in spite of himself. In spite of everything that made this the worst time for them to be having a baby.

She moved first, standing so close to him that he could smell the mint on her breath. Neither of them spoke. Words could not convey how grateful he was to see her, here in this place, on Christmas Day. When his parents hadn't shown up for family day last week, Luke had resigned himself to no holiday visitors.

And now here was Abby. His anchor that kept him from floating away forever in a drugged haze. He touched her cheek, and she smiled.

Luke's heart stirred with gratitude and wonder. In this moment, everything and anything seemed possible. Even his full recovery. *Thank You, Jesus.*

Abby stepped closer, and her baby bump pressed against him. She tilted her face to him, her eyes filled with unspoken questions.

Luke couldn't bear seeing her afraid. Not caring who saw them, he lowered his head, his mouth covering hers in a sweet, trembling kiss. Her lips moved against his, gently at first. Then she wrapped her arms around his neck, surrendering. He deepened the kiss, stirring her passion as well as his own.

How had he not noticed how much heroin had dulled his sex drive? He pulled her closer.

A sharp "Harrumph," from a new resident reminded

Luke of their lack of privacy.

He instantly released Abby. "Merry Christmas, honey." Searching his eyes, she caressed his face, her hand smooth as silk. A pretty pink blush colored her cheeks, and she sighed. "I'm sorry I couldn't come before."

"That's okay, babe. I'm just glad you're here now. I've only had visiting privileges for about a week anyway." He took her hand and led her to a couch that was only slightly longer than a loveseat. He sat with his leg deliberately pressed against hers, wondering if she wanted him as much as he wanted her. "I can't believe your parents let you come."

"Dad drove me. He's arranging a day-pass for you."

Shocked, he blurted out, "You're kidding, right?"

"I'm not. We're bringing you with us to my grandparents, if you want to come." Her voice shook with surprise and doubt.

"I don't ... think that's a good idea." His stomach twisted into a tight knot, and feeling like a coward, he averted his face so she wouldn't see the fear in his eyes. "Your grandparents probably hate me." That wasn't the real reason, and he knew it.

She gripped his forearm, urging him to face her.

He resisted. How could he possibly spend the whole day—Christmas Day of all days—with her family? It was too much to ask of them. Of him. He couldn't handle the strain. Especially if they all knew he was in rehab. And how could they not know?

"Luke, honey, everyone's praying for you. My parents. Your parents. No one hates you. No one wants to see you fail. We're all pulling for you to get well. To leave rehab and start your life over."

She was talking fast, the way she always did when she was unsure of his reaction.

Start your life over, she'd said. Why hadn't she said, start our life over? The muscles in his shoulders tensed into throbbing knots. If he failed again, what then? How many chances would she be willing to give him? She had already given him more chances than he deserved.

"Luke, did you hear what I said?"

"I heard you, but I haven't heard a word from my dad, and my mom's only written twice. I should have known she'd never buck my dad." He didn't, couldn't add, especially after I stole her great-grandmother's jewelry. Luke couldn't bear Abby knowing how low he'd actually sunk.

Abby frowned.

Was she angry at his parents? Or did she feel sorry for him? He didn't want her pity. And he definitely didn't want her to think he was bitter because he wasn't. "I'm beginning to understand, Abby, how deeply I've hurt my parents. And how deeply I've hurt you." He hesitated, needing her to believe he'd made real progress in the last six weeks. "But I'm not ready to leave the center yet."

She said nothing. She had come all of this way, and he didn't want to go with her. What did he expect her to say? He couldn't blame her for being upset with him. If only she'd get mad. He could handle her anger more easily than her disappointment.

He laid his hand on her thigh, awareness sparking between them. He wanted to lose himself in her, but that wouldn't fix anything. "If you really want me to come with you, I will. I just ... it's the stress, babe. Imagining their thoughts. Their judgment. Not that I blame them. I deserve whatever they think about me."

Whatever they imagined he had done, the truth was far more disgusting. Besides, that wasn't exactly the issue. Could he resist the temptations? Probably not. He wasn't ready for a social gathering.

"Luke, they're not like that."

Surprised at her naiveté, he rubbed her stomach, hoping to feel the baby move. "Babe, the last time we saw your grandparents was at your parents' Labor Day picnic. I wasn't exactly very nice to you that day. So I wouldn't blame them if they didn't like me. And getting you pregnant in your senior year of high school ... they probably hate me."

Pink flooded her cheeks again. She was so beautiful when she blushed. He wanted to kiss her again and again until ...

"It takes two to get pregnant, Luke."

"But it's my fault. I should have told you no." Apparently, there was no end to his lack of character.

"*I* knew we were taking a big risk, but at the time ..."

He took both of her hands and held them, marveling again that she had actually come to see him. "I know I've said it before—so many times, but I'm sorry, Abby. I really am. I love you, babe. I'd do anything to erase the past two years." His eyes held hers. "Do you ... can you ever forgive me?"

She tried to smile, but her lower lip started to tremble. Tears trailed down her cheeks and slipped off her jaw. His heart clenched at the pain in her beautiful eyes. His Abby. He ran his thumbs from her jawline to her lower lashes to stop the flow of her tears.

"I already forgave you, Luke." She turned her face to kiss his palm, then looked up at him again. "The only thing I want from you is ..."

Her dad appeared, his big frame filling the doorway, effectively stopping Abby in midsentence. What had she been about to share? Luke held her gaze, needing to maintain the connection between them for as long as he could.

"Merry Christmas, Luke," Mr. Collins said. He glanced at Abby, who was drying her face with a crumpled tissue. "We're all set. As long as this is what you both want to do."

Abby stood on her toes to kiss her father's cheek. "Thank you, Dad."

Sizing up Luke, the older man added, "We just have to bring you back by seven thirty."

In that moment, spending a few hours with Abby was worth the risk of relapsing. "I'll get my coat and be right down."

Abby's smile was the best Christmas present Luke had ever received.

*

Abby's grandmother rushed to greet them as they entered house. Luke had barely helped Abby out of her jacket before her grandmother swept her away. The scowl her grandfather leveled at Luke started the whispers in his brain. *Just a little something to take the edge off. A drink. Weed maybe.* He scanned the room. All of Abby's cousins appeared too young to be using.

That left one option. The medicine cabinet.

He couldn't do that. Not here. Not at her grandparents'. Abby would never forgive him.

But if he *could* manage it without being caught ...

What about tomorrow's urine test? The unwelcome thought prompted him to reconsider.

No. It wouldn't be worth it. He'd come this far. The worst was behind him, wasn't it? He couldn't endure withdrawal again.

To silence the argument in his head, he searched the crowded room for Abby. Where had she disappeared to so quickly? At the far side of the living room, seated together on a navy leather couch with oversized plaid pillows, Abby and her grandmother clung to each other. They were both crying. He cursed under his breath. If they didn't get it together fast, her whole family would start asking questions. He was in no shape to face an inquisition.

On cue, his skin started to crawl.

He surveyed the room, gauging the reactions to the emotional scene playing out between Abby and her grandmother. No one seemed to have noticed. Yet. Not wanting to appear overly concerned, Luke allowed his gaze to shift past them and back again. Still crying. Two weeping females must not be that unusual for this family, or somebody would have said something by now.

Yeah, right. Tell yourself whatever you want. The proverbial crap would hit the fan any minute. He didn't want to be here when it happened, but he couldn't exactly walk out on Christmas. Anxiety twisted to the brink of panic.

Then he spotted an older man—an uncle maybe—pulling a cigarette from a pack of menthols. Thank God. Luke crossed the room, prepared to bum a cigarette from this complete stranger. He thrust out his hand, and the man shook it with a boxer's grip.

"Hey, I'm Luke. Abby's boyfriend. Got an extra smoke?"

The older man's forehead crinkled in obvious surprise. His eyes narrowed. "My name's Ed. Abby's Uncle Ed."

So much for winning points for social etiquette. His mother would be mortified. In this setting, bumming a cigarette *was* pretty lame, but desperation trumped good manners. For him anyway. "I'm all out. I forgot to ask Abby to stop at a convenience store."

"No problem, but we better head out back to the patio, or my mother will have a cow." He shot a look in the lady's direction. Grandmother and granddaughter were both blowing their noses and drying their splotched faces.

Luke cringed. Why did Abby have to make a scene, here, today? His first day away from the center. He should have listened to his instincts. This was a bad idea.

The older man held out the pack of menthols. "You might want to fly under my mother's radar, since my niece is obviously pregnant. You have heard of birth control, right?"

Luke didn't even raise an eyebrow at that. Ignoring the man's smirk and the dig, he tamped down his irritation, accepted the smoke, then followed Uncle Ed through the dining room and out the patio doors. There was no point in telling the man that Abby's grandparents already knew about her pregnancy. Obviously, the news hadn't reached the entire Collins clan, not until they saw Abby's pregnant belly.

Bracing himself against the sharp December air, Luke waited as Ed lit his own cigarette first and then passed the lighter to Luke.

Seconds later, ignoring the sub-zero temperature, he dragged the smoke into his lungs, counting on the nicotine to take the edge off his cravings. He'd been right. He didn't belong here. Especially with so many people he didn't know. So many people who probably couldn't stand the sight of him, and for plenty of reasons.

The whispered voice in his head grew louder, more seductive. *Just one more time, and then you can get clean for good. You got this. You can control it.*

Luke ground the spent cigarette on the flagstone beneath his feet and watched the butt sputter in the crystals of new-fallen snow. Uncle Ed hadn't said a word since they'd come out here five minutes before, but who knew what questions he would launch at Luke? "I think I'll head inside and look for Abby. Thanks again for the smoke."

The man clasped Luke's arm with controlled strength, and he forced himself not to wince.

"See you don't hurt her. Any more than you already have. Or you'll answer to me, and I'm not the gentleman my brother is." He dug his fingers into Luke's bicep. "Do we understand each other?"

Luke noted the steely glint in Uncle Ed's dark eyes. He would make good on his threat. "I love your niece, sir, and never—"

"Cut the crap. You and I both know what you really love."

Bile rose in Luke's throat. "You don't know me."

"I do know you. I see guys like you every day. I'm a public defender."

Luke backed up toward the sliding doors, itching to extricate himself from this no-win conversation.

"You're lucky your parents have money, because if I had to defend you ..."

Ed trailed off, leaving Luke to imagine what the other man would do.

"Thanks again for the cigarette. And Merry Christmas."

The man's lethal look scorched Luke's bare neck as he strode back into the house. He needed to get out of here. At this rate, he would never make it through dinner and presents. Where was Abby? At least, she wasn't still sitting on the couch crying with her grandmother.

He found her in the family room, talking to another cousin whose name he couldn't remember. Abby's darting gaze and tight lips suggested her concern. For him? He was about to go to her when a toddler grabbed her before she saw Luke. She dropped to her knees, her full attention on the youngster. She was going to be a good mom.

But he wasn't going to be a good dad. Not now, and maybe not ever. His patience was shot. The volume in the room thundered in his ears. But not loud enough to drive out the voices in his head. Could he sneak upstairs without anyone noticing?

He returned to the front hall. The view of the staircase in the foyer was visible to only a fraction of people gathered in the living room. He could make his escape undetected. Abby's mother was reading aloud to two toddlers. One twin sat on each of her knees. Two middle-school-aged girls were laughing about some You-tube video or chat or some other crazy message on their phones. Mesmerized by their technology.

Addicted. Just like him. He suppressed a laugh.

Not just like him. They could stop anytime. And they weren't destroying their bodies, though being glued to electronics couldn't be good for their brains.

But Luke was destroying his body and his brain. Doctor Jefferies said the damage wasn't permanent. Not yet. Luke could still turn it around. That's what everybody at Ellis said, every day, to remind themselves they could get control of their lives and keep it.

But today, he needed something stronger than a cigarette to take the edge off, so he could hang out with Abby and her family without turning into a crazy man.

So he slipped past the living room and climbed the oak staircase unnoticed. A whisper in his head urged, *Go back downstairs, now.* He clenched and unclenched his shaking, sweaty hands. If someone asked, he would say he was looking for the bathroom. Four doors lined the second-floor hallway, and an oriental runner in earth tone colors covered the hardwood floor. Every available wall space featured family photographs that spanned several decades and three or four generations. A legacy he could never live up to. On his left, he spotted a photo of Abby and her brother fishing off a dock.

Luke remembered that day. He'd kissed her for the first time. Sitting on the warm sand, the sun sparkling in her dark hair, she'd been the most beautiful girl he had ever seen, and he had known he would love her forever. Was it true what her uncle said? Did he love his drugs more than her?

He should go back downstairs. Right now. Be honest with her. Tell her sharing Christmas with her family stressed him out so much that he was desperate for drugs. Any drugs.

He'd take a pain pill or a muscle relaxer. Just something to even him out. He wasn't planning to shoot up. He had no intention of screwing up that badly. He could control this. As long as he stayed focused.

He sucked in a sharp breath and studied the hall. Two doors on his left and two on his right. Hounded, he headed for the one on the far left, hoping that was the bathroom. He inched the door open and groaned. Inside, shelves of fabric and yarn and a table cluttered with photos, colored paper, and assorted decorations met his desperate eyes. Her grandmother's craft room. Disgusted, Luke backed into the hall and silently closed the door. He pivoted to try the room across the hall next.

Finally.

He heaved a sigh, entered the bathroom, and locked the door behind him. He flung open the medicine cabinet to discover ... nothing? Not a single prescription bottle in sight. The shelves were lined with creams, first aid supplies, assorted floss and tooth care items, and rows of nail polish. Where the heck did these people keep their drugs? They were old. They had to have pain killers somewhere.

Go back to the center. They'll help you.

He hadn't screwed up yet. Could he talk himself into

doing the right thing? For Abby and the baby.

God, where are you?

Luke splashed water on his face and dried off the excess with a red, green, and white towel. Fighting a sudden pang of homesickness, he stared at the wreath and holly berries printed on the terry cloth. His mom hung Christmas towels in the bathroom, too. For as long as he could remember, she had decorated every room in the house, on the Saturday after Thanksgiving. He and his brother always helped, suspecting she sometimes missed not having a daughter. And now, thanks to his stupidity and weakness, she didn't even have two sons.

Angry at the tormenting voices in his head that would not stop, he muttered, "No. That's not true."

But it could be, if he started using again. The odds of dying rivaled Russian roulette. He'd already overdosed once. He would need to be more careful.

Worry about that later, fool.

In case someone was waiting to use the bathroom, Luke flushed the toilet to avoid suspicion, pasted a smile on his face, and wished with every cell in his body he could find their stash. But where else could he look? Ready to give up, he trudged to the head of the stairs, then halted. The bedroom. Of course, old people kept their medication in their nightstands beside their bed.

The hallway was empty. Christmas music and conversation created a hum of happiness that Luke had no part of. He opened the first door on the right. The master bedroom. Mounds of coats were piled on a king-sized bed flanked by matching mahogany nightstands, each with three drawers. Drugs would be in the top. He headed for the side of the bed farthest away from the master bathroom. He slid open the drawer to discover only a pad of paper, pencils, and a hardbound copy of *Pride and Prejudice*. Should he skip the other nightstand? The drugs were probably in their bathroom. He should have figured that out before. He marched to the other side of the bed anyway and checked the other nightstand. Nothing but books. James Patterson mysteries and a rectangular magnifying glass.

Luke hurried into the bathroom, yanked open the medicine chest, and feasted his eyes on two shelves of prescription bottles. For a moment, he considered sweeping them all into the sink and dumping them in a plastic bag, but that would be difficult to hide in his ski jacket.

Besides, taking it all would be stupid. Most of it would be garbage anyway.

Breathe, man. You know what you're looking for.

The third bottle he touched was it. Oxycodone. A new refill, the red pills skimming the cover. 60 mg. He'd been hoping for 80, but these would have to do. He twisted the cap off and swallowed two tablets, closed his eyes, and waited for the calm to seep through his body.

That's when he heard a noise.

"Who's in here?"

No. Not Sam. *God, can't I catch a break?*

Standing in the bathroom door, the boy still carried a load of coats, scarves, and hats draped over his arms. "I told my sister not to trust you." His face was red with fury. He growled, "You'll never change. I'm going to get my dad."

The kid tossed the coats on the bed and whirled toward the open door, almost before Luke could react.

But he closed the space between them, grabbed the kid's arm, and jerked him back so that their faces were inches apart. "Don't. Think of Abby. She'll be devastated. I just took a couple pain pills. That's all. Forget you ever saw me up here."

Sam glared, his eyes shooting daggers. "Give me the bottle."

Luke scoffed. The kid was smart. He had to give him that.

"Give me the pills, and I'll keep your secret. As long as you don't mess up again."

"Sam, I love your sister."

"You don't know anything about love." Sam ground out the words, pulverizing Luke.

It was the second time that day he'd been told he didn't love her. Was it true? He stuffed his hands in his jeans. The fingers of his right hand closed around the prescription bottle containing the pills that had started it all, that had turned him into a loser addict who couldn't function without chemical help. Self-loathing burst like fireworks in his brain.

The kid held out his hand. "Give me the bottle, then go downstairs. I'll be down in a few minutes."

Luke had no choice but to go along and hope the kid kept his word.

CHAPTER EIGHT

One look at Luke ambling down the stairs, and Abby knew. She placed her right hand protectively over her stomach and willed her pulse to slow down. Her baby's father shot her a restrained smile, one that might have been a grin, had he not realized how well she knew him. The unnatural glow of his eyes confirmed her suspicions and sabotaged her hopes. He had taken something, but what? He had been out of her sight only twenty minutes. Surely, he couldn't have had anything on him when they'd left the center. That meant … no! No way. He wouldn't do that to her.

She would not let her mind go there. Not until, not unless she heard it from his own mouth.

Their baby girl kicked, three short thrusts that reminded Abby of her number-one responsibility. *Stop fooling yourself. Luke is an addict. He can't be the man you want him to be. Not now, no matter how much you think you need him.*

Her heart sank. Scolding herself changed nothing. She still loved him. She couldn't stop loving him. He needed her. They needed each other. Didn't he love *her* enough to stay clean for one single day? She searched his gaze for the truth, and his eyes pleaded for her forgiveness. She should have listened when he said he wasn't ready to leave the center. She had been naïve to think spending Christmas with her family would encourage him, maybe, even help him. She had wanted to remind him of what they could share. Instead, she'd provided him with the means and the opportunity to slip up. Big time. *God, what am I supposed to do now? Dad's going to be furious. I should have stuck to Luke like glue.*

He stood on the last stair, gripping the rail, watching her and waiting.

Not knowing what else to do, she mouthed the words "I love you" and hoped he understood.

"Abby, where does this piece go?" five-year-old Timmy asked, holding up a slanted gray Lego.

"That's part of the roof, honey." She pointed to the appropriate spot, then glanced at each of her three youngest cousins in turn. "I'll help you guys more later. I have to go talk to my boyfriend. He doesn't really know anybody."

"But he's talking to Daddy."

Timmy was right. Luke and Uncle Leo were standing near the foot of the stairs, so absorbed in their conversation that she couldn't catch Luke's eyes.

"Besides," seven-year-old Ethan added. "We're your family. If you like Luke, we like him, too."

Abby smiled. If only life were that simple.

Luke crossed the room then and rested his hand on her shoulder. His fingers twitched. Did he think she didn't want him to touch her? That alone confirmed that he felt guilty about something. He *was* guilty. He was on something. The only question was would her family notice? Surely, not everyone. But definitely Uncle Ed.

At that moment, Sam marched down the stairs, wearing his angry face, confirming Abby's suspicions.

Acting as if everything were perfectly normal, Luke

grinned at her cousins. "Maybe after dinner, Abby and I can help you finish your police station."

Silas, the oldest, shook his head. "No way. We need to open presents after dinner. We've been waiting for hours."

Luke laughed, a little too loudly, and Abby cringed, hoping no one had noticed.

"What was I thinking? Of course, you want to open presents first." He winked at Abby. "But right now, I'm going to steal my girl away from you."

She watched the boys process this remark, and satisfied that they had no inkling that anything could be wrong, she started to rise from her cross-legged position on the floor.

Smiling down at her—did he really believe she was completely clueless—Luke reached for her hand to help her up. He eased her against his side, wrapped his arm around her shoulder, planted a kiss on her cheek, and before she could protest, led her into the hallway.

Grateful for a moment of privacy, she opened her mouth to confront him.

Before she could get a word out, he said, "Miss me, babe?" in that sexy way of his and trailed kisses down her neck.

Abby's knees buckled. Luke caught her, wrapping both arms around her back and hugging her close. She blinked back angry tears and tried to push him away. Instantly, the muscles in his arms tensed. Holding her against the length of his lower body, he leaned back to look at her but didn't quite meet her eyes.

Was he hoping she wouldn't notice that he was high? They had been down this road so many times before. Who was he kidding?

She couldn't do this anymore.

"You all right, babe?" he asked, his voice even.

He didn't sound different. Not high anyway. Maybe no one *would* notice. She sighed. No sense kidding herself. He might fool everyone else, but Uncle Ed would take one look at Luke's glassy eyes, and it would be all over. Her uncle and her father would be driving Luke back to the center before they even sat down to dinner, leaving Abby to deal with the repercussions.

How had this happened?

She cupped Luke's face, hoping he'd be honest with her, maybe tell her what had sent him over the edge. Had someone said something? Abby should never have pressured him into coming with her. He had tried to tell her he wasn't ready. Was this her fault?

"I saw you crying earlier." He met her gaze and bit his lower lip. "Is everything okay with you and your grandma?"

She pressed her mouth closed to keep from screaming at him. He was trying to distract her, to keep her from asking what he had been doing upstairs. Which was completely unfair. Because she already knew, and he knew she knew.

"How could you, Luke?" She pushed at his chest, shoving him away.

"Babe, what are you talking about?"

She grabbed his hand and pulled him further down the hall. "Don't lie to me, Luke Bradford. You're on something."

His brows knit in a frown. "Keep your voice down."

His slight nod alerted her to the fact that they were no longer alone. The pressure of a hand on her back confirmed this. She pivoted to discover who had witnessed their argument.

Mom's polite smile declared she had heard at least part of the conversation between Abby and Luke. "Sorry to interrupt, but I need to steal my daughter for a few minutes. No one makes mashed potatoes as creamy as she does."

Abby opened her mouth to deny this, but the frosty glint in her mother's eyes silenced her.

"Luke, why don't you go into the den and watch the football game with the guys?" her mother suggested with polished courtesy. "Dinner will be on the table in fifteen minutes."

He shrugged. "Yeah, sure."

When he was out of earshot, Abby laid her hand on her mother's arm. "I'm sorry, Mom."

"I know you are, honey, but now is not the time or the place for this discussion."

Mom was right. Christmas was about peace and good will. The last thing Abby wanted was to shame Luke by making a scene. Unfortunately, Uncle Ed would not feel the same way. She could pray that he wouldn't say anything to Luke, but if he did, she had no idea how she could prevent their confrontation from spoiling Christmas.

*

By some miracle, Luke held it together for the rest of the day. Now, her dad was driving twenty-five miles per hour through the blinding snow. Soft Christmas music on the car radio competed with the whirring and slapping of the windshield wipers. Otherwise, the car was silent. Abby hadn't said a word to him since they'd climbed into the backseat of her dad's car. Twice, he had caught her wiping tears off her cheekbones when she thought he wasn't looking. How could he have been so stupid as to steal from her grandparents? He had stolen from his own family, and they couldn't forgive him. How could he expect her family to forgive him?

When he had caught sight of Abby talking with her uncle after dinner, Luke almost panicked. Popping the oxies without factoring in the man's experience with addicts had been crazy. One second of eye contact with Uncle Ed told Luke how wrong he'd been to underestimate the public defender. Ed Collins was ready to defend his niece and throw Luke out in the streets, snowstorm or no snowstorm. Walking back to the center would take about four hours. But didn't he deserve that and worse?

Sitting next to Abby in the backseat, Luke searched his brain for something to say to her. I'm sorry wouldn't cut it. She'd heard that too many times before. He reached for her hand, laid it on his thigh, then covered her hand with both of his.

She moved closer and rested her head on his shoulder. "I love you."

Her voice was a low whisper he barely heard. She was fading out of his life, saying goodbye. He couldn't blame her. Who knew how long it would take for him to fully kick his addiction?

He should give her any easy way out. Let her go. But a picture flashed in his mind—Abby walking beside another guy. He had one arm circled around her slim waist, and his other hand pushed a stroller. The two of them knelt down to kiss Luke's precious baby girl. Luke squelched the cry that rose in his throat.

He wrapped his arm around Abby's shoulder. "I love you, too, babe. I'm so sorry about today."

She lifted her face, and their eyes met. Her lips parted, and he kissed her, his mouth tender, his tongue seeking her life-giving warmth. She was the best part of him. He owed her everything, but if he couldn't kick his habit, he wouldn't be able to .... His body wasn't responding to her passionate response. Just a couple of pills could dull his nervous system that much? He deepened the kiss, hoping he was wrong.

She drew apart first, her cheeks flushed with

embarrassment over kissing him with her dad less than two feet away. "When can I come and see you again?"

How could he answer that question? He didn't even know if he'd be at the center. If they drug-tested him tomorrow morning, he'd be thrown out. No questions. No explanations. Just, pack up your stuff and leave. *God, if You can do anything for me, don't let me be in tomorrow's rotation.*

Abby stared at him. "Luke, I asked when I can visit again."

"I'm not sure about the schedule. I'll try to call you. And we can write. Send me a picture of the baby when you get a new one."

"I wish you could go with me." Her face glowed with excitement. "Hearing the baby's heartbeat is so awesome. You should be there."

Ignoring the sharp pain in his chest, he cupped her face with his hands. "It's okay."

"But Luke—"

"I'm sorry you're going through this pregnancy alone. Dealing with school and doctor's visits." Wishing this conversation could be a private one, he lowered his voice to a whisper. "I want to be there with you, helping you."

Her blue eyes glistened with tears. How many times had she cried today? And every time, it was his fault. With his thumbs, he wiped the moisture from her face.

"You can help me, Luke. By getting better. Maybe … maybe you can even be with me in the hospital when the baby comes." She sobbed and covered her mouth.

"Everything okay back there?" her dad asked.

"Yeah, Dad, I'm okay." She gulped a breath. "I miss Luke. I miss being able to see him every day, talking with him on the phone, hearing his voice, just … all of it."

Luke cringed. Her words were a slap on his face. Didn't

she know she was embarrassing him, talking to her dad like that? He almost said something, but one look at her silenced him. Tears like a spring flood coursed down her cheeks. Not knowing what else to do, he pulled her into his arms and held her while she wept as her father drove silently the rest of the way to the center.

*

The following morning, Luke slouched in a chair in the common room, waiting to find out whether he would be tested. His brain was going to explode. Desperate not to fidget, or worse, leap from the worn armchair and pace the crowded room, Luke sucked in a deep breath and begged God for mercy. *For Abby's sake, don't let them kick me out.*

Dustin settled into the lumpy, plaid love seat directly across from Luke. "Hey, man. Calm down," he said in a low voice. "I was the last guy for today."

Luke's shoulders sagged in relief. He resisted the urge to put his head in his hands and cry like a baby. Even now he couldn't believe he'd stolen those pills. Talk about a moronic move.

"Want to tell me what happened yesterday?" Dustin's remark was more a command than a question.

Luke couldn't look at his friend. Nobody caught an addict in a lie faster than another addict. "The usual. Christmas dinner, unwrapping presents, lots of noisy kids."

"You handle the pressure okay?"

Meeting the other man's scrutinizing gaze, Luke ground out the words, "Back off."

"That's what I thought."

The other residents were all heading into breakfast. No way did Luke want to call attention to himself, but his gut still churned, whether from withdrawal or anxiety he had no clue. He didn't think he could stomach any food.

"Let me give you some advice." Dustin stood over Luke. "Be careful who you talk to. You don't want to be the victim of smoke-screening." He gave Luke a long look. "Let's go get breakfast. I'm starved."

Smoke-screening? Why did his life feel like walking through a mine field? He followed his friend into the dining room without acknowledging the cryptic remark, but after they'd gone through the food line and taken their plates to an empty table in a far corner, Luke couldn't wait any longer. "What did you mean about me being a victim of smoke-screening?"

Dustin dunked his toast into the yolk of his fried egg. Focusing on his meal, he whispered, "You think you're the only one finding a way to use?"

Luke swallowed hard around a half-chewed piece of bacon. So that was it. Throw someone else under the bus to save your own hide. Made sense. He might do it himself if he were desperate enough.

"Take it from someone who learned the hard way, keep your business to yourself."

"But Dr. Jefferies is going to ask me how yesterday went."

"So, tell him just enough that he thinks you're confiding in him." Dustin looked up from his plate. "The best lie is 99% truth."

Luke dumped his egg on top of his toast, folded it in half, and took a bite. "That's ridiculous."

"Is it? People generally hear what they want to hear. You mix in enough truth, and the lie will go undiscovered." Dustin forked a clump of hash browns into his mouth. "*So, how was your Christmas, man?*"

Luke assessed the other guy's composed features. His friend was offering him a chance to practice his story.

Pondering how best to begin, he tested the temperature of his coffee with one finger. Finding it lukewarm rather than scalding, Luke drank a long, satisfying draught. It was probably just psychological, but after last night, he welcomed the instant effects of the caffeine. Willing the knot in his stomach to uncoil, he stole a glance at the staff standing around the perimeter of the dining area. Their relaxed postures suggested none of the residents were under surveillance, no more than usual anyway. He released the tension knotting his shoulders and neck. For the moment, he'd successfully flown under the proverbial radar.

Almost giddy with relief, he made eye contact with Dustin. "Just like I thought it would be. Tense and uncomfortable. The minute Abby unzipped her bulky jacket I became the enemy. Her grandfather gave me a look that would've withered a seasoned Marine, and her grandmother ... let's just say Abby and her grandmother ended up crying on the couch. One of her uncles took pity on me, and we went outside for a cigarette."

Under his breath, Dustin said, "Nice touch about smoking. Only natural given the pressure you felt." Approval shone in his eyes. "That must have been rough," he added, loud enough to be heard by the guys at the next table.

"Yeah, it was, more than I expected. But it would've been worse if her dad had not had the decency to give his parents a heads up. Seeing their favorite granddaughter visibly pregnant pretty much ruined their Christmas. You can imagine how tense everybody was, and you know, they blamed me."

Dustin smiled. "You got this. Share your normal frustration. If you try to hide how you felt, Jefferies will probe for the truth until you've revealed too much."

Luke polished off the last of his sandwich, surprised he'd

been able to eat at all. He pondered Dustin's assessment of his predicament. "What makes you so sure that's how it will go down?"

"Because I got kicked out last spring for running my mouth about stuff I should have kept quiet about."

From the grieved look in his eyes, what had come after must have been pretty bad.

"Like I said before, be careful who you trust. You and I both know an addict's first priority is himself."

Luke wanted to argue about that, but picking a fight with the only person he could call friend in this place would be stupid. Besides, Dustin really was trying to help. He was a much better friend than Cole ever had been. Comparing the two startled Luke, but he didn't have time to think about that now.

He and Dustin had just finished their coffee when Dr. Jefferies announced that the morning group session would begin in five minutes.

Showtime.

"Stay quiet during the meeting." Dustin's voice was low, so low Luke barely heard him. "Don't offer any information unless you're asked a direct question. Plenty of people will want to vent about how stressful or lonely their Christmas was. All you have to do is pay attention to their conversations. If we're lucky, maybe someone will break down. That'll take up a chunk of time."

Luke's brow knit in tight lines, and he massaged his temples to ease the beginning of what could easily turn into a pounding headache. If only he could quiet the panic roiling in his gut. Abby was counting on him. He had screwed up royally yesterday, but she'd forgiven him, though he hadn't deserved it. The last thing he wanted to do was have to tell her he'd gotten kicked out of rehab and totally ruined her chances of getting any money from his dad.

"Relax. You look like you've been hauled downtown for questioning."

Needing to do something with his fidgety hands, Luke piled Dustin's plate, mug, and silverware onto his tray then slid Dustin's tray underneath his, picked them up, and headed for the kitchen.

By the time, they reached the meeting room, half the residents were already seated in the large circle that contained forty some chairs. Dustin headed to two empty chairs about thirty degrees away from Dr. Jefferies. His buddy was quite the strategist, choosing seats where they wouldn't be in the Doc's direct line of vision.

"I can't screw this up." Luke lowered his voice below the chatter in the room. "Abby's counting on me to be clean by the time the baby comes."

"How far along is she?"

"More than four months, I think."

Doubt flickered in Dustin's eyes. "When's the baby due?"

"May 15th."

"She's asking a lot."

Luke scowled at his friend. "You don't think I can do it." The irritated edge in Luke's tone reflected his recent quick temper. Was he angry at Dustin or himself? It didn't matter. Luke had to maintain control for the next thirty minutes. "You don't know me."

Amusement flashed in Dustin's eyes, replaced instantly by an expression as serious as death. "Maybe not. But I know how addicts think, and I know what the traps are. And there's no bigger trap than a deadline."

The truth of Dustin's words was a kick in the gut. That's exactly how Luke had been feeling ever since Abby had given him her ultimatum. *You have to be clean, or you can't see the baby.* Her words echoed in his head, making him feel more desperate as the weeks passed. 44 days of sobriety had seemed a significant victory, a decent start on the road to full recovery. But one day outside of rehab, a few hours away from the restrictions and safe environment of the center, and Luke had fallen off the wagon big time. Stealing pills from her grandfather. How insane could he be? Classic addict move.

"I'm not trying to discourage you, Luke." Dustin kept his voice low. "I just want you to be realistic."

Luke nodded. Hadn't he thought the same thing? Hadn't he wished a thousand times over that Abby would be more realistic, that getting clean by the baby's birth was a lot harder than she made it sound? He'd proven that at her grandparents' house. In spades.

"One day at a time," Dustin said.

It sounded like a platitude, but Luke acknowledged it was the lifeline they all clung to. He could beat himself up about yesterday's failures, or he could concentrate on making it through today, starting with the morning meeting.

Relax. You can do this. Just keep your mouth shut. Listen. Smile and laugh at the right times.

God, help me not to blow this.

With an easy smile, Dr. Jefferies scanned the room, probably counting heads to make sure everyone was present. After a brief exchange of good morning greetings, he said, "So, would someone like to share their thoughts about yesterday? Christmas can be a tough day."

Luke's body tensed, stiff as a plank of wood. The urge to race from the room pounded in his veins, but an image of Abby rocking a newborn appeared in his head, then dissolved in an instant. Losing them would kill him. He forced himself to breathe slowly, relax his shoulders, and slump back as much as was possible in a folding chair. He crossed one ankle over his knee like he didn't have a care in the world. That was a gross exaggeration that would describe no one in this room. He would have laughed out loud if he wasn't so keen on being invisible.

No one spoke up.

Several more minutes of uncomfortable silence passed. Luke flinched, knowing from experience what was coming.

"All right, then. We'll go around the room, and each of you will share one high and one low."

The residents emitted a collective groan, but everyone cooperated when his or her turn came. Luke listened to the usual highs and lows. Getting to see family. Not getting to see family. Everyone's story was remarkably similar. Even those who had left the center to visit family and friends expressed a range of bittersweet emotions. On the one hand, they were grateful to spend time with loved ones, and on the other, the pressure of family expectations often made a recovering addict feel doomed to failure.

One girl, a new resident named Sheila who didn't even look old enough to be in high school, started sobbing the minute Jefferies called on her. Turns out her best friend had died of an overdose on Christmas Eve. The teen had been alone in her room, and by the time her parents found her sitting on the floor with the needle stuck in a vein between her toes it had been too late. Sheila's whole family had been warned not to say anything to Sheila, but in the middle of a screaming match, her older sister had blurted out the whole story. Sheila's dad brought her right back to the center. "They couldn't help me like you guys." Sheila blew her nose, and the girl sitting to her left grabbed her hand, then pulled her into a hug.

Almost every resident knew at least one person who had

died of an overdose. The papers called it an opioid epidemic. No kidding. Luke hadn't known anyone personally who had died, but Dustin insisted that was just a matter of time. Addicts kept company with addicts, and one of two outcomes awaited them all—get clean or die. Luke suppressed a shudder.

After Sheila's story, he tried to focus on what the others were saying. Only two more people and it would be his turn. What could he say? Too bad Dustin had been wrong. Luke wouldn't be able to lay low.

If You help me, God, I'll try harder next time.

Jefferies turned in his seat and eyed Luke. "Your high and low, Luke?"

He scrambled for the briefest answers to both questions. "My high was seeing my girlfriend. We're ... we're having a baby." He scanned the room, expecting to see disapproval on the faces of the girls, but their expressions said so what. Apparently, compared to the struggles of addiction, pregnancy was a cakewalk in their eyes. Some of the guys stared at him like they couldn't believe he would be that stupid. A few wore a cocky, you-go-man expression, like he'd accomplished something worth being proud of. He wasn't. Not about the baby. Not about anything much at all. He'd been proud of his 44 days, but he'd ruined that with one stupid move.

Dr. Jefferies was staring at him. How long had Luke zoned out? Long enough for the doc's radar to kick in. *Focus, Luke. Make it short and sweet.*

"The last time I saw her she didn't look pregnant. Now she does. My low was her uncle threatening me. He's a public defender, so he thinks he knows me."

"How did you handle that, Luke?" Doctor Jefferies asked.

"I told him that I love his niece."

"Did he accept that?"

Sensing he was treading toward the undertow, Luke shrugged. "It doesn't matter what he thinks. Abby knows I love her."

Doctor Jefferies nodded, but his dark eyes were sharp. He would probe in their private session, and Luke better be ready with believable responses or the truth would tumble out.

CHAPTER NINE

Abby wanted to forgive and forget, but Luke stealing her grandfather's pain meds had shattered her trust, and she had no idea how to reassemble the pieces of her heart. Was this how his parents had felt? Was that why they'd kicked him out? Because they didn't know how to survive the paralyzing pits of desperation that inevitably followed the briefest heights of hope? Because trusting a recovering addict required the faith to move a mountain?

Abby tucked a bookmark into *What to Expect When You're Expecting*, placed the book on her nightstand, and keyed in a group text to Megan and Lisa. "Want to go to a movie?" She desperately wanted to do something normal so that she could *feel* normal, like an ordinary teen instead of a soon-to-be unwed mother whose baby daddy was in drug rehab.

Her phone signaled a reply. "Meeting Ryan, Ian, Lainie, and Jack for pizza at noon. Wanna come?"

Did she? She hadn't talked to Jack since she had started on home instruction. Maybe, Lainie had finally let Jack know how she felt about him. That didn't seem likely. Meg or Lisa would have told Abby if Lainie and Jack were dating.

Hanging out with Jack, and worse, comparing him to Luke, would not help her or Jack and wasn't fair to her boyfriend. If he found out that Jack wanted more than friendship from her, Luke wouldn't handle that well at all. Abby couldn't risk doing anything else to upset his recovery.

His slip-up on Christmas day had been partially her fault. He'd tried to tell her that he wasn't ready for a big social gathering, but she had been so focused on trying to convince her family that even though she was pregnant, everything was going to work out because she and her boyfriend were committed to each other and their baby. Uncle Ed had seen through her ruse in a matter of minutes. He didn't consider Luke boyfriend material, let alone father material. As for the rest of the family, they'd been too polite to call her out on her lie.

But it wasn't really a lie. It was a dream. A dream she couldn't let go of, for her baby's sake. She just needed more faith to hang in there with Luke, to believe that God planned a miracle for them.

Her phone pinged with another text, this one from Jack. Abby's face heated with frustration and aggravation, but she opened the message anyway. "Heading to Tony's for pizza. Shall I pick you up?"

Abby read between the lines. He was asking her out on a not-date that really was a date. "I have my own car, remember?" she texted back, which was her way of tactfully reminding him that even a not-date was inappropriate because it could give people the wrong impression. It would give him the wrong impression.

His reply instantly popped up on her screen. "I'm already in your driveway."

She groaned. Not wanting to fight with him, she texted, "Give me five minutes." He didn't need to know that even though it was 11:35, she was still in her navy and white snowflake pajama pants and one of Luke's baggy t-shirts.

Five minutes later the doorbell rang. Mom or Sam would get it. Abby still hadn't decided what to wear. She had tried on two outfits, but both made her look noticeably pregnant. Her baby bump seemed bigger every day. She couldn't buckle her jeans—not even the pair that was two sizes bigger than she normally wore. That left black yoga pants worn low enough on her hips so that the waistband didn't bind her stomach or hurt her back, or a pair of her dad's sweatpants that she'd absconded from the dryer last week. Wearing men's sweatpants around the house was acceptable, but wearing them outside? Someone might think she was homeless. She shuddered. "Black yoga pants it is," she muttered to herself, tugged them back on and topped them with a soft, purple tunic that fell to the middle of her thighs. At least she hadn't put on weight in her legs. She ran a brush through her hair, grabbed her purse and her phone, and opened her bedroom door to find Jack smiling on the other side. Their eyes met, and he tucked a loose strand of hair behind her left ear.

Startled at the electric current sparked by his touch, she stepped back into the room and nearly stumbled on the Oriental rug. Jack's arms surrounded her, pulled her against his chest, and brought their faces so close she could smell his watermelon gum. He wasn't looking into her eyes. He was staring at her lips, still parted in surprise. He leaned his head a fraction of an inch closer.

God in heaven. He was going to kiss her.

She couldn't let that happen. She freed her arm, placed her right palm against his muscled chest, and shoved. "Let me go."

He raised his gaze to hers, and she saw everything—his

love for her, his embarrassment and regret over crossing the line they'd both agreed to, his panic that she would banish him from her life. His eyes glistened with grief and remorse.

Tears welled in her eyes, too. "Jack, I—"

"Don't say anything." He released her and took a step back.

She closed the distance between them, stood on her toes, and brushed a kiss on his cheek. She'd meant to give him a sisterly peck to let him know she wasn't mad, but before she could back away, he turned his head and covered her mouth with his. His tongue slid past her lips, driving every reasonable thought from her head. He kissed her like a man who'd been deprived for years, kept from the woman he loved by circumstances beyond his control, and now that he held her in his arms, he intended to draw every ounce of passion from her. Her body awakened as he pulled her closer.

She wanted to stop him, but she didn't want the kiss to end. Jack kissed her like she was the most precious thing in his life. How long had it been since Luke had kissed her like that?

Luke!

Horrified, Abby squirmed and pushed out of Jack's embrace. What had she done? She skirted around to the opposite side of the bed, snatched up a pillow, and held it like a shield.

"Abby, please, we need to talk about this."

"No. No, *we* don't need to talk about anything. There is no we. Just leave me alone," she barked.

"I'm sorry. That wasn't supposed to happen. It won't happen again. I promise you." Jack's words declared his regret, but the husky timbre of his voice suggested an altogether different emotion.

She glared into his dark eyes. "I'm used to guys breaking

their promises."

Jack's face paled as if she'd slapped him. She should have slapped him the second he dared to put his mouth on hers. Why hadn't she stopped him? This was as much her fault as his. "I think you'd better leave."

"Leave?" He backed up toward the door, his eyes reading her. "You're serious. What am I going to tell Megan and Lisa?"

She sighed. "Tell them I'm too nauseated to eat pizza today." That wasn't too far from the truth. She was sick to her stomach over what she had done. Jack had been wrong to kiss her, but she had kissed him back, and it hadn't been a quick, overcome-by-the moment kiss. She'd kissed him with a hunger for more and then blamed him when he responded with passion that nearly obliterated her reason. "I'm not mad at you, Jack. I just can't talk to you or see you right now."

Composing his features, he said, "I'll call you later, okay?"

She nodded. He would keep his word.

Unlike Luke.

But she was done comparing the two guys. Look at the trouble it had gotten her into.

*

Luke slouched in the worn upholstered armchair. Silence wasn't an option. Dr. Jefferies had worked at Ellis Rehab for five years. The man had seen and heard every conceivable lie an addict could concoct.

The doctor made a few notes in his laptop. He steepled his hands, elbows resting on the uncluttered desk. After a few minutes of studied silence, he asked, "How did you handle the temptation to use?"

Luke sat up straight, meeting the other man's questioning eyes with what he hoped was a transparent look.

"What makes you think I was tempted?"

Jefferies sighed. "All addicts are tempted to use. Especially their first time outside the center. Your situation, packed with stress and expectations, would be hard for anyone, Luke."

He wanted to say, not me, but the words stuck like peanut butter in his throat.

"If you'd been drug-tested this morning, you would have failed, wouldn't you?"

Here it comes. The boot out the door. So long. You're past help.

His silence shouted the truth so that it bounced off the walls in the 15-foot by 15-foot office. He couldn't make eye contact with the man who had borne with him for over six weeks. Luke rose to leave. "I'll pack my stuff."

Dr. Jefferies stood and gestured to the armchair. "Sit back down."

Great. The man was going to lecture him before kicking him out. So be it. Nothing Jefferies said could be any worse than what Luke had already called himself. *Scumbag. Loser.*

"Why do you think I made sure you weren't in the rotation?"

Luke could play dumb and pretend he didn't know what the doctor was implying, but he didn't see any advantage to dissembling. Still, he shook his head. Two slow, barely felt movements. Just drawing in a full breath took all of his focus. *God, where are You?*

"I'm giving you another chance." Jefferies paused, waiting for Luke to process what he had just said.

Weak with relief, Luke uttered a soft, "Thank you, sir." Abby could still get that money from his dad. Luke only needed to stay clean for 45 more days. He was half-way there. He wouldn't slip up again. Even if it meant no day trips outside the center. "I ... I ..." He trailed off. What more could he say?

"Are you ready now to share what really happened yesterday?"

Luke nodded, then he told the doctor the entire sordid story without leaving out a single detail.

*

Sam's voice, punctuated by insistent pounding, penetrated through Abby's fog of quasi sleep. "Abby! Open up."

She tossed the blankets aside and half stumbled to the door. With a perplexed frown, she faced her brother. "What's going on? The way you're screaming and beating on my door, you'd think the house was burning down."

Sam grabbed her arm to pull her into the hall. "I've been trying to wake you up for five minutes. Grandma and Grandpa are downstairs talking to Mom and Dad. They kicked me out of the room, but I could still hear them."

No sense pretending her grandparents' visit had nothing to do with her. "They didn't see you?"

"Nope. I hid in the hall closet with the door open just a crack."

Abby's stomach rumbled. She had skipped lunch and fallen asleep, mostly to escape the dreadful scenarios playing out in her mind like a low-budget drama. There would have been no way Megan and Lisa would have missed the tension between Jack and Abby, but she couldn't think about that problem now. She marched to her nightstand and stuffed two crackers into her mouth, then faced her little brother, who had once again appointed himself her protector. For a split second, she considered how different her life might have been if she had an older, rather than younger brother. No sense bucking reality. After all, Sam *was* trying to help. "I repeat, what's going on?"

"Grandpa and Grandma know."

Not wanting to say anything that would reinforce any suspicions Sam might have, Abby worked to keep her voice calm. "Know what?"

Sam shot her an incredulous look. "You mean *you* didn't figure it out?"

Dear Lord, can this get any worse?

Sam shuffled his sneakers with a squeak on the hardwood floor. "Grandpa noticed some of his pills were missing."

Suddenly lightheaded, Abby leaned against the door frame. "Do they want me to come down?" If they did, what could she say in Luke's defense? That it was partly *her* fault because she had insisted that he leave the center before he was ready?

"I don't think so. But if they did, they wouldn't send *me* to get you. They think I'm just a kid."

She resisted the urge to remind him that he had turned nine only last month, and that, by everyone's definition, made him just a kid, albeit a very smart one.

Her brother's eyes twinkled the way they always did when he believed he had devised a fabulous plan. "Your friend Megan is next door at Trevor's. You could sneak next door through the bushes like me and Trevor."

Sam was getting pretty crafty for a third-grader. "I better not, squirt. But thanks for the warning."

He smiled, basking in her appreciation. "Want me to tell Mom and Dad you'll be right down?"

She shook her head. "It might be better if I surprise them." She wanted to get a feel for everyone's reactions before she headed into the lion's den. "Why don't you go watch a movie in your room? Maybe, we can talk Mom or

Dad into playing a game after supper." More than likely her grandparents wouldn't stay for dinner. Grandpa probably wanted to make sure that Dad kept Abby as far away from Luke as possible. Once he'd obtained an iron-clad promise, her grandfather would usher her grandmother out the door before she could mess up his plans with her more compassionate heart. Grandma Collins wasn't as understanding as Grandma Elise had always been, but at least she understood Abby's need to give Luke every chance, for the baby's sake.

After Sam left, Abby took several minutes to compose herself and to pray for the right words before heading downstairs. She slipped into the kitchen for a banana, unpeeled it, and nibbled two bites before Mom startled her by marching in with a bare dessert platter and what must be an empty coffee carafe.

"Hi, honey. I didn't know you were up. Are you feeling any better? Jack told us you were sick to your stomach—his words, not mine."

Hoping her face hadn't colored at the mention of Jack, Abby tried to gauge how the conversation in the living room was going by her mother's expression. Unfortunately, like her tone, Mom's face revealed nothing. "Are Grandma and Grandpa staying for dinner?" Maybe, Abby could play dumb. "I can bake macaroni and cheese. Grandpa loves that."

Mom laid her hand on Abby's arm. "They aren't here for dinner, Abby."

"Mom, please, you have to be on my side. What happened is partially my fault. Luke tried to tell me he wasn't ready, but I insisted he spend Christmas with me."

Her mother squelched a flash of anger, placed her hands on Abby's shoulders, and held her gaze with a now-you-listen-to-me look. "Nothing Luke has done is your fault,

Abigail."

She laid her hand protectively over her rounded stomach, and shook her head. "Nothing is ever only one person's fault in a relationship. That's what Grandma always said."

Mom's eyes darkened with grief, anger, or both. "Grandma wasn't talking about drug addiction, Abby. She was talking about conflicts and disagreements that can split up two people who love each other. Not placing blame within the context of a committed relationship and enabling a drug addict are two different things entirely." Mom turned her back, rinsed the carafe, and started a new pot of coffee.

Making more coffee wasn't a good sign at all. It meant the four of them were determined to hash out a plan for Abby, with or without her input. No way was she going to let them plan Luke right out of her life. She owed it to him and to their baby to take up his side, especially if everyone else was against him. She opened several cookie tins and started refilling the dessert plate, then she poured herself a tall glass of milk, picked up the artfully arranged display of Christmas cookies, and headed out of the kitchen to face her family.

God, help me to convince them to give Luke another chance.

For a moment, she felt God's peace settle her mind. Until the next thought kicked her budding faith in the shins. How long did she plan on giving him another chance? Exactly how many chances would it take? Only God knew the answer to that, and He wasn't telling her. She bit her lip to keep from sobbing in frustration and marched into the living room to advocate for the man she loved. It was the right thing, the only thing she could do.

Grandma stood first and wrapped Abby in a rose-scented hug. "How's my beautiful granddaughter feeling? I hope yesterday wasn't too much for you."

Tempted to ask what her grandmother meant by that remark, Abby decided to lay low and wait to see how the conversation would go. "I'm fine, just a little tired is all." She prayed God would forgive her lie.

Grandpa harrumphed, which was never a good sign.

"Have a seat," Dad said. "We want to talk to you about Luke."

Abby lowered herself to the couch with all of the terror she might feel if she were the one that had stolen and taken her grandfather's oxies. The urge to bolt coursed through her, but she crossed her legs, folded her hands in her lap, and waited for the edict.

"Your father told us everything," Grandma began.

"Which he should have done months ago," Grandpa growled.

Was he implying that she wouldn't be in this predicament if her dad had confided his concern about Luke's drug use to his father earlier?

In an obvious attempt to keep the peace, her grandmother placed her weathered hand on her husband's leg just above his knee and patted him the way she would a child.

He shot her an impatient look. "Annabelle, let me handle this."

Grandma withdrew her hand, her face momentarily stricken, as if he had slapped her. She folded her hands together on her lap and straightened her back, her lips compressing into thin lines. Her quick glance at Abby contained sympathy and regret. There would be no help from her.

Grandpa marched to the fireplace, rested one forearm on the marble mantel, and faced his son. "How you allowed this to happen, practically under your own roof—"

"Ethan, that's not fair." Mom moved closer to Dad. "We told Abby that she couldn't see Luke anymore."

"After his parents kicked him out. I imagine there were plenty of signs *before* that that the guy wasn't good enough for my granddaughter."

"Grandpa, please, you don't know Luke. After his accident and the surgery, he was in so much pain."

Grandpa's dark eyes softened. "Do you think I'm a stranger to pain? Do you think I don't know how tempting it is to take more of those blasted pills than the doctor prescribed?"

Abby blinked back the tears pricking her eyes. "He's trying to get better, Grandpa. He's been in rehab for six weeks. If I don't believe in him, who will?" Afraid nothing she could say would convince him, she covered her face with her hands, muffling the sobs she could not control.

Grandma slid around Abby and pulled her close. "Ethan Collins, you are making a dreadful situation worse."

"Dad's right, Mom," her father said.

His words fell like a boom, crushing any hope Abby had of persuading her family she and Luke should be allowed to see each other as much as possible.

"But Dad—"

"Visiting Luke—at least right now—isn't good for you, Abby. You're under enough stress and pressure trying to finish all of your schoolwork a month early. I think we can all agree that taking care of yourself has to come first." Dad glanced around the room.

Abby followed his gaze. They were united in one purpose—to keep her away from Luke, and nothing she could say was going to change their minds.

"We understand how you feel about helping Luke. Your

loyalty is one of your best character traits. But you need to let the professionals at Ellis Rehab help him. Your job is finishing high school and taking care of yourself so that you have a healthy baby girl."

As if she'd heard her grandpa talking about her, her daughter fluttered in Abby's womb. "Mom, the baby's moving."

Grandma laid a hand over Abby's belly, and Mom knelt down next to Abby's knees. "Hello, little one. We can't wait to meet you. We all love you so much."

"So does Luke," Abby dared to add.

She glanced up at her father's drawn face. He had never looked sadder. And it was all her fault.

*

Luke unfolded Abby's letter, lifted the pink stationary to his nose, and breathed in her sweet floral perfume. His pulse raced at the flood of memories. Losing himself in her kisses night after night in his dreams only intensified his need for her. Now that the drugs were out of his system, his senses had returned in full force, and his body ached to be satisfied in her arms.

With one leg outstretched and the other knee bent, Luke sat on his bed reading and rereading Abby's letter, which was dated January 1st. It had taken four days to reach him, but the postmark was only two days ago, which meant she hadn't mailed the letter right away. She hadn't wanted to mail it any more than he wanted to receive it. The pages were splotched with her tears. Had she tried to change her parents' minds? Would she come to see him in spite of their insistence that she promise them she would have no contact with him until after the baby was born? Luke raked his hands through his hair and yanked hard, with enough force to block out for the briefest second the complete and utter abandonment that threatened to swallow him whole.

She promised that she would keep writing. She just couldn't visit him. And he couldn't visit her, which meant he'd be stuck in here for the next thirty-five days because sure as hell his parents wouldn't pick him up for a visit. They hadn't come one time, and he'd had only two letters from his mom, the last one written on Christmas morning and mailed the following day. He had broken his mother's heart when he'd stolen the jewelry that had belonged to his great-great grandmother. Heaven knows how much those pieces been worth. They'd been gifts from her husband who had returned from fighting in World War I without a scratch on his body, but with scars on his heart from which he'd never recovered. He'd watched his younger brother get shot and held him while he'd bled out from a stomach wound the size of a dinner plate. The raw grief in Mom's eyes when Dad informed her that the pawnbroker had already sold the heirloom pieces to a vintage jewelry collector from downstate New York had nailed Luke to the floor. At the time, he'd been angry, thinking she cared more about some old jewelry than her own son. What an insensitive, selfish idiot he had been.

His fingers itched to tie a rubber strap around his arm and shoot up one more time, just to escape the self-loathing and the gut-wrenching pain of being without Abby. But he wasn't stupid enough to believe one hit would be enough. One hit would be the first disastrous step down a slippery slope into the quicksand of chasing one high after another. He knew it. But still he craved the sweet peace and oblivion heroin promised.

"God, I can't do this alone."

A knock sounded on the door. Was this the answer to his desperate plea or more bad news?

"Hey, Luke, how about a game of pool?"

Dustin's voice was easy, relaxed, unconcerned. Clearly, the other man had learned to take recovery one day at a time, something Luke couldn't afford to do. Not if he wanted to see his baby born. He climbed off the bed, opened the door without a word, and handed Abby's letter to his friend.

Dustin shook his head. "I don't want to read your mail, man. What you and your girl got to say to each other is private, and there isn't much that's private in this place."

Luke took the pages back, refolded them, slid them into the envelope, and tucked it in his Bible, smack dab in the middle of "Song of Solomon." No sense trying to hide his thoughts from God. He already knew how Luke felt about Abby, how going back wasn't possible. Or was it? Not that it mattered now. He wasn't even going to get close enough to hold her hand. Maybe God had a plan to help Luke through this because he couldn't imagine not seeing Abby until after their baby's birth. Hell, that was more than four months away. An eternity for an addict.

"I take it the letter was bad news." Dustin shut the door behind him. "If you want to talk about it, I'll listen, but I don't want to read her words."

Luke shrugged, defeated. "I get it. There isn't much to say. Abby promised her parents and grandparents that she wouldn't see me until after the baby comes. They all think she's under too much stress."

"She probably is." Dustin laid one hand on Luke's shoulder. "She loves you, man. She's still going to write to you, isn't she?"

"Yes, but it's not the same." Luke started at the sound of his voice cracking. He struggled to maintain a semblance of control. "Besides, I need to be with her when the baby comes."

"I get it, man. You're trying to prove yourself, and it

seems like her family won't even give you a chance." Dustin tightened his grip on Luke's shoulder, demanding that he snap out of his funk. "But it could have been worse. They could have forbidden her to have any contact with you. They could even take legal action to keep you away from Abby and the baby."

Luke's heart slammed against his chest. "They still could." What would he do then?

Dustin stepped back, his eyes boring into Luke. "They won't. Not unless you give them a reason."

Luke wanted to put his fist through something. A wall. Dustin's gut for daring to speak the truth. Or maybe his own skull to drive the desire for drugs forever from his brain. He would do just that, if it had a prayer of working.

God. A one-word cry for help. If He didn't answer, Luke couldn't go on another minute.

He drew in three sharp breaths to steady his nerves and slow his stampeding heart. He couldn't fight. He couldn't run away either. And his patience was nearly gone. Stuck in rehab, dragging himself through each day, trying to regain control of his own will as the drugs released their physical hold had revealed how weak Luke really was. Admitting his utter helplessness had done nothing to rebuild his self-respect. Dr. Jefferies insisted that being brutally honest with oneself was as integral to recovery as clean days logged.

One day at a time was a lot harder than most people knew. One minute at a time was Luke's current reality. If only Abby had been strong enough to stand up to her parents, but how could he criticize her when he could barely muster the strength to face each day? He needed a distraction, a brief break from the discouraging, demoralizing thoughts that plagued his days and haunted his dreams. "How about that game of pool?"

A slow smile spread across Dustin's face. "You in the mood to lose?"

Luke laughed. Dustin had never once in the last eight weeks beaten Luke, but his friend improved a little with each game. "Whatever. Let's make it best two out of three." They didn't have anything to bet with, but that didn't matter. Shooting pool required focused concentration and allowed them to forget where they were and who they were, if only for a few hours.

CHAPTER TEN

Abby considered calling Jack. It had been almost two weeks since they had kissed. Because she was on home instruction, avoiding him was easy. Seeing him at school would have been horribly awkward. It was bad enough that Megan and Lisa kept pressuring her to fess up about why she and Jack weren't speaking to each other.

On Saturday night, in the middle of watching *When Harry Met Sally,* Megan insisted she already knew—a tactic she'd refined in elementary school to get Abby to spill her secrets. It wasn't working this time, which seemed to convince Meg that her suspicions were correct. Abby half wished her friend would just come right out and accuse her of cheating on Luke with Jack. Then she could finally talk to *someone* about what had happened. Her thoughts vacillated between a simple kiss is no big deal and only a horrible person cheats on her boyfriend when he's trying to stay off heroin. Was the truth somewhere in between?

Her phone pinged a message. Jack. "When are you going to forgive me?"

There was only one answer to that question. *When I forgive myself.* Since that wasn't happening any time soon,

Abby put her phone on airplane mode. One message from Jack was all she could stand to read tonight. She would have to talk to him sooner or later but not before she talked to Luke.

She hadn't answered a single call or responded to one text from Jack since that awful day she'd let him kiss her. He probably thought she was fuming mad that he'd broken their unspoken agreement, but that wasn't it at all. If she could lay all of the blame on Jack, then maybe the nightmares would stop. But she couldn't lie to herself. She should have stopped him. Why hadn't she shoved him away, slapped him, told him he was out of line? That's what haunted her. Maybe, telling Luke what had happened between her and Jack would stop the nightmares, but how could she do that when she had agreed not to see him? Writing something that disgusting in a letter was too cruel. She was a cheater, but she wasn't a nasty witch.

If she told him, it would have to be in person, and the only way she could make that happen was to explain everything to her mother. Mom would be disappointed in her, but she would understand how much Abby needed to see Luke. Not talking to her boyfriend was causing her way more stress than seeing him. This morning, the obstetrician had grilled her for five minutes on all of the possible reasons for her elevated blood pressure and the dangers to herself and the baby if she didn't do something about it.

Abby set aside her physics textbook and made her way reluctantly downstairs to her mother's study. Seeing the open door, she rapped on the jamb. "Mom, do you have a few minutes?"

Her mother leaned past her computer screen and gestured to the rocking chair. No one but Mom knew why she wanted a rocker in her study. Rockers suggested the importance of relaxation, a concept, according to Dad, that Mom had yet to comprehend or implement. The spring semester hadn't even started yet, and already, she was holed up in her study several hours a day, probably refining her course syllabi.

"Honey, I still have one more class to ..."

The concern in her mother's cool violet eyes convinced Abby that she must look dreadful.

"But it can wait. Let's go out to the kitchen for some tea."

Herbal teas tasted gross, but Abby would force down a cup if she could have her mother's undivided attention. On the other hand, Dad or Sam could barge into the kitchen at any moment. "Could we bring the tea up to my room? Please."

Mom frowned then nodded. "No problem. You go on up, and I'll brew some chamomile tea and cut a couple of pieces of carrot cake."

Abby smiled with relief. Carrot cake would make the tea palatable, and trained to respect what Mom called their girl time, neither Sam nor Dad would interrupt.

In the sanctuary of her room, Abby tried to figure out how to convince her mother that she needed to talk to Luke. She didn't want to discuss what had happened between her and Jack, but if she couldn't tell her mom, how would she ever tell Luke? That one kiss threatened all of her dreams. If only she could get past the guilt, she would never breathe a word of her betrayal to Luke. But what if he found out from anyone other than her? God alone knew what would happen then. She had to tell Luke as soon as possible.

Mom knocked, but without waiting for a reply, she entered the room carrying a silver tray with teacups, a teapot, and two slices of cake, forks, and napkins. Abby took the heavy tray and set it on her desk. She poured the tea, handed a cup to her mother, and settled, cross-legged at one end of the window seat. Her gaze never leaving Abby's face, Mom sat at the opposite end of the cushion.

Stalling, Abby forked a bite of the dessert into her mouth. Where was her courage? Mom sipped her tea and chewed a forkful of cake. Abby tried to eat, but the cake tasted like stale bread in her mouth.

"Are you ready to tell me what this is about?"

Tears pooled then slid down Abby's cheeks. Frustrated, she swiped them away with the back of her hand, ashamed to meet her mother's questioning gaze. Abby couldn't remember the last time she had done anything to make her parents proud. And she wouldn't be doing anything praiseworthy in the immediate future. If Grandma were alive, Abby would have begged her to take her some place where no one knew her, where no one would judge her a failure at seventeen.

Mom laid one hand on Abby's knee. The familiar pressure of Mom's hand was meant to reassure her that nothing was as bad as Abby imagined. Still, the truth stuck in her throat like a piercing fishbone. If only she could convince herself that Luke would forgive her, that this wouldn't devastate him and drive him back to—

"I can't help if you won't talk to me, honey."

Abby lifted her face. "I kissed Jack." *Not Jack kissed me.* There was no point in lying to her mother.

Surprise furrowed her mother's smooth brow. "And you think you've betrayed Luke?"

"Yes! Yes, I do." Disgusted with herself, Abby jumped from the window seat, knocking two pillows to the hardwood floor. Feeling like a trapped wildcat, she paced from one end of her room and back—twice, desperate for her mother to understand. "I cheated on him. At the worst possible time. When he's in rehab. And I'm having his baby, *his* baby. Not

Jack's. Who does that, Mom?"

"Abby, stop. Sit back down, and tell me how this happened."

Choking back an angry sob, Abby complied. She backed up against the headboard and drew her knees as close to her chest as her swollen belly would allow. "He kissed me, and I didn't stop him. I kissed him back. Mom, everybody knows how Jack feels about me. How could I have done that to him? To Luke?" She sobbed, letting the grief and the guilt have full sway. "I have to tell Luke what happened."

Without a word, her mother enclosed her in a soothing embrace. Her soft hands stroked Abby's hair, and her gentle voice cooed, "It'll be all right, honey," over and over until Abby had no more tears left. All that remained was her ache to be in Luke's arms.

Several minutes passed and her need for the bathroom took preeminence. "I'll be back in a minute."

When she returned to her room, her mother was waiting, a confident expression suggesting that she'd been praying the whole time Abby was gone. "Why do you want to tell Luke about kissing Jack?"

"I don't know." Telling him was the last thing she wanted to do. She would give almost anything if that kiss had never happened. "He needs to know."

"Why? Are you planning to break up with him, to start dating Jack?"

Her mother's tone wasn't hopeful, and Abby was grateful for that. "No. I love Luke. Kissing Jack was a mistake. Mom, it's just so hard being away from Luke, not knowing if we can ever be together like we were before ... before he started—"

"I know, honey. It's a lot. It would be a lot to deal with even if you weren't pregnant."

"Jack's a good friend, and now, we've ruined it because

Luke won't want me to even talk to him anymore."

"Are you sure you want to tell him? If kissing Jack was a mistake—"

"I don't know. I feel so guilty. Keeping this from Luke feels like I'm lying. I've never lied to him, Mom. Not one time."

"Honey, maybe it would be better if you didn't tell him. You don't know how he'll take it."

Abby heard loud and clear what her mother wouldn't say out loud. "Well, what should I do? Are you saying I should lie to Luke?"

"No, I'm saying it might be better for both of you if he doesn't know. You and I will pray about this tonight, and tomorrow, if you want to talk to Luke, I'll drive you to the center."

"But Dad and Grandpa and Grandma … they'll be mad. I promised not to see Luke until after the baby comes."

Mom patted Abby's knee with a tender touch. "Leave them to me. Now, you get some sleep. You look exhausted."

Abby felt like a wrung out sponge, utterly drained. She held her arms out to her mother and hugged her tight. "Thank you," she whispered against her dark hair, "for understanding. And for not thinking I'm a horrible person."

Mom pulled back, and their eyes locked. "I could never think that about you. You're one of the most compassionate, generous people I've ever known, and Luke knows that about you."

"Maybe, but if I tell him about kissing Jack … Mom, will Luke believe I still love him?"

"I can't answer that question, honey. But forgiveness, forgiveness takes time."

They didn't have much time. Their baby would be here in four months.

*

Luke couldn't believe it. Two visitors in one day. He hadn't seen anyone outside the center since Christmas, nearly three weeks ago.

"Who would you like to visit with first?" Leah studied him, probably to assess how well he would handle the stress of seeing his mother for the first time since he had entered rehab sixty-five days ago. Why was she here? Did his father know?

"I need to talk to Abby first." Luke had to see for himself that everything was fine with her and the baby. Her recent letters had been newsy, mostly about school, but he couldn't dismiss the nagging feeling that something wasn't right. He didn't want to name it, but now that he was finally going to talk to her, he did. Abby's letters sounded evasive, like she was hiding something, and he couldn't wait another minute to discover what it was. "Ask my mother if she can come back in an hour."

Leah frowned, her eyes troubled. "I think you should see your mom first. Abby said she didn't mind coming back after lunch. She could eat, she said, because she's hungry all of the time." Leah laughed. "I definitely remember those days."

Her light-hearted remark did nothing to dismiss his mounting anxiety. "Okay. We'll do it her way. Tell my mom I'll be down in five minutes."

Leah closed his door, and Luke sank to his knees beside his bed. *God, I'm scared. Whatever Abby has to tell me, it's bad. I can feel it like a jagged boulder in the pit of my stomach.* He covered his face with his hands and pressed his thumbs into his temples to ease the sudden throbbing. Instinctively, he reached into his pockets and came up empty. Drugs weren't the answer. Drugs were the problem. *Jesus, please don't let go, even if I try to yank free.*

Luke rested his forehead against the mattress and waited for peace that didn't come. Until he remembered God's promise, "I will never leave thee, nor forsake thee."

Taking three deep breaths, Luke stood and squared his shoulders against whatever was coming. He'd rather talk to Abby first, to get it out in the open, so he could begin to deal with it. He wouldn't rely on drugs. Not anymore.

*

Mom pulled him into a hug and kissed both of his cheeks. "Luke, I … I'm sorry."

He set her away from him to study her expression and was shocked to see tears tracking her lined cheeks. "What's wrong? Is Joe all right?"

"Your brother's fine. He loves fifth grade. He started violin lessons this past fall. You knew that, didn't you?"

How could he? Luke hadn't lived at home in over a year, and his father strictly forbade any contact with Joe. The old resentment reared its demanding head, until Luke acknowledged that Dad had every right to protect his younger son from danger. Luke was seeing things more clearly now after weeks of listening to the others admit how their addictions had hurt their families. Everyone's story contained the same ugly truth—every one of them had chosen drugs over family, at least once, if not countless times. Joe wouldn't have been safe hanging out with Luke. His choices had put everyone he loved at risk. He knew that now. *God, forgive me. Help me make it up to them. Starting with my mom.*

Eager to begin now, Luke laid his hand on her forearm. She smiled up at him, drinking in the sight of her firstborn as if she'd been deprived of life-giving water. In a sense, she had. Her role as their mom was the only role her husband didn't dictate, until Luke messed that up for her. A flash of anger at how controlling his father had always been momentarily obscured Luke's focus. Why, after so many weeks, had Mom chosen to defy her husband by visiting her son?

"Why did you come, Mom?" Luke held her gaze until she was forced to look away. The sorrow in her eyes—sorrow he had put there—made him more determined than ever to stay clean. "Dad wouldn't approve of your being here." Luke stated the obvious, but it wouldn't do either of them any good to ignore the truth. Ignoring the truth had gotten him into more trouble than he'd ever imagined.

He watched his mother, hoping against hope that his drug use hadn't irrevocably harmed their family. Seeing her brokenness roused fresh tears of shame, but he refused to let them fall. This wasn't about him. It was about his mother. From the day they had discovered he'd stolen her jewelry, Mom had followed Dad's edict—minimal to no contact with Luke as long as he was still using. She'd rarely resisted her husband's decisions, even before Luke's addiction had strained their family to the breaking point. "Does Dad know you're here?"

Staring at her trembling hands, she whispered, "I told him I was coming to see you." She raised her eyes to his and bit her lower lip.

Luke clasped her hand and led her to the sofa. He sat beside her, and she shifted to face him. "And he was okay with that?"

"He had to be. This has gone on long enough."

"What's gone on long enough, Mom?" Were his parents getting a divorce? Luke wouldn't be surprised by that. His mother was a shadow in their home, at least that's what his Aunt Julia said. He'd been twelve at the time and hadn't understood what she meant. "Tell me what you're talking about."

With perfectly manicured fingers, his mother brushed frosted bangs out of her eyes, her expression revealing her newfound determination. "I'm talking about your father holding your recovery over your head as if you could comply with his timetable simply because he willed it. It's too much pressure on you and completely unfair to Abby."

So that was it. She'd stood up to her husband for Luke's sake. He couldn't even imagine what that had cost her. Willing his heart rate to slow down, he waited to learn what this would mean for Abby and for him.

"I called Abby's mother yesterday and told her we would give Abby one thousand dollars every month until she no longer needs our help. I mailed a check for three thousand to cover November, December, and January. Going forward, your father agreed to deposit one thousand in Abby's checking account on the first of each month."

Dad rarely altered any plan once he'd set his course. What had roused this surge of compassion? "Why? What changed?"

"It's the right thing to do. We can afford it, and if Abby wants to get her own apartment, pay for daycare, or save for college, she's going to need that much and more. Of course, her parents will help her as long as she needs it, but your father and I want to contribute."

His mother was right. Abby would probably need double or triple that amount. "She's not going to live with her parents after the baby comes?"

"Yes, she is. She's decided to start college at Niagara Community because they have a daycare facility for their students."

Apparently, Abby had it all figured out, how she and the baby would manage without his help. A twinge of anger pierced his heart until he recognized the toxic thought behind his flaring temper. Abby didn't, couldn't love him anymore. Stealing her grandfather's drugs had been the final straw. He shouldn't be shocked, after all he'd put her through. She was done with him. That's what she wanted to tell him. That's why it didn't matter that she wasn't supposed to visit him. A craving for drugs of any kind roared through his mind like an impending tornado. His hands started to shake, and he gripped his knees. *Jesus, help.*

Mom covered his hands with her soft ones. "What's wrong, Luke? You're so pale."

Luke closed his eyes and followed his breath in and out, in and out. "Mom, did Abby say anything about me?"

A puzzled frown knit his mother's brow. "What do you mean? Of course, we talked about you."

He didn't want to ask, but he couldn't wait another second. "Did she say anything about breaking up with me?"

"Heavens, no. She loves you, Luke. Surely, you don't doubt her love. She's stuck by you when most girls would have—"

"I guess I'm just paranoid." He struggled to dismiss the feeling that something was terribly wrong, but the foreboding persisted. "I haven't seen her since Christmas day. Three weeks is a long time in this place."

Guilt flickered in his mom's eyes, and he immediately regretted his thoughtless words.

"I didn't mean you, Mom. I know you were only doing what Dad wanted."

"That's the trouble. He never asked me what I wanted, but those days are over. Richard Bradford will have to get used to an entirely different wife from now on because I'm through staying quiet when something needs to be said."

Impressed by her courage, Luke pulled her into a hug. "I

love you, Mom."

"And I love you." She squeezed him like she never wanted to let go. "You can plan on my visiting at least once a week."

He smiled. "I'd like that."

She gave him another kiss on the cheek then released her bear hold. "Maybe, next time Joe can come with me."

Luke doubted his father would agree to that, but then again his mother might insist.

*

Her mother turned the key in the ignition, shutting off the Subaru outside of Panera Bread, Abby's favorite restaurant. They placed their orders, Abby hurried to the rest room, and by the time, she came out Mom was already seated, waiting for her to eat.

They enjoyed their meal in silence for several minutes until Mom, said, "Are you sure want to tell Luke? If what happened between you and Jack is never going to happen again, it might be easier for Luke, and for you, too, if he doesn't know."

Her appetite gone, Abby pushed her half-eaten turkey sandwich aside. Not for the first time, she considered whether she would want to know if the situation were reversed and Luke had kissed another girl. Part of her preferred to remain blissfully ignorant of her boyfriend's indiscretions, but that hadn't worked out very well so far. Every time she'd believed him when he'd said he was through with drugs for good, he had lied to her. He'd probably meant every word, but that didn't change facts.

She cringed. Did that mean she would slip up, too? Was it possible that she would find herself in Jack's arms again, unable to resist the simple pleasure of being held by a man she could fully trust? "Mom, what if Jack and I can't be friends anymore?"

"Only you and Jack can answer that question. Unless you tell Luke about the kiss. Then you and Luke will have to decide what's best for both of you." Mom took a long swig of her coffee and bit into her cheese pastry.

If only Luke were as reliable as Jack, she never would have found herself in this position in the first place, because if everything was good between her and Luke, Jack wouldn't have hugged her. He never would have kissed her, and she would not have kissed him back. Reluctantly, she met her mother's eyes. "What if it happens again, Mom?"

The words sounded horrible and ugly when Abby said them aloud, but the possibility had popped into her head several times this morning, nearly sending her careening into a panic attack.

"Honey, you are under a lot of pressure right now. You didn't kiss Jack because you want to be with him." Her mother let the words sink in. "Did you?"

"No. I told you last night. I love Luke." She squeezed her eyes shut against the tears. "We're having a baby together."

Mom's smile didn't reach her eyes. "This isn't an easy time for either of you. I know you don't want to hear this, but it might not be the best time to be in a committed relationship. On the other hand, if you decide that you want to stay with Luke, like I told you last night, I don't think you should say anything about what happened between you and Jack."

Was it possible that Luke didn't need to know? She wasn't going to give Jack a chance to kiss her again, and if he tried, that would be the end of their friendship. Jack wouldn't want that. He'd follow her lead and comply with whatever she wanted. Why should she tell Luke about something that was never going to happen again? An anxious knot formed in her stomach. "If I don't tell Luke, and he finds out from someone else … I don't want to lose him, Mom."

But what if she had already lost him? Tears spilled down her cheeks. She grabbed a napkin, dried her face, and blew her nose. "I love him. I want to build a life with him and make a home for our baby."

"I know you do, honey. Whatever you decide, Dad and I will support you. But only if Luke's behavior doesn't jeopardize the baby's safety or yours."

Abby wanted to defend Luke, to promise her mother that Luke would never do anything to endanger her or their baby, but the reassurances stuck in her throat. If only she could trust him.

Mom studied her with concern. "Maybe, you and Luke need to take a break, concentrate more on the baby, and less on your relationship. Give Luke the time he needs to put his life back together."

Fighting the fear sucking the air from her lungs, Abby clutched her hands together in her lap. "What if the baby and I are the only reason he has to even try to put his life back together?" The raw emotion in her words seemed to rouse her daughter, who kicked like a world-class soccer player. Responding to her maternal instincts, Abby massaged her stomach to comfort her child.

"Honey, Luke has to do this for himself."

Her mother's soft tone did little to calm Abby's rising terror. "If we break up, what if he doesn't want to live anymore?" She choked back a sob. "What if he tries to …?" She couldn't speak the words. A world, her world without Luke, was inconceivable.

"Tries to what?"

"Kill himself," Abby whispered.

"He would never do that, honey." Mom reached across

the table and rested a comforting hand on Abby's shoulder. "He loves you too much."

Abby closed her eyes a moment, silently praying her mother was right. Outside the crowded restaurant, the lightly falling snow looked like a postcard, but the beautiful sight didn't have its usual, soothing effect. "I have no idea how we're ever going to survive all of this." Luke's addiction, her cheating on him, the baby—it was all too much. "I'm scared, Mom."

"I know you are."

Abby was desperate for answers. She'd prayed last night until she'd drifted into a restless sleep, but she hadn't gotten a clear answer. "I still don't know what the right thing to do is. Keeping this from Luke feels like lying."

"Abby, your desire to tell Luke everything is more about easing your conscience than being honest with Luke."

"So, you think telling him is selfish? That I only want to tell him so I'll feel better?"

"Yes, that's what I think. But trust me, honey, you won't feel better. You'll feel much worse, especially if Luke can't handle it. He's stuck in rehab, and Jack can be there for you when he can't. If you tell Luke about the kiss, he isn't going to want you to spend any time with Jack."

"Oh, Mom, I wish I'd never kissed him."

"Forget about it. It was one kiss. Ask God to forgive you and move on. God loves Luke even more than you do. You can trust His plan for you and Luke, and for my granddaughter."

Was it really that simple? Could Abby leave it all in God's hands, trusting that everything would work out eventually? The trouble was she had no idea how long eventually would be, and she couldn't shake the horrible feeling that they were running out of time.

*

One look at Abby's red-splotched face, and Luke knew what was wrong. She couldn't forgive him for stealing her grandfather's drugs. She'd come to tell him it was over.

Could he change her mind? If only they could take a walk. But twenty-five degrees was too cold walking. He needed to hold her, kiss her, and tell her how much progress he was making. He could get a day pass for an hour or two. "Do you want to go for coffee? Somewhere quiet, so we can talk."

"Mom dropped me off. She went to Tim Hortons."

"I thought you told Leah you were going to get something to eat."

"We did, but Mom didn't want to sit in the car for a half an hour."

Thirty minutes? He hadn't seen her in three weeks, and that's all the time they'd have? He touched her face, his fingers grazing her cheek, her hair like shimmery silk against his skin. Trembling at his touch, she blinked back tears. He pressed a quick kiss to her lips and took her hand. "Let's sit."

Her frazzled, distraught expression sent chills down Luke's spine. *God, what can I say that would make this easier for her?*

With a weak smile, Abby lowered herself onto the worn sofa. Her belly was much bigger than the last time he'd seen her, but she had never looked more beautiful to him.

"Are you feeling okay? How's the baby? Did you bring me a new sonogram picture?"

He was firing questions at her, trying to act like this was any other visit, though she'd only come to see him that one time. "I can't believe you're past the halfway point. You look great, even more beautiful than before you got pregnant. I guess it's true, what they say about pregnant women glowing."

But she wasn't glowing now. Her skin was pale, and when she glanced up at him, the light in her eyes was gone. His addiction had done that to her. If he didn't ask what was bothering her, maybe she wouldn't tell him what was wrong. Maybe, they could go on as if … as if what? As if he hadn't screwed up his life and hers, too? That wasn't likely.

Her silence was killing him. She hadn't even thanked him for the compliment. She probably knew how dreadful she actually looked. He had to do something to lift her spirits and infuse some hope into this visit. "I'll be out of here in twenty-five days. Can you believe it?"

She smiled, but her eyes were hiding something. Something more than her disappointment over his stealing her grandfather's drugs? But what?

He frowned. "Aren't you excited about my getting out?"

"I miss you so much, Luke." She laid her cold hand over his.

He threaded their fingers together, desperate for any connection with her. His body and his heart ached at the memory of those perfect moments with her in his arms, rocking his world with her love. "Babe, I know it's hard, but if you can just hang in there a little longer. I'll be released on February 9th. Then we can make plans."

"Oh, Luke …" She pulled her hand free and averted her face.

Why didn't she want to talk about their future? Had he completely destroyed her faith in him? "I understand that it's going to be hard for you to trust me after what I've done, but I'm determined to do whatever it takes to earn your trust back." He ran his hand down the length of her hair, his fingers tingling at the silky texture. She turned to look at him, her cheeks flushed with a soft blush. He captured her hand again and kissed her palm. "I want to be everything you need, Abby, everything our baby needs. You have to believe that."

She slid across the sofa into his arms and buried her face against his neck. A soft sob escaped her trembling lips pressed against his skin.

He inhaled the light floral scent of her hair and rubbed his hands up and down her back, surprised at the tight knots of tension that failed to yield to his fingers. "I love you, babe."

She raised her face to his, and his heart wrenched at her troubled look. "Don't cry. I won't let you down again. I promise."

Doubt flashed in her eyes, but she nodded.

He battled doubts, too. Could he succeed as Jake and Leah had? With God helping him, could Luke stay clean outside the sanctuary of Ellis Rehab? He was scared, and he saw his fear reflected in Abby's eyes.

He checked the wall clock. Thirty minutes were up. "I know your mom's waiting, but we need to do one more thing before you leave."

"But, Luke—"

"Just text her that you'll be out in ten minutes. Please."

Her brow knit with indecision, then when he had about given up, she pulled her cell from her purse and typed a text to her mom. Luke stood, offered Abby his hand, and helped her to her feet. He couldn't let go of her hand at that moment any more than he could stop breathing. He led her to the end of a quiet hall to an open door on the left. Trying not to think of how she would react, he ushered her into the small chapel. A single cross constructed of two pieces of rough barn wood hung on the cream-colored walls. Quiet instrumental music played from the speakers overhead—an old familiar hymn that he couldn't quite place from his childhood.

Abby shot him a questioning glance, her mouth open to speak, but he couldn't bear to have her refuse his request. With a slight tug, he urged her to sit beside him on the front pew. "Pray with me before you go."

Her eyes widened, and she gave him a wobbly smile before wrapping her arms protectively around her stomach. He didn't wait to see if she would close her eyes or bow her head. He simply tucked his chin to his chest, and spoke to God in a soft but firm voice.

CHAPTER ELEVEN

"Jesus, I know this is all my fault. Abby has every right to be afraid to trust me. I've made her life miserable for more than two years now. But it isn't just her I'm hurting. I'm hurting my little girl. She needs her daddy ... God, she needs a daddy who isn't ... an addict. I need Your help. I'm counting on you to change me. I can't do this without You."

The desperation in Luke's prayer roused a storm of conflicting emotions in Abby. Guilt. Shame. Hope. Compassion. Love. Without opening her eyes, she groped for his hand, found it covering his face. Moisture dampened her palm. Luke was crying.

"Lord, please help us." The words escaped her lips without forethought.

Luke squeezed her hand, clearly reassured by her praying with him. "Jesus, we both need You," he continued. "We can't make it without You. I know it's going to take time for Abby to trust me again, but if You can make me the man she needs ..." Luke's voice cracked with emotion.

Abby leaned close and wrapped her arm around his bent shoulders, stunned to discover he was shaking with muffled sobs. "I love you, Luke. I'm not going to leave you."

He straightened and faced her. "Do you mean it? You still love me after all I've put you through ... even stealing drugs from your grandfather? You still want to be with me?"

She did. Kissing Jack had been a horrible mistake, one she was determined to forget. Telling Luke would only hurt him. God had forgiven her.

"I do. I do want to be with you." Gently, she wiped the tears from his face with her fingertips, hardly noticing the prickly stubble of his beard. "I love you, Luke. I'll always love you."

He captured her hands and kissed her palms. "Someday, I'm going to make you proud of me again."

"I already am. I know you're trying. For me and for the baby." She paused, afraid he might misunderstand her next words. "But, honey, I need you to do this for you. I need you to recognize that you're an addict, and I need you to be determined to stay drug-free for yourself. Not just for us."

His gaze shot to hers, but she couldn't read his thoughts. Desperate to make him understand, she ignored the fear that urged her to be quiet, to stop pushing him so hard. She clung to his hands, hoping to infuse her strength into him. "You have to do it for yourself, not just for me and the baby."

He yanked free. Anger and hurt battling in his eyes, he backed up to the end of the short pew, putting as much distance as possible between them. "I understand. You're trying to tell me—"

"No. That's not what I'm saying. I believe we can be a family, get married the way we planned."

"But not until you're sure I've kicked heroin and oxies for good, right?"

She scooted closer and laid her hand on his thigh.

He stiffened at her touch. His mouth formed a hard, resistant line.

"I want to be with you, Luke, but your parents and my parents won't—"

"Won't help you if you and the baby are living with me. They won't give you any money. Is that what you're saying?"

She averted her eyes, her gaze on her rounded belly. "They won't let me see you at all unless you can prove you've been clean for at least four months."

"And how do they propose I prove that?"

She raised her face to him, knowing he would need to see in her eyes that she believed he could succeed. "After you're released from Ellis, your father wants you to take a drug test three times a week, every week until the baby comes. If you pass every test, they'll let you be with me for labor and delivery."

Defeat replaced the anger in Luke's eyes, transforming them to a stormy blue. "You agreed to this?"

The anxiety in his voice made her want to weep. She squeezed her eyes tight against the tears. Should she have fought them all? She should have realized that these terms would make him feel pressured to be perfect, even though their parents were trying to help ensure his recovery and protect her and the baby. Everyone, her grandparents included, thought they knew what was best for her and Luke and the baby. But no one had asked what she wanted.

Luke cupped her chin and lifted her face to his. With his thumb, he wiped the moisture from her face. His touch filled her with longing. She opened her eyes to look at him.

"Is this what you really want? If I mess up, even once, I don't get to see our baby born?"

She leaned close to kiss him, but he jerked away. Apparently, a kiss couldn't make anything right for him any more than it could for her. "What do you want me to say, Luke? I'm seventeen years old. In four months, I'm going to have a baby. This is not how I imagined my life would be. I need their help. I can't do this alone."

"Translation—you need their help because you can't count on me. That's what you're really saying."

The resignation in his tone awakened the fear that was never silent for long, the fear that plagued them both. What he said was true. How could she deny it?

"Abby?"

Silently, she prayed God would give her the words to explain what she barely understood herself. "I'm scared."

"Of me using again?"

"Yes. And of the labor and the delivery. If I'm planning on you being with me, coaching me through the pain, and then ... then you're ... high or passed out somewhere. I couldn't bear that, Luke. If I plan on Mom being my coach—"

"I want to see our baby the minute she enters this world. I want to hold her in my arms, watch you nurse her for the first time. Those are memories I can never get back. Why would I chance missing that?" He grabbed Abby's hands and held on as if she were his lifeline. Tears slid down his cheeks.

Her heart was breaking. Why? Why had this happened to them? "I know you want to be there. I want you to be there, but ..."

Her phone vibrated in her purse, he released her hands, and she pulled out her cell to check it. There was a message from her mom, telling her to take as much time as she needed. She slipped it back in the outside pocket.

"Why can't you plan on us both being there?" Hope illuminated his face. "That way if I screw up—which I won't—you'll have your mom."

"If you're clean when my labor starts, you *can* be with me. Nobody wants to keep you out of the delivery room, Luke. If you slip up once or twice, well ..." Her stomach churned. She wasn't giving him permission to take drugs, but she didn't want him to think that one mistake would ruin everything. "You can't be actively using."

He nodded. "Fair enough. I'm not going to let you down, Abby." He captured her face in his hands, slanted his mouth over hers, and kissed her gently.

His lips on hers felt right—perfect, sweet, and exhilarating at the same time. She didn't want the kiss to end, but suddenly, kissing in a chapel felt too weird, inappropriate somehow. She broke off the kiss, leaned her forehead against his, and sighed. "I love you."

"And I love you."

She stared into his eyes, and knew it was true. He did love her. More than his drugs. This man, right here at this moment, was the Luke she had always loved. He was struggling to come back to her, and she could, she would take this leap of faith with him. She would believe in him in spite of everything, and she wouldn't let anyone cast doubt on their relationship again.

"We can make it, Abby. I promise."

She needed to believe him, to believe his love for her and the baby was stronger than the iron grip of heroin and oxies, but fear drummed in her ears with a sense of imminent horror. *He's going to end up dead.*

"What is it? Your face is so pale. Is it baby? Are you all right?"

She nodded, but she wasn't all right, and she had no idea when she would be because how would she ever know that Luke was completely cured of his addiction. Did anyone ever know? Were there any guarantees?

There was only one course of action she could live with. "I'll be back next week."

"What about your parents and your grandparents?"

Abby managed a smile for him. "We need to spend time together, and they're just going to have to understand that."

Luke wrapped his arms around her, and they clung to each other until the vibration of her phone interrupted them again.

*

Abby stepped carefully across the well-salted parking lot. She wasn't afraid of losing her footing. Not really. But chancing a fall that could hurt her baby wasn't worth rushing against the biting, sub-zero winds to reach the car. Falling snow whirled in strange and beautiful patterns, like the flutter of angel wings—a comforting reminder that God was watching over them.

Luke couldn't see the lot from the chapel or the common room, but she imagined him watching her go, more encouraged now that she'd promised to visit him every week. She sighed, reluctant to confront her parents. She didn't have the energy to fight with them. *Lord, please help them— all of them—to understand.*

Exhaust poured from the CRV. Good. Mom had kept the car running to keep the interior warm. Being pregnant felt like having her own personal, portable heat source, so Abby was rarely cold. Today wasn't one of those days. She sneezed then ducked her head against force of the wind pushing against her.

A patch of ice near the passenger door caused her to slide. A few seconds of panic stole her reasoning before she gripped the door handle and righted herself. Relief rushed through her as she leaned against the car to catch her breath then opened the door.

"Are you all right? What happened?" Mom's tone mirrored Abby's fear from moments before.

Abby climbed in the car and buckled her seat belt. "I'm

fine. I saw the ice too late. But I didn't fall."

"Thank goodness." Mom's features visibly relaxed. "We need to get you boots with better traction. We'll stop at the mall on the way home. How was your visit with Luke? Did you tell him about kissing Jack?"

"No, you were right. It's never going to happen again, and telling Luke would hurt him too much."

"I think you made the right decision."

Abby prayed silently that her mother would understand. "I made another decision, Mom. Luke and I decided ..."

"What? What did you decide?"

Abby swallowed to ease the scratchiness in her throat. "I can't keep my promise to stay away from Luke. I know that's what everyone wants, but it's not the right choice. Not now, while he's still in rehab."

Her mother shook her head. "We agreed—"

"Mom, Luke asked me to pray with him. He's trusting God to make him the man that the baby and I need, but he and I need to spend time together, to talk. I'm practically his only visitor. So, I promised him that I would visit him at least once a week. He needs my support, and I need his. The next four months are going to be hard enough without missing each other."

Mom's forehead creased as she raised her eyebrows, then drew them together in a frown. "I'm not sure how supportive Luke can be."

"I know you have doubts, but I have to do what's best for me and Luke. If I'd been visiting him every week, if I hadn't shut him out after Christmas ... what happened between me and Jack ..." She shook her head in disgust. "It was my fault, Mom."

Mom narrowed her eyes. "Jack wasn't entirely innocent."

Abby didn't want to think about Jack's motives. In fact,

she preferred to believe he'd reacted impulsively. "Maybe not. But that doesn't matter anymore."

Mom reached to touch Abby's cheek then withdrew her hand. "What about the baby? She has to be your first priority, not Luke. I thought you understood that, Abby."

The rebuke stung. "Mom, please, I need you on my side. Spending time with Luke *is* best for the baby. When I talk to Dad, I need you to back me up." Abby paused, staring into her mother's eyes, willing her to understand what her support, or the lack of it, would mean. "You know I'm not going to put myself or the baby at risk."

After a moment, Mom nodded. "All right. I understand, and I trust you, but you have to realize that we don't trust Luke. There's no guarantee that *he* won't put you and the baby at risk."

"That's exactly why I need to visit him. He needs encouragement. He knows you don't trust him, and his dad is barely speaking to him. He just saw his mom for the first time since he started at Ellis. And maybe months before that."

Her mother's eyes widened in surprise, but she didn't comment. Instead, she put the car in gear and headed out of the parking lot. "I don't know if I can fully support your choice, but I'll talk to your father about how you're feeling."

*

The following morning, her father greeted Abby with a kiss as he wrapped one arm around her expanding waist. "Morning, honey."

"Hi, Dad, did you … did Mom talk to you?"

"Yep."

Reluctant to examine his tone or his cryptic reply, she poured a mug of coffee for him and a tall glass of milk for herself. "I was going to make omelets, if you want one."

"I have to get to the office, but first, we need to talk." He took his mug and her milk and set them on the table. Then he pulled out a chair for her.

Here it comes.

Obediently, she sat, hands clasped together on the table. "Dad, please try to understand. I know you think I'm making a mistake, that I should cut Luke completely out of my life, but that's not the right choice. Especially when I believe he's getting better."

Her father laid one hand on her shoulder, his gaze filled with concern. "There are no guarantees, Abby. Luke could be fine, for months, years even, and then one day, something will happen, something he can't handle, and he'll start using again. And then where will you and the baby be?"

Abby couldn't deny her father's concerns. She'd been up for hours last night praying about what she would do if Luke slipped up again. About two a.m., she made her decision. If Luke started actively using, she and the baby couldn't be around him until he'd been clean for at least six months. But she wasn't prepared to tell her father this. She wanted to be optimistic.

"That's true," she whispered. "But I don't think that's what's going to happen. Luke isn't trying to do this alone. We prayed together, Dad. I believe that God can set Luke free, and he believes it, too."

"I admire your faith, and I'm certainly happy that Luke is learning to lean on the Lord, but you're my only daughter." Dad leaned forward on his elbows, his presence large in the breakfast nook. "And you're carrying my granddaughter, and it's my job to protect you. Both of you."

She resisted the urge to correct him, to tell him that protecting her and the baby was Luke's job now. But Dad must have read her thoughts in her expression. A sheen of tears in his eyes softened her next words. "I love you, Dad. I appreciate everything you've ever done for me, but Luke and I ... we have to do this together."

"What you're asking me to do is very hard."

He was silent for several minutes. Abby finished her milk. "Please, Dad."

"Okay, I will give Luke the space and time he needs to get this right." The words came out weighted with regret and anxiety. He gripped his mug until his knuckles turned white. "But if you need anything, anything at all ..."

"I'll ask you, Dad." The baby stirred in her womb, and a glimpse of what she was asking him to do tempered her next words. "I promise you I won't put myself or the baby in jeopardy. Not even for Luke."

Dad stood, pulled her into a hug, and kissed the top of her head. "I'll tell your grandparents our plans have changed." His tone was matter-of-fact, almost resigned.

"You will?" She lifted her head from his chest and met his gaze, then looked quickly away before his doubts could shake her resolve.

"I want to believe this is going to work, and I'm agreeing because I trust *you*. Trusting Luke is another matter entirely."

She nodded, her heart sinking. Her father was right. Trusting Luke would not be easy. Even for her. "Thank you, Dad."

He smiled then filled his travel mug with hot coffee and a tablespoon of sugar. A moment later he was gone, and unable to ignore her hunger another minute, she gathered the makings for a ham and cheese omelet and fixed herself a quick breakfast. She had to do her online economics final exam and submit it by noon, and she definitely couldn't accomplish *that* without food in her stomach. Even using her notes and the textbook, the exam wouldn't be easy because Mr. Davies preferred essays to multiple choice questions. Her final wouldn't be exactly the same as the in-class version, but according to Lisa, the written portion was 50% of the grade. Abby's writing skills weren't the problem. Her comprehension of the content would probably earn her thirty-five out of the fifty points at best. The baby fluttered like a synchronized swimmer in her womb, and Abby patted her stomach. "Don't worry, little girl. Mommy's got this." Striving to be valedictorian was a goal she'd given up months ago. Passing this class with an 85% would be just fine with her.

*

Luke wanted to plan something special for Abby's birthday, but without internet privileges he couldn't even shop online, not that he had much money to spend anyway. His mother was willing to help. She had offered to pick out something that Abby would like, but what? A bracelet? Perfume? A designer purse in her favorite color? Maybe, but what was her favorite color? Blue? Purple? Green? Why hadn't he paid more attention? He was a typical guy, that's why.

"You seem distracted this morning." Dr. Jefferies drummed a pencil on the desk blotter. "Want to talk about it?"

Luke shrugged. He leaned back in the upholstered chair, feigning resignation and staring out the windows through the wrought iron bars at the slivers of light overcoming the dismal gray sky. "It's my girlfriend's birthday next week, and I don't have a present for her."

"Hmm. Well, you're eligible for a day pass, aren't you?"

Dr. Jefferies knew the classification of every resident in the building, so the question was purely rhetorical. Luke nodded.

"Abby's had it really hard …" He stared at his scuffed sneakers, reluctant to meet the older man's discerning gaze. "Being pregnant, not being able to go to school, dealing with the challenges of home instruction."

The weight of it all tightened around Luke's neck like a hemp noose. Self-flagellation was a slippery slope for any addict. Fighting desperation, he met the counselor's gaze, wanting advice but fearing he could not do whatever the older man would suggest.

Dr. Jefferies leaned forward across the piles of papers on his desk, a question in his dark eyes that Luke preferred to ignore. The doctor wouldn't press—not exactly—but the man's silence was more compelling than his questioning. His ability to draw out the truth, no matter how unpleasant or shameful, made him good at his job. He looked totally composed leaning back in his leather swivel chair, resting his elbows on the arms and steepling his fingers like he had all day, though their session would end in forty minutes.

Envious of the doctor's calm demeanor, Luke paced the small office for a few moments. His frustration was about more than choosing the right birthday gift. Searching for answers, he stared out the window then faced his counselor. "I want to be able to make it up to her, but I have no idea how." Placing his palms on the edge of the massive desk, he leaned into the doctor's personal space and met the man's probing gaze with his own intense stare. "How do I prove to her that I'm not going to do heroin anymore?"

Dr. Jefferies pushed his horn-rimmed glasses up to the bridge of his nose. "That's a good question, but it shouldn't be the first question."

"It shouldn't?" Sensing he was being led where he might not be ready to go, Luke hesitated, praying for courage. "Then what is the first question?"

"How do you prove to *yourself* that you're not going to use anymore?"

That question was stated with compassion, but still, the cold, clammy hand of fear clutched the back of Luke's neck. He tensed. He didn't have an answer.

"That's the first question every addict must confront." Jefferies' tone was matter-of-fact, his voice low and gentle, as if he knew he was asking Luke to climb Mount Everest without any training.

Defeated, he sank back into the chair, his head in his hands, the voices plaguing him with desperate scenarios from which he could never escape.

I died to set you free.

Luke turned that thought over in his mind. Jake had mentioned just last night that the Pharisees were angry because Jesus had stood up in the synagogue and claimed that He had come to set the captives free.

Maybe, the voices in Luke's head were lying.

Light spilled through the office windows, drawing Luke's attention. The sun had broken through the clouds, which were suddenly framed in soft blue where moments before there had been only bleak shades of gray with razor-thin streaks of light. He would be leaving Ellis in less three weeks. No way was he ready. He was wise enough to admit he would need a lot of support. "Can you recommend a good outpatient program?"

"Several are very good. In the beginning, you may want to live with other recovering addicts in a group home with counselors on staff 24-7." He paused, clearly to give Luke a moment to consider this option. "For the long haul, recovered addicts need ongoing support. You'll need to find an NA group—Narcotics Anonymous. Get a sponsor, and go to meetings. Every day, more than once a day if you need to."

Luke drew in a long breath, sighed, and nodded, thinking of the list of local groups he'd made three months ago, before he had overdosed. Suddenly, the burden on his shoulders seemed less like a semi and more like a pickup. The suffocating, crushing defeat gripping him eased off just a little. "Mind if we end our session early, Doc?"

The counselor raised his eyebrows, waiting for an explanation.

"I want to go to the chapel before the afternoon group meeting."

Dr. Jefferies smiled in approval and nodded toward the door.

"Thank you, sir."

"It's what I'm here for."

Luke tried to smile but couldn't. He was counting down the days—nineteen—until he would be free to leave Ellis, but how would he ever adjust to sharing his struggles with a new counselor? Revealing the sordid story to Dr. Jefferies had been a slow, excruciating journey, one Luke wasn't anxious to revisit. Still, he would do whatever it took to stay clean for Abby and the baby.

Dustin had tried to make it outside of Ellis twice before. So many addicts ended up coming back here. They couldn't manage on their own. Their families had given up on them and had stopped trying to intervene. For the first time, gratitude for his father's deal with Abby replaced his resentment. Understanding Luke better than he did himself, Dad had maneuvered Luke into the place where he felt compelled to get the help he needed.

With one hand on the office door, Luke pivoted to face his counselor. "Dr. Jefferies?"

The other man glanced up from the notes he was typing into his laptop. "Yes, Luke?"

"I just wanted to tell you … you're good at your job."

A broad smile brightened the doctor's tired face. "That's good to hear. Thanks for the compliment."

*

Abby was not looking forward to her birthday. She turned sideways in the mirror to view the basketball shape of what used to be a very flat, muscular stomach. The baby kicked hard—probably protesting Abby's off mood. Turning eighteen when she was five and a half months pregnant was about as far from her dreams as she could possibly get. Reality sometimes demanded new dreams. That's what Grandma Collins had said last week when they'd shared a quiet lunch at Bravo's restaurant before shopping for baby things. Abby had acknowledged the wisdom of her grandmother's words without having a clue how to implement them. Could God give her a new dream? That must be His plan because now she was responsible for a child who would depend on her for absolutely everything.

Thank goodness, she and Luke were in a good place now. They hadn't done anything but talk during their last two visits, deciding against leaving the center for any outing, primarily because he hadn't want her driving on snowy roads any more than was absolutely necessary. More than likely, he felt guilty that she'd come at all, and guilty that he hadn't told her not to come. Part of him, he'd said, couldn't wait for February 9th to get here. But he was nervous. He couldn't hide his feelings from her, which was okay because they needed to confide in one another. Keeping secrets would destroy the fragile trust they were working so hard to rebuild.

Luke had admitted leaving the center wouldn't be easy, for any number of reasons. He wanted to get a job, but his parents insisted he go back to school, and since they held the purse strings, Luke intended to do both. Abby had tried to talk him out of working. Returning to classes would mean deadlines and more than enough stress, but Luke wanted to contribute to their baby's expenses, and nothing Abby could say would change his mind.

A sharp fear pricked her even now. What if he wanted his own money for drugs? No. She refused to believe it. Luke was determined to stay clean. That truth was the foundation upon which they were building a new life together.

The one thing they hadn't discussed yet was getting married, not even for the baby's sake. At this point, they couldn't afford an apartment, not without their parents help, and Luke didn't want their financial help. Not for himself. He was glad his parents were helping Abby and the baby, but he intended to prove that *he* could manage on his own. Addiction had shredded his pride and all but destroyed his belief in himself. Accepting his parents' help with school expenses was a necessity, though.

Maybe, recovery would be easier if he took some time off from school, but then he might have too much free time. His parents were probably right. Working to get his grades up and to get off academic probation would keep Luke busy. But would the struggle be too much?

How long and what would it take to restore his confidence? And her confidence in him?

Abby shook her head at her reflection, startled anew at how quickly she'd transformed from ordinary high school student to very pregnant teen. They'd messed things up so badly. She rubbed her belly in gentle, swirling motions. "Don't you worry, little girl. Mommy's going to make sure ..."

What was she going to make sure? That the baby didn't suffer for her parents' mistakes? No matter how hard Abby tried, she wouldn't be able to make everything fine for her daughter. "A baby needs two parents." She patted the spot where a heel or an elbow had momentarily bulged the surface of her sweater. "Did you hear your grandpa and your great-grandpa talking about adoption? Don't you worry. I told them absolutely not."

Her cell rang. Abby glanced at the caller ID on the screen. Caroline Bradford. Why would Luke's mother be calling her? She swiped the screen to connect the call. "Hello." Her voice sounded thin and nervous. "Mrs. Bradford, is something wrong? Is Luke all right?"

"Luke is fine. In fact, I just dropped him back off at the center. He and his brother and I had lunch together."

Abby felt a surge of joy. Luke had missed his little brother terribly. But why was Luke's mother calling her now, especially with Joe in the car? "Thank you for calling," Abby said, her remark sounding stupid even to her own ears.

"I'm calling to invite you and your mother to lunch on Saturday."

Abby couldn't answer for her mother, but she had nothing on her calendar that would provide an excuse to decline the invitation. Why did she want to wriggle out of a simple lunch with Luke's mother? Hadn't she hand-delivered a check to help pay for the expense of setting up the baby's room in what used to be the guest room? Abby appreciated the effort Luke's mother was making, especially for Luke's sake. He had all but given up on restoring his relationship with his family, until his mother told her husband she intended to visit her son regularly.

"Lunch sounds … good."

"Say one o'clock at the Cheesecake Factory?"

Abby drew in a silent breath and slowly released it. "I don't know my mother's schedule. Can I have her call you tonight?"

"Certainly, dear. We have a lot to discuss."

The call was disconnected before Abby could ask what Mrs. Bradford meant. Had the signal been lost or had the older woman deliberately and abruptly ended the call before Abby could respond?

She sat down on her neatly made bed and leaned back against the mound of pillows. Under normal circumstances, she would call Luke and ask him if he knew what his mother wanted to talk about. Abby was half tempted to get in her car and drive to the rehab center, but a quick glance at her watch told her she would arrive in the middle of the afternoon group session. No resident could be excused from group, unless it were a true emergency, which this definitely wasn't.

Abby keyed in Megan's number. The call went directly to voicemail. Then she tried Lisa, who picked up on the third ring.

"Abby! How are you? Megan and I were—"

"Luke's mom wants to have lunch with me and my mom."

"That's so nice."

"Is it? I have no idea what she wants." A burst of conversations muffled Lisa's reply. "What did you say? Where are you? I can hardly hear you."

"The cafeteria, silly. Let me step out into the hall. I said, Mrs. Bradford probably wants to talk about your baby shower."

Abby hadn't even thought that far ahead. "You're probably right. I'm just being paranoid."

"Maybe you're not. What's been happening with Luke?"

"I'm visiting him at the rehab center once or twice a week. And we're talking about the future."

Lisa groaned. "You two aren't thinking about getting

married, are you?"

"Not now."

"Not now? What does that mean?

"Lisa, I can't talk about this on the phone. Can you and Megan come over after school?"

Abby held her breath. She hadn't realized how much she'd been missing her two best friends. They might not have as much in common as they'd had in the past, but they loved her, and she loved them.

CHAPTER TWELVE

Four hours later, Megan and Lisa were sitting cross-legged on Abby's bed. The three of them munched on freshly popped kettle corn and drank pomegranate and cherry juice—Abby's newest craving. They chatted about school, and how many games the basketball team had won so far this season and whether or not both the girls' and the boys' teams would make it to sectionals.

In spite of the typical teen conversation, an unspoken question hung in the room, draped like damp wool around Abby's shoulders. Nothing in her life was simple anymore. Absolutely nothing. She couldn't even just hang out with her two best friends. The baby kicked to confirm her thoughts, and Abby grabbed one of Lisa's and one of Meg's hands and laid them on her stomach. "Do you feel that?"

Lisa giggled. "Wow."

"Amazing." Meg's brown eyes sparkled with wonder. "Does that happen often?"

"Yep. Especially when I'm trying to fall asleep. Or when I'm feeling sad or stressed. It's like she's saying, hey, mom, I'm in here. Life's not so bad."

"You really think your baby is trying to communicate

with you?" Lisa asked skeptically.

"I don't know, but I talk to her all of the time."

"Have you and Luke picked out a name yet?" Meg asked.

"I want to name her Elise after my grandma. Luke wants to call her Grace."

"Hmm. I like them both." The baby hadn't moved for several minutes, and Lisa removed her hand from Abby's belly. "Is Grace his grandma's name?"

Abby smiled, a sense of burgeoning hope soothing her heart. "No. He wants to call the baby Grace because without God's grace he wouldn't be here."

"Truly?"

"Yes. Luke knows he can't stay drug-free without God's help. He's counting on God's mercy and forgiveness every day."

Lisa and Megan exchanged glances.

"Jack asked about you." Lisa leveled Abby with a perplexed look. "When are you going to forgive him?"

"I don't know what you're talking about."

Lisa scoffed, and Meg looked uncomfortable. Abby should've known she couldn't hide the truth from her friends. "I don't ... I can't ... talk about this."

"You don't have to talk to us, but you can't pretend forever." Lisa grabbed Abby's arm. "We know something happened. You've been ignoring his calls and texts for over a month."

"What? Don't look at me like that. I've been busy." Abby scrambled off the bed as quickly as she could manage and busied herself refilling everyone's glasses.

"Lisa's right. You haven't talked to him since you ditched us the day after New Year's Day."

A surge of renewed guilt churned in Abby's stomach. *God, I know You forgave me. Why can't I forgive myself?*

"Jack … and I … we kissed."

The shock on her friends' faces made Abby want to scream or cry or both. "It happened so fast. It was … over so fast. But Jack …. It didn't mean anything. Jack and I … we've always had this agreement that we'd never talk about his feelings for me. Jack knows I'm with Luke. He … I just can't talk to Jack. Nothing I can say will make this better. We can't go back to the way we were before. It's too weird, and—"

"You're afraid of what will happen to Luke, of what he'll do if he finds out." Lisa put her hand on Abby's shoulder.

Abby shifted away, needing to deny their valid concerns. "There's nothing for Luke to find out. It was a terrible mistake that is never going to happen again."

Megan stared, stunned. "Is that why you won't see Jack or even talk to him? Because you're afraid something more will happen between you two?"

Tears pricked Abby's eyes. "No. It's because I'll see it in Jack's eyes."

"See what?" the other girls said in unison.

"I'll see how much he wants to kiss me again, how much he wants me to break up with Luke." She sniffled and snatched a tissue from the box on her nightstand. "Jack wants to be the one to take care of me and the baby. He can't hide that anymore. Not from me. And not from himself. Not from anyone else who sees us together. That's why I can't talk to him."

The girls enveloped her in a hug. "Oh, Abby. We're so sorry."

"It was my fault, too," she muttered. "I should have stopped him. Then, we could still be friends like we've always been."

Megan, ever the optimist, tried to smile. "Maybe you can

be friends again. Someday."

Abby shook her head. "I don't think so."

"But won't Luke think it's weird that you and Jack don't hang out anymore?" Lisa asked.

"I don't think so," Megan said. "Luke has too many other things to deal with to wonder about Jack."

*

Luke could hardly believe that in eight short days he would be leaving Ellis. His palms started to sweat just thinking about the pressure he would be under. Dustin would be gone in three days. The guy had become a good friend, someone Luke could be honest with. They had discussed getting an apartment together, but neither man felt strong enough to live with another recovering addict. Ex-addict wasn't a term they used because it implied that their addictions were over and done with—a problem they no longer had to contend with, which simply wasn't true. Luke understood that he would need to continually guard against the temptation to relapse into his old patterns. That meant he could no longer live with Cole. If he didn't already have a new roommate, Cole wasn't going to take that news well, and Luke dreaded going to the apartment to pack up his stuff. What if he couldn't resist the pull?

But he didn't need to stress about that battle today.

Today, his beautiful Abby would be coming to celebrate her eighteenth birthday. He'd managed to buy her a small gift—a silver Claddagh promise ring. If only he were in a position to place it on her left hand as an engagement ring. He planned for her to wear it on her right hand as a symbol of their love for each other and their dreams for their future. He intended to give it to her at the restaurant when he took her out to lunch. It would be the first time they'd shared a meal since Christmas.

Remembering the events of that day still pained him, but beating himself up over his own stupidity would only sap his strength, strength he needed for today. One day at a time wasn't accurate though. Most times, Luke managed one hour, or even one minute, at a time. Sometimes, his prayers were *I can't go on another second without Your help, Lord.* The anxious thoughts would stop pummeling him, and then, Luke could breathe.

He took his fleece-lined leather jacket from the closet, checked his tie in the mirror above the dresser, and stared down his reflection. "Well, Bradford. The true test is coming. You think you got what it takes?"

A resurgence of anxiety crashed through his mind with tsunami force. Eight days was too soon. Could he even handle an afternoon out with his girl?

He covered his face with his hands and prayed for courage and peace.

I will never leave you.

It was Luke's favorite verse, his anchor when the likelihood that he would ever be totally free seemed as impossible as parasailing off Mount Everest.

*

Abby wore a green and black plaid flannel tunic that graced her knees over black leggings with suede boots. She pulled her long hair back into a tortoise-colored clip and swiped clear gloss over her lips. Then she sprayed her favorite floral perfume on her wrists and rubbed some of the fragrance onto her neck and behind her ears. She encircled her arms around her belly, surprised at how fast the baby was growing. Luke said pregnancy made her more beautiful. Most times, she felt self-conscious and tired, so his compliment meant a lot. She smiled.

Mom and Dad had agreed to Abby driving herself to the

center so that she and Luke could have time alone. She wanted to snuggle up to him without the watchful eyes of the Ellis staff chaperoning them.

Soon enough, they would have time alone, as long as Luke passed his thrice weekly drug tests. In a little over a week, he would be moving back in with his parents—a temporary solution to his housing problem. Abby still couldn't believe the Bradfords were allowing Luke to come home, but clearly, everyone believed this arrangement was Luke's best chance for success. No one, least of all his father, wanted Luke to spend any time with Cole Marchman. At first, Richard Bradford had insisted on packing up his son's things himself, or at the very least, accompanying Luke to the apartment, but his mother vetoed both of those plans. Trusting their son was key to his recovery, she had insisted.

Of course, Abby heard all of this second-hand from Luke. She'd kept quiet about her opinion—that avoiding temptation whenever possible made the most sense. Taking unnecessary risks, especially so soon after his release from the security and supervision of the center, seemed reckless and stupid. She believed Luke wanted to stay clean, even that he intended to stay clean, but trusting him to resist the pressure of free drugs—and Cole would definitely push heaven knows what at Luke—didn't seem reasonable to her.

Her anxiety took the form of the recurring nightmare— the same one she'd had months ago when she'd first confirmed her pregnancy. She was running after Luke, trying to stop him from carrying their daughter into Cole's apartment where her baby girl would be exposed to second-hand marijuana smoke. Abby had awakened in a cold sweat three out of the last five nights. She'd prayed herself back to sleep, asking God to protect her baby and to help Luke stay drug-free. She refused to think about the staggering relapse rate for heroin addicts. Several websites claimed 90% of heroin addicts relapsed within the first three months after detox. If only she'd never researched recovery statistics. She'd been naïve to hope that the statistics would bolster her faith. The opposite had happened. Emotionally, she was surviving on prayer and her parents' support.

"LORD, couldn't You just make sure that Cole isn't around when Luke goes to the apartment?"

Of course, He could. God could do anything, but she had learned He didn't always answer her prayers the way she wanted. If he did, her favorite grandmother would still be alive.

But Abby couldn't think about that right now. Feeling as if God had let her down would weaken her faith even more, and she couldn't let that happen. For her baby's sake and for Luke's, Abby needed her faith to move mountains because she really wanted him to be with her for their baby's birth, and there was no way their parents would let him anywhere near the hospital if he tested positive.

She descended the stairs, one hand firmly gripping the bannister, then retrieved her oversized khaki parka from the hall closet. The coat was ugly, but it was the only one that closed around her belly.

Her Mustang started on the first turn of the key—one of the many benefits of their heated garage. She eased the car to the end of the driveway, taking care to avoid the snow banked on either side where the plows had dumped mounds high enough for the neighborhood boys to slide down with their plastic saucers.

She switched on the radio in time to hear the latest weather update. The meteorologist warned commuters that a lake effect storm starting around five thirty could dump eight to ten inches by nine o'clock. Ugh! She was so sick of snow.

By February, Abby dreaded the dreary, overcast skies. Where was the sun hiding? She could scarcely remember the brilliant blue sky accented with fluffy white cumulus clouds. After her birthday on the first, there was nothing to look forward to. The February break from school meant nothing to her. She planned to work straight through, determined to plow through the majority of her academic requirements before the baby's arrival in mid-May. She would still have to take two Regents exams, Physics and Math, in June, but otherwise, she wanted to be finished. Her mother had warned her that she'd be exhausted for months after the baby's birth, between the stress of labor and getting up during the night with her infant daughter.

If only she could control what Luke did. He said he wanted to be with her for the baby's birth, and she believed him. The determination in his eyes and the set of his jaw punctuated his words but not enough to completely erase her fears. For that she relied on prayer—short S.O.S. prayers that filled her mind with a peace she couldn't quite explain.

*

Holding Abby in his arms, Luke soaked in the sense of peace he'd lost so many months ago, when he'd first lied to her about shooting up. He swallowed the shame of the man he'd become. God's mercies were new every morning. Luke couldn't afford to let his past mistakes define the man he wanted to be.

"I miss you." She stood on her toes and kissed him then snuggled into his neck.

He tightened his hold on her, the baby large between them. He cupped her chin, catching her gaze, grateful for the longing in her eyes that mirrored his own. "Happy birthday, babe."

"Are you ready to leave?"

He wasn't sure if she meant leave for lunch or leave the center. The answer to both questions was finally the same. He couldn't postpone facing the real world any longer. "Definitely. I can't wait to celebrate with my favorite girl."

Her eyes sparkled with mischief. "I may not be your favorite girl come mid-May."

"Right." He brushed a kiss across her lips.

His quick, playful kiss that made her erupt in giggles. "So, I am right. I will be replaced."

"No, I'll have *two* favorite girls."

"I can live with that," she murmured against his lips and kissed him so passionately that for a long moment, he almost forgot where they were. He released her long enough to capture her hand in his, and they headed through the crowded common room, down the hall, and outside into the brisk February air. The sky was a mass of dark clouds, portending heavy lake effect snow, but nothing could dampen his mood. The storm wasn't scheduled to dump any significant precipitation until after five o'clock. Abby would be safe at home long before then.

They crossed the parking lot to where she'd parked her Mustang in a row with only one other vehicle several spots away. With relief, he noted that she'd had snow tires put on. "Still taking great care of your car, I see."

She smiled. "I'm trading it in before the baby comes. Dad wants me in an all-wheel-drive car that will be safer for the baby."

Luke hadn't thought of that. Selling her Mustang wouldn't be easy for her. Abby had made so many sacrifices already, sacrifices she never would have needed to make if it weren't for his selfishness. "I'm sorry, babe. I know how much you love this car." He held the door open for her and waited for her to pull her seatbelt around her expanded waist. Then he bent down and pressed his lips to hers. She had popped in a stick of gum and tasted like mint, sunshine, and possibilities. "Someday," he said as he broke off the kiss, his heart straining to be a better man.

"Someday what?"

"Someday, I'm going to make it up to you." He didn't wait for her to ask for an explanation. He walked around the back of the vehicle and got in the passenger side.

She was staring at him, her lips parted as if she wanted to reply but had no idea what to say.

Had he hurt her, again, because she wasn't convinced he could ever make it up to her?

"Don't look at me like that," she said, laying her hand possessively on his thigh.

The gentle squeeze of her fingers drove every thought from his head save one. He wanted so much more than her gloved hand caressing his jean-encased thigh, but this wasn't the time or the place. God expected Luke to cherish Abby by waiting until after they were married to make love to her again. Could he do that? Not if she kept rubbing his leg. He captured her hand, pulled off her glove, and kissed her palm. "I love you, Abby. I'm determined to be the man you and the baby deserve."

"I love you, too, Luke Bradford."

Their gazes locked, and the urge to kiss her senseless swept through him. "Let's go to the restaurant."

He wanted to give her the ring while they were alone in the car, but the desire to pull her onto his lap would become too strong to resist if they sat here much longer. Lucky for him, this car was way too small to do anything remotely inappropriate.

She smiled, her face flushed pink. She had recognized the look he'd given her. They knew each other well.

Once again, Luke was amazed at how heroin had dulled his body's responses to her. Even though he had no intention of following through, he rejoiced that once again he wanted her with a consuming passion. A passion God expected Luke to restrain. Which would be almost as difficult as resisting the temptation to use. The only difference was one day he would no longer have to restrain his feelings for Abby, but he would always have to guard against the temptation to use drugs.

He eased the car out into traffic. Abby was chattering about the baby shower their mothers were planning, but he couldn't focus on her words. He clutched the small box in his right coat pocket. The possibility of marrying her was so far off in the distant future that he nearly panicked. The urge to shoot up, to feel the sweet release of every tension and desire returned with relentless force, and with it, a shame that would have driven him to his knees had he been alone.

Parked at a stoplight, Abby glanced over at him. "Are you all right?" She put his hand on her arm. "Do you want me to pull over?"

"Definitely not. I'll explain when we get to the restaurant."

*

Luke helped Abby out of her coat and waited while she maneuvered herself into the booth. He kissed her cheek and whispered, "Pray for me."

She shifted in her seat to look up at him, startled by the tension creasing his forehead. "What's wrong?" He didn't answer. She wanted to kiss away his distress, but this wasn't the time or the place. "Is it … you know?"

His face colored with embarrassment. That was her answer. She wanted to ask what was stressing him out, but did it matter? Talking about what triggered him might help, and it might not. She waited until he slid into the booth opposite her, then reached for his hand and closed her eyes, dismissing her twinge of embarrassment at the thought of praying in public. "Jesus, please help Luke." Her voice was low, but his soft "yes" encouraged her to continue. "Take away the cravings. Nothing is too hard for You, God. Nothing is impossible."

Luke tightened his grip on her hand. "Please, Lord," he whispered. "I need You. Now."

With her eyes still closed, Abby waited, allowing Luke's silence to settle her pounding heart. A soft light emerged like a sunrise in her mind, and with it, an image of Jesus leading her out of this dark place. But where was Luke? She couldn't leave him behind. *Father, help him.*

"You promised to set the captives free," Luke whispered.

After a long moment, their soft, simultaneous "amen" was barely audible in the crowded restaurant, but Abby was sure God had heard every word they'd spoken and even the requests that they couldn't put into words. Especially those.

The server, a twenty-something guy named Mike, brought them water and took their orders, lasagna for Luke and chicken parmigiana for her. When they were alone again, Abby studied her boyfriend. A small smile touched his lips with an excitement she hadn't seen in far too long. What was he thinking? She couldn't stand the suspense another second. "A dollar for your thoughts."

He laughed, his blue eyes sparkling with triumph. "Isn't it a penny for your thoughts?"

"Well, yeah, but I didn't think you'd tell me if I only offered you a penny." She ran her hand over his sleeve, rousing an altogether different spark in his eyes, one she remembered with a flash of heat in her cheeks. She sucked in a deep breath and blew it out.

A full-fledged Cheshire cat grin spread across his face.

They hadn't flirted like this in so long. She almost didn't want it to end, but they couldn't end up where they usually did. "Are you going to tell me or not?" She tried but failed to sound stern.

His eyes never leaving hers, Luke reached under the table then set a black jewelry box in front of her.

She gasped. "It isn't? You didn't—"

"Not yet, babe. The timing isn't right."

The regret in his voice brought pricks of tears to her eyes, and she blinked them away. Luke's addiction was only part of their problem. She rested her hand on the spot where the baby pushed against her with a tiny fist or maybe a foot. Abby couldn't deny the truth. They had both messed this up. Getting pregnant while she was still in high school was something that happened to other people, but not to her. This was her fault as much as his, though he continued to insist on shouldering all of the blame. They would need to talk about that, but not today. She fingered the jewelry box. "Then what is in here?"

"Open it, and you'll see."

The excitement was back in his voice, and she smiled. The box was too small for a bracelet. Maybe, it was a necklace, perhaps with her birthstone set in a silver heart or something equally romantic.

Before she could open the gift, the server returned with a basket of bread and seasoned olive oil. Ignoring her hunger, Abby captured the box in her left hand and flipped it open. A silver Claddagh ring nestled in the black velvet. "Oh, Luke, it's beautiful." She slipped it onto the ring finger of her right hand, held the ring close to the soft glow of the hurricane lamp, and sighed. "It fits perfectly."

"I had it sized to match your high school ring."

Her first thought—how much longer would it fit—was followed by a much darker one, one that shamed her. "You still have it?"

Instantly, his eyes dimmed with deep sorrow. She would give almost anything to take the words back, almost anything to not have imagined the worst. He needed her trust.

"You thought I'd sell your class ring."

It wasn't a question. It was a statement of profound regret and disappointment. Was he disappointed in her for doubting him or in himself for giving her so many reasons? Probably both. "Luke, I'm sorry. I'm glad you still have it. But you aren't wearing it, so I thought maybe—"

"I wanted to wait to put it on again when you would be proud to have people see it on my hand." He pulled a gold chain from beneath his crew neck sweater. Her amethyst class ring hung from the end.

So that was the lump she'd felt earlier when they'd hugged hello. If they weren't in a restaurant, she'd wrap her arms around him and squeeze him like she never wanted to let go. She had no intention of letting him go. With God helping them, maybe she wouldn't have to. She blinked back tears as the baby kicked twice. Hard.

Glad for any excuse to be close to Luke, Abby slid out of the booth, slipped in beside him, and laid his hand over the place on her stomach that protruded with their daughter's tiny fist or foot.

Luke's eyes widened in wonder.

"Do you feel that?"

He nodded, his hand radiating warmth through her tunic. "Amazing." He gazed at her, his blue eyes bright with love. For her? Or for their baby? He had never looked at her quite like that before, with his soul so transparent.

Completely gone was the shrouded look that feared her scrutiny. He kissed her cheek, and she turned her face until their mouths met.

She kissed him then, and he responded with a passion that quickened her breath and her heartrate. "I love you, Luke."

"I love you, Abby. I never stopped."

She knew it was true. She laid her hand over his where it remained pressed against her swollen belly, and together they waited for their daughter to move again. The baby gave another sharp kick, and Luke laughed. For the first time since Luke had met Cole Marchman, Abby believed that everything was going to work out, that their happily ever after had not been destroyed after all.

CHAPTER THIRTEEN

Luke said goodbye to Jake and Leah. Their words of prayer and encouragement buoyed Luke's mood but couldn't eradicate his anxiety about leaving Ellis in less than two hours. Needing one last session with the man who had helped him see his addiction in all of its horror and ugliness, Luke headed for Dr. Jefferies' office. He rapped twice on the door.

"Come in, Luke."

He stepped inside, standing with his hands hanging at his sides, suddenly uncertain whether the doctor would have time to talk with him. "Do you have a few minutes?"

Dr. Jefferies gestured to the chair on the opposite side of his desk, the same place Luke had sat every other day for the last three months.

Grateful, he sank into the comfortable armchair, wishing he had another week in the center before he had to face Cole. "How'd you know it was me?"

"Like most recovering addicts, you're nervous about leaving rehab. The prospect of being on the outside, where drugs are readily accessible, is scary. I'd be concerned if you weren't scared." With his elbows on the desk blotter, Dr.

Jefferies rested his chin in his folded hands. "But I believe you're ready."

Several moments of silence passed. Apparently, he was waiting for Luke to articulate his concerns. He swallowed hard, ashamed of the utter helplessness he felt at the thought of seeing Cole again. Had the guy ever been Luke's friend? "I have to go back to the apartment and pack up my stuff."

"And you don't want to face your roommate."

Luke shook his head vehemently. He'd rather face a firing squad. "Cole ... he ... supplied me with whatever I wanted. Heroin, cocaine, marijuana."

Dr. Jefferies came out from behind his desk and placed his hand on Luke's shoulder. "You're afraid he'll pressure you into using again."

Luke nodded. "I want to be strong—for myself and my family, for Abby and the baby, but what if I cave? One slip-up and I'll be right back where I was three months ago. The truth is I'm terrified."

"You have my number. You can call or text me, anytime, night or day. And you plan to attend an NA meeting tonight, right?"

Luke drew in a deep breath. "I'm going to two meetings a day until ... until I feel like I can make it with only one meeting a day."

Dr. Jefferies nodded. "That's a good plan. Even so, my offer holds. Text or call me day or night. Now what's your plan for reducing the temptation you'll experience when you see your roommate? Do you really need to go there today? If you wait until after you've attended an NA meeting or two, you'll be assigned a sponsor. That person would probably be glad to go with you for moral support."

"My cousin, Ian, is going to the apartment with me

tomorrow afternoon." Luke wanted to get the uncomfortable conversation with Cole over with as soon as possible. He couldn't stand having it hanging over his head. His imagination had already conjured up too many disastrous scenarios, all of them involving him using and being instantly sucked back into the deadly cycle.

"Tell me why you think having Ian along will help."

Luke considered his response for a moment. "I don't want to go alone."

"Why not one of your parents?"

"My father wanted to go with me, but my mother insisted they needed to trust me to do this alone. And there's no way I want Abby involved. She's never liked Cole, and he can't stand her. I asked my cousin, and he said yes. Before I started abusing oxies, Ian and I spent a lot of time together. We were more like brothers than cousins."

"I see. You want to get this over with, and Ian offered. But that still doesn't answer my question. Why the rush?"

Luke willed his fidgety hands to be still. He gripped his knees. "I want to put that life totally behind me as soon as possible."

"And severing ties with Cole is your first step?"

"He's the one who started me on heroin. I never want to see him again after tomorrow."

*

Abby had wanted to see Luke the minute he left the center, but they had agreed he should spend his first evening home with his parents and his little brother. She didn't want to encroach on their family time, but she kept wondering how it was going. She composed a quick text: "How are things with you and your dad?"

Her phone beeped to signal his reply as she was checking the biscuits. The tops were golden brown. To make sure they were completely baked on the bottom, she slid the metal spatula beneath one biscuit. Perfect. She removed the biscuits to a cooling rack on the counter then read Luke's reply. "Okay, I guess. No serious discussions about the testing schedule or anything else."

"That's good, right?" she texted back.

"Yeah, but I'd rather be with you."

"I miss you, too." She set her phone on the kitchen counter. If she didn't pay attention to dinner, she'd end up burning the soup. She typed one last message: "Getting ready to eat dinner with Sam. Call you later."

His reply was an emoji of a kiss.

She smiled and rubbed her belly. "Well, baby, I guess your daddy's doing okay on his first day home." *Thank You, Lord.*

She stirred the beef and barley soup leftover from the previous night. Trying to gauge the temperature by the steam rising from the savory broth didn't seem too reliable. She dipped in her spoon, blew softly on the beef and broth, then tasted it to see if it was hot enough. Definitely. She set the table for two. It was only going to be her and Sam tonight. Both their parents were working late, as they so often did, and Abby was tired of eating at the kitchen island, sitting on uncomfortable stools that provided zero support for her aching back. She placed the biscuits in a towel-lined basket on the table next to the softened butter. She considered lugging the soup kettle to the table but decided against it. Instead, she ladled generous servings into two bowls and carried them into the dining room.

"Sam, dinner's ready," she called from the bottom of the stairs. Then she returned to the kitchen to pour two tall glasses of milk, one for herself and one for Sam. He'd probably complain and argue he'd rather have water, but she wouldn't back down. He needed the calcium as much as she and the baby did. His bones were still growing, after all.

She smiled to herself. She was actually starting to think like a mom.

Sam appeared in the dining room moments later without her even having to call him a second time. "What's that smell? Biscuits?"

"Yep."

"Just for us?"

"Why not? Soup tastes better with some kind of bread." She smiled, happy to please her little brother. "It was either pop biscuits in the oven or serve marble rye, and you hate that."

Sam wrapped one arm around her middle and kissed her cheek. "You're going to make a good mom, Abby."

Tears sprang to her eyes. She blinked and swiped away the moisture with the back of her hand. "Thank you."

"Hey, don't get all weepy on me." He looked at her like he had no idea what she'd do next.

She laughed. "Weepy?"

"That's Dad's word. He said now that you're past the halfway point you'll be crying about everything."

"Don't count on it. Just because Mom was super emotional doesn't mean I will be." Though defending herself was a knee-jerk reaction, the irony was she had a lot more to cry about than their mother ever did, what with their father's support and the fact that both Abby and her brother had been planned babies, despite the eight-year difference in their ages. Mom had had two miscarriages between Abby and Sam, who they all viewed as their miracle child. Mom had just about given up having another child when she got pregnant with Sam. Clearly, her mother had stresses and heartaches of her own. Had she feared she'd lose Sam like she'd lost the other two? It was something she and Abby never discussed. She laid her hand protectively over her stomach, eager for the moment she would hold her baby girl for the very first time.

"Hey!" Sam snapped his fingers in front of Abby's nose. "Where are you? The soup's getting cold. Let's eat."

With a newfound understanding of what her mother had endured to bring Sam into the world, Abby felt her heart swell with love for her brother. She leaned close and kissed his cheek.

With his face screwed up in a grimace, Sam pulled away. "I'm not your baby brother anymore. Save those kisses for your own baby, okay?"

Abby laughed outright. "I love you, you know that, right?"

Sam wrinkled his nose. "Stop talking mushy."

Abby didn't take offense. When they were both seated, she reached across the table and clasped her brother's hand before asking a blessing. She opened her eyes to discover her brother staring at her with a quizzical expression.

"What?"

"We don't usually pray unless Mom or Dad are home."

It was true. But recently Abby had come to believe that God cared about everything that mattered to her, and that conviction made her feel more loved than ever before. "You know how much Mom and Dad appreciate it when you thank them without being reminded?"

Sam wiggled his mouth back and forth, then his eyes lit with excitement. "Thank You, God, for giving me only one sister." He laughed until he doubled over.

Abby should scold him, but she didn't have the heart. She reached across the table and mussed up his hair instead. "Eat your soup before I decide to give you a chore to do after dinner."

Sam opened his mouth but closed it just as fast.

Maybe, her little brother was right. She did know a few things about kids.

*

On Sunday morning, Luke woke with a start. Darkness cloaked the room, his bedroom. He was home. He had been released from Ellis yesterday afternoon. Was he ready? He shivered beneath the plaid flannel comforter but sat up to check the time. Six thirty. Anxiety pummeled his nervous system, and he rolled out of bed and onto his knees. He half wished Mom had let Dad pack up his stuff—anything to avoid his drug-pedaling roommate.

"God," he whispered, "I need You. Take away this awful fear. Make me strong enough to say no to Cole. For Abby and for our baby. For my parents. For Joe. For You."

Luke slowed his breathing, matching inhales to exhales. He trusted God to defeat the desperation, to conquer the doubts. God had brought him this far, and He wouldn't leave Luke now.

Seeing Cole again wouldn't be easy, but with Ian there, Cole wouldn't resort to his high pressure tactics. "Jesus, thank You that I don't have to do this alone. I don't have to do any of it alone because You promised to never leave me." Luke reached for his Bible, sliding it off the nightstand and onto the bed. It was too dark to read the words without turning on a light, so he laid his hand over the worn leather and mentally recited his favorite verse from II Timothy: "For God hath not given us a spirit of fear, but of love, and of power, and of a sound mind." Luke was especially grateful for the amazing gift of a sound mind.

He rose from his knees, turned on the nightstand lamp, and reached for his phone. "Abby, can I pick you up for church today?" He ended the text with, "Please," and then touched the send arrow. She wouldn't be up for another couple of hours, so he didn't expect a response. He opened his Bible to the book of John and read aloud until the soft glow of morning light brightened the room, then he took a shower and waited for Abby's reply.

He was pouring his first cup of breakfast blend coffee when his cell phone rang. "Hi, babe. Can we go to church together?"

"I want to ..."

"But?"

"I need to ask my parents, and they're not up yet."

Luke dumped two spoons of sugar into his coffee and stirred it, tamping down his frustration. Surely, they wouldn't object to him attending church with them. Didn't it prove he was trying to get his life in order? "What time should I pick you up?"

"Nine thirty. I don't think they'll say no."

Luke couldn't read Abby, and that scared him. Before his knee surgery, they had talked about everything, sharing their fears and their dreams. They'd been more than a couple. Abby was his best friend, and he was pretty sure she had felt the same way about him. Not anymore. She had withdrawn, but he'd been too high for too long to notice. He'd been so close to losing everything that now he finally understood how extraordinary their relationship was. Was. Thinking of the best time in their relationship as past made him all the more determined to restore all they had lost. "Do you want *me* to ask your dad if it's all right?"

"No. I'll let you know in a half hour."

"I love you, Abby. I want to start going to church with you. Not just today, but every week."

"I'd like that, Luke."

*

Abby felt the disapproving glances of several church members as she and Luke followed her family to their usual pew about midway down on the right. She squeezed Luke's hand, leaned close, and whispered, "Thanks for coming with me."

He nodded and slipped his arm around her middle, his fingers grazing her ribcage. But he dropped his hand quickly, almost as if he, too, sensed the harsh judgment leveled against them.

Her father waited at the end of the pew and gestured for Luke to follow her mother, who was already seated at the end of the row. Her boyfriend and her father exchanged a glance that Abby couldn't decipher, and Luke complied with Dad's request. She moved to sit next to him, but Sam jostled past her and plunked down beside Luke. One look at her father told her this was no accident. First, he'd insisted they all come in one car, and now he wouldn't let her sit with Luke. "Seriously, Dad?"

He bent to whisper in her ear. "You don't need to fuel the gossip."

Gossip? What more could people possibly say about either of them? She was six months pregnant, and Luke had just gotten out of drug rehab yesterday afternoon. But there was no sense arguing with her father. She slid into the pew next to Sam, reached across her brother's lap, and squeezed Luke's good knee. She hoped her smile reassured him, but the earnest expression in his eyes was hard to read. How she missed the days when they seemed to know each other's minds with almost no effort.

Pastor Schwartz took his sermon from the fourth chapter of Luke, verse 18, almost as if he had known in advance that her Luke would be here. "Jesus came to preach deliverance to the captives, not to condemn them. He came to offer hope, hope that leads to joy, not shame or disappointment. You may be struggling with something in your life, something that's kept you captive for months, possibly years. But I'm here to tell you something that Satan doesn't want you to know." The pastor glanced in their direction. "God wants to set you free from whatever has you bound."

Overcome by her need to *see* Luke's reaction to Pastor Schwartz's words, Abby held her body perfectly still and resisted the urge to turn in her seat and face her boyfriend. *God, I know You hear my prayer. Please help Luke. He needs You.*

She opened her eyes as the baby kicked her just under her ribcage. A small smile turned up the corners of Abby's mouth as a deep peace settled her soul. God was watching over all three of them.

Pastor Schwartz moved to their side of the church. His eyes rested on hers for the briefest moment. "If you're bruised and broken, He wants to heal your body and your heart. He wants to put your life back together. He wants to restore your dreams. He has good plans for you."

Was it God's plan that she and Luke marry someday and make a home for their baby girl? How she hoped so. She couldn't imagine being the wife of any other man. Ever. Her heart belonged to Luke, and before he had become an addict, she was sure his heart belonged to her. Could God restore all they had was lost? Even their dreams of a happy future together? Especially that?

The congregation stood as one, and Abby felt her cheeks heat with embarrassment. Her mind had drifted off, and she'd missed the end of the sermon.

Pastor Schwartz looked over the congregation, his gaze filled with loving acceptance. He seemed to be trying to make eye contact with everyone in the sanctuary. "You can come to him today. Just as you are. With absolutely nothing to offer him but your great need and your willingness to accept His help. Won't you all bow your heads and pray with me? In your own heart, tell Him everything. He already knows. He didn't send His Son to condemn you but to save you and give you abundant joy beyond anything you could ever imagine."

*

After the service was over, Luke once again took Abby's hand, and together they made their way out of the church. He wanted to tell her what God had shown him, but he preferred to take action, rather than to try to persuade her with words. At the door to the vestibule, he reached for the pastor's outstretched hand. "I'm Luke Bradford, the father of Abby's baby."

Her hand trembled in his, and she tried to pull away, but he couldn't let her go. They were going to be parents in three months. From this moment forward, he intended to take responsibility—for himself, for Abby, and for their daughter.

Pastor Schwartz gripped Luke's hand in a firm shake. "I'm glad to have you with us, son."

The man's gentle tone encouraged Luke to speak freely, something he hadn't known he could do outside of the shelter of Ellis Rehab. "Thank you, sir. I'm grateful to be here. Your sermon really spoke to me."

Pastor Schwartz smiled warmly and seemed about to respond, but Luke needed to declare his intentions before his resolve faltered. "I'd like to meet with you soon, Pastor Schwartz. With Abby."

The pastor nodded his approval. "My secretary can set up an appointment for you sometime this week."

Luke's shoulders relaxed as another weight lifted from his battered heart. He turned to Abby, surprised to see her eyes flooding with tears. Without breaking eye contact with her, Luke told the pastor, "We'd like to meet with you once a week."

She wiped the moisture from her face with a tissue she pulled from her pocket then turned to look at the pastor. "Yes … we … have a lot to talk about."

Her tone, tinged with shame and insecurity, tore at Luke's heart. *He* had done that to her, on top of everything he'd put her through over the last two and a half years. His confident Abby was unsure of herself and unsure of him. Repairing *that* damage would take time and a lot of help, from God, and maybe, from this kind pastor as well.

*

Luke longed to accept Abby's parents' invitation to join them for lunch after church, but he wanted to pack up his apartment more. The faster that unpleasant task was done, the sooner he could move forward into the new life God had planned for him and for Abby. Standing in her front foyer with her family discreetly waiting in the kitchen, Luke hugged her and pressed a quick kiss to her sweet mouth. His heart swelled with love for her and with determination to do right by her and the baby. With God's help, Luke would succeed.

Abby linked her arms around his back to hold him close, but he captured her hands and reluctantly eased out of her embrace. "I'll call you as soon as I get back home with my stuff, assuming Cole hasn't sold everything I left behind." The fear in her eyes unsettled him. He breathed a silent prayer that he wouldn't let her down and that God would give her peace. "I'll be okay. Ian and I are just going to toss everything into boxes and leave. We'll be out of there in thirty minutes, an hour tops."

She tried to smile then bit her lower lip.

"Maybe Cole won't even be there." It was wishful thinking, and Luke wasn't about to lie to himself or to Abby.

"You think?"

He didn't. The best he could hope for was that Cole would already be passed out. Luke's prayer was to get in and out without having to talk to Cole at all.

"Luke, please let me go with you." Her voice shook with fear.

He folded her in his arms again, their faces inches apart. "Not a chance. Things could get—"

"That's why I want to come." She leaned back and looked up at him. "You might need me. You know how Cole is."

"Yeah, I do, and there's no way I'm exposing you to any of his crap." He tucked a strand her silky hair behind her ear and tried to ignore the tears glistening in her eyes. She'd been crying a lot, and it was his fault. "You can't be with me 24-7, babe. Ultimately, it's just me and God. If you can't trust me, then trust Him."

The indecision on her face stirred his regret, bringing fresh shame, but Luke sloughed off the guilt. He had asked for and received God's forgiveness, but he needed her forgiveness, too. "I know it's going to take time, but one day, I promise you, you'll be able to trust me again the way you used to. No matter how long it takes, Abby, I'm going to show you that I will *never* choose drugs over you again."

A long moment passed. He laid his hand on her cheek, and she leaned into his touch. "There's no excuse for what I put you through. Can you forgive me?"

Her tears tracked her cheeks. "I forgive you, Luke. But … I don't want to be afraid anymore."

The pain in her words seared his heart. "You won't. After today, I promise you that I will never willingly go anywhere where there's any kind of drugs."

She smiled and kissed him, her lips salty from her tears. "Do you believe me?"

She studied his face, clearly probing for the truth. "Yes, I believe you, Luke."

He took a breath, the first deep breath he had taken in years, then kissed her goodbye, promised to call her later, and strode to his car. Ian would be picking him up in fifteen minutes. He turned on the Bluetooth and called his cousin. "Hey, Ian, I just left Abby's house."

"I'll be waiting in your driveway. I got six empty boxes from the grocery store. Do you think that'll be enough?"

Luke eased out into traffic. "If it isn't, we can throw the rest in a garbage bag or leave it behind." For several minutes, Luke considered leaving it all behind. After all, it was just stuff. His family, Abby, and the baby—they mattered most, and Luke prayed he would never give them any cause to doubt him ever again.

CHAPTER FOURTEEN

Standing before the apartment door, Luke paused to pray for strength to resist whatever temptations awaited him inside this dark place. Dropping the stack of boxes he carried, he turned his key in the lock for the last time. He'd leave it on the kitchen table for whomever Cole found to kick in rent money, if he hadn't already found someone. Luke pitied the poor sucker who would mistakenly believe Cole was his friend. And yet, the man had been a companion of sorts, and Luke cared what happened to him.

"You all right?" Ian gripped Luke's shoulder.

"As good as I *can* be." He turned to face his cousin. "Thanks for doing this with me."

Ian shook his head. "You don't need to thank me. I'm glad to have your back. I've missed hanging out with you, cuz." He yanked Luke into a quick bear hug.

"I've missed you, too." He started to open the apartment door but hesitated. He needed to be sure everything was cool between them before he faced Cole. With only three younger sisters at home, Ian had always been closer to Luke than to his own siblings. Until after the surgery. Ruled by his addiction, Luke had alienated everyone. Everyone but Abby.

He had been angry, bitter, foolish, and reckless. "I'm sorry, Ian. I made a horrible mess of everything. I … I lost sight of what's important. My values got all screwed up. My thinking was wacked for a long time. I hurt a lot of people, you included." He searched Ian's face, anxious then pleased to see understanding in his cousin's eyes. That compassion gave Luke the courage to ask what he most needed to know at this moment. "I know I'm sorry doesn't cut it, but can you forgive me?"

Ian nodded, clapping his hand on Luke's shoulder. "Let's get this done."

Luke grabbed his boxes and opened the apartment door to the smell of rotting food. The aroma of spicy incense lingered but didn't begin to mask the stench emanating from the kitchen. Thank goodness, he hadn't contributed any kitchen items. He didn't even want to see the source of the foul odor. He would leave his key on the coffee table instead.

He headed down the hall, straight for his old room, opened the door, and found everything exactly as he'd left it. Ian's footsteps followed across the hardwood floor. Suddenly, Luke regretted bringing his cousin along. He'd see with his own eyes how Luke had lived for over a year. There was drug paraphernalia and who knows what all else. "You mind taking the closet while I tackle the dresser and the desk?"

Ian shrugged. "Whatever you want."

Relief surged through Luke. Maybe, Ian wouldn't notice anything beyond the messy room. Not worried about how wrinkled his clothes would get, Luke pulled the dresser drawers out one at a time and dumped the contents into cardboard boxes until each box couldn't hold another item.

Meanwhile, Ian tossed everything from the closet onto the bed and wrapped the comforter around the stack, creating an unwieldy bundle. Next, he scooped up shoes, sneakers, and boots and threw them into a third box.

With his back to his cousin, Luke slid open his center desk drawer. Needles, spoons, lighters, and a roach clip were scattered among pens and other school supplies. Disgusted, he shoved the drawer closed with a bang.

"You all right, man?"

Shame burning his face, Luke glanced over his shoulder. "No, I'm not. I just want to get out of here. Where's Cole? His car was in the driveway. I can't believe he hasn't stormed in here with welcome home junk."

Ian frowned. "Junk?"

"Heroin."

Ian's eyes widened. "Oh. Well, maybe, you were right. He's probably already passed out."

A sick feeling coiled in Luke's gut. "It's barely past noon. I don't think ..." His gaze swept the cluttered bookshelf. "Can you pack up those books and the stuff from two side drawers in the desk? I need to see ... I need to face Cole one last time ... so he'll know not call or contact me."

Ian looked past Luke to the open door. "If you're sure."

"If you find any drugs, dump them in the trash, okay?" He didn't want to ask his cousin to clean up after him, but a nagging need to cut all ties with Cole drove Luke down the hall to the other guy's room.

The master bedroom door was ajar, so Luke walked in without knocking, calling out, "Hey, Cole, it's me." The guy's bed was a rumpled mess of blankets, sheets, and discarded clothing. Nothing new about that. Shoes littered the floor— no surprise there either. Luke bent to pick up the desk chair that had fallen over, his eyes taking in several packets of brown H, a bag of weed, and another of cocaine laying on the desk with an envelope stuffed with cash and a neat stack of bills, as if Cole had been counting his money. Apparently, the man was dealing to more than just his friends these days. Gratitude and relief that he had never been talked into selling drugs welled up inside Luke. He had wanted no part of profiting from the addiction of others, even when he hadn't wanted to admit that he himself was an addict.

Dreading what he would find, he inched closer to the master bathroom. Its door was slightly ajar as well. A distinctly unpleasant odor reached Luke's nostrils, and his stomach clenched. Body wastes. His feet turned to lead. "Lord, no. Not … not like this."

Luke grasped the door, yanked it open.

His mouth gaped wide enough for a train to plow through. Cole slumped against the wall. A yellow rubber strap was still tied around his left bicep, and a needle dangled from the crook of his arm. His eyes stared, vacant and lifeless.

Still, Luke couldn't be sure. Maybe, there was still a chance. Ignoring the stench, he knelt next to his roommate and placed his fingers on the man's neck. Nothing. No pulse. Not even a faint beat. Desperate to be wrong, he checked again, this time on the other side of Cole's neck. Nothing. The man was dead. Luke had no idea for how long. Hours, probably.

He covered his face with his hands, overcome with dread and raw grief. Had Cole ever met Jesus? Did he know that God could make a way out of heroin's sinister clutches? Luke would never know. Bile rose in his throat. He scrambled to the toilet, vomited what remained of his breakfast. He wiped his mouth, stood, opened the linen closet, and retrieved a fresh washcloth and towel. He rinsed his mouth with mouthwash, washed and dried his face and hands, and stared at his face in the mirror.

"That could have been me, Lord. It would have been me."

"You all right, man?" Ian called out, piercing Luke's shocked mind.

"Don't come in here." He exited the bathroom and slammed the door shut. "Cole's dead."

"What? Are you sure?"

"Yeah, I checked. He's been dead for hours."

Ian's faced paled in horror, but Luke couldn't worry about his cousin.

Taking his cell out of his pocket, Luke sat on Cole's unmade bed, and called 911.

An operator picked up on the first ring. "911, what's your emergency?"

Luke inhaled then slowly released the breath. "My roommate, Cole Marchman, is dead. Heroin overdose."

Luke answered the woman's questions, a part of him entirely detached, as if he were watching a tragic movie. The rest of him was a numb mixture of disbelief, anger, and grief. It didn't have to end this way, and yet, it had. He was alive. Clean for 47 days. It would have been 91 days, if he hadn't taken the oxies. 94 if he counted the days in the hospital following his own overdose in October.

The last thing he told her was the hardest of all. The temptation to say nothing was like sitting on the beach on a warm summer day, watching the tide roll in and out, drawn by the deceptive promise of utter and unending freedom. "Tell the police Marchman had a stash—heroin, cocaine, and marijuana."

At the corner of his eye, Luke saw Ian standing motionless. He was staring in disbelief at the desk. He shook his head, and muttered something Luke couldn't catch. The operator confirmed the address. "That's it. Thank you." He disconnected the call and pocketed his phone.

"Thank God I came with you," Ian said.

"I'm sorry you got dragged into this."

His features composed, Ian met Luke's look. "Better me than Abby or your parents."

Abby. He needed to call her. She would be worried. Heaven only knew how long it would be before he and Ian could leave. "Why don't you wait in the living room? I need to let Abby know what's happened. I promised to call her as soon as I got home. She's probably already anxious that she hasn't heard from me."

*

Abby was scrolling through her various social media accounts when her cell rang. Luke's face smiled at her from the screen. She connected the call with a tap, and before she could even say hello, Luke blurted out something that couldn't possibly be true. "What did you say? I couldn't hear you." She muted the music streaming through her flat screen TV. "Are you okay? Are you home yet?"

"Cole's dead. Overdosed. Maybe three, four hours ago."

Abby clenched the phone, holding the screen away from her cheek, so she wouldn't accidentally disconnect the call. "Are you sure? Was anybody with him? Is Ian still with you? Did you call the police?"

"Abby, I'm all right."

He was all right? He had just found his roommate dead from a heroin overdose, and he was all right?

"The police are on their way. Ian's here with me. We have to wait for the ambulance and the police. They'll want to question us."

Dread chilled her veins, but she couldn't think what to say. *God, this can't be happening.*

After several seconds, he said, "I don't know when I'll be home or when I can call you."

"Don't go straight home." She gulped back a sob.

He sighed. Because he knew she was crying and trying to hide it from him.

"Come here first. I need to see you. Please."

"Babe, I'm okay."

She wanted to hug him, to comfort herself as much as him. "I don't care what time you get here. Just promise me."

"I'll come if I can."

What did that mean? Did he think he would be arrested? Thank goodness, he hadn't gone to the apartment alone. Ian was Luke's witness that he'd had nothing to do with Cole Marchman's death.

"I love you, Luke."

"I love you, babe."

The silence lengthened. Had the police arrived? "Are you still there?"

He sighed, a mournful, resigned sound that chilled her even more. She wrapped her arms around herself to suppress the shudder, and the baby stirred in her womb. Did their daughter sense her mother's distress? Was that even possible? The baby kicked. Hard. Abby pressed her hand to the spot. "Luke, talk to me. What's happening?"

"If I'd been here, Cole would still be alive."

She shook her head. He couldn't blame himself. She wouldn't let him. "No! If you had been there, you would be dead, too." She sounded unbelievably selfish. She recognized *that* even through the fog of fear. But she couldn't lose him. Not after all they'd been through.

"Maybe. Maybe not. Maybe, I could've saved him the way he saved me."

Abby didn't know what to say to that. Cole *had* called 911 when Luke overdosed. "Do you want me to call your folks?"

"No, I'm sure Ian took care of that already."

"What can I do?" She had to do something. Something to prevent this from causing Luke to—

"Pray," he said then disconnected the call before she could ask what he wanted her to pray for.

She knelt beside her bed and begged God for mercy, for them all.

*

The police interrogated Luke and Ian separately and then together. Obviously, their stories aligned perfectly. The only difference lay in Luke's statement regarding what had happened when he found Cole dead on the bathroom floor. Luke thanked God that he hadn't touched anything on Cole's desk. The drugs and cash remained undisturbed, exactly as Cole had left them earlier that day. Seated with Ian on the couch opposite the two officers, Luke squelched the urge to cross his arms over his chest. He didn't want to give the impression that he was resistant to their questions. He had nothing to hide.

The older officer, a man in his late forties with dark eyes, a receding hairline, and an inscrutable expression, folded his hands and then rested them on his knees. "Is there anything else *either* of you think we should know? Any ideas about who may have been here with Marchman before he died?"

"Like I told the other officer, I've been in a 90-day inpatient rehab program at Ellis Rehab. You can confirm that with the center. I was released yesterday afternoon, and I spent the remainder of the day with my family. This morning, I attended church with my girlfriend's family, and I left her house at twelve fifteen, drove home where my cousin was waiting for me, and we arrived at the apartment about thirty minutes later. We went straight to my room to pack up my stuff. After about ten minutes or so, I started wondering why Cole hadn't come in to say hello, so I went to check on him." Luke's eyes never left the senior officer's face. Maintaining eye contact conveyed confidence and sincerity— a lesson both of his parents stressed. Luke kept his hands still, his fingers resting lightly on his knees. "And that's when I found him dead."

Ian laid his hand on Luke's forearm. "You aren't being accused of anything, Luke. They just want to know if you have any information that may help them in their investigation."

He ignored his cousin's attempt to soothe him. Show no weakness—his father's creed, particularly in a situation where the odds were seemingly stacked against him.

The younger officer smiled at Ian, but his smile did little to reassure Luke. There had been no drugs in his room, but that didn't mean they couldn't charge him with ... who knows what? But wouldn't they take him to the police station for further questioning if they were planning to charge him with possession, or worse, dealing? This was one time Luke would be grateful to see his father stride into a room.

Almost on cue, a knock sounded.

The older officer opened the door. "Are you a family member?"

Luke's heartrate slowed to a normal range. "Dad."

With squared shoulders and an expression that exuded confidence, and in most circumstances, commanded respect and cooperation, his father introduced himself to the officers. "My name is Richard Bradford. This is my son, Luke, and Ian, my nephew. If they've answered all of your questions, I'm here to drive them both home. This has been an unfortunate ordeal, and my wife and sister-in-law are anxious to have our boys home."

His father shot Luke a reassuring look then returned his attention to the officers. "Naturally, my son realizes that his belongings will need to remain here until you've completed your search of the apartment."

The younger officer shook his head. "We've already searched through your son's personal items. You can take the boxes and clothing with you."

Luke breathed easier at that news. Maybe, he didn't have anything to fear.

The older officer stared Luke down once more. "You have no idea who may have been with Marchman or where he would have gotten the drugs laying out in plain sight on his desk?"

Luke glanced at his father, grateful for the trust in his eyes. "I haven't talked to Cole in over three months. I can't help you."

The officers exchanged a look that set Luke's nerves on edge. They clearly didn't believe him. They wanted a name, any name.

After a tense moment, the younger officer said, "I trust you'll give us a call if your memory improves."

A hard glint flashed in his father's eyes. "My son has already told you that he has no idea with whom his former roommate may, or may not, have been spending time."

The older officer nodded slightly, a conciliatory gesture if Luke had ever seen one.

"You're all free to go. You can collect the items from your son's room, then I will escort you to your vehicles."

Five minutes later, all of Luke's stuff was stowed in the back of Dad's SUV. The officers had returned to the apartment, probably to wait for the coroner.

Ian stood next to his car. "I'm going to head home. My mom's probably worried sick."

"If you're sure you're up to driving." Luke's father gripped Ian's shoulder. "Your dad and I can pick up your car later."

"I'm good. I just want to get out of here."

Luke agreed. This favor had turned out to be a lot more than either of them ever imagined. "I'll text you later, Ian. Thanks for everything."

His cousin smiled. "Obviously, God wanted me here, to make sure this incident didn't cause … you know."

"I do."

His father hugged Ian.

"Thanks for coming, Uncle Richard."

"Well, your mom and your aunt were getting ready to come get you themselves if I hadn't intervened, and your dad was growing crazy, stuck at the Chicago airport with no way to get here soon enough to do anything."

"I can only imagine." Ian opened his car door, climbed inside, and started the engine. "Like you, Dad always wants to … have an impact in a crisis."

"You can say the word. My brother and I like to be in control."

Ian shot Luke a that's-an-understatement look, but neither of them gave in to the urge to laugh. Then, Luke headed to his dad's vehicle and settled in the passenger seat. He couldn't wait to get home.

Dad joined him a minute later. "Let's go home, son," was all he said.

But the warmth in those words wrapped Luke in a feeling of security he hadn't felt in a very long time. "Dad?"

His father turned the key in the ignition, and the engine purred instantly. "Yes, Luke."

"I …" He paused, unsure how much he wanted to share with this father.

"I know this was hard for you, seeing your friend dead with a needle in his arm."

The memory of waking up in the hospital after his own overdose skittered through Luke's veins like an electric shock. "It could have been me, Dad. Cole was there to save me, but there was no one to save Cole. At least no one who cared enough to try."

His father shifted in his seat to grip Luke in a bear hug.

"I know it could've been me," Luke choked out.

Dad held Luke tighter. The smell of aftershave and coffee filled his nostrils. He wanted to cry like a baby, but he wouldn't. He disengaged himself from his father's embrace and met his eyes. "I'll never put you or mom through that. God willing, I'll never touch another drug. Ever. I mean that Dad."

"I know you want to try, and your mother and I will do everything we can to help you, son."

Dad meant what he said. Something had changed. Suddenly, Luke knew what it was. His father believed in him again. "I'm so sorry for everything I put you and Mom and Joe through. I hurt the whole family. And Abby. I have a long road ahead of me, but with you all praying for me, and believing in me ..."

Dad gripped Luke's shoulder. "We love you, Luke. We'll all help you, whatever you need, whatever way we can. Because that's what family does for each other."

Luke cried then. Tears of repentance and hope welled up from what had been the darkest place in his soul. With God's help, restoration was possible. All Luke had to do was walk on water every single day. With his eyes on Jesus.

*

Abby couldn't stop shivering. She pulled the down comforter up under her chin. She shouldn't be afraid. Luke had done nothing wrong. Had he?

She stared at the time on her phone. 3:57. Almost four. It

had been almost two hours since Luke had called to tell her that Cole was dead. She keyed in a frantic message, then erased it, and typed the exact message she'd sent twice in the last hour. Two words. "Call me." Swiping away the tear tracking down her right cheek, Abby set her cell phone aside, opened her Bible to the Psalms, and started reading. Her breathing slowed as a gentle peace enveloped her, and the baby, who had been karate kicking moments before, quieted. At five o'clock, Abby headed downstairs to see what her mom had decided to do about dinner. She wasn't hungry, but the baby needed nourishment.

Abby found her parents sitting at the kitchen table, drinking coffee, and talking softly, their words barely audible from her vantage on the opposite side of the spacious room. When they spotted her in the doorway, their conversation stopped instantly. Just as quickly, her father rose from his seat and pulled out a chair for her to sit. "Can I get you something? A glass of milk or a yogurt, maybe?"

She shook her head. Food wasn't her first priority. "Did Luke's dad call?"

"Not since he let us know he was heading out to get Luke and his cousin," Mom replied, her tone carefully even.

"What about his mom? Can't you call her? I've tried texting Luke, but he hasn't gotten back to me." She bit her lower lip to keep from crying. "I can't stand this waiting anymore."

Sam stood in the doorway. "Look who I found." Her brother stepped aside.

"Luke!" The tremble in her tone conveyed her fear even more than her words. "Where were you? I texted you so many times."

His drawn face lit with a smile just for her, but the exhaustion in his eyes urged her close. She flew into his arms. No longer caring who heard her cry, she sobbed and clung to him.

"It's okay, babe," he whispered as he kissed her forehead.

She lifted her head from his shoulder, her eyes locked on his. "When I didn't hear from you, I thought—"

"I'm here now." He cupped the back of her head, pulled her close again, and stroked her hair. She nestled as close as the baby would allow and savored the feeling of his arms wrapped around the small of her back. She suppressed a small chuckle. There wasn't much about her that was small at six-months pregnant.

Dimly, Abby became aware of her parents and little brother talking. She sniffled, kissed Luke's neck, then leaned back to search his eyes again. He looked exhausted ... and ... relieved.

He led her to the table, pulled a chair out for her, and sat beside her. "Buddy, you don't mind if I talk to Abby and your folks alone, do you?"

Sam shrugged. "I know everything I need to know."

"What's that?" Mom asked.

"Luke's okay. He's not going to jail." Sam's confident tone dared them to disagree.

Talk about getting the elephant out in the open. "No, Sam," Luke agreed. "I'm not going to jail."

He probably wanted to say he'd done nothing to deserve going to jail, but Abby could see by the twitch in his left eye that he didn't believe that. She wanted to tell Sam to go next door and play with Trey for a while, but it was dinnertime. "Dad, please ..."

"Sam, go upstairs and finish your book report."

Her brother laughed. "How do you know I didn't finish it already?"

Mom shot Sam a stern look. "Quit stalling and get

upstairs, young man."

Accepting defeat, Sam turned to go then shot back over his shoulder, "I'm glad you're back, Luke. Just make sure you don't hurt my sister anymore, or I'll—"

Dad glared, crossed the room, and with his hands on Sam's shoulders, pushed him into the hallway. "Go now, or no video games for a week."

"I'm going. I'm going." Clearly, being viewed as grown up wasn't nearly as important as triumphing in the latest video battle.

Mom reached across the table to rest her hand on Luke's arm. "Are you all right?"

He gazed at Abby, his eyes resting on hers. "I am now."

For the next several minutes, Abby and her parents listened as Luke shared the horror of finding Cole dead with a needle stuck in his arm, the rubber strap still tied. Guilt laced his words as he repeated three times that he should have been there. It was her dad that got through to Luke. "God sees your heart, Luke. He knows that you would have done everything you could to save your friend."

"He was never my friend, but he didn't deserve to die like that … alone."

Abby reached under the table and gripped Luke's knee. He shot her a grateful look, then began to tell them about the police questioning him and Ian. The officers seemed convinced that he and Ian knew something, and Luke forced his voice to remain calm, though he'd answered the same questions the same way at least three times. His fear that they would all end up at the police station had intensified exponentially as the minutes ticked by. Finally, his father arrived, and the officers agreed that Luke and Ian could go home. Luke had never been so glad to see his dad in all his life.

*

As they stood together in the foyer, Luke didn't want to leave Abby. She clung to him, pleading for him to stay just a few more minutes. A few minutes had turned into thirty. Thirty minutes holding her close, stroking her back and her silky hair, whispering words of comfort. He wanted to make love to her in the worst way. His body pulsed with his need for her, but he had promised God not to treat her like his wife until they were legally married. His heart belonged to her, and he had vowed to love her and only her for as long as they both lived, but their wedding seemed a distant future. Neither his parents nor hers had even suggested they get married simply because Abby was pregnant. The baby would be here in three months.

Three months during which he would have to be drug tested thrice each week. His father had wanted Luke to do the test at home under his direct scrutiny, but Mom had persuaded Dad that the outpatient facility associated with Ellis Rehab would be just as diligent about ensuring that the urine sample tested actually belonged to Luke. And so, the matter was settled to everyone's satisfaction. Luke was grateful to avoid the added humiliation of providing samples with his dad watching.

Abby tightened her arms around his waist, and Luke sighed, his thoughts drifting back to the pleasure of lying in Abby's arms.

She lifted her head from his shoulder, her questioning eyes meeting his. "What's wrong?"

Warmth flooded his cheeks, and he answered her question with a look she knew well, a look mirrored in her own eyes.

"Oh, Luke." Her face colored, and she brought her hand to his cheek. "Me, too."

Her touch sent an electric surge through him. Surprisingly, the urge to draw her into his arms was as powerful as his craving for any drug had ever been. How could he have ever put his need for drugs ahead of his love for Abby?

A sudden, radical solution popped into his head. "What if we eloped?"

Her eyes widened. "You're kidding, right?"

He exhaled, her response dampening his exhilaration. "Not really, but I know we can't."

She kissed him then, a kiss that did nothing to cool his desire. He forgot all of his good intentions and deepened the kiss, reveling in her response. His hands yearned to explore her curves, but slowly, his reason returned. "Abby," he whispered against her mouth. "We have to stop."

"Yes, you do," her father commanded.

Luke turned to face the other man. "I'm sorry, sir. We—"

"I can see that." His gaze moved from Luke to Abby and back to Luke again. "Until your situation changes, you will confine your visits to the first floor of the house, and you will visit Abby here at a time that's convenient to her mother or myself. She may not, under any circumstances, go to your house." He paused, his expression demanding compliance.

Was he waiting for Luke's reply? Weren't his parents equally capable of chaperoning? He was about to say something to that effect, but one look at the man's hard expression silenced any objections Luke could reasonably make.

Ray Collins' eyes bored into him. "Are we clear?"

Crystal. "Yes, sir. I … you … we all want what's best for Abby." This had become the primary criterion for his every decision, his every action. "You can trust me, sir." *With God helping me.*

Collins' expression declared *that* remained to be seen. He studied Luke for a tense moment. "I'm glad we're all in agreement."

Agreement about what? Whether Luke was trustworthy? Or whether they all wanted the best for Abby? Candidness might go a long way toward improving his relationship with Abby's parents. "I realize you have no reason to trust me at this point, but as the days pass, I intend to prove to you that I will never do anything to hurt your daughter again."

Collins did not smile. "You do know that your father and I will be keeping in touch?"

"Dad, please, you're making Luke uncomfortable." Abby sounded as if she were about to cry.

Luke reached for her hand and intertwined their fingers. "It's okay, babe. I'd feel the same way in his position." And he knew it was true. God help any guy who dared to hurt his daughter the way he had hurt Abby.

Her father extended his hand to Luke, and he shook it with a firm grip. "I'm glad we understand each other, Luke. In time ..."

Luke nodded. In God's time, everything Luke had lost would be restored. He had read that in the Old Testament the day he'd given his heart and life to the Lord.

"Your mother ordered pizza." Mr. Collins laid one hand on Abby's forearm, but his eyes never left Luke's. "You're welcome to stay a bit longer and eat with us, Luke."

He shook his head. "My mom's eager to have me home."

Collins smiled approvingly. "Then, I'll leave you two alone for a minute to say goodbye."

Abby opened the door to the front closet, and Luke retrieved his coat. He stuffed his arms inside his down jacket and yanked the zipper up to his chin. Abby grinned and snatched both ends of his wool scarf in her hands, then tugged him as close as the baby allowed. She giggled. "Did you feel that?" She grabbed his hand and placed it on her belly over her tunic sweater. The baby kicked hard.

Luke pushed down a wave of emotion. He would do anything for his two girls. Abby and their baby. No matter how much he might be tempted to use, he would never go down that road again. There would always be someone to call. Someone to stay with him until the relentless urge passed. Someone to remind him that he had everything to live for.

He kissed Abby goodnight, promised to call her later, and headed home to spend time with his parents and his brother. Then he would end the day on his knees, bowed before God—his Savior and Deliverer.

If only he had the chance to tell Cole how different *his* life could have been.

CHAPTER FIFTEEN

The birds outside his bedroom window greeted the morning with songs of praise to God. On this warm April day, Luke envied them their carefree worship. He was about as far from carefree as a man could get. If he hadn't overdosed, he would be close to finishing his fourth semester at UB, but he had sabotaged that opportunity, along with so many others. Even his father's phone calls couldn't persuade the powers that be to give Luke another chance to prove himself a worthy student. Not back in February when he'd been released from rehab and not this coming fall either. Getting his four-year degree would take longer than he'd hoped, but he refused to let himself be defined by other people's opinions or judgments. Accepting defeat would mean giving up on God, which was not an option. Luke was fully persuaded that God would never give up on him, so he'd found another way to reach his goal. He would start at ECC North in the first summer session the third week in May right after his daughter's birth. In a year, he would have an Associate's Degree in General Studies. After that, he'd apply to UB again.

"One step at a time" was Jake and Leah's mantra ...

actually the mantra of every one at Ellis Rehab. One step, one moment, one second at a time, whatever it took. Luke missed his friends, but Zeke, his NA sponsor, kept Luke grounded. Recovering from his heroin addiction was like the weather, unpredictable and subject to countless external forces outside his control. Thank goodness nothing was out of his heavenly Father's control.

Luke sat up in bed and stretched, grateful to be alive. "Jesus, thank You for giving me the strength to stay clean. Help me today. People are counting on me." He had prayed the same prayer every morning since that awful day he'd found Cole dead on his bathroom floor.

The very next day, Luke had found an NA group and had attended the meetings without missing a single day. He checked in with Zeke often, at least once a day, sometimes four. The older man, clean for eleven years, took tough love to a new level. Five weeks ago, Zeke had recognized how close Luke was to falling off the wagon and had urged him to check back into Ellis for at least thirty days. Sloughing off the near defeat, Luke had followed his sponsor's advice, and now, back home for barely a week, he acknowledged that he'd made the right decision. There was no shame in knowing when he needed help.

Less than six months ago, Luke had actually considered taking his own life. A wave of horror shook him at the anguish he would have caused Abby and his family had he bought the lie that they would all be better off without him. Worst of all, he would have never met his baby girl. Thinking of his daughter was a constant reminder that he had so much to live for. As angry as he'd been at his father, Luke knew with absolute certainty that Dad's insistence that he enter an inpatient drug rehabilitation program had saved Luke's life.

As had become his habit at Ellis, Luke began and ended

each day leaning heavily on God for strength. The sun was barely up. Just a soft glow of white light seeped around the edges of the shades that covered his bedroom windows. He turned the light switch on his bedside lamp and reached for his phone. Abby's due date was still more than a month away, but he checked his cell often to be sure he hadn't missed a call from her. He smiled at her text, an animated bear blowing kisses. He sent her a heart then opened his Bible to his favorite verse in Jeremiah. He read aloud, "For I know the thoughts that I think toward you, saith the LORD, thoughts of peace, and not of evil, to give you an expected end."

Luke smiled, awed that God was thinking about him. The wonder of this amazing reality never faded. He clung to that truth whenever he feared he would never be totally free from the temptation to use some kind of drug or another. If the hunger for heroin wasn't dogging him, he would get the urge for coke or weed. Before he reached for his phone to call Zeke, first Luke would stop and imagine God, the Creator of the universe, sitting on His throne and thinking about him, Luke Bradford. Then the Holy Spirit would whisper in his heart, *I have plans for you, my son.*

Luke had plans, too. A new dream, one he scarcely believed he could fulfill. During their weekly meetings, Pastor Schwartz spoke often to Abby and Luke about God giving His children the desires of their hearts. Luke's daily prayer had become simple. *Lord, give me the desires of Your heart so that what I want for myself is what You already want to give me. Line up my desires with Your desires.*

But nagging doubts sometimes crept in to shake his determination. A sense of his own unworthiness, even the weight of his sins—his addiction and how much pain he'd caused every person he loved—made him question whether or not God could actually use him to help others. After all, he hadn't even been clean a year himself. He could ruin it all in a single moment of weakness. The knowledge kept him continually on guard, like a soldier who never quite knew from which direction enemy fire might come. "Lord," he whispered. "I need you today. Not just for me, but for everyone I love. Don't let me mess up."

Luke walked over to his desk, sat down, opened his laptop, and clicked on his favorite Bible app, then keyed in Jeremiah 29:11, AMP. Somehow, the Amplified brought him even more comfort than the King James. "An expected end" seemed vague, and for some reason, not altogether positive. His own end would have been drastically different had Dad not used Abby's pregnancy to maneuver Luke into "voluntarily" entering the rehab center. "Thank You, God, for making my dad such a wise and stubborn man."

One day, Luke hoped to be as good a father as his dad was. But even that—maybe especially that—wasn't possible without God's help. "I'm counting on You, Lord, to make me the man You want me to be."

Ignoring his increasing desire for his morning coffee, Luke locked his hands around the back of his neck, leaned back in his chair, focused on the screen, and read the verse aloud three times. "'For I know the plans and thoughts that I have for you,' says the LORD, 'plans for peace and well-being and not for disaster, to give you a future and a hope.'" Luke drew in a deep breath and released it slowly. Pastor Schwartz insisted that there was power in spoken words, and Luke agreed. Speaking the truth out loud seemed to disarm his doubts and fuel his faith. He closed his eyes and waited for the words to wash over him. God had a plan for his life, a peaceful future. Luke didn't have to live fearing the worst and bracing for the next disaster.

For some reason he couldn't begin to fathom, God had laid the seeds of an amazing dream in Luke's heart, a future in which everything he'd gone through wouldn't be for nothing.

A dream in which he would help others who struggled as he had.

He tamped down his frustration over the delay. He wanted—no, needed—to move forward in the direction of his goal. Next month, he would take two classes at ECC and two more in the second summer session. A community college was a definite step down from the university, but what did that matter? He would take this one step at a time, one day at a time, and eventually, he'd get where he wanted to go, where God planned for him to be. Luke was determined to make a difference in someone's life, the way Dr. Jefferies and Jake and Leah had made a difference in his life. He wanted to shine light in the darkness, to bring the message of hope and deliverance to those who had surrendered to nodding out of their own lives.

His phone pinged with a text interrupting his thoughts. He crossed the room and checked the screen. He smiled when he saw the text was from Abby. "Are you up?"

He hadn't shared his vision with her yet. Only his dad knew of his long-term plans, and the only reason Luke had told him was that he had hoped his father could talk the dean into giving Luke another chance. Mom and Abby were just happy he was going back to school, keeping busy. Keeping his mind off doing drugs is what they meant. He couldn't blame them. Even working part-time at the clothing store and volunteering at the center left Luke with far too much free time. And Abby didn't need him underfoot while she was doggedly working to finish her coursework before the baby came.

He touched the receiver icon, and in a few seconds she said, "Hey, you are up."

He grinned. "Do you have time for breakfast? Maybe pancakes or that crepe place you like on Main Street." It was already fifty degrees, so standing outside in line waiting for a table wouldn't be an issue. "I have something I want to talk to you about."

Abby laughed. "I've already had breakfast, but I could eat again. Pick me up in a half hour."

It was his turn to laugh. "I haven't showered yet. I'll be there in an hour. How's our little one this morning?"

"Doing summersaults all night keeping her mommy from getting a decent night's sleep. I feel like a beached whale with no energy to get back in the water."

She was referring to her weight. Nothing he could say would make her feel better about that. "We'll take a walk through Glen Park after breakfast. That'll rock her to sleep."

Abby sighed. "That's the problem. I rock her to sleep all day, and then, the minute I lie down in bed, she starts her gymnastic routine."

Luke covered his mouth to muffle a laugh.

"You better not be laughing at me, Luke Bradford."

"Of course not. Even I know laughing at a pregnant woman is very dangerous."

"Very funny. I'll be ready at 9:30. Don't be late or I'll end up eating three breakfasts, and when I get on the scale next week, the doctor will be all over my case about how the baby isn't gaining more than a half pound per week. She'll narrow her eyes and remind me that I'm the one packing on the pounds."

Luke scrambled for a safe reply. "I'll be there. We can walk off the extra calories."

"So, you *do* think I look fat?"

He drew in a sharp breath. Open mouth, insert foot. "You look beautiful. More beautiful every single day."

"That's better," she said, the pout in her tone disappearing.

He hadn't realized how much she needed his reassurance. Maybe he should spend some of his spare time reading up on what to say and what not to say to a pregnant woman. "I love you, babe. Let me get in the shower, so I can pick you up before 9:30."

"Good idea," she said and disconnected the call.

Luke breathed a sigh of relief. He would get on that research first thing this afternoon.

*

"Do you want to go with me to the doctor's on Tuesday?" Abby asked around a mouthful of ham, cheese, and mushroom crepe.

Luke's startled look made her drop her fork onto her plate with a clatter that made other diners turn to stare at them. She didn't give a hoot what they thought. Luke should've been with her all along. Now that she had only five appointments left, she was determined to have him beside her every time. *If* that's what he wanted. His pale expression, not to mention his pin-prick pupils, made her wonder.

"What? Go with you?" he stammered. "Your parents are okay with that?"

Abby reached across the table and squeezed his hand. "You haven't failed a single test since you left the center in February."

"True, but I don't know if that's enough. I'm not sure your parents understand why I checked myself back in." He paused, drained his coffee mug. "I don't know if they see that choice as a sign of strength or weakness."

Abby regretted having this conversation in a public

place. She needed to wrap her arms around Luke, to gaze into his sad eyes until every doubt disappeared. "Knowing when you need help and having the courage to admit it is a sign of strength. I'm proud of you, Luke. And my parents are proud of you, too. But this isn't about them. *I'm* deciding. *I'm* okay with your coming with me. I have a sonogram scheduled, and I want you to see the baby moving. I want you to hear her heartbeat. This is *our* baby, not theirs."

Luke smiled, but he blinked several times, teardrops catching in his gorgeous burnished lashes.

If she weren't so big, she'd jump out of her chair, sit on his lap, and kiss him, right then and there in the crowded restaurant, with other diners barely two feet away in every direction. Instead, she would have to reassure him with her words. "So, we've decided—you and I. You'll come with me. My appointment is at ten o'clock. Pick me up at nine thirty, and plan on taking me to the mall and lunch after."

His smile disappeared, replaced by the grim set of his mouth that she knew so well.

"You won't come?" Her voice trembled. Her heart sank. Confronting her parents had taken more out of her than she'd anticipated. She wanted Luke with her, but she didn't have the energy to fight him.

He touched the back of her hand then laced his fingers through hers. "I didn't say that."

Frustration changed what should have been a sweet couple moment into what could morph into a full-blown argument. Arguing with Luke was the last thing Abby wanted, but almost without thinking, she yanked free of his tender, pleading grasp and slipped both hands under the table, clasping them on what remained of her lap. The hurt in his eyes made her regret pulling away from him.

"I didn't say that I didn't want to go to the doctor with

you."

"Then what are you saying?" She wanted to spend today with him, doing things a normal couple would do to get ready for their baby. They weren't supposed to be arguing. Heat rose up her neck to her cheeks. She didn't want to be angry at him, but her emotions seemed to have a mind of their own, disregarding all of her attempts to maintain self-control. "It's my decision. I told my parents that I need you with me for the rest of this pregnancy. I need you to be all in."

Luke frowned. "I am all in, Abby. But that's not our arrangement. That's not what I agreed to. Our parents agreed that if I could stay clean, I could be with you for the birth, but if it's that important to you—"

"That important to *me*? This is our baby we're talking about."

"What I was about to say before you cut me off is that I will talk to my dad and your dad. If they're comfortable—"

"What about what makes me comfortable? You haven't been there for me at all."

Pain clouded his eyes, and she felt a check as certain as if God had gripped her shoulder, but she couldn't seem to stop. "I need you, Luke. I don't care what our parents think. They don't understand that this is our baby."

Luke folded his napkin and placed it over his half-eaten food. "I care what our parents think. I respect their judgment. And you should, too."

Shame and regret silenced Abby. She did care what their parents thought. After all, they were looking out for her and the baby, and even for Luke.

He signaled the server. "Check please."

She reached for her hoodie and her purse. "I need to use the restroom."

Once she was safely inside a stall, she covered her face

with her hands and released a torrent of sobs. Fighting with Luke shredded her heart.

"Are you all right, dear?" came a voice from the next stall.

Embarrassed, Abby swallowed hard, her breath ragged. "Yeah, I'm fine."

A lady, who appeared to be about seventy or even eighty, was washing her hands as Abby emerged from the stall. "Are you sure you're all right?"

Abby nodded.

"I cried a lot toward the end of my pregnancies, too. Over nothing most of the time. How much longer do you have to go?"

"About six weeks. But it seems like forever."

"So, what made you cry just then?"

Abby stared at her splotched face in the bathroom mirror. She dropped her gaze to her hands, pretending to focus on rinsing off the soap. "A fight with my boyfriend."

The lady patted Abby's arm, her cool hand comforting Abby's raw nerves. "My husband used to irritate me so badly that I'd grouch at him every single day. I'm surprised he didn't pack me off to my mother's." Her wrinkled hand flew to her mouth. "Oh, I apologize, dear. That was very insensitive of me. Bernie always said I shouldn't be butting into other people's business. Especially when I don't know the circumstances."

Abby dried her hands and wiped her face with the paper towel. "I know you didn't mean anything by it. You were only trying to help."

The lady smiled. "Maybe try again ... to talk about whatever it is. First babies are hard on men, too. Their protective instincts surge to dizzying heights that drive the women they love completely crazy."

Abby laughed. If only her life were that simple. "We aren't married."

The woman's hazel eyes softened. "That makes it even harder—"

"Harder to what?"

"Harder to learn how to love each other through all of the changes."

Abby wanted to hug this stranger, who suddenly sounded exactly like Grandma Elise. Instead, she smiled and let her shoulders relax. "What's your name?"

The twinkle in the lady's eyes washed over Abby like a gentle wave. "My name is Daisy. Daisy Shank."

"Thank you, Mrs. Shank. I'll remember your advice."

"Why, I didn't give you any advice."

"Yes, you did. You told to remember how much I love Luke and how much he loves me. That's the first step in resolving any conflict we have."

Mrs. Shank smiled. "You haven't told me *your* name."

"I'm Abby. Abby Collins. And my boyfriend is Luke Bradford."

"Abby Bradford. It has a nice ring to it." The lady moved to open the restroom door, then she faced Abby again. "I'll be keeping you and Luke in my prayers. I have a good feeling about you two. God has amazing plans for you. Promise me you'll remember that."

Startled by the certainty in the woman's proclamation, Abby whispered, "Thank you. I'll pray for you, too."

Mrs. Shank brushed her fingers over Abby's belly, but she didn't mind the way she usually did when strangers touched her without asking first. The baby stirred, and the small bump of a hand or foot pressed outward at the exact spot where the elderly woman's fingers had rested a moment before. The tension in Abby's soul vanished. Who was this stranger?

The woman held the bathroom door open for Abby, and her eyes met Luke's concerned gaze. She smiled and started walking toward the man she loved with all of her heart. Bolstered by the lady's kindness, Abby turned to thank her again, but Daisy Shank was nowhere in sight.

*

After breakfast, Luke insisted on parking farther down Main Street to be closer to the entrance to Glen Falls Park. Abby linked her arm through Luke's and smiled at his solid grip on her elbow. He hadn't been around during the early months of her pregnancy, and he'd missed most of her seventh month, too. Now his watchful care was a bit over the top. The slow speed at which they descended the stone steps to the daffodil-lined walkway made her tempted to complain that she wasn't an invalid. "I'm pregnant, but my legs still work fine, thank you very much," she teased.

He didn't laugh. Instead, he released her arm, stepped away from her, and cupped her chin. "Let me take care of you, Abby."

His soft words, weighted with regret, drew her gaze to his. A sheen of tears highlighted the silvery flecks in his blue eyes, and she longed to wipe away all of the pain of the last two and a half years. Her heart swelling with love, she reached up to brush the moisture now sparkling like tiny diamonds at the tips of his long lashes.

The tender touch of her fingers brought his strong arms around her. "I love you, babe. I'll never put anything before you ever again. No matter what—"

She covered his mouth with her fingers, and he pressed a kiss against them. "Honey, we have to move forward. I forgive you. You know that, right?"

He hauled her as close as the baby would allow. "I don't

deserve you."

Maybe, *she* didn't deserve him. Six months ago she'd been terrified that he would destroy any future they hoped to share, and that fear had birthed fantasies of splitting up with him for good. Things were different now. They were both different. Luke's courage, determination and faith in God had transformed him into the man she always believed he could be, and she'd found the strength to trust God with their love. Even during their darkest hours, her heart had clung to Luke, though her head had insisted she should leave before he destroyed her, too. Now, she knew she could spend the rest of her life loving him. "No more talk about not deserving me. I'm proud of you." She stood on her tiptoes until their mouths were inches apart. "Kiss me, Luke."

For a long moment, their eyes locked, searching for truth deeper than words could convey. He lowered his mouth until their lips met in a kiss that began like the caress of a warm breeze. Her body awakened to the dance of his tongue in her mouth, and every thought but being in his arms left her. Then the baby kicked her. Hard.

Luke lifted his mouth from hers and stared into her eyes. "Maybe our girl wants to be a soccer player."

"Or a gymnast." She giggled, and Luke laughed, too. They hadn't laughed together in so long that she couldn't remember the last time. "Or a stuntwoman."

"Or a ninja warrior."

Abby stifled her laughter with her hand. "Stop. I can't laugh anymore. I need to go to the bathroom."

Luke took her hand and started back the way they had come. "We'll go for ice cream, and then you can use the restroom."

She hoped she could wait that long. Hadn't she just gone to the bathroom thirty minutes ago? Their baby must be pressing against her bladder.

Once they were back in the car, and she could sit, Abby felt better. Luke turned the key in the ignition, and the engine started with a low purr. She laid her hand on his right arm, and he turned to look at her. "Are you … okay?"

"Actually, yes. And no." She didn't want to pressure him or stress him out. Should she back off and go to the sonogram appointment by herself or with her mother? A knot clenched her stomach, and she resisted the urge to squirm in her seat. "Luke, I really want you to come with me."

He leaned close and brushed a kiss over her forehead then gazed deep into her eyes. "All right, babe. I'll have a conversation with my dad, and if that goes well, I'll talk to your dad." He caressed her cheek and ran his fingers over her lips. "But if they're against my going to your doctor visit with you, then—"

"But, Luke, I need you with me. I … I'm scared. Labor is going to hurt like crazy. What if I can't do it? What if I panic?"

He placed one hand on each side of her face. "Abby Collins, you are the bravest person I've ever met. You can do this."

"Not without you."

His hands dropped to her shoulders. "Babe, I promise you. I will be there. Nothing and no one can keep me away."

"But you said—"

"I said I need them to be onboard with this change in our plans."

"But what if they are still … Luke, what if they still don't trust you?"

Pain flashed in his eyes followed by a resolute strength she hadn't seen before now. "Let's ask God to help your dad and my dad see how important this is to you."

She nodded, and Luke took her hands in his. "God, we need Your help. Give me the words to help our dads understand that Abby and I need to be together. She's already had to go through so much of this pregnancy without my help, and I'm sorry for that, Father. I know you've forgiven me. Please help our dads to forgive me, too, and help them to see that I am committed to staying clean for Abby and for our baby, Lord. Help them to see that I'm not trying to do this in my own strength, that I'm counting on Your strength to sustain me every single day. Day by day."

Luke paused, and Abby waited to see if he would say more before she spoke. "Father, help Luke say the right thing, and help our dads to believe him. I ... I understand they're afraid. Sometimes ..." She put on the mental brakes. "Sometimes, we forget that You are in control, that when we ask for Your help, You show up in amazing ways."

"Amen," Luke whispered.

Abby opened her eyes, smiled at Luke, and clasped his hand. Together, they would expect God's amazing grace, no matter what temptations Luke might face.

CHAPTER SIXTEEN

Luke had just finished layering the lasagna when Joe burst through the kitchen door and flung his gym bag in the general direction of the back hall. "Are you kidding me, buddy? You know Mom's going to flip out on you if she finds your stuff on the kitchen floor."

Joe scowled. "You're not my boss."

Luke sucked in a breath. His relationship with his younger brother wasn't what it had been before Luke started on oxies. The kid no longer looked up to him as the wise, older brother, and Luke had no idea if he ever would again. "Right. Not your boss. I get it." He marched into his brother's physical space and hazarded a light punch to his upper arm. "But I have lived with Mom eight years longer than you, so I've learned a few things about what bugs her."

Joe's brown eyes lost some of their defiance, and he reached for his bag, slung it over his shoulder, then headed into the back hall to hang it with the collection of coats lining one wall.

Luke sighed. "You probably want to take your gym clothes to the laundry room—maybe even start a load of darks for Mom. Cold water."

"You really are bossy." Joe's tone held a hint of teasing—a big improvement over the scowl of a few minutes ago.

"Just trying to help you get on Mom's good side."

Emerging from the back hall, Joe laughed, opened the basement door, and trudged down the steps to the laundry room. He probably found that remark pretty ironic, considering that, until recently, Luke hadn't been on Mom's good side for quite a while.

He shrugged. Accepting the fact that he couldn't change the past was a daily struggle. Focusing on the present and the future was almost impossible, whenever he let guilt and shame crowd out God's forgiveness and grace. Luke had been slipping into that pit this morning, until he read Jake's Tweet about "forgetting those things that are behind" and pressing "toward the mark for prize of the high calling of God." Those words had lifted Luke out of his funk, and now, he wanted to reread Philippians, chapter three. Maybe later, after his talk with Dad.

Luke glanced at the clock. Five fifteen. Forty-five minutes until dinner. Shifting his focus to getting dinner on the table by six, he retrieved the makings of a green salad from the fridge, rinsed the romaine under cold water, and put the lettuce in a colander to dry. Next, he started chopping carrots. A sense of uneasiness—not dread, exactly—rose like morning fog in his brain, distracting him from his task. He stared hard for a moment at the still knife in his hand, drew in breath, and sliced the ends off the last carrot, nicking his index finger.

Get it together, Bradford.

Usually, the silence in the house soothed him. He avoided the radio and his personal playlists on his phone because that music reminded him of doing drugs. Funny, how a song could resurrect emotions and thoughts, rouse his old mindset, stir a need to go back to the sweet oblivion. Luke didn't want to spend another minute checking out of his own life. Even a few bars of some songs threatened to transform him into an addict again. He refused to even approach the edge of that slippery slope.

Today, the quiet made him restless ... probably because he hadn't yet talked to his dad, and tomorrow morning, Abby expected him to drive her to the sonogram appointment. Luke tuned in the classical radio station and a full orchestra filled the kitchen with expansive music. Vivaldi's "Four Seasons" maybe? Luke had barely passed Music Appreciation in his senior year, maybe because he'd nodded off in too many classes. Too bad. This stuff was actually energizing. Maybe, that was why his mom loved classical music.

Luke dumped the remaining chopped carrots into a bowl and started slicing cucumbers.

Luke's cell played Taylor Swift's "Love Story," the ringtone Abby had set for herself on his phone. He had tried to tell her that her father wouldn't approve of the lyrics, but she'd shrugged and said, "What are the chances he's ever going to hear your phone ringing when it's me calling?" He connected her call.

"Hi. Did you tell him yet?"

Luke swallowed the urge to correct her. He had no intention of "telling" his dad anything. He planned to ask him to renegotiate their original terms. Again. With Richard Bradford, word choice mattered. Especially when he wanted his dad to change his mind.

"Not yet. He's not home."

"Oh." She was trying, unsuccessfully, to hide her disappointment.

He wanted to take her face in his hands, look into her eyes, and will her to be patient. "Babe, my dad's due home in an hour. I'm going to talk to him after dinner, alone."

"But your mom ... she'll understand better than your dad how important this is to me. To us."

"Trust me, Abby."

The silence on her end of the line frustrated him, but Luke didn't want her to know that. What else could he say? He wanted what she wanted, to be there with her, for her, as much as possible. *Jesus, help her understand.*

A soft sob reached his ears. Oh, no. "Babe, are you crying?"

"Yes. I ... I'm sorry. I know you'll try to convince your dad you deserve—"

"Not deserve, Abby. But I think my dad will see how important my seeing our baby on the sonogram is to you. And to me."

"What's this I hear? Abby has another sonogram appointment?"

Luke pivoted to see his dad, his broad shoulders filling the kitchen doorway, his dark leather briefcase in one hand and his trench coat in the other. "Dad, you're home early." Luke regretted the nervous edge in his voice. Already, he'd managed to give his father the upper hand.

A half-smile appeared and disappeared so fast on the man's face that Luke might have imagined the conciliatory gesture. "Obviously."

Squarely meeting his father's gaze, Luke said, "Abby, I have to go. Dad's home."

"Okay. Call me later?"

"Sure. Love you. Bye." He slipped his phone into his pocket, pulled the romaine out of the colander, and started ripping it into bite-size pieces. Before he could gather his thoughts, Dad rounded the center island and strode into the back hall to hang up his coat.

In the next moment, he stood eye-to-eye with Luke. "I'll make a fresh pot of coffee, and we'll talk while the lasagna's baking."

Suddenly, Luke wanted to delay this conversation. No way was he prepared to present his case. "I still need to make the garlic bread."

Dad placed one hand on Luke's shoulder. "Son, the first rule of negotiation is never let your opponent see you hesitate. If you don't believe you have a legitimate case, convincing someone else is next to impossible."

Luke didn't know how to respond to that, so he tossed the salad fixings, placed the bowl on the middle shelf of the refrigerator, took out the butter, and sliced a chunk into a small frying pan to melt. The sound of the coffee percolating eclipsed the soft music of an oboe and violin piece. Luke drew in a sharp breath, peeled, and minced garlic, then stirred it into the melted butter. How could he convince his father that he had earned the right to go with Abby?

"Unless your nose is better than mine, you better turn that off." Dad held a full coffee mug in each hand and gestured to the breakfast nook.

The butter was speckled brown. Luke shut off the burner, put a cover on the pan, and took a seat across from his father.

"Present your case."

His dad was all business, as usual, which was not what Luke needed. "Dad, do you remember when Mom was pregnant with me? Or with Joe?"

A faraway look flashed in his father's eyes for a few seconds. "Of course."

Two words? That was all? Dad was drawing on another of his negotiation strategies—keep your opponent talking and gather as much information as you can. Wasn't that what Luke needed to do? Get his father talking? "Did Mom need you? I mean, more than usual."

"She did. Especially in the last two months with you." He sipped his coffee then folded his hands on the hardwood table. "With first babies, women don't know what to expect from labor, and they're terrified because they have no idea how much pain they'll have to endure. They have no frame of reference."

Luke nodded. "Abby's scared, Dad, and for some reason I can't begin to fathom, she thinks my mere presence will make everything easier and less frightening."

Understanding softened his father's expression. "It will."

Luke hadn't expected his father to capitulate so quickly. Was he actually consenting to a modification of their agreement? Or was he simply acknowledging that Abby needed Luke? "Dad, I haven't failed one drug test."

"I know. Your mother and I are proud of you, of how quickly pulled your life back together."

"You're proud of me?" The catch in his voice was audible, so he sat up straighter and met his father's eyes. "Even though I had to check myself back in?"

"Yes. Especially because you were wise enough to know when you needed more help than we could provide. You've fought your addiction, and right now, you are winning."

Luke opened his mouth to reply, but his father held one hand up. "You're winning now, but, Luke, don't let your guard down. Ever. You've won many battles since you entered Ellis Rehabilitation back in October, but those victories don't mean the war is over for you."

His dad was right. Luke could still screw up and ruin everything. "You're right." He paused to let his agreement momentarily disarm his dad. "But that doesn't mean I'm going to back away from my responsibilities. I won't be a coward. What I need right now is to be the man Abby needs me to be." He watched his father's face for a flicker of acquiescence then pushed ahead. "Which is why I want you to change our terms. Abby can't wait for me to just support her during her labor and delivery. She needs me now."

"All right." Dad unfolded his hands and drank a long draught of his coffee. "I'll call her father after dinner."

"Thank you. You won't regret this. I promise." Dad didn't respond, and Luke did something he had never done before. He asked his father to pray with him.

*

Abby stuffed another pillow behind her back. Printouts and books on historical, cultural, and literary influences on Shakespeare took up every available space on her double bed. She should have listened when Mrs. McNamara advised her that her research topic was too broad. Her tutor had been an English teacher for forty plus years. Why hadn't Abby heeded her warning?

The baby kicked, and Abby tried to capture the bump of a heel that pressed beyond her belly. Her daughter shifted in the small space that remained in Abby's womb. She was hungry, and aching all over. She'd need to move to her desk soon. Working in bed too long made her left leg go numb. She massaged the icy spot where her leg met her torso. Dr. Liselle said the baby was pressing on a nerve. Whatever. Abby was done being uncomfortable. She picked up her computer, cleared away textbooks and papers from her desk, then set the laptop far enough from the edge that she wouldn't accidentally knock it to floor. She needed a break and some ice cream. And maybe a peanut butter and banana sandwich.

With food in her stomach, she could trust herself to compose a coherent email to Mrs. McNamara requesting a modification of her research topic. What on earth was her essential question anyway? That no author writes in a vacuum? No wonder she'd gathered way too much material for a ten-page paper.

Abby held the railing as she cautiously descended the stairs. She could barely see her feet. She was so ready for this baby to be born. Five weeks. Thirty-five days. Maybe, her daughter would be eager to meet her mommy and daddy and would come early. Never mind that Dr. Liselle had said that first babies rarely arrive early.

Just outside the kitchen, Abby stopped. The low voices of her parents interrupted her daydream of an early delivery. She drew in a deep breath to fortify herself. Dad must have heard from Mr. Bradford. She hesitated a few seconds before strolling into the kitchen with feigned nonchalance.

Mom's gaze settled on Abby with a look that declared she wasn't fooling anyone. "Sit with us for a few minutes. We need to talk."

Abby nodded, her craving for ice cream vanished. She snagged a banana from the fruit bowl on the counter, peeled it and took a bite as she settled her aching body onto the chair opposite her parents. She shifted slightly so that the rails of the chair back didn't aggravate her tense muscles. She longed for a throw pillow from the living room couch, but she wasn't moving from this spot until she heard what they had to say. She reached behind her and pressed her fist against her lower back. It didn't help. Why didn't Mom buy those cool chair cushions like they had at Lisa's house? Ignoring the pain in her back, Abby waited for her parents to begin the conversation.

Dad's smile was tight. Which probably meant this conversation would not go well at all.

Mom rested her hand on Abby's forearm in a gesture

meant to soothe. It didn't. "We've decided that Luke has ... has demonstrated ..." Mom paused, clearly searching for the right words. "We've decided to trust Luke ... for a trial period."

"A trial period?" Abby jumped from her chair. "What does that mean?" Incredulous, she stared at her mother then turned to her father for support. "Dad, what is Mom talking about? Hasn't Luke already passed your trial period? He hasn't failed one drug test. You know that wasn't the reason he went back to rehab."

Her parents exchanged the look, the one that meant they would back each other up no matter what Abby said. Frustrated at the doubts in their eyes, she marched from the table to the fridge and took out the jug of skim milk. She needed a minute to corral her ranging emotions. They didn't understand. No one understood. Even Luke didn't completely get it. She was only eighteen, for crying out loud, and in six weeks she would be a mother. She simply could not do any of it any more without Luke. And she shouldn't have to. Luke had been clean for three and a half months.

Fighting tears, she poured herself a tall glass of milk and stared out the kitchen window to compose herself. Her mother's daffodils, a myriad of yellow, white, and pale orange in various color combinations, formed a pretty contrast amongst the bright green grass swaying in a breeze not quite strong enough to bend the flowers. Abby envied their stalwartness. Why couldn't she be as steady? *Cut yourself some slack. You've been living in a storm for more than two years.*

Wasn't that the truth? A breeze she could handle, but she was living in a hurricane, carried along by the force of Luke's mistakes. Her breath caught in her throat. She had made mistakes, too. Getting pregnant in high school was proof of that. She drank half of her milk and carried the glass to the table. Getting her parents to ease up on Luke clearly required a different approach. She returned to the table. "This isn't all Luke's fault, you know."

Frowning, Mom reached for her hand, but Abby pulled away. "Hear me out."

Her parents nodded. It was crazy how in sync they were. Would she and Luke ever be that close? Would they ever know each other so well that they could tell a story like two actors in a musical singing a duet? How did her parents do that and make it look so effortless?

Dad leaned back in his chair. "We're listening, Abby."

She couldn't suppress a smile. He always did that when he wanted her to open up. This time she was ready to talk, but *was* he ready to listen? His posture said yes, but his eyes didn't agree. She forged ahead anyway. "I'm not saying Luke's drug use is my fault. I know *I* didn't do anything to give him a reason to use drugs. He may have blamed me for stuff or used what was going on with us as an excuse, but that's all on him."

Mom released a slow sigh. "We're relieved to hear you say this. We were worried you felt guilty."

"I do. I mean, I did feel guilty. But not about Luke's addiction."

Her mother met her gaze. "You feel guilty about having sex before you were married and about getting pregnant. But we've talked about this, prayed about it." Her lips pursed in concern. "You need to let this go, Abby. God has forgiven you."

"It's not about God forgiving me, or even about me forgiving myself." Abby paused, praying that her parents were ready to take this next step in the rocky journey that had begun at the Homecoming game when that two hundred pound guy slammed into Luke, destroying his knee and any hope he had of playing football in college.

Her parents exchanged a questioning glance, but neither said a word. Did they already know what she would say next?

She forged ahead. "It's about you guys forgiving Luke. I know you both want to blame him, but this baby is more my fault than his." She looked from one parent to the other. Their expressions confirmed her suspicions. They needed to understand what really happened. "The night Grandma died, I knew I wasn't thinking clearly. Luke and I … had always been responsible. Until that night. If only I'd gone home, instead of falling asleep in his arms."

"You don't have to tell us this." The pink tinge of her dad's cheeks signaled his embarrassment. He did not want to *think* about his daughter having sex, let alone hear her talk about it.

"Dad, *I* put Luke and myself in a vulnerable position … because we were out of—"

"He could have insisted that you go home."

The intensity of his anger shocked her, but she shouldn't be surprised. "Really, Dad? Would you have sent Mom away?"

A slow dawn of understanding relaxed her father's tense features. "Okay, I see your point, Abby, but—"

"It's not that easy, after all he's put you through," Mom interrupted.

Her mother's anger discouraged Abby more than her father's had a moment before. What she said next would determine how things would go for the rest of her pregnancy. And after the baby came, too.

Lord, give me the right words. She took a deep breath and plunged ahead. "Pastor Schwartz said that forgiveness is a choice. Remember? When we decide to forgive someone, because that's what God requires of us, the feelings follow."

Dad reached across the corner of the table and took Mom's hand. "She's right, Steph." A single tear slid down Mom's cheek, and Dad wiped it away with his thumb.

Once again, Abby shuddered under the weight of pain she had caused her family. She opened her mouth to apologize.

But Dad held up his hand as if he'd read her mind. "We've said enough for tonight. Luke can go with you to your appointment tomorrow."

Abby wanted to ask if they would be willing to forgive Luke, but her parents clearly needed more time for that. At the very least, they wanted to discuss the matter alone. Later, they would tell her what they had decided. For now, she had to be content with a single step in the right direction. Luke would see his daughter on the sonogram monitor for the first time. He would clasp Abby's hand, and they would cry tears of joy. That much she knew about the man she loved.

*

Luke couldn't take his eyes off the screen. His baby. She was a living part of him and of Abby. To his astonishment, his daughter was the most beautiful person he'd ever seen. Her sweet mouth wrapped around her tiny thumb swelled the love in his heart that had begun the first time he had laid his hand on Abby's belly and felt his child move. Tears pricked his eyelids, and for a brief moment, he looked to Abby to see if she felt the same all-consuming love for their daughter. Abby smiled and took his hand, and he leaned down to kiss her. A quick brush of his lips against hers and Luke stood to his full height and faced the screen again. He couldn't get enough of looking at his daughter. The 3-D view surpassed the photos he'd clung to during his first time at Ellis Rehab. Looking at her now, his mind filled with images of holding her in his arms, rocking her to sleep, staring for hours at her precious face. In that moment, he understood Abby's eagerness for their baby's arrival. Well, maybe not quite. He had no real idea of how uncomfortable Abby felt. "How much does the baby weigh now? She looks big enough to be born."

The technician turned from the monitor. "About six pounds, but her lungs aren't fully developed yet. She needs this last month for her respiratory system to be ready to handle breathing on her own."

Luke remembered reading about that in health class. "Yeah, I forgot that." Out of the corner of his eyes, he caught movement on the screen. The baby shifted slightly, and her bent legs tucked tightly to her chest tensed with her effort to push against Abby.

"It's getting pretty crowded in there." The technician smiled. "I need to measure your girl, and then Dr. Liselle wants to examine you."

Abby tugged on his hand, her cheeks flushed with embarrassment. "You can wait for me in the waiting room if you don't want—"

"No way. I want be there when she tells you how much longer it will be before the baby comes."

The technician chuckled softly. "It's a little early for the doctor to detect signs of impending labor, but she will be able to tell you if Abby has started to dilate."

Luke met her eyes. The woman, who was about his mom's age clearly found his eagerness, or maybe his ignorance, amusing. "So, when will we know?"

The blonde woman shook her head back and forth a few times. "A week before. Maybe ten days. Plus or minus a few days."

His disappointment must have been visible on his face. "Seriously?"

"Babies come when they come." The technician set aside the wand she'd been using to examine the baby.

When the woman left, Abby sat up, and he held her hand while she climbed down from the table. "You really can wait in the waiting room. I won't mind."

He captured her face in his hands, noting again the rosy blush of her cheeks. "Babe, I'm going to see everything in the delivery room."

She nodded, sighed loud enough for people passing in the hall outside the door to hear, and met his gaze. "I just feel so vulnerable being ..."

Luke put his index finger over her lips, pulled her into his arms, kissed her hair, and held her close until she relaxed against him.

*

Two hours later, after a leisurely stroll through the Botanical Gardens, Abby and Luke were sharing a banana split at Anderson's. The entire time her eyes had feasted on the gorgeous displays of spring bulb flowers, Abby had been craving curly fries and ice cream. Now, she was searching on her phone for the latest romantic comedy showing at a local theater. She couldn't remember the last time they had gone to a movie together. She wanted to sit and relax with her boyfriend, and for just a while, enjoy their relationship without talking or even thinking about the baby. Which was, of course, nearly impossible to do this late in her pregnancy.

She suppressed a chuckle and smiled at the romantic picture she'd created in her mind. For a moment, she studied Luke's face. With his dark hair, blue eyes, and amazing smile, she could stare at him forever. He'd put on a few pounds over the last six months, losing the gaunt look of a heroin addict. She breathed a silent prayer of thanks that that part of their life was over because Luke would do whatever he had to do to stay clean. Sticking her spoon into the caramel sauce and swirling through the chocolate, she shot him a mischievous look. "It tastes better that way."

He raised his eyebrows at her and scooped up the last maraschino cherry.

"Hey, I wanted that."

"You ate the other two, remember?" Luke reached under the table and patted her belly, probably hoping to feel the baby move. She didn't.

"Okay, one for me, one for baby Elise, and one for you."

He lowered his eyes at her in a mock scowl. "So, I see how it's going to be. You girls get two votes, and I get one."

She laughed out loud, and the elderly man in the booth behind Luke shifted to face them. "You better nip that in the bud right now, son. Two females united against a man ... well, they're a force to be reckoned with."

Luke twisted in the booth so that Abby could no longer see his expression. "Thanks for the advice, sir. I'll take it to heart starting right now."

The gentleman's gravelly laugh filled the restaurant, creating an atmosphere of merriment. Another man, probably in his mid-thirties, whose twin girls were enjoying vanilla cones with rainbow sprinkles, chuckled. "He's right to a point. Daughters instinctively know how to persuade their daddy, but whatever you do, don't cross their mother."

One five-year-old cast a mischievous glance in their direction. "Yeah, we're worn to secret."

"That's sworn to secrecy, honey." The dark-haired man ruffled his daughter's curls, and she shook them out of her eyes.

"Daddy, stop. I can't see my ice cream."

Luke smiled. "Thanks for the advice, gentlemen. I'll remember it."

Abby sighed. This was a side of Luke she hadn't seen in a long time. Decisive. Confident that he could persuade her to his way of thinking. "What's going on in that head of yours, Luke Bradford?"

"We're *not* going to the movies today."

Her eyes widened in surprise. "We're not?"

"Nope."

The twinkle in his eyes put her in a malleable mood. "Then, where are we going?"

"Shopping."

"What?" She dropped her spoon with a clang against the glass dish. "You hate shopping."

"This is different. I want to go with you to pick out the outfit we're going to bring our baby home in."

Abby blinked back tears, but in seconds, rivulets streaked her face. She tried to respond, but nothing came out of her trembling lips. Through the blur of her tears, Abby watched confusion transform Luke's features from happy expectation to dismay.

"Why are you crying? I thought you'd want to do this with me."

She swiped the tears away and captured his hand. "I love you. I ... of course, I want to go with you to pick out our daughter's coming home outfit."

*

Watching Luke hold up yet another frilly pink dress and add it to the pile draped over his arm, Abby put her hand on his back to gain his attention. "Honey, you have at least ten outfits already."

He pivoted to look at her. His bemused expression was

priceless. "Maybe, we should get them all."

She stood on her toes, enclosed his face in her hands, and pulled him down for a sweet, brief kiss. "You are nuts. She doesn't need that many dresses. She'll grow out of that size before she gets to wear them all." Abby pointed to the hangers, each one with a yellow tab. "Every dress you picked out is for newborns. By June, she'll be in zero to three months."

Luke stared at the pile of pink dresses and lavender dresses then scanned the length of the rack. "Why are there so many sizes?"

Abby laughed. The hurt in his eyes sobered her. She'd read the baby book about what to expect in the first year. Luke had not. While she'd been preparing for their child, he'd been working on his recovery. She took his free hand and rubbed her thumb over his knuckles. "Babies grow a lot in the first year, Luke."

"Everybody knows that."

In Luke's defense, he had almost no experience with babies, with the exception of his little brother, and that was twelve years ago. "Let's lay all of those dresses out on that display table over there." She pointed to a table piled with stacks of shirts and pants. "We can choose two or three we both like."

He shook his head, his brow wrinkled into his characteristic, I-don't-think-so look. "I say we get two or three in each size."

"That's not a good idea."

"Why not? She'll need new dresses as she gets bigger."

Abby suppressed the urge to laugh again. "She'll need warmer clothes by October. These dresses are for late spring and summer."

"I should have thought of that." Luke carefully placed

the dresses in two rows then stepped back to study them. He turned to Abby. "Which ones do you like?"

"They're all pretty, but I like the white one with the pink roses best."

Luke handed her the dress. "What about this light purple one with the white dots?"

His soft tone revealed his need for reassurance, and she wanted to hug and kiss him until they were both breathless. Yikes. Not what she should be thinking about now. "I like that one, too." She scooped up the other dresses and replaced them on the rack. "Let's get white leggings and a hoodie, too, just in case it's cool the day we bring her home."

Luke nodded, but his eyes looked sad.

She didn't have to ask what had dampened his happy mood. He would be bringing her and the baby to her parents' house and then he would return to his parents' house. She was sad about that, too, but neither of them were ready to make a life together in their own place, and she had no intention of living with him before they were married. Megan and Lisa had argued for hours that she was being old-fashioned, but Abby didn't care what they thought. Going forward, she wanted to please God by doing things in the proper order. Sharing a home with Luke and the baby was a distant dream, probably two or three years down the road. Maybe longer, if they waited until they were both through with college. Luke wanted to be practical. She did, too, but that didn't stop her from praying that somehow they could get married sooner. She took his hand again and pressed a kiss to his palm. "We're going to be okay. As long as—"

"As long as I stay clean."

She met his gaze and saw a mix of pain and resignation. "That's not what I was going to say."

"What then?"

The defensiveness in his tone alarmed her. "As long as we talk. I need to know how you're feeling, and I need you to know how I'm feeling."

Luke slipped his arm around her, drew her close to his side, and kissed the top of her head. "I want to come home to you every day, fall asleep with you in my arms, and wake you every morning with a kiss."

His eyes, dark with desire, stirred her, but she needed to diffuse the passion arcing between them. "Before I brush my teeth?"

"Yep." He took her hands in his. "But it's not about making love to you. It's about loving you, as my wife, through every moment of every day. And we can't have that yet because I screwed up."

Abby pulled her right hand free and rested it on the top of her swollen belly. "We've talked about this. I—"

"I know. You think you are as much to blame. But that's not how I see it."

*

Silencing any argument she might make, Luke led Abby to the cash wrap. Once the cashier had wrung out their purchases—who knew two baby dresses would cost thirty dollars?—Luke guided Abby to a door that exited not into the mall but outside. At her puzzled expression, he squeezed her hand. "I want to go to the gym before work, and to do that, I need to get you home." He unlocked and opened her door, waited for her to get comfortable, then got in on his side. One glance in her direction confirmed his concerns. She was exhausted. "Why don't you take a nap when you get home, babe?"

She yawned. "I might, but I still have—"

He put a finger over her lips. "A lot of schoolwork to do. I know, but you'll think better after a nap."

Her response was another yawn.

He started the engine, tuned the radio to the classical station, set the volume on low, and made his way out of the parking lot. His phone rang in his pocket, but he ignored it, thankful that he had disconnected from the car's Bluetooth. Whoever it was, he could call them back. Beside him, Abby shifted in her seat. One sidelong glance told him she was already asleep. Her features were relaxed, though with the baby's increased size, he didn't see how she could be comfortable anywhere, and definitely not in a bucket seat. A newfound appreciation for all his own mother had endured to bring him and his brother into the world welled up in Luke. Wegmans was two blocks out of his way.

A few minutes later, he pulled into the busy lot, parked the car, and shut off the engine.

Abby's eyes fluttered, and she whispered, "Are we home already?"

He patted her thigh. "Not yet, babe. I'm running into Wegmans. Do you want to come in with me or wait in the car?"

She shifted towards him, opened her eyes, and smiled. "I'll wait in the car."

That suited him just fine. He would buy flowers for her as well as a bouquet for his mother. Should he get some for her mom, too? Probably not. Stephanie might think he was trying too hard to get on her good side. Which he definitely was. But he couldn't win Abby's mother over with thoughtful gestures. She was watching to see if he would fall off the wagon. The apprehensive way she studied him every single time she laid eyes on him made him nervous, but he did his best to conceal his anxiety. More than likely, she was judging him for that, too, interpreting his guardedness as a sign that he was on something or thinking about using.

Luke dismissed the resurgence of regret. He couldn't undo the past. At every NA meeting, someone said something that reminded him to focus on the present and his dreams for the future. One day, Stephanie would greet him without suspicion. But how long would that take? Abby believed in him. His mom did, too, and maybe, even his dad. Their confidence in him would have to be enough for now. Hadn't Zeke said just last night when Luke had called to discuss his challenges with his brother that some people take longer to convince?

Zeke's wisdom continued to amaze Luke. He hoped Dustin had found as good a sponsor. If he were attending NA meetings. Luke prayed that Dustin was getting the support he needed, but no one at Ellis had heard from him in over a month.

Abby stirred, her moving on her belly. Luke leaned over the console to kiss Abby's cheek. She sighed but didn't open her eyes. The urge to protect her pulsed in his veins. Never again would he put anything ahead of her.

Lord, forgive me.

I forgave you the first time you asked.

Startled, Luke looked up through the sun roof into the clear blue sky. But God wasn't in the sky. His still, small voice rose as a soft, gentle thought, a word of encouragement or direction, and often, simply an awareness that Luke wasn't alone. "Thank you, Jesus."

"God is good all of the time," Abby whispered.

"I'm sorry, babe. I didn't mean to wake you." He pressed a kiss to her mouth, but apparently she wasn't really awake. He let his lips linger for a few seconds. She tasted like cinnamon, her favorite gum. He lifted his face to look at her. She was so beautiful, brave and strong and loyal. If he could spend the rest of his life keeping her and their daughter safe, he would be a happy man.

It could have turned out so differently. He could be dead. Like Cole.

Grateful for God's mercy, Luke climbed out of the car, mulling over Abby's words. If God was good all of the time, then why was the world in such a mess? How had Luke nearly destroyed everything? Dark clouds filled the western sky, portending a coming storm, but the eastern sky, with fluffy, white clouds scattered across soft blue, seemed to promise a rain-free day. Hadn't he read somewhere that high above even the darkest sky, the sun shines with comforting light?

As he entered the grocery store, something Jake had said about free will surfaced in Luke's mind. "When a person's free will takes them away from God, they can't see His goodness. Sometimes, they don't even remember that He is good."

Luke understood. He'd been that way, too. He had believed God didn't care about him and had even doubted his own family's love. Worse, he had tested Abby's love over and over again. Why had this happened? The drugs had warped his thinking. Satan had duped him into believing so many lies.

Thankful that part of his life was over, Luke strode directly to the floral section. The abundant selection of flowers surprised him. Countless were out of season, shipped from down south, but Easter was less than a week away, and spring flowers outnumbered the others. Most of these flowers were pink, yellow, or some shade of purple. At the Botanical Gardens, Abby had oohed and aahed over the display of daffodils, tulips, and hya—, hya-something. He perused this section twice, hoping to find one pot with all three flowers but ended up disappointed. On his third circuit, he spotted a basket with pink and white tulips interspersed with pale yellow daffodils. Some kind of moss surrounded and separated the flowers, and a bow made from skinny pink ribbons and wider white ribbons was tied to the handle of the pale green and cream basket. The color combination celebrated spring. Abby would love it. His decision made, Luke handed the pretty basket to the woman working in the department. "I want this one. And I need another for my mother."

"What's her favorite flower?" The dark-haired woman's green eyes clearly expected his answer.

Luke didn't know. His mom always gushed over whatever he and his brother brought home. But when exactly was the last time either of them had brought her flowers? Years, probably. "I'm not sure."

"Roses are always a good choice."

"Her favorite color is purple."

The woman—her tag said her name was Irene, and she looked to be his grandmother's age—pointed to a glass bowl filled with five tulips. Three of them were blooming a bright purple.

"Yeah, she'd love that one."

"So, no roses?"

"You don't have purple roses. I'll take the tulips."

Irene picked up the glass bowl and set it on her work table. Then, she gestured with a tilt of her head to a display of small cards. He chose two, wrote a brief note on each one, signed them both, and handed them to Irene.

Resisting the urge to glance at his watch, Luke waited impatiently while she wrapped both arrangements in plastic and tied a complicated bow on each one. Then, he headed directly to the "7 items or less" line. He hadn't even considered the price when he'd made his choices. He opened his wallet, not surprised to see that he didn't have enough cash. Quickly calculating his bank balance minus the cost of the flowers, he stuck his bank card in the chip reader. It was a good thing this Friday was payday, or he would have had to borrow thirty dollars for gas from his father.

*

A gust of cold air startled Abby out of her sleep. She shuddered, disoriented and suddenly needing the bathroom. She opened her eyes to see Luke carrying two reusable shopping bags.

"What on earth did you buy? How long was I asleep? I really have to go to the bathroom. Right now."

Luke's eyes widened the way they always did when she rapid-fired questions at him. He held one bag out to her.

But she was already opening her car door, her mind entirely focused on getting to the bathroom before she had an accident. "Be right back," she called behind her.

*

Amused, Luke set Abby's flowers on her seat and his mother's on the floor in the back. Then he reached in his back pocket for his cell. Who had called? He'd actually missed *two* calls. One from his mother and another from he had no idea who. He stared at the strange number in the recent call list. It looked vaguely familiar, but he couldn't place it. He pressed the phone icon to return that call first.

"Merriweather Middle School, how may I direct your call?"

Luke's brows scrunched together in confusion. Someone from Joe's school had called? Why? He was absolutely certain he was at the bottom of the emergency contact list. "This is Luke Bradford. I'm returning—"

"Yes, let me connect you to Mrs. Renfield."

Mrs. Renfield, the school counselor, wanted to talk to

him? Why? Anxiety tripped through his veins, and he gripped the steering wheel with one hand and his phone with other.

"This is Faith Renfield, who's calling please?"

"Luke Bradford. Has something happened to Joe?"

"Your brother is fine. For the moment. He's still in class, but we need you to pick him up. Can you get down here immediately?" Mrs. Renfield's voice crackled with frustration and concern. "We called you nearly an hour ago, and—"

"Why did you call *me* and not one of my parents? What's happened?"

"Luke, I'm sorry to have to tell you this, but there's been an accident. Your parents were rushed to ECMC."

Luke's brain felt like it had been chopped in a blender. His parents? A car accident? "How bad was it? Does Joe know?"

"No, your mother asked us to contact you so that you could tell your brother."

If his mom called Joe's school, she had to be all right. "What about my dad? What did she say about Dad?"

"Your father is in surgery."

Luke's hands shook uncontrollably. Emergency surgery. That meant life-threatening, didn't it? He couldn't lose his dad. Not now when they were only starting to get close again.

"Luke, are you still there? I asked if you could please pick up your brother as soon as possible."

"I'll be there in ten minutes." He disconnected the call, covered his face with his hands, and begged God to spare his father.

Luke barely noticed the car door opening, but the familiar touch of Abby's hand on his thigh brought his head up. His eyes sought hers for a lifeline.

"Luke, what is it? What's wrong?"

His lips trembled. His world rocked like a row boat assailed by four-foot waves. Without his dad, they would all capsize, especially his little brother.

Abby's hands enclosed his face, her eyes infusing strength into him. "Luke, talk to me, honey. I can't help if I don't know what's wrong."

"My parents were in a car accident. Dad's …Dad's in emergency surgery."

Abby dropped her hands to her lap, shook her head. "How bad is it?"

"I don't know yet. Mom wants me to pick up Joe and meet her at the hospital. I …" Luke swallowed around the lump in his throat. "I need you to come with me."

Abby captured his hand. "Of course, I'm coming with you."

*

Fifteen minutes later, Joe burst through the school's main entrance doors, sprinted to the car, and buckled himself into the backseat before Luke even started the engine. Abby twisted herself so that she could make eye contact with Luke's little brother. He wasn't exactly little. At twelve, he appeared to have grown three inches and twenty pounds since she'd seen him last summer. His face, bleached white with shock, was streaked with tears that he swiped away with the back of his hand at her concerned look. What could she say? She couldn't promise him everything was going to be all right. They didn't have enough information yet for her to say much that would encourage the boy. She bowed her head and prayed silently as Luke headed the car in the direction of Erie County Medical Center. The ten-minute drive was ten minutes too long for Joe and Luke. And for her, too.

God, what will happen if they lose their dad? Can Luke hold up under that?

Be strong and courageous.

Abby trembled with fear. How could she be strong or brave? *Help me, Jesus. I can't, none of us can do this without You.*

CHAPTER SEVENTEEN

Two hours in the waiting room and they hadn't heard a word about his dad. Luke squelched his frustration and tried to take comfort in the whole-no-news-is-good-news outlook. With a sidelong glance, he assessed his mother and brother. Joe had stopped crying, but he was practically sitting in Mom's lap. The kid had stuck to her like Velcro since he'd first spotted her in the nearly empty surgical waiting room.

Luke was glad they were the only family here. The silence made it easier to wait. Talking led to speculation, and that ... well, they didn't have enough information to speculate on the outcome of his father's surgery. No one had said anything for at least thirty minutes. Abby had called her parents to let them know what had happened, and her mother had arrived about forty-five minutes ago with sandwiches, coffee, an herbal tea for Abby, and a sports drink for Joe, but only Abby had eaten. His own appetite was non-existent, but the coffee churning in his stomach demanded he eat something. He took a bite of the ham and Swiss on rye, surprised at how good it tasted, surprised he could even think of eating at a time like this. "Thanks for bringing the food, Mrs. Collins."

Abby's mother smiled. "No problem." She rose from her chair. "I'm going to check on Abby. She's been gone a while."

Luke nodded. She'd gone to the bathroom twice since her mother arrived. Apparently, tea was a bad choice for a pregnant girl. The doctor had said the baby was pressing on Abby's bladder. Luke couldn't even imagine how that might feel.

The moment Mrs. Collins was out of earshot, he crossed the room to his mom and brother. "You guys should eat something. This sandwich is really good."

"I'll puke if I eat anything." Joe's screwed up face was a tornado shade of yellowish-green, suggesting that vomiting was a distinct possibility.

"Mom, *you* should eat. We don't know how much longer Dad will be in surgery."

She nodded, reached into the basket for a sandwich, unwrapped it, and took a tentative bite. Then she clasped Luke's hand. "Honey, you … you've been so … helpful. I don't know what I'd do without you." Tears shimmered in her eyes.

He bent down to kiss her cheek. "Dad's going to be okay. I know it."

She tried to smile but couldn't quite manage more than a momentary turning up of the corners of her mouth. "Of course, he is," she whispered but the doubt in her eyes belied her words.

His decision made, he sat down on her other side and reached for his brother's and mother's hands. "Let's pray together."

"Right here?" Joe glanced around the room. "But someone might come and—"

"Hear us praying for your dad." The tense lines between Mom's brows smoothed out. "I'm ashamed I didn't think—"

Luke squeezed her hand, silencing her self-reproach.

"Lord Jesus, we're together, asking You to help the surgeon help Dad. We need him so much. Please don't take him. We're counting on You for a miracle. We know You love us and want what's best for us." Luke wanted to promise that he would do anything if God would let his father live, but Jake had said bargaining with God was the wrong approach because human beings could never keep their side of the bargain, couldn't be that perfect. Luke was about as far from perfect as a man could get. "Please be merciful, Jesus, and heal Dad."

Joe sucked in a breath and released a sob. "God, please don't take my dad. You don't need him like I do."

Luke gripped his little brother's hand, and Joe responded with a quick squeeze.

"Thank You, Lord, that even now You are watching out for Richard. Thank You that You are healing him and will restore his strength. My children and I are so grateful. Help us not to be afraid of bad news but to trust that the doctor will be here very soon with good news. Amen."

Luke felt Abby lean into his back, her baby bump big against him. "He's going to be all right," she whispered for his ears alone. "I know it."

Luke released his mother's and his brother's hands and encircled Abby in a hug that he surely needed more than she did. "I love you, Abby." He almost said Abby Collins, but he wanted to say Abby Bradford. That day would come, sooner, rather than later. An inner strength, not his own, but God's, would help Luke rebuild his life so he could make her his wife. In the last six months, he had learned the most important lesson of all. He couldn't do anything at all in his own strength. He needed to rely on God for everything.

*

Standing with her mother at the opposite end of the

small waiting room, the walls of which seemed suddenly to close in on her, Abby prayed. The surgeon, looking totally spent, explained to Luke and his family that his dad had suffered a lacerated lung from a broken rib. Using a procedure called a wedge resection, the surgeon had successfully repaired the air leak and stopped the internal hemorrhage.

"That's good, right?" Abby whispered to her mom.

"Yes, that's good."

The surgeon was still talking, and Abby refocused on his words. Richard had a severe concussion with minor brain swelling and bleeding. They had removed the blood clots by drilling a small hole through his skull. The image brought a wave of nausea that made her dizzy. She backed up a few steps and collapsed into the nearest chair. Taking comfort in her mother's hand on her shoulder, Abby sucked in several deep breaths. Luke didn't need her fainting or running out of the room to throw up. *Lord, help me.*

The ringing in her ears stopped, and the surgeon's words became clear again.

"Mrs. Bradford, your husband should be out of surgical recovery in about an hour."

Caroline leaned heavily on Luke as though *she* would collapse at any second.

The doctor touched her arm. "The surgery went well, ma'am," he soothed. "You'll be able to see your husband soon."

"Thank you, doctor," Luke said.

Abby marveled at his steady tone. Was his heart equally calm? She prayed it was so, prayed that the stress of this situation would not make him vulnerable to temptation. No, she refused to doubt him. Not now when he needed her more than ever.

Caroline wept, a soft sobbing that echoed her relief. "Thank you, doctor. I can't believe I almost … lost him." She covered her mouth with one hand.

The surgeon squeezed her shoulder. "Your husband will make a full recovery. He's a strong man, physically fit, and healthy until this accident. I expect to keep him in the hospital for three or four days. After that, he'll be in moderate pain for several weeks as a result of the surgery on his lung, but he'll be fully recovered in time to hold his new grandbaby." The surgeon caught Abby's gaze, his eyes drawing her into the family circle.

Caroline turned her head to Abby, something akin to joyous expectation in her eyes. Abby nodded, pleased that her baby would be part of Richard's recovery. He had been harsh with Luke, had maybe taken his tough love approach too far, but his course of action had forced Luke to get the help he needed, and for that, Abby would be forever grateful to the man who she hoped would someday soon be her father-in-law.

"I'll arrange for a bed to be brought into your husband's room so that you can stay through the night, Mrs. Bradford, if that's what you want."

"Yes, I do." Her voice trembled, and both Luke and Joe moved closer to her. "Can my sons see their dad, too?"

"Of course." The surgeon looked beyond the tight family semi-circle to Abby and her mother. "Immediate family only. Once, your husband's out of intensive care, then he can have additional visitors."

Overcome with relief, Abby rose to go to Luke, but his arms encircled his mother and brother. Abby turned to her own mother. "I was so scared, Mom. I prayed he would be all right—"

"And he is." Her mom's words revealed amazement and

gratitude.

Abby had not heard thanksgiving in her mother's voice since before her grandmother's brain tumor had been diagnosed nearly three years ago. Losing her mother had clearly shaken Mom's faith.

"God is good all of the time, even when we don't understand. Maybe, especially when we don't understand what's happening and why."

Mom smiled then hugged Abby until the baby kicked, hard enough to bring a startled look to her mother's eyes. She inched away and rested her hand on Abby's belly. "I remember how happy I was whenever I felt you moving inside of me. It was the most marvelous experience of my life, carrying you and then your brother."

The wistfulness in Mom's tone tugged at Abby's heart. "Grandma always said being a grandmother was a thousand times more fun than Christmas morning."

"Yes, she said that a lot. You and your brother and your cousins brought her so much joy." Mom's eyes glistened with unshed tears, her grief too new for words.

"I love you, Mom. You're going to be an awesome grandma."

"I hope so."

At Abby's questioning expression, Mom added, "I work too much. I'm going to need to make some changes after my granddaughter is born. But enough about us. I think we should head home. I'll speak with Caroline for a moment while you say goodnight to Luke."

The clock declared that it wasn't quite five thirty, but Abby was exhausted. Her legs trembled. She massaged the icy spot where her left leg met her torso. The baby must be pressing on that nerve again. She walked like a newborn duck toward Luke, touched his back, and he turned into her arms. They clung to each other for several minutes until Luke's mother's voice penetrated the circle of their love.

"Luke, can you take Joe home?"

"No way. I'm not leaving here until I see Dad." Joe's tone was petulant.

"Buddy, I know you want to see Dad, and probably after supper you can. We'll head home for a few hours to eat, and I'll help you with any homework you have. Then, we'll come back to the hospital."

"Promise?"

"I promise."

Two little words but Luke hadn't been able to say them to anyone, not during those long years of addiction when his promises meant little more than morning fog burned off by the sun. Now, the boy she had fallen in love with had emerged from his drug haze, transformed into a man they could all rely on. Her heart rejoiced before God, for He alone had restored their hope and confidence in Luke. She could trust him because every day he trusted God to give him strength to resist heroin's enticement.

*

Two days later, Luke stopped at the hospital on his way to work. He and Mom had devised a schedule, dividing the day into three sections, making sure one or the other of them spent chunks of time with Dad. He wasn't a patient man, which basically made him a lousy patient. Whenever he was left alone too long, Mom feared he would take his frustrations out on the nurses, and she was probably right.

Luke had barely exited the elevator when his father's angry voice pierced the quiet. Quickening his pace, he strode to the end of the hall to the last room on the right. His father's door was ajar.

"I won't take oxycodone," Dad growled. "No narcotics. It's

not happening."

Luke's body absorbed the barrage of his father's words as if he had been slammed by an Atlantic wave. He leaned against the wall to steady himself. Why hadn't he seen this coming? Of course, Dad would need pain meds. NSAIDs wouldn't cut it.

"You are going to be in a lot of pain," the doctor warned, "especially during your first week home. A lung resection takes six to eight weeks to heal."

"No way will I ever let that poison in my house again—"

"But, Richard—"

"No buts about it, doctor. I won't have that poison in my house."

"At least let me prescribe enough pills for the first three days you're home."

Luke needed to end this conversation. Now. His decision made, he yanked the door wide open.

The doctor turned to see who had interrupted their private conversation, and Luke noted the man's frustration in the tight set of his jaw. Too bad. Ignoring him, he met his father's startled gaze. "I figured it was time I made my presence known." His voice sounded cool, surprisingly calm. Good. They had to resolve this, once and for all. "Since I am the elephant in the room."

The obvious dismay on his father's face declared his regret. "How long were you standing out there, son?"

"Long enough." Luke shrugged. He wasn't angry or hurt that his dad didn't trust him. He was smart enough to realize trust wasn't the issue. "I know you don't want me to be tempted, but Dad, if you need pain meds—"

"I need my son more."

Understanding dawned in the doctor's dark eyes. "You were addicted?"

"Yes, for more than two years. I've been clean since Christmas."

"That's a good beginning."

"My point exactly, Dr. Santoro. My son hasn't even been clean four months. I'll take the 60 milligram ibuprofen, but not the ones mixed with codeine. And definitely no narcotics. Taking oxies turned my son into a heroin addict."

Though the words stung, Luke wasn't sorry he'd stumbled upon this conversation. It was better for him and for his dad that he'd disclosed his fear that Luke might not be able to resist the temptation of having oxies in the house. "Thanks, Dad."

His father turned from the surgeon to meet Luke's eyes. "Thanks for what? For not making sure you never took that poison in the first place?"

Distressed by the suppressed rage in the word "poison," Luke moved to the bed and laid his hand on his father's shoulder, surprised to be the one offering comfort. "That wasn't your fault, Dad."

"If I had been here after your surgery, I never would have let them prescribe narcotics for you, but your mother—"

"Mom didn't know, Dad. It's in the past. We need to put it behind us and not let misplaced guilt drag us down. You have no reason to feel guilty. I'm taking responsibility for my own actions."

Dad briefly covered Luke's hand with his own then folded his arms over his chest.

Luke didn't know how to relieve the anguish in his father's eyes. Reaching behind him, he dragged the chair closer to his father's bed. *God, what should I say? How can I help him?*

"I haven't been the father you needed, and I have to live with that."

"No, you don't. You've been a good father. I probably wouldn't be alive if it weren't for you making me check into Ellis."

The sheen of tears clouding his father's eyes was almost Luke's undoing. "Thank you for being willing to endure pain so that I won't be tempted to steal your pills."

"Son, I would have pushed through this pain without narcotics, even if you had never been addicted. I know enough that I wouldn't take the chance that I'd get hooked."

"All right, Richard," the doctor interrupted, "I'll prescribe ibuprofen."

The man's words startled Luke. He'd completely forgotten that he and his father were not alone.

"If that doesn't work, try icing your ribs and chest, twenty minutes on, twenty minutes off."

"That I can do."

The doctor looked to Luke. "Make sure he doesn't overdo it. No lifting anything over ten pounds. Not until after his six week checkup."

Luke wasn't sure how he could guarantee that, but he nodded anyway, mostly so the doctor would leave, and he could be alone with his father.

*

The following day Luke met Jake for breakfast.

"It's good to see you, man." Jake set his menu on top of Luke's on the end of the table to signal the server that they were ready to order. Break'n Eggs Creperie was packed as usual, and another dozen people were waiting for a table. "I'm glad you called."

Their waitress, a twenty-something with too bright eyes named Maddie, showed up to take their orders. With a sinking feeling, Luke deduced she was on something. One glance at Jake, and Luke realized the older man saw it to—

an excitement, almost an agitation in the girl's expression that had nothing to do with how busy the restaurant was on this Friday morning. "I'll take the chicken, ham, and Swiss savory crepe with black coffee," Luke said.

The girl scribbled down his order then turned to Jake. "I'll have the chicken, bacon, apples, and cheddar crepe. And coffee with cream and sugar."

Maddie rushed off to put their orders in, and Luke met Jake's eyes. "It gets to me every time."

"What gets to you, Luke?"

"The horrible waste. And the sense that the person has no idea that death is lurking around every corner."

"You're thinking about your roommate?"

Luke twisted his napkin with barely leashed fury. "Cole thought he was invincible. Every addict does—at least until their first overdose. You know that. Then there's this sick feeling that cheating death once is no real victory." He shook his head, his anger cooling. "It's just Satan toying with them, making them believe the lie that they have luck on their side. Luck has nothing to do with it."

Jake listened, attentive, focused, obviously waiting for Luke to get to the real reason he had asked to meet. Maddie brought their coffee, interrupting his rant. She moved on to the next table, offering refills to other patrons.

Finally, Jake asked, "Why did you want to see me?"

"My parents were in a bad car accident." Luke broke eye contact, momentarily distracted by the piercing scream of a toddler, followed by a man's firm command to stop yelling. "Dad got t-boned on his side. He got hurt pretty bad. He almost didn't make it."

Jake reached across the table, tapped the top of Luke's hand. "That must have been awful for you. And your family. How's your mom?"

"She's good. Just a few cuts and bruises. But Dad ... he needs to go home with pain meds."

Jake's brows knit in a frown so brief Luke almost missed it, but the man's eyes held no judgment. "That's a problem for you, isn't it?"

Luke sipped the hot coffee, needing the brew to calm his ragged nerves. "Yeah, but not in the way you think."

Jake waited, drank his own coffee, and held Luke's eyes in a steady gaze, one that declared he understood.

But how could he know? "My dad refuses to take oxies. He's in a lot of pain, but he ..."

"Doesn't want you to be tempted?"

"He doesn't want to get hooked." Luke's stomach tensed in frustration. "Surely, he could take oxies for three days and not get hooked, right?"

"Probably. Maybe. I don't know if the researchers really know how long it takes for a person to get hooked or whether some people are more susceptible."

Maddie approached their table, a large oval tray with their food balanced on her left forearm. "Chicken and apples?" she asked, lowering the plate in front of Luke.

"That's mine."

The girl opened her mouth, perhaps to apologize, but Jake offered her a smile. She set Luke's plate in front of him. "Can I get either of you more coffee?"

They both declined, and she moved on to her next table.

Jake bowed his head first to ask a blessing that ended up as plea for strength, wisdom, and peace. Luke was grateful. He would need all of that and more to navigate the next week with his dad.

*

The morning of her baby shower, Abby moved the seat of her Mustang back again. She had room for her belly, but she needed to stretch her arms to their full length in order to grip the steering wheel properly. She was tired of driving like this, tired of being so hungry and then barely having room in her stomach for any food, tired of being the size of a beached whale. She had heard that the last month was brutal but hadn't wanted to believe it. She should have let her mom come back for her. There'd be no room in her little car for many shower gifts anyway. Better still, she should have listened to dad and gone with him to the dealer last week to trade in her beloved car for a more practical SUV, a vehicle suited to a mom, which she would be less than three weeks.

"Shoulda, woulda, coulda." Even as she muttered her grandmother's words, the dear woman's voice echoed in her mind, and with it a deep longing to snuggle into the comfort of her arms, arms that would never again hold her on this Earth. Fresh grief assailed Abby at the picture of Grandma holding her namesake in her arms—a picture that would never happen. Tears filled Abby's eyes, cascaded down her cheeks, and blurred her vision. She covered her face with her hands, laid her head against the steering wheel, and gave in to the sobs. She was so weepy lately it was absurd, but she couldn't seem to stop.

She should think of something she was thankful for, starting with the Richard's rapid recovery. Contrary to the surgeon's fears, Luke's dad tolerated his pain so well, he had labeled it merely discomfort, and Luke had believed him. Richard had managed with prescription-strength ibuprofen, alleviating any residual guilt Luke felt about putting his dad in a position of suffering when oxies could have completely knocked out the pain, even though the man didn't consider narcotics an option. Abby thanked God for that, shuddering at the dark trap Satan may have planned for Luke. God was good all the time. That's what Grandma always said, and

Abby was starting to see how true that was.

Sniffling, she shifted slightly to pull a tissue from the box on the passenger seat. A hand on her shoulder shocked her into instant attention. She twisted to see who had touched her. Startled to her core, she blurted, "Jack? What are you doing here?"

His dark eyes pierced her, accusing her of abandoning their friendship.

No way did she want to deal with this today. Today was supposed to be fun, opening baby presents and celebrating with her family and friends. Of all days, Jack had to choose today. She had imagined, hoped, that they were past this, this awkwardness between them.

But how could they be when they'd never actually had a real conversation?

"Lisa told me you were home, that they were all at Mangia waiting for you. For your baby shower." His gaze dropped to her enormous belly. "I guess it won't be long now, right?"

Abby tried to smile, but talking with Jack about her baby, Luke's baby, made her uncomfortable. Having Luke's baby had changed everything between her and Jack, but not in the way he imagined. "My due date is in three weeks."

Jack nodded. He didn't smile either, didn't seem happy for her. His restraint suggested that he didn't approve.

What right had he to judge her? If she wanted to raise her own child, if she wanted to build a life with Luke, what right had Jack to attempt to shake her confidence with his disappointed look? Irritated as she was, the sadness in his eyes tugged at her heart, reminding her that they'd been friends since the sixth grade, reminding her that she had betrayed him nearly as much as she'd betrayed Luke. Kissing Jack had given him a moment of false hope, even though she'd promised him it would never happen again.

"You were never going to call me."

His rebuke stung, but she forced herself not to look away. This was Jack. One of her oldest friends. "Kissing you was a mistake." He'd kissed her first, but that didn't matter. She'd kissed him back, something that never would have happened if she and Luke hadn't been in such a bad place. But with God's help, she had finally forgiven herself. "I love Luke. I've always loved Luke. He and I—"

Jack held up his hand. "Yeah, I know. But ... it doesn't matter now. I only wanted to find out if ..."

She knew what he wanted to say. Putting it into words was necessary. For them both. "I don't feel that way about you, Jack."

Abby rested her hands on the top of her belly, soothing herself as much as the little one straining for room in the tight space of her womb. "Things change, would have changed anyway. We weren't planning to go to the same college, and well ... our lives were bound to go in different, separate directions."

"But if you hadn't gotten pregnant ..."

There was no accusation in the words. Just a lingering longing mingled with regret.

She ignored the temptation to touch his hand where he'd rested it on her car door, invading her space. Instead, she massaged her belly to soothe the baby, who seemed to sense her mother's agitation. "You'll meet the perfect woman someday, Jack, and you'll forget loving me."

The corners of his mouth turned up in a skeptical smile. "She won't be you."

Abby shook her head. "Jack, you know you and I were never meant to be more than friends." Pain flashed in his eyes, but she had to finish this. "When you meet the right woman, you'll know. She will be perfect for you in every way. She'll adore you and won't be able to live without you. You'll drive her crazy, of course, but she'll always forgive you."

"I'm going to miss you, Abby."

"Me, too." The words sounded final—goodbye and an end to their six-year friendship.

"Promise me one thing?"

Dread flicked, stung like a mosquito in her mind. "What's that?"

"If he hurts you again, leave him." The words were hard, razor sharp.

Abby shook her head. "Love isn't like that, Jack. Love is patient. Love endures all things. Love never gives up hope."

She heard a vehicle pull into the driveway, checked her rearview mirror, and saw Luke in the driver's seat of his mother's SUV. Her face flushed with embarrassment to be caught with Jack. Thank goodness she had never told Luke she'd kissed Jack. Her boyfriend climbed out of the car and strode toward them.

Making his presence known, he joined Jack, who still stood beside her car. "Hey, man, didn't expect to see you here." Luke's tone was easy, but his left eye twitched once, an indication of tension coiled like a cat ready to pounce on its wary prey.

Jack backed away. "I was just—"

"Saying goodbye," Abby said. That sounded lame, but she didn't know what Jack would have said, and she had no intention of letting him blurt out something stupid to Luke. Especially not today. Not ever, actually.

Luke bent down into the car to kiss her lightly on the mouth. "Your mom suggested I pick you up. My mom's SUV will have plenty of room for the bigger items—the crib, changing table, high chair, stuff like that." Standing to his full height, he took in her tight position in the Mustang, opened her door, and reached for her hand.

Jack was quiet, and Luke seemed to be ignoring him entirely. The awkwardness increased until he said, "Thanks for coming over, Jack. I know you and Abby had some things you needed to clear up." He pulled her closer to his side and draped his arm possessively around her shoulder. "I'm glad you had a few minutes to talk, to put things to rest, once and for all."

Jack's face stilled, the message clearly received. "I'll see you at the graduation, Abby. If you decide to walk across the stage."

"The baby and I will be there, too," Luke said. "Cheering Abby on. She's one determined woman."

Being called a woman when she was only eighteen sounded odd to her, but Abby didn't miss Luke's point. Which was, she was his, and Luke intended that Jack acknowledge that fact.

"I'm happy things are working out for you, Luke. Abby's the best. She deserves the best, and I know you won't ever forget that."

The steely look in Jack's eyes made Abby want to squirm, but she leaned into Luke in spite of the rigid way he held his body. Someone had told him what had happened between her and Jack. But who?

CHAPTER EIGHTEEN

Luke and her father were setting up the crib in the baby's room, while Abby and her mother sorted baby clothes by size in stacks on top of the dresser. "Do you want to put everything bigger than six months in the plastic bin in the closet the way we planned?" Mom asked.

"Yeah, let's do that."

Abby tried to catch Luke's eyes, but he was bent over the crib, screwing a leg to the frame. At the moment, she didn't care what they did with all of the cute baby clothes that she wouldn't need before winter. She had enjoyed her shower, oohing and aahing over adorable sleepers, pretty dresses and even everyday outfits, but now ... now, she couldn't get Luke's last words to Jack out of her mind. He hadn't exactly said he knew, but the interchange between the two guys flowed with electric messages, messages about her, messages she wasn't sure she wanted to decipher.

"It's five o'clock. Time to take a break." Mom emptied the last gift bag and set the items atop the appropriate piles. "Let's go downstairs and see what we can scrounge up for supper."

"I'm not hungry, Mom." Food was the last thing on her

mind. She wanted the nursery completely set up so she and Luke could go somewhere to talk. A walk would work, as long as they were alone. She felt like she'd been underwater, holding her breath until her lungs threatened to burst.

"I could eat." Luke straightened to his full height, rubbed his knee for a few seconds, then winked at Abby. "I can't believe you're not hungry, babe. You're always hungry."

She tossed a stuffed lamb at him, hitting him squarely in the nose. "I am not."

He flung the toy back at her, bouncing it off the top of her belly. She giggled, a nervous laugh that released some of the tension that had her wound as tight as her ponytail after a long ride in her Mustang with the top down. She sounded like her English teacher, spouting similes at herself. *Yikes, pull yourself together, Abby.*

Dad glanced up from the crib assembly directions. "We should be done here in another ten minutes. How about that leftover pulled pork and grilled sweet potatoes with a salad?"

Mom laughed. "Nothing wrong with your appetite. Do you want a cupcake with that, too?"

"I never turn down cupcakes."

Of course, he didn't. Her father had a ridiculously high metabolism and the lean body of an athlete who ran several times a week.

Abby smiled, her attempt to focus her attention on anything other than finding out where she stood with Luke futile. She needed time alone with her boyfriend. ASAP. "I could help Luke finish the crib while you and Mom put dinner together, Dad."

Her father actually laughed, and Luke winked at her again.

That was a good sign. He wasn't mad at her. She was fairly certain of that. Maybe she shouldn't bring up his exchange with Jack. Unless Luke brought it up himself, and then she would find out what he knew about that morning, the one she wanted to erase from the pages of her life.

Still torn, she followed Mom out of the baby's room, but instead of heading straight downstairs, Abby stopped at the bathroom. When she came out, Luke was waiting. He pulled her into his arms and kissed her, a soft, gentle kiss that made her feel as if everything were right in their world. Needing his closeness, she deepened the kiss, and massaging the muscles in his back, she tried to meld her pregnant body into his. She giggled.

He groaned, lifted his lips from hers, and enclosed her upper arms in his hands, effectively putting enough distance between them that she could see what her kiss had done to him. "What's so funny?" he complained, his voice husky.

Her cheeks heated in a blush. If they were already married, they could come together and heal this rift she had created when she'd kissed Jack. "I can't get as close to you as I want to." The words had a double meaning.

Luke knew it, too. His dark gaze held hers a moment. Then he enclosed her face in his hands and kissed her again, shutting out everything and everyone else, bringing their bodies as close as the baby would allow. The kiss and his hands in her hair made her dizzy with longing.

Until he broke away.

What was between them couldn't be mended by lying in his arms, even if she were willing to make love again before they married. Abby had never felt so bereft. Tears threatened to burst the dam of what little control she possessed. If he said one harsh word to her, if she couldn't make him understand that ... that what? That kissing Jack didn't mean anything, when it clearly had? That it didn't matter now because she and Luke were in a good place again?

Tenderly, he lifted a lock of her hair off her shoulder and ran his fingers down the length.

"We're good, babe." His intense expression conveyed confidence, confidence in her and confidence in them.

Confidence she wanted to feel, but didn't. She reached for his hand and held it. "Luke, I—"

"Abby, stop worrying about something that's over and done with. Whatever happened between you and Jack doesn't mean anything." He ran his thumb over the back of her hand. "I love you, and I know you love me."

Abby's heart pounded. They couldn't have this conversation in the hallway. Sam or one of her parents could interrupt them at any moment. "Can we take a walk? Please."

"After dinner?"

She shook her head, tears pooling in her eyes, drizzling down her cheeks.

He wiped them away with the pads of his thumbs. "Don't cry, babe. We really are okay. I promise."

She sniffed, nodded, offered him a trembling smile.

"Give me a minute. I'll let your dad know."

She rubbed her belly, soothed by the movement of her daughter straining at the close quarters of her world. But Abby's world was closing in on her, too.

God, please. I didn't mean to hurt him. To hurt us.

When Luke reappeared, his tender look was a balm to her aching heart. "I told him we were going to walk for twenty, maybe thirty minutes, that you needed some fresh air. The crib's nearly finished. He doesn't need me."

She wanted to say, good because I need you more, but she couldn't force a single word past the lump in her throat.

Downstairs in the foyer, he wrapped a plaid blanket scarf around her shoulders and led her out onto the front porch. "Do you want to just sit on the swing?"

She shook her head.

"Okay, let's go out back to the gazebo."

And have this conversation in full view of her parents? No way. "Let's go to the park."

"That's at least two miles from here. No way am I letting you walk that far. He marched her to his mother's SUV, held the door open for her, waited until she was settled, and then got in on his side. "We don't need to do this," he said, his eyes on the back-up camera as he navigated their driveway.

She didn't respond. Not for the entire drive to their favorite park. Abby stared out the front window at the tiny yellow-green leaves that reminded her of rosebuds opening. "Nature's first green is gold, her hardest hue to hold."

"That's Robert Frost, right?"

English had never been Luke's favorite subject. "It means the first bloom of innocence is easily lost." Every sweet and precious moment between her and Luke seem shattered like fine crystal in her traitorous heart. How could she have kissed Jack?

"I thought it just meant spring is the shortest season of the year."

"It means that, too." Apparently, he hadn't been paying attention to Mrs. O'Malley's discussions on symbolism.

Luke turned onto Glen Avenue and pulled into the Glen Falls Parking lot.

She didn't wait for him to open her door. She gripped the handle above her head and climbed out before he'd made it to her side of the car. She wanted to take his hand, wanted him to reach for her in the worst way, but she twirled away from him, and trudged across the parking lot, forcing him to follow.

Luke caught up to her in seconds, wrapped his arms

around her belly, and urged her to lean against his chest. He kissed her hair, lifted it from her neck, and pressed his mouth against the sensitive spot behind her ear that usually made her shiver with anticipation. Now, she felt only anxiety. He said he wasn't mad, but how was that possible?

With his hand gripping her elbow, he led her to a bench that faced the creek.

His eyes were patient, calm, and steady. He pressed his thigh closer to hers. His heat warmed her body, but the cold place in her heart remained untouched.

For a moment, she allowed the water rippling and gurgling over the rocks calm her. *Jesus, help me. Help Luke understand how sorry I am.*

Finally, she shifted to see his face. "Who told you?"

"Ian."

Of course. Ian was a wide receiver, the best Easton had had in two decades. He and Luke had racked about over three hundred and fifty passing yards in the two years they had played together. Ian would be loyal to Luke. So, why would Jack tell Ian? Unless, Jack wanted Luke to find out. Anger at Jack eclipsed her fears. After six years of friendship, how could he have betrayed her?

"We don't *need* to talk about this, Abby. I know it only happened one time. I'd be a fool to let one kiss ruin what we have."

Tears cascaded down her cheeks. He knew everything. Everything but her side of the story. She forced herself to meet Luke's eyes. "I love you, Luke. So much. I have to tell you ... what happened."

He slid to the end of the bench and leaned back against the wrought-iron arm rest, but his body was coiled for quick action. "Okay, I'm listening."

His tone was ... even, calm, accepting, resigned? She

couldn't read him. "It happened the day after New Year's Day. Lisa, Meg, Ian, Lainie, and Jack were going out for pizza and a movie. I … I thought maybe Lainie and Jack were … she'd always liked him. I hoped they were finally dating. Lainie's liked him forever." Abby tugged the blanket shawl around her belly, more to quiet her nerves than for added warmth. "Still, I didn't want to go. Not really. But I hadn't done any normal teen stuff in so long. And I was—"

"Mad at me."

Abby met Luke's gaze, saw the pain in his deep blue eyes, and swallowed the sob rising in her tight throat. "Yes. I didn't want to be mad at you. I wanted to understand how hard being at my grandparents' house was for you. And you'd tried to tell me you weren't ready, but I wouldn't listen. What happened … was just as much my fault as yours."

Luke slid next to her again, put his hands on her shoulders, and leaned so close she could feel his breath on her face. "It was *not* your fault. None of it was your fault. *I* always had a choice."

"But—"

"No, buts, Abby. I'm an addict. I stole your grandfather's oxies. I did that, to you, to your family. On Christmas Day of all days."

This conversation was careening off track. They weren't supposed to be talking about what he'd done wrong. She was the one who needed his forgiveness. "I missed you so badly. I missed us, and the way we used to be before … before your injury."

"Oh, babe, I know." Sorrow ravaged his handsome face. "I stopped … needing you like I had before."

She bit her lip to keep from sobbing, to keep from revisiting those days when she had felt rejected, unwanted, almost forgotten altogether, if he hadn't needed her money to buy drugs. She had done her research now and knew what opioids did to a guy's sex drive, and knowing that, the baby in her womb seemed more like a miracle than a mistake, a miracle that was meant to change their lives in amazing ways. If only Luke could forgive her.

He kissed her then, teasing her mouth open with his tongue, and she yielded to him. The same way she'd yielded to Jack that awful afternoon. Abby pushed at Luke's shoulders. "Let me finish."

He sighed. "I just wanted to let you know that I'm my old self again."

She laughed. "Yeah, I've noticed."

When he placed his hand on her belly to wait for the baby to move, she rested her head on his shoulder for a moment, drawing on the courage God had poured into her. She shifted to look at Luke, to watch every expression that would tell her what she needed to know.

"Jack showed up at my house. Literally, outside my bedroom door. I was so startled I tripped over the Oriental rug, and Jack caught me, kept me from falling. He tried to kiss me then, but I shoved him away." Should she tell Luke how hurt Jack looked? Would that make any of this any easier for her or for Luke? Probably not.

"He's in love with you, Abby. I can't believe you didn't know that." Luke's frustration snapped like a whip. His stormy gaze accused her.

Of what? Of leading Jack on? Of being blind to what she had not wanted to acknowledge? Of setting a boundary that could crumble? She pressed her lips tightly together, sighed, and forged ahead. "I did know, but I thought we could be just friends. But that day, I saw it in his eyes—the hurt, the hopelessness of loving me when he knew I would always love you."

"What happened after he tried to kiss you?" His hands on his knees, Luke leaned in close, peering at her like a detective. "Why didn't he just leave?"

If only she could go back and do that day over, but she and Jack had been friends for more than six years. How could she have let him leave without trying to fix things between them? "I ... I didn't mean for ... it to happen. I'm sure I never did anything, at least not until that day, to give him any indication that I felt more than friendship for him."

Luke was taking it all in, his brows still knit in a frown. "I believe you. So why didn't the guy respect that?"

"He was so hurt. I ... I kissed him on the cheek, and the next thing I knew—"

Luke covered his face with his hands, and his shoulders shook.

His anguish pierced her heart. "It didn't mean anything. I ... he made me feel—"

"Loved," Luke declared, facing her once more. "He made you feel loved. Something I hadn't done for a very long time. Not since ..." His gaze dropped to her belly, then his eyes met hers. "Not since the night we made our baby."

Tears dropped off Abby's jaw, chilling her neck. She hung her head and sobbed.

He lifted her chin with his index finger. "Oh, Abby. I did this to you. To us. Can you ever forgive me? Please say you can forgive me."

"Forgive you?" She shook her head. "I need you to forgive me."

They were both crying, heart-wrenching grief, grief she had no idea how to heal.

He took both her hands in his, their eyes locked in their own private world. "I love you, Abby. I forgive you for letting Jack kiss you. Now, I need you to tell me you forgive me for making you so vulnerable, for making you feel as if I didn't love you anymore."

Her mind flashed to the many nights, nights she'd needed him, and he'd nodded off, completely oblivious to her presence. "I forgive you, Luke. I'll never hurt you like that again. Not as long as I live. I don't want anyone but you." For several seconds, she just looked at him, into those blue eyes that reflected their shared dreams, dreams that had been shattered by drugs and betrayal, dreams that were awakening with renewed hope. "I never did, and I never will want any man but you, Luke Bradford."

She wanted him to kiss her, needed him to kiss her, but he pulled her into his arms and held her close for several minutes. Finally, she couldn't stand the ache in her heart another second. She leaned back to look into his dear face. "Kiss me, Luke."

He started to lower his mouth to hers, but she captured his face in her hands, and pulled his head down until their lips met in a kiss that cleansed away every doubt, every concern.

"Marry me, Abby," he whispered so softly she barely heard.

*

It was a crazy thing to say. Luke knew it the minute the words were out of his mouth. His retail job wouldn't even buy groceries, let alone put a roof over their heads. But he could put a ring on her finger. His grandmother's gorgeous emerald engagement ring. His dad had retrieved it from the safety deposit box in the bank, and Luke had been carrying it in his pocket for three weeks now. His hand closed around the velvet box, and he bent down on one knee, heedless of the cold concrete footer beneath the bench.

She stared at him in startled disbelief.

His eyes never left her beautiful face. Corralling his nerves, he unfolded his hand, palm up, and flipped open the box. The emerald marquise flashed in the late afternoon sun. Abby's eyes, red from crying, instantly shone with what he hoped were happy tears. "I know we can't get married right now, but we *can* get engaged."

She covered her mouth with her hands, and her surprised sigh cheered his heart. Maybe asking her wasn't so crazy after all.

He took her hands and held out the ring. "Say yes. Say you'll marry me, Abby."

She looked down at the emerald and back up at him. "But I'm only eighteen. You're twenty, not even twenty-one. Getting married now would be crazy and impossible. Our parents would never approve. Where would we live?" She was talking fast, the way she always did when she was excited about some new adventure.

But this would be more than a new adventure. It would be a whole new life. But not altogether new. Jesus had already given Luke a new life, a second chance to live as if every day mattered, because it did. What could possibly matter more than to stand alongside the girl he loved, the mother of his child, all the days of their lives? He grinned with sudden assurance. "We'll figure all of that out. Just say yes."

Doubt, joy, and worry played across her beautiful face. "I want to say yes."

Here was his practical Abby. But he had prepared for her obvious objections.

She ran her fingers along his jaw. "We'd have such a long engagement. Years maybe."

She was right, of course. He had three more years of college, but married people often worked while getting their degrees. Most of them probably didn't have a baby to care for, so making ends meet would be tougher. Acknowledging that reality only increased his determination. A deep confidence settled every doubt in his mind. God had a plan for them. Luke reached for Abby's left hand and rubbed the pad of his finger up and down the length of her ring finger. "Babe, I promise you that I will be the husband you deserve. And I'll be a good dad. You and our daughter will always come first."

Her eyes softened, and he could see their future reflected in their blue depths. "Wear this ring." He slid it onto her finger. "And we'll wait until after the baby is born to talk about setting a date."

Abby held out her hand, turning it back and forth to watch the light catch the perfectly cut green stone nestled between two rows of tiny diamonds. "It's beautiful, Luke. I've never seen a more beautiful engagement ring. Ever."

"It belonged to my mom's great-grandmother. With so many girls in Mom's family, I'm the first male in three generations."

Abby glanced at the ring again. Then she gave him a brilliant smile that illuminated every dark place in his mind. The bleak hopelessness of his addiction, the sharp knife of jealousy, even the self-loathing that sometimes reared its ugly head even after he'd been clean for four months, all that darkness scattered in light of her love. Luke reached for her hands and helped her to her feet. "Abby, I know we've done things out of order. Having a baby before getting married wasn't part of my plan, but marrying you always was."

She stood on her toes, looped her arms around his neck, and stared up at him. "Do we really have to wait until after the baby's born?"

"What are you saying?"

She giggled.

"Wait. Is that a yes?"

She caressed his cheek, her fingers as smooth as satin. "Yes. Yes, Luke, I want to marry you, too."

He let out a whoop, twirled her around so many times her laughter filled the park. Luke had never imagined he could ever be this happy.

Then she let out a soft whimper.

"What's wrong?"

Abby backed several steps away from him and stared down at the ground.

His eyes blinked twice at the puddle spreading on the concrete. Instantly, his playful mood disappeared. "Is that what I think it is?"

She nodded. "My water just broke."

"But the baby isn't supposed to come for three more weeks."

"Tell that to our daughter." Abby grabbed his hand, practically dragging him across the rain-soaked grass. "We need to go. Now!"

*

Grateful to his mom for her commitment to living green, Luke covered the passenger seat with four reusable shopping bags he found in the hatch. Then he helped Abby into the SUV. She buckled her seat belt, retrieved her phone from her purse, and called her mom. Without even saying hello, she blurted out, "Mom, my water broke. Should I come home or go straight to the hospital?"

"Have your contractions started?"

"I don't know. Maybe. I have been feeling crampy all day, and I've had more Braxton Hicks than usual."

"That sounds like you could already be in labor. Am I on speaker? Put me on speaker. Luke, go right to the hospital. We'll meet you there."

"I don't have anything packed." The fear in her voice threatened to morph into full-blown panic. "Mom, it's too early."

"Abby, calm down, honey. You and the baby will be fine. It's not that early."

Abby bit her lip. How could she possibly be in labor three weeks before her due date? She wanted to finish all of her schoolwork before the baby came, and the nursery was barely ready. "I can't have the baby yet. I'm not ready."

"Of course you can, honey. Try to relax. Luke, tell her to relax."

"Relax, babe." He gave her hand a quick squeeze and exited the parking lot heading east. "Everything is going to be all right."

"But she isn't supposed to come for three more weeks." Twenty-one more days to prepare herself to be a mother. Twenty-one more days that she apparently was not going to have. *Lord, help me. I'm scared.* She balled her hands into fists but couldn't make the trembling stop.

"Honey," her mom said, "Luke's right. The baby will be fine. She probably weighs at least six pounds by now, and her lungs should be fully developed."

"Should be? What if they aren't?"

"The doctors know what they're doing. Try to relax."

Abby cringed. If she heard that word one more time, she was going to scream.

"Dad and I will see you in less than an hour."

Abby disconnected the call. Tears pooled in her eyes then trickled down her cheeks. She swiped them away. The gorgeous emerald sparkled on her left hand. Never in her wildest imaginings had she envisioned becoming engaged and having her baby on the same day. But the baby probably wouldn't come until sometime early tomorrow morning. Her mom's labors lasted about fifteen hours, and there were less than seven hours left in today. Abby turned on the radio and scanned for some music to soothe her nerves. Trace Adkins was singing "You're Gonna Miss This." Abby laughed out loud at the irony then selected the classical station.

Luke navigated past several slow cars, but the tail end of rush hour traffic slowed their progress. They stopped at practically every red light. She could have walked faster, which was ridiculous, of course. She was going to scream if they got stuck at one more light.

"How you doing, babe?" Stopped at yet again another red light, Luke leaned over the console and kissed her cheek.

"Okay." Her answer came out like a toddler's whine.

He didn't say a word. He knew her well enough to realize nothing he could say at this moment would help much. The light turned green, and he squeezed her hand and proceeded through the intersection.

The first hard contraction hit her a block away from the hospital. She drew in a deep breath. Maybe, she wouldn't have the mind-blowing pain other mothers talked about, the pain they claimed she would forget the minute she held her baby. If she would forget, why did they all say that labor was more painful than they had ever imagined it would be? She and Luke had agreed that she wouldn't have an epidural, but maybe she should have drugs. Yeah, she should have drugs. If it got much worse than this, no way would she be able to handle the pain.

Three minutes later, Luke pulled up to the front entrance, jumped out of the car, and leaving it running, handed the keys to the valet. "We're having a baby."

Abby couldn't hear the man's reply. When Luke reached her side of the SUV, she was already climbing out.

"How are you doing? That last contraction was a lot

stronger, wasn't it?"

How did he know? She was the one in labor. She shot him a look that silenced any more stupid questions.

Moments later, they were standing behind an older couple at the admission kiosk when the next contraction struck like an Atlantic wave, buckling her knees. She gripped Luke's arm, pinching his bicep until he winced.

Through the blur of pain, Abby noticed the older couple stepping aside.

"We're in no hurry," the woman insisted.

"Thank you." Luke led Abby to the admission desk.

"Name, please," the hospital attendant asked.

"Abby Collins," Luke answered. "We're having a baby."

"I can see that. I'll get a wheelchair down here ASAP. Date of birth, please."

Luke rattled off her birthday as the pain finally subsided to dull cramping.

She released Luke's arm and looked up at him. "Don't you dare leave me."

"Babe, I'm right here." He leaned toward her, easing her to his side.

The attendant shook her head. "You aren't pre-checked in. I need photo IDs."

Luke slid his driver's license across the counter. Abby fished around in her purse until she snagged her wallet. Where was her license? After several frantic seconds, she found it tucked between a Tim Horton's gift card and her a Target receipt for several duplicate baby outfits she planned to return. She handed her ID to the attendant.

With a sympathetic smile, the woman passed their IDs back to them. "You need to go to admissions and answer a few questions before heading up to the maternity ward."

Abby patted her belly. "You're making Mommy's life

difficult already, little girl."

Unfortunately, Abby was scheduled to do all the paperwork on Monday, so that she wouldn't have to worry about it when she was in labor. There was no way around it. They would have to stop at admissions. The woman at that desk took one look at her and ushered her into a small room where she started asking Abby questions about her medical history. She lost track of how many questions she answered with "no."

She rubbed her stomach, surprised at how tight her muscles were. "Well, baby, you are an impatient one."

The older woman smiled. "Some babies are like that. My first was two weeks early."

"My baby isn't due for three more weeks."

The woman glanced up from her paperwork. "You and the baby will be just fine. My granddaughter had her baby here yesterday, and everyone took very good care of her and my great-granddaughter. Don't you worry. By this time tomorrow, it'll be all over, and you'll be holding your little one in your arms."

The woman's smile soothed Abby. Until she thought of her own grandmother, who would never see *her* great-granddaughter. Tears spilled down Abby's cheeks.

Luke massaged her shoulders. "We're planning to name our daughter after Abby's grandmother."

"How wonderful! I'm sure she's happy to have a namesake."

Abby willed Luke not to say the words.

They tumbled from his mouth anyway. "She passed away last summer."

Fresh tears cascaded down Abby's cheeks as her abdominal muscles clenched, signaling another mind-blowing contraction.

A man in light blue scrubs finally arrived with a wheelchair. Abby stared at him through a blur of agony. No way could she stand. She gripped the arms of her chair and tried to breathe. When the pain released its grip, she glanced up at Luke. "This is so much worse than I thought it would be. I ..." She hoped he wouldn't be disappointed in her. "I changed my mind. I want the epidural."

Luke nodded. "Whatever you want, babe." He helped her into the wheelchair, and with the attendant pushing the chair, they headed down several halls to the elevators.

They had barely exited the elevator onto the maternity ward when another contraction squeezed her stomach in a vise-grip. This one encircled her entire midsection. Why did her back hurt? Was that normal? She ground her teeth together but failed to block out the escalating pain. Luke was squatting in front of her and telling her to breathe. She obeyed, matching her breaths to his.

*

"The baby's crowning." Dr. Lisette announced as Abby's strongest contraction subsided.

After eight hours of labor, Abby's desperate expression told Luke the epidural was beginning to wear off. She fell back against the pillows. He mopped the sweat from her face then turned to look at the doctor for some indication of how many more contractions Abby would have to endure.

The wonder in the woman's eyes surprised him. She had probably seen hundreds of births. A new truth drew him, the magnetic pull of his child. Awestruck, he stared at the baby's head, covered with wet blonde hair.

Abby screamed.

Luke returned to her side, leaning down so that he could maintain eye contact with her. "Breathe, babe."

"I ... can't ... do this ... anymore."

Seeing the pain in her eyes, he wanted to pour his strength into her, but that wasn't possible. "Yes, you can."

"Push," Dr. Lisette commanded. "Come on, Abby. You can do this. That's it. One shoulder's out. Keep pushing."

Luke glanced back just in time to see Dr. Lisette's gentle hands welcome his daughter into the world. Overwhelming gratitude illuminated his mind and heart like pristine light after a deadly storm. Tears rolled down his face. *Thank You, Jesus.*

"Is she okay? Can I hold her?" Abby tugged Luke close. The exhaustion on her face was gone, totally erased by bright eagerness. "I need to hold my baby."

"Your daughter is perfect. You can hold her in a few minutes." Dr. Lisette looked to Luke. "Do you want to cut the cord?"

Did he? What if he did it wrong?

The doctor discerned his indecision. "Cut right between the clamps."

Luke took the offered shears and cut the umbilical cord, his daughter's lifeline to her mother. Severing that connection created a new, stronger bond, their three-fold cord. His family. He could have missed it all. This moment and every one after. He could still ruin everything. He wasn't as strong as Abby believed he was, and he definitely wasn't as strong as he needed to be. He was clean today, had been clean for four months. But the struggle wasn't over, and he wasn't sure if it ever would be.

Jesus, keep me.

God's peace settled Luke's anxious heart, and he focused his attention on his baby girl who was wailing as the nurse tended to her needs and evaluated her overall health. After a few minutes, the woman wrapped Elise in a warm blanket and handed her to him. Tears filled his eyes again as he carefully supported her head, held her close, and bent to kiss her cheek. "Hi, Elise. I'm your daddy." A tear splashed on the baby's cheek, and she screwed up her mouth like she was about to cry.

"I want to hold her," Abby insisted.

The nurse nodded. "Let's see if she wants to nurse."

Luke stared in amazement as his baby daughter instinctively latched on to Abby and started to suck.

"She's a natural," the nurse proclaimed. "We have to help some babies get the hang of nursing, but your daughter—"

"Is a survivor." Abby patted Elise's back. "Just like her daddy."

Luke met Abby's gaze. "And her mommy." Overcome with joy and gratitude, he kissed his girls. "I love you, Abby, and I love our daughter, and I'll never let you down, ever again."

Abby touched his cheek, her eyes locked with his. "I love you, Luke. We're going to be okay. I know it."

CHAPTER NINETEEN

Abby tried to keep her eyes open, but the whole room kept going dark, maybe because she'd slept less than five hours last night, what with the baby coming at 3:11 a.m. Following her nurse's advice, whenever Elise slept, Abby tried to sleep, too, but she had only managed two short naps, one in the morning and the other just after lunch. She squelched a sigh. Since five thirty, a steady stream of visitors had arrived to meet Elise and take pictures. After Luke's parents and his brother, followed by two sets of his aunts and uncles with a half dozen cousins Abby had never met, not to mention several friends, she wanted to be alone with Luke and the baby.

Abby gestured to her fiancé, and he sat beside her on the bed.

His face filled with concern, he asked, "Are you all right?"

"Not really. Honey, can you please ask everyone to go home, so I can get some sleep?" Her request sounded more like the whine of a toddler than the reasonable request of a new mom.

Luke frowned. "You want me to just ask them to leave?"

"Please. You look tired, too."

He planted a kiss on her forehead then stood. "Thanks for coming to meet our girl, but Abby is exhausted, so ..."

Meg and Lisa exchanged understanding glances. Luke's Aunt Hannah—actually Great-Aunt Hannah, waved a hand toward the door. "Everybody out. They'll be plenty of time to snuggle the baby later, when y'all stop by with food or to help Abby out while she finishes her schoolwork."

She shot Aunt Hannah a grateful look.

Mrs. Jamison, Abby's favorite English teacher, said, "We should have realized how exhausted you would be."

Abby smiled. "That's okay. Thank you all for coming."

Five minutes later, each person had hugged or kissed her goodbye. With Elise contentedly nursing, her sweet, warm body snuggled against her, Abby drifted into a welcome doze. Luke touched her shoulder, and she opened her eyes.

He pulled the blanket aside and lifted Elise into his arms. Then he patted her back to encourage her to burp. "I got this, babe. Go to sleep. I'll be right here watching out for my girls in case either of you need anything."

Abby tried to focus. The sight of Luke with their baby girl cradled against his shoulder brought tears of joy, and she brushed them away. The intensity of her love surpassed any she had ever known. She would do anything—move mountains, forge rivers, fight fires—for these two people. Her family. "Let's get married tomorrow," she whispered so low that she wasn't sure Luke even heard her. Then she sank against the pillow, pulled the blanket up under her chin, and silently thanked Jesus for the best day of her life.

*

Was she serious? Get married tomorrow? Literally? Even if she were serious, Luke couldn't agree. He pressed a gentle kiss to Elise's forehead and laid her on her back in the bassinet next to Abby's bed. His daughter stirred, opened her mouth, and released the tiniest whimper. He patted her tummy a few times, and she quieted.

He sank into the recliner to watch his girls sleep. The image of leaving them at Abby's parents' house made him bite his lower lip to keep from crying out his anguish. It wasn't supposed to be this way. If he had never been an addict, maybe …

Maybe what? Maybe they would already be married. Maybe Elise wouldn't even be here. Luke couldn't imagine his world without her. God had used Abby and Elise to save Luke's life. He knew that as sure as he knew he couldn't marry Abby tomorrow. Or any day soon.

He opened up a Bible app on his phone and started to read, praying for peace, patience, and guidance. God was in control. Even if Luke couldn't see the whole length of the road he needed to travel, the goal—being married to Abby and together raising Elise and any other children God planned to give them—shined like a beacon on a dark winter night. The tension gripping Luke from the second Abby had suggested they get married tomorrow left him. His mind quieted, and his body relaxed.

*

Luke awoke the next morning to the piercing cry of his daughter's wailing. He leaped to his feet and lifted his daughter into his arms. Snuggling her close, he whispered, "Shh! Let's not wake Mommy yet."

"I'm awake. Bring her to me. She might be hungry."

Luke met Abby's gaze. "Let me check her diaper first." Gently, he unwrapped his daughter from her swaddled cocoon, removed her sleeper, and felt the outside of the diaper. It was gushy. Was he about to change his first poopy diaper? Not his favorite father moment but a necessity. He tore back the tabs and to his relief discovered a very wet diaper but nothing more.

Abby laughed. "You're doing fine, Luke. Poopy diapers are no big deal."

"How would you know? You've never changed one. I've seen … never mind." She'd find out soon enough. Unlike Abby, Luke had an older cousin who already had two babies within two years. He had observed first hand just how big of a mess a baby could make, a mess that often required a total change of clothes.

A nurse entered the room and strode past Luke to the side of Abby's bed. "How are you feeling this morning?"

Abby sighed. "Still tired. Weepy."

"Any cramping?"

"Only when the baby's nursing."

"That's normal. It'll pass in a day or so. It's just your uterus contracting back to its normal size. How's the nursing going? Do you need the lactation specialist to come in and help you?"

Luke laughed, snapped up the baby's sleeper, tucked her securely in her swaddling blanket, and snuggled her against him. "Elise is a natural. She figured it all out on her own in the delivery room."

The nurse, a thirty-something ginger named Allison, smiled as she checked Abby's blood pressure, then her pulse. "Perfectly normal," she pronounced. "Are you hungry? Breakfast won't be served for another hour, but I can get you some juice and graham crackers."

"Sure. Can Luke get something, too?"

He shook his head. "I'm going home for a shower. I have to work today." He had had the presence of mind last night to let Jake know he wouldn't make it to the center this morning. "I'll be back around six. Do you want me to bring you anything? Maybe a sandwich?" The thought of eating anymore hospital food brought back awful memories of his own hospital stay.

Abby reached for the baby. "No thanks. I'll be hungry before you get here."

Allison smiled. "Being ravenously hungry is normal."

Abby's face screwed up in distress, and Luke suspected she was anxious to get back to her pre-baby weight.

"Your body needs the extra calories to make milk," Allison added.

After the nurse left, Abby slid over to make a spot for him on the bed. "Come sit with me before you leave."

Here it comes. She's going to bring up getting married. "About what you said before you fell asleep last night ..."

Her blue eyes met his, and he didn't want to look away. They couldn't avoid this conversation. "I know you want to be with me. And I know you feel bad that we can't live together right now. But Abby, your parents wouldn't support us, and I don't mean financially."

She opened her mouth to argue.

But he placed one finger over her lips. "They don't trust me. Not fully."

Tears tracked down her cheeks, wrenching Luke's heart out of his chest. "They need more time, time to be sure that I'm not going back to ... that I'm never going to use drugs again." He handed her two tissues, and she blew her nose. "We need to give them that time."

"I love you so much, Luke. *I* know you're going to stay clean. *I* believe in you." She gulped back a sob. "Why can't they trust *me*?"

He wiped fresh tears from her face with his thumb, but he could not erase the pain in her heart, pain he had caused. Careful not to disturb the baby sleeping with her head on

Abby's breast, he kissed Abby. She tasted sweet and salty from her crying, and he ached to claim her for forever. "Babe, they do trust you, but you can't control what I do. And we can't be together 24-7."

"How long do you think it's going to take for my parents to trust you?" Her eyes pleaded with him.

But he didn't have the answer, at least not one she wanted to hear.

"This isn't about them. It's about you and me and our baby."

"Babe—"

"I don't want to wait until we've finished school to be a family. So tell me, how long *do* you think it will take before my parents will give us their blessing?"

He resisted the urge to remind her that she hadn't even finished high school yet. "I'm not sure. A year maybe?"

"A year? That's too long." Her voice broke, and she started crying again.

Elise stirred and let out a wail. Abby moved her to the other breast, and a moment later, the baby suckled, eyes closed. Watching them, Luke fell more deeply in love with both his girls. He would move heaven and earth to make them happy, but so much lay beyond his control. "Let's take it one day at a time for a while."

Her blue eyes flashed with a moment of anger. "I don't need a big wedding, if that's what you're worried about."

"Abby, you know that isn't it. We can have whatever kind of wedding you want. But we need our parents' blessing first."

Abby cupped her hand around the back of his neck and kissed him, a kiss designed to remind him what he could have whenever he wanted. If he would agree to marry her now. Passion surged through him. Thoroughly frustrated, he pulled away, scooching back to the end of the bed. His eyes met hers in a plea. "Play fair, babe. Please."

"I don't want to play fair. I want you. I want you in my bed at night. And I want you with me, helping to take care of our daughter. I don't want to do this alone."

Guilt swept through him, bringing dark regrets and black hole desires. He remembered how easy it was to slip away from the pressure and pain. But, with God's help, Luke wouldn't make that choice ever again. "No more, Abby. Laying on the guilt doesn't change the facts."

"This wouldn't be happening if—"

"Go ahead. Say it. I know what you're thinking. If I weren't addict, you could have the life you want. Right now. But that's not how it is with us. And if you don't trust me enough to wait, to believe that we can have the life we both want—"

"No! I do trust you. I just don't want to be alone."

"You won't be alone. You'll have your mom and dad. And I'll be there as much as I can. You know that. This is killing me as much as it is you. But getting married right now is not the answer."

Elise wailed, her cry a painful reminder that everything that happened to him and Abby would affect their baby. "I don't want to fight with you, babe. I love you."

Abby bit her lower lip. Tears tracked her cheeks again. "I love you, Luke. I didn't mean to … I'm sorry. I'm just … my emotions are all over the place … like a roller coaster."

He tucked a strand of her hair behind her ear, and she leaned against his hand. Her eyes drew him in, but he didn't like the panic marring their blue beauty. "I'm going to head out. I'll be back in a couple of hours."

Abby reached up and cradling his face in her trembling hands, tugged his head down for a sweet see-you-later kiss. "I really am sorry. You know I didn't mean—"

"I know. I forgive you. We're good." He kissed the top of Elise's head, grabbed his coat from where he had flung it over a chair, and headed for the door. There wasn't anything more that he could say to make this easier for either of them. "Try to get some sleep while I'm gone."

"Yeah, I will."

One thought pressed in on him during the entire thirty minute drive to his parents. What if Abby really couldn't handle being a mom without him beside her? What if … if she decided giving up Elise was the only answer for them?

Luke couldn't let that happen. Because if they gave their child away, she might never forgive him, and he had no idea how he would forgive her.

*

Luke found his mother watering the plants in her sunroom. Soothing harp music filled the comfortable room, which was decorated in pale blues and greens. Mom was a firm believer in the calming properties of those particular colors. He wasn't entirely convinced, especially today. Exhausted and discouraged, he sank into a plaid chair and rested his elbows on his knees, his head in his hands.

"What's wrong?" The gentle touch of his mother's hand on his back roused him.

But when he looked up at her, he didn't even try to smile.

"Is something wrong with the baby? Is Abby okay?"

Instantly, he regretted distressing his mom. He didn't want to worry her, but he needed her advice. "Abby and the baby are fine. Abby promised to take a nap, and Elise was sleeping when I left the hospital."

His mother studied him, her expression grave. "Something's bothering you, Luke." She set her watering can on the glass coffee table then sat in a chair opposite him. "What's happened? If Abby and the baby are fine, then why are you so upset?"

How he wished she could fix this. All during his childhood, Mom had always come up with sensible plans, plans that convinced him that no matter how awful things might look, everything would work out. But he wasn't a child anymore. He was a grown man who had no idea how to take care of the woman he loved. The mother of his child. She should be able to count on him, but she couldn't, and that was killing him. "Abby wants to get married."

Mom sighed with relief. "Of course she does. She loves you, and she just gave birth to your child. Her emotions are going to be all over the place."

Luke studied his mother's relaxed features. How could she be so calm when he saw a tidal wave threatening to destroy all of his hopes and dreams? "Abby wants to get married tomorrow. We can't do that, Mom. Every time her dad looks at me ... he thinks—"

"He doesn't."

"Yes, he does. So do you. So does Dad. And Abby's mom, too. None of you are convinced that I won't ..." He couldn't even say the words. The devastation he had already wreaked by his selfish actions shamed him every time he thought of the horrible cycle of using and looking for his next fix. If he fell back into that life, which was no life at all, they would all be better off if he overdosed. Dark despair pulled at his sanity with a magnetic force nearly impossible to resist.

Jesus!

The light of God's forgiveness and keeping power instantly banished the bleak scenarios that had played out in his mind like a horror movie only a moment before. He let out a long breath. *Thank You, Jesus.*

Luke raked his hand through his hair. "Mom, what if Abby and I set a date? Even if it's more than a year from now. She needs to know that I'm committed to her and the baby. Setting a date would do that."

Mom's pensive expression stirred his doubts.

"I know I can't support her yet. I have at least five more semesters before I finish my business degree." The impossibility of their finances nearly suffocated the hope kindling in his heart. But he was determined to make Abby happy. "Maybe, if I found a better job, worked full time, and went to school part time ..."

His mother cupped her chin and laid one finger over her mouth the way she always did when she was exploring options or formulating a plan.

"Mom, what are you thinking?"

She smiled and patted his knee. "Let me talk to Dad."

Luke wanted to press her for details, but exhaustion clung to him like drenched clothes. He'd been through a storm with Abby, but if his mother had an idea ... "I'm going to shower and take a nap. If I'm not up by eight, pound on my door. I need to be at work by nine."

"Of course. There's leftover ham and cheese quiche if you want to eat breakfast before you shower."

He crossed the room to kiss her cheek. "Thanks, Mom. Have I told you lately how much I love you?"

"Not recently." She stood and pulled him into a brief hug then gave him a push toward the door.

With a much lighter heart, Luke headed into the kitchen. He couldn't wait for his work day to end so he could share his plan with Abby. Wearing his great-grandmother's emerald engagement ring hadn't been enough to ease her fears. Setting a wedding date would encourage her. Taking that concrete step would be good for him, too. Moving toward his long-term goal of being the husband and father he knew he could be, with God's help, made Luke want to shout as if he'd won a championship against an arch rival.

*

Abby couldn't take her eyes off Elise. She was so beautiful. At six pounds, her sweet, little face was perfect. Abby kissed the satiny smooth skin of her baby's cheek, the soft down of her light brown curls, and momentarily considered undressing her to kiss each one of her adorable toes, but she had fallen asleep. "Mommy loves you, baby girl," Abby whispered as she gently laid her daughter in the bassinet. "To the moon and back."

"Daddy loves you, too."

Luke's warm breath on her neck made her shiver, and she whirled to face him. His eyes sparkled with some secret he could scarcely wait to share.

"Hi, handsome." She had pushed him so hard that morning and regretted how unreasonable she'd been, but she felt more like flirting than apologizing. "You look good for a guy who slept in a chair last night and then worked all day."

He grinned. "I always knew you loved me for my looks and not my brain."

She laughed. Academically, Luke was as capable as she was. His grades had dropped after the accident—a direct result of his drug use. "Kiss me before someone walks in the door."

He lowered his face to hers, a teasing grin bringing out his dimples.

She wrapped her arms around his neck, easing him closer until their breaths mingled, and he pressed his lips to hers at last. She yielded instantly to his seeking tongue.

Voices outside her door signaled more visitors. Luke broke off the kiss. "I have something to ask you, as soon as we have a moment alone."

A blush warmed Abby's cheeks, and she reached for his hand. "I love you to the moon and back."

He kissed her nose. "To the moon and back."

It felt more like she had loved him to the brink of hell and back, but she would never say that out loud. She didn't need to. They both knew it was true.

"Hey, are you decent?" her dad cried.

Luke shot her a perplexed look.

"He means am I nursing the baby."

Luke smiled, amused.

But Abby understood and appreciated her dad's thoughtfulness. "The baby's sleeping. Come on in."

Her parents rushed into the room. Their exultant expressions reminded her of her little brother's face on Christmas morning. Sam held back, studying the baby as if she'd been dropped from another planet.

"Hey, Sam. How are you?"

"Good." He moved closer to the edge of the bed.

"Come closer so you can see her."

Sam peered at Elise. "She's so tiny."

Abby studied her brother. His expression, a mix of curiosity and hesitation prompted her to encourage him. "You can hold her, if you want."

Sam shook his head. "Later, when she's bigger."

"Well, I have to hold my grandbaby now." Mom picked up Elise and cradled her close. "I can't wait another second to kiss her," she announced as she pressed a kiss to the baby's cheek.

Abby laughed. "She just finished nursing, and I couldn't get a burp out of her. Maybe, you'll have better luck, Mom."

"Not yet." Dad held up his phone. "I want a picture of my three girls."

"Oh, yes. We need one we can enlarge for the stairwell."

"Where do you want us, Dad?"

"Sitting on the bed will be good."

Obediently, they took their places.

"I want both of you looking down at the baby." He snapped three pictures. "That's good. Now, give her back to Abby, Steph. Luke, sit next to Abby. I need one with the three of you."

After her father had taken several shots, Luke took a few with her and her parents. Then, Elise started to whimper. "Dad, let Mom burp her."

Dad shook his head. "Your mother has held her long enough. It's my turn now."

Watching her dad gently rubbing her daughter's back brought fresh tears to Abby's eyes. It seemed like anything and everything could make her cry. Was this normal? She would ask a nurse later, after everyone went home. Abby reached for her glass of water and drained it. She was so thirsty, which was good because the nurse insisted she drink an eight-ounce glass of water every time the baby nursed. Apparently, she needed to do this to stay hydrated and produce enough milk for Elise. That part of motherhood, Abby could handle. She wasn't so sure about the rest, especially the late-night feedings, which she would have to manage without Luke's help.

*

The following morning, Luke pulled his mom's SUV up to the front door of the hospital. Yesterday had not gone as he'd planned. Too many visitors had left no time for a private conversation. Today would be different. He was taking Abby and Elise home, her parents were both at work, and Sam was at school. Once, Elise settled in, Luke would talk with Abby about their future.

The valet, a twenty-something named Evan, approached Luke. "Give us about ten to fifteen minutes. We're checking out today."

Evan smiled as he took Luke's keys. "Sure thing."

Luke entered the hospital with mixed emotions. He understood Abby's frustration and disappointment. He, too, chafed against their circumstances, but if he could be patient, maybe she would follow his lead.

Look where you led her before.

The caustic thought tackled him to the ground, slamming him into that dark corner of his mind that he struggled to avoid. He wished God would wash his mind clean, the way Christ's blood had washed his heart clean the day Luke had finally surrendered his life to Him. Luke didn't want to remember the havoc his addiction had wrought in not only his life but in Abby's and his family's lives, too. But he didn't dare forget.

Forgetting would be ... would make him vulnerable to the nagging lie—*just one hit can't hurt you, man. You can control it. You need something to take the edge of all of this pressure.*

"Name, please."

Luke stared at the security guard waiting behind the admission desk. "Luke Bradford, here to pick up Abby Collins and Elise Bradford."

The guard smiled, typed in the information in his computer then handed Luke a visitor pass. "Bringing your baby home?"

Luke nodded.

"Congratulations. Have a nice day."

"Thank you. You have a nice day, too." What he really wanted to say was, I will because I'm bringing my wife and baby home today. But he wasn't Abby's husband. Not yet. His conversation with his dad had gone far better than Luke ever hoped. He still didn't have a job that would cover their expenses, but he could put a roof over his family's heads.

Alone in the elevator, Luke prayed silently. He asked God to help him be strong for Abby and to silence Satan's voice in his head. Condemnation and temptation weighed Luke down on what should have been one of the happiest days of his life.

Resist the devil, and he will flee.

Under his breath, Luke declared, "I'm doing this God's way. No more using drugs to get me through."

The oppressive pressure pounded in his head like a migraine. "Jesus, help me," Luke whispered. A reverent peace settled his heart and mind just as the elevator doors slid open.

He couldn't believe who was waiting to get on the elevator. "Pastor Schwartz. Wow, I didn't expect to see you this morning."

"Good morning, Luke." Abby's pastor extended his hand. "I was hoping to run into you today."

Luke stepped from the elevator to shake the man's hand. "Sir, I realize we were supposed to meet with you yesterday, but the baby—"

"There's plenty of time, son. Satan pressures people, but God leads. Abby invited me to her parents for dinner on Thursday night. She said that works with your schedule, right?"

Filled with gratitude, Luke nodded. "It does. But I'd actually like to meet with you before then."

The pastor studied Luke for a moment. How much had Abby already shared with the man?

"How about an early breakfast, say about seven? There's a little diner in the plaza at Main and Transit that makes the best spinach and feta omelets."

Breakfast Luke could manage. He didn't have to be at work until nine forty-five. "I know the place. I'll be there."

Pastor Schwartz gripped Luke's shoulder. "You're in my prayers, son. All of you."

Luke stood alone for a moment after the pastor got into an elevator heading down to the main floor. Luke would rather talk things over with Jake. The older man might not understand the daily struggles Luke faced, but he had known Abby since she was a baby. Talking to Pastor Schwartz would be a good thing, maybe even a very good thing.

CHAPTER TWENTY

Abby had cried three times since breakfast. Frustrated with herself and with the harsh, unforgiving bathroom lights, she frowned at her face in the mirror. Luke would be here any second. A minimalist when it came to makeup, Abby dabbed concealer under her eyes then blended it with tinted moisturizer. Her pupils were constricted, making her blue irises appear unusually large, but at least the red splotches from crying were no longer visible. She ran a brush through her hair and tried to see herself as Luke would. Would he know how much she was struggling? She hoped not. He had enough to deal with.

"Abby, are you almost ready?" Luke tapped on the bathroom door. "I have Elise all bundled up and secured in her car seat.

He'd done all of that? How long had he been here? Apparently, she'd been so lost in her own thoughts she hadn't heard him moving around in the hospital room.

"Shouldn't we get going before the baby starts fussing to eat or something?"

Abby checked her face one last time in the mirror. Her smile looked forced. Knowing she wouldn't be able to hide her distress from Luke, she opened the door, walked into his outstretched arms, and pressed her face against his chest. The steady beat of his heart slowed her own until she could speak. "I'm ready to go home."

He stepped back, lifted her chin with one finger, and stared into her eyes.

She willed him not to say anything that would make her cry. "Thanks for getting Elise ready. I didn't even hear you come in. Did you let the nurse know we were ready to go? They won't let me walk out, you know. I have to sit in a wheelchair. Isn't that silly?"

He silenced her with a kiss, and she wrapped her arms around his muscled back.

A man's voice interrupted them. "Are you folks ready to go?"

Luke broke off their kiss, and Abby stepped out of his embrace. "We're all set." She picked up her overnight bag and sat in the wheelchair, allowing the attendant to place her feet on the footrests. Luke carried Elise in the car seat, and Abby glanced around the room to make sure she hadn't forgotten anything. Thank goodness, her parents had taken all of the flowers home last night. "I'm ready."

But she wasn't. Not really. How could she possibly be ready to care for her baby without Luke's help? She hadn't even finished her schoolwork yet. Who would take care of Elise when Abby went in to school to take the last of her final exams? More importantly, who would hold her at night when she was terrified that she wouldn't be a good mother?

Luke studied her for a moment. His eyes declared he had something to tell her, something he hoped would make her happy, something he couldn't share right now. Carrying their daughter, he led the way to the elevators. "Come on, baby girl. Daddy and Mommy are taking you home."

*

Elise hadn't uttered a peep during the car ride home, but the moment Abby lifted their daughter out of the car seat, she opened her sweet blue eyes. Right now, they were the exact shade as her daddy's, but the nurse had warned her that babies' eyes often changed as they got a little older. Abby hoped Elise's eyes would stay exactly the same as Luke's, as blue as the prettiest summer sky.

Elise screwed up her tiny mouth, a precursor to a cry so piercing Abby had wondered more than once how so loud a sound could come from such a little person. Having read in several places how important a mother's smile is to a baby's well-being, Abby smiled down at her, hoping Elise didn't realize how sad her mother really was.

Luke caught her gaze, kissed her cheek, and patted the baby's back. "I'll make some lunch. How does tomato soup and grilled cheese sandwiches sound?"

Abby was ravenous, a normal consequence of producing milk for her baby. At least some things in her life were normal. "Good. Maybe, I can get Elise to nurse now, so she doesn't interrupt our lunch. Our daughter has a sixth sense about when her mommy is eating."

Luke chuckled.

Abby scowled. "It's not funny. Most hot foods taste better hot." That didn't come out the way she intended, and Luke laughed again. Deciding she'd better use the bathroom before settling in to nurse, Abby handed the baby to Luke. "You hold her for a few minutes."

He grinned. "Glad to." He tickled Elise's chin. "Hey, baby girl, Daddy loves you to the moon and back."

Mesmerized, Abby watched the enraptured look on Luke's face as he held their daughter. "I see I've been replaced in your heart."

"No way. My heart is big enough for both of my girls."

His smile chased away her gloom. Perched on the arm of the couch, she leaned in to kiss his cheek. "Have I told you today how much I love you?"

"Not yet." With a mischievous twinkle in his eyes, he captured her hand and twirled her so that she plopped onto the couch beside him. He drew her into the crook of his free arm. "I love you, too, Abby. I always have, and I always will."

A dark image of Luke with a needle piercing a vein in the crook of his arm formed in her mind. She frowned. There had been many days when she had doubted his love. Would he ever cause her to doubt him again? Ashamed of her abrupt mood swing, she averted her eyes to avoid his scrutiny.

But Luke cupped her chin and turned her face toward him.

His distressed expression told her all. He had seen her heart in her eyes. "Luke, I have to go to the bathroom before we start this conversation."

Several moments later, when she returned to the living room, Abby found Luke crouched on the thick carpet, the baby lying on her back on a soft blanket with her daddy blowing raspberries on her bare belly. Elise's little face screwed up into an expression that might be a precursor to laughing or crying. Abby wasn't sure which to expect. Then she remembered that babies don't laugh before four months old. Would they all be living together by then? Probably not. Luke would miss so many firsts.

She knelt beside them and captured Luke's face in her hands. "This is what I want." Tears pricked her eyes, and she blinked them back. "Moments like this. Every single day."

Luke turned his head and pressed a warm kiss against her palm. "I know, babe. Me, too."

She didn't want to burden him, but she couldn't hide the

truth from him, even if she tried. He knew her too well for that. She took a deep breath then plunged ahead. "I'm scared, Luke. I've been … depressed. What if I get postpartum depression and can't take care of Elise? I've been researching it on the internet and—"

"That's not going to happen. But if it does, we'll deal with it. You have your family and mine to help you." He brushed away the tear tracking down her cheek. "And I plan on being here every day."

"It's not the same."

Elise started to cry, too. Was she already picking up on her parents' distress? Abby picked up the baby, carried her to the couch, and positioned the nursing pillow comfortably, then lifted her sweater and unhooked her nursing bra. The baby latched on immediately.

Luke watched as Elise suckled as though she hadn't eaten all day. Fighting a blush, Abby stroked her daughter's silky hair.

"I want you to be able to count on me, babe." Luke placed one hand on her thigh. "But even if we were married and living together, I would still have to go to school and work."

"I know that." She despised the whine in her voice. "Look, I don't want to talk about this while I'm nursing the baby. Let's wait until she takes a nap." She was over a week behind in all of her subjects, but schoolwork could wait a few more days. She had just had a baby, after all. And she and Luke really needed to get on the same page.

Luke studied her a moment. "All right. But we need to talk. I have something to tell you that I hope will make you feel better about everything." For a nanosecond, he waited for her response then kissed her on the cheek and headed out to the kitchen to make their lunch.

When they were alone, Abby massaged Elise's back as

she continued to nurse. "I'm sorry I messed things up for you, baby girl. If I had only known …"

"Known what?" Luke stood in the archway, his broad shoulders signifying steady strength. His expression was inscrutable.

"I thought you were making lunch."

"You're out of tomato soup. Do you want cream of broccoli or Italian wedding soup with your grilled cheese?"

"No broccoli. It might give the baby gas."

Luke smiled, his dimples coming out in full force. "See, you're already thinking like a mom."

*

Taking care not to awaken her, Abby laid Elise in the pink bassinet a few feet from her bed. Luke had ensconced himself on "his" side of the bed. With his hair slightly askew, he looked irresistibly handsome. Abby ached to rake her hands through his hair and hold him in her arms as they'd done so many times before, but she switched on the baby monitor, picked up the remote, and held her hand out to Luke. "We can't talk in here. She'll wake up."

Luke winked at her then laughed outright. "You just had a baby, remember? What do you take me for, a selfish cad?"

She blushed. "I didn't mean that." Why did he insist on reminding her of what they could no longer have? Not until after they were married. There had been days when the temptation had nearly overwhelmed her convictions. Which was one of the reasons she wanted to get married sooner rather than later. Backtracking in their relationship, especially since they had no idea when they could have the wedding she had always dreamed of, drove her crazy. Luke's eyes, dark with desire, didn't help.

He clasped her hand and pulled her onto the bed.

She shook her head. "You're just making it harder. On

both of us."

"Just let me hold you for a minute, and then we'll go downstairs." Without waiting for her reply, he eased her onto his lap.

Unable to resist the comfort of his arms, she rested her head on his shoulder and kissed his neck.

He moaned. "If you don't stop …"

She lifted her head and studied his dark blue eyes. It had been so long. Too long. She jumped off the bed, putting a safe distance between them. "Let's talk in the kitchen."

He nodded.

His boyish look of disappointment and resignation made her want to kiss him until neither one of them could breathe. "Luke Bradford, don't you dare give me that look!" She grabbed his hand and yanked him off the bed.

"What look?"

"The one you always use to get what you want."

He laughed but sobered immediately. "What I want is to talk to you about our future." He slipped his arm around her waist and led her from the room without waking the baby.

*

A few moments later they were sitting across from each other at the kitchen table, a pot of berry herbal tea between them. Satisfied that the bags had steeped long enough, she filled two mugs.

Luke screwed up his face at the red-violet tea. "You really expect me to drink that stuff?"

"If you don't like it, make coffee for yourself." She gestured to the Keurig on the gleaming countertop. "There's at least three different k-cup flavors."

He shook his head. "For you, I'll be a good sport and try it." He took one taste, grimaced, and marched to the coffeemaker. "How can you drink that stuff?" he grumbled as he waited for his coffee to brew.

She laughed. "I'd rather have coffee, but the lactation specialist warned me that consuming caffeine might make Elise wake up more during the night. I don't want to find out if she's right. Getting up twice is enough for me."

"Twice? You must be exhausted." He stirred a generous amount of sugar into his coffee and reclaimed his seat, dragging the chair close to her. He touched her arm. "Babe, I have news that I think will make you happier."

She slid her chair beyond his reach and crossed her arms over her chest. "You already said that before lunch. So, are you going to tell me? Or do you want me to guess?"

A startled look was his only response.

Her hand flew to her mouth. When had she become so sarcastic? "I'm sorry, Luke. I don't mean to take my frustration out on you, but *nothing* has turned out the way I always imagined it would." She loved him, needed him, wanted to be his wife. Most of all, she wanted to raise their daughter together, under the same roof. "Do you really think we can make it, Luke? Can we make a good life together? In spite of … everything?"

"Yes. I do. But you need to believe it, too."

She wanted to get out of her chair, sit on his lap, and kiss away the pain she'd put in his eyes. Frustrated that she couldn't conquer her doubts, she straightened her back and uncrossed her arms. "I'm trying, Luke."

He smiled then—not his full-dimples smile, but an encouraging one that prompted her to smile back.

"I know it's been brutal. But we have a beautiful, healthy baby girl. God's been so good to us." Luke leaned across the corner of the table and touched Abby's cheek. "We're going to be together, sooner than I thought."

"I want that, Luke. It's all I think about."

He captured her face in his strong hands and planted a quick kiss on her mouth.

"Luke, you look like a kid on the last day of school. What's going on?"

"My grandparents have decided to buy a house in Florida. They don't want their house here to be empty, but they don't want to sell it because it's been in our family for three generations. Abby, we can live there, rent-free until we get on our feet. You, me, and Elise."

Abby had only met his grandparents a few times, and they were willing to let her and Luke live in their house? It was wonderful and impossible. "That's so generous, but, honey, we need more than a place to live."

His eyes pleaded with her to believe in him.

But she had no words to reassure him. Not now with their daughter needing so much from them both. "We need money for food, and utilities, and gas. We need money to take care of our baby."

Luke's fingers trailed through her hair, and her senses stirred at his gentle touch.

"I know that, babe. I just need a little more time to figure that part out."

She leaned against his hand and willed herself not to cry again. How many times had she cried today, and it wasn't even two o'clock in the afternoon? She bit her lower lip.

Luke studied her, his eyes concerned. Was he assessing her emotional state? She wanted to be strong for him, to believe everything she ever wanted was still possible.

"So, when do you want to get married?" he asked.

"I can't figure that out right this second. There's a lot of things we have to think about."

An amorous twinkle sparkled in his eyes. "Then, don't think right now." He lowered his head until their lips met.

The pressure of his mouth on hers urged her to yield— yield to his kiss and yield to his plans. She wrapped her arms around his neck, stood, and stepped into his embrace. With her body pressed against his, she believed that everything would work out. Eventually.

But when exactly would eventually be? She'd been very short on patience recently. And the reason was upstairs asleep in her bedroom.

The piercing wail of their baby over the monitor interrupted them.

Luke broke off the kiss. Disappointment flashed across his face, followed immediately by acceptance. "Our girl needs her mommy. And her daddy." He took Abby's hand and led her out of the kitchen, but stopped at the bottom of the stairs. "We'll pick a date soon, right?"

Elise cried louder. Abby glanced up the stairs then met Luke's gaze. "Okay. I trust you to figure everything out."

"You do?"

Shocked by the moisture welling in his eyes, she caressed his face. "I do."

*

Contrary to what she had dreaded, her baby blues lifted by the end of her second week at home with Elise. Luke had been faithful to his word. He stopped by nearly every morning before heading to school or work, and he spent several hours with them each night, sometimes rocking the baby or driving her around the neighborhood, nestled snuggly in her car seat until she drifted off to sleep, while Abby sat at her desk, completing the last of her high school coursework. Rather than dragging, the weeks leading up to her graduation had zipped past.

She'd bought a new dress for the ceremony, a deep rose that accented her blue eyes and brown hair. Rather than opting for curls that would be limp long before her party that evening, Abby accepted her sleek, straight hair. Her fingers deftly created a perfect French braid while Elise continued to nap in her crib. At nearly two months old, she had settled into a semi-predictable routine, and Abby's energy level had begun to rebound. She slipped the gold locket around her neck then opened it. Inside precious faces smiled up at her from two pictures, one of Luke and the other of Elise. He had given it to her, her very first Mother's Day gift.

He'd accepted a position as a Math tutor at the community college, a job that paid three times as much per hour as his retail job had. To celebrate quitting Abercrombie, Luke had cooked a special dinner for the two of them. With the house all to themselves thanks to the thoughtfulness of her future mother-in-law, Luke had grilled steaks, zucchini, and potato wedges on his parents' patio. She smiled at the memory of him grinning in pure delight as she pronounced the meal "the best she had ever eaten." Only one thing marred their happiness that night—their mutual struggle to remain true to their agreement to wait until their wedding night to be together.

Balancing school, work, and family, they hadn't had much time alone recently, which made their promise a little easier to keep. Luke tutored thirty hours a week. He was saving every penny, except for a minimal allowance and, of course, gas money. He wanted them to have several thousand dollars in savings before their wedding on the Saturday following Thanksgiving.

Her wedding. Her broad smiled reflected in the mirror shone from a joy and gratitude she could scarcely contain. She and Luke would be married in five months. In her girlhood dreams, she had always imagined getting married after college, but Elise had changed that. Combined with the on-site day care provided by the community college and four grandparents who adored her, Elise would be well-cared for while Abby and Luke worked on their degrees. Their path *now* differed drastically from her original dream, but that was okay.

Her cell vibrated on the dresser top, and she snatched it up before the rumbling noise could awaken her daughter. "Hi, Luke."

"Why are you whispering?"

"Why do you *think* I'm whispering? I'm trying to get ready in peace. Are you on your way?"

"I'm heading to my car now. Are you ready for your big day?"

Abby paused to consider her answer. After giving birth, graduation day paled as a milestone. Still, she'd worked hard to get here. "I'm ready."

*

Abby smiled as she received her Regents diploma and shook Principal Williamson's hand. Her mom snapped several pictures, then winked to let Abby know she'd gotten enough shots. Heat suffused her cheeks until she acknowledged that her mom was not the first, nor would she be the last parent, to hold up the ceremony.

Elise's soft whimper drew Abby's attention to Luke and the baby. Hopefully, she wouldn't start wailing. When Abby looked back on this day, the last thing she wanted to remember was the embarrassment of her milk letting down and hoping her graduation gown could conceal the evidence that she was the only girl in her graduating class who had become a mother in her senior year. Much to her surprise, she didn't feel judged by her classmates. Several girls and even a few boys had approached her before the ceremony to applaud her courage.

"It wasn't me. It was all God, and my family." When she tried to tell them about Luke's help, a few people shook their heads in disbelief, and one guy had the audacity to say, "I can't believe you're still with that loser."

Abby restrained her temper. People could be so judgmental. God had shown her that people who believed they were perfect on their own, without having accepted His grace and forgiveness, often cast the first stone at others. "I know you don't mean to be unkind," she replied to the teen she'd known since kindergarten. "I'll pray for you."

"Pray for me?" he sputtered. "I don't need that."

"I'm sorry you feel that way, Tom. I hope you enjoy graduation day."

A nudge from Lisa jarred Abby back to the moment at hand.

"Stand up, Abby. The ceremony's over. Mr. Williamson wants a photo of all of us for the school website."

Pictures took another ten minutes, then Abby hurried off to join Luke and Elise, her family. Grandma Collins had insisted on hosting dinner at her house, even though Abby had tried to persuade her mother to nix that idea for Luke's sake.

Reaching across the console, Luke took Abby's hand and placed it on his thigh.

For a brief moment, she regretted setting a November wedding date. She missed him so much, more now that she was fully recovered from giving birth. Five months seemed like forever. She sighed, but the expression in Luke's eyes jilted her out of her selfish impatience. "Are you okay?"

He started the engine.

Wasn't he going to answer her question? That couldn't be good. She should have insisted they celebrate at home. Her parents' house was smaller, but they could have easily rented a tent to set up in their backyard. Her mother's roses bloomed in a riot of reds, yellows, pinks, purples, and white. Mom kept the gardens encircling the fenced yard in pristine condition, and their flagstone patio could have accommodated a buffet table. The backyard was peaceful, familiar, languid with new happy memories she and Luke had made together with their baby. Why hadn't Abby pushed harder for what would be best for her and Luke?

He hadn't stepped into her grandparents' house since Christmas day, the day Sam had caught him stealing Grandpa's pain pills. Why, oh why hadn't she considered how hard this would be for Luke?

He shifted the car into reverse, but she gripped his forearm. "Not yet. We need to talk."

He cut the engine and turned to face her, his expression resigned. "Talking about it won't help, Abby."

She slid to the edge of her seat and reached up to enclose Luke's face in her hands. She opened her mouth to disagree but kissed him instead. His hands cupped her head, holding her, drinking in her kiss, drawing strength from her until she melted into him, and they were one, the world fading away. When he lifted his lips from hers, she felt bereft. A tear spilled over her lower lashes before she could stop it.

He brushed it away with his thumb, and she shivered at the familiar caress. "I love you, Luke. We don't have to go if it's too hard for you. Really we don't."

He shook his head, his mouth forming a tight line in his tense face. "I have to go back eventually. Now is a good time, when your whole family will be congratulating you, and oohing and aahing over Elise."

"But—"

"No buts. I'll stay downstairs and then—"

"Luke everyone knows you've been clean for six months."

He sighed and took her hand in his. "They've heard that, babe, but I don't know if they believe it."

"Then show them your NA coin."

"I could, but I'm pretty sure your Uncle Ed still thinks I'm not good enough for you, and a six months recovery chip isn't going to change his mind."

Abby stared into Luke's eyes. The expression clouding their blue depths would be inscrutable to everyone but her. "You are my choice, Luke Bradford. And don't you ever forget it. My family will ... accept you ..."

"And forgive me eventually? Is that what you were going to say?"

Tears pooled in her eyes again. "Do you need their forgiveness? Isn't it enough that I forgive you?"

"Yes. And no. We're asking them all to entrust me with you, and with the baby. I don't know if they're ready to do that."

She touched his face. He turned and pressed a kiss to her palm. How she wanted to lie in his arms for a while and forget everyone but the two of them, but they couldn't escape this by surrendering to an hour of passion. "They have five months before our wedding to get used to the idea. Then you'll have been clean for almost a year."

He smiled at the confidence in her tone. "We better get going before your family starts to worry, before your grandmother starts complaining that her beautiful catered feast is getting cold."

Abby smiled at his attempt to lighten the mood. "Promise me one thing first."

"Sure, I'll lasso the moon for you." He grinned, that boyish expression that first made her fall in love with him. "Do you want a few stars, too?"

Her steady gaze sobered him.

"Promise me that as soon as you want to leave, you'll let me know."

"Okay, Abby, but we need to stay for a couple of hours at least. It is your graduation dinner after all, and everyone wants to celebrate your accomplishment."

CHAPTER TWENTY-ONE

Abby opened her grandparents' ornately carved front door without knocking, crying out, "We're here," before Luke could fortify his nerves with one more prayer. He followed meekly, carrying Elise in her car seat. He would forge a raging river to protect them. He could face her family, even if they met him with steely disdain. He wouldn't blame them if they did that and worse.

Wearing a bright smile, Annabelle Collins swept into the foyer, her lavender dress swirling around her legs like the dancer she'd been before Ethan had captured her heart and changed her dreams—Abby's way of telling her grandparents' love story.

At that thought, Luke smiled. Until he imagined what his own granddaughter might have to say about her grandparents' love affair. Fresh shame washed over him, but he resisted its quicksand pull. "Hi, Mrs. Collins."

"Hello, Luke, welcome."

He blinked, met her keen eyes, and saw cautious acceptance. It was more than he had expected. He was about to thank her, but she turned her attention to Abby.

"Congratulations, sweetheart." She kissed Abby's cheek.

"We're so proud of you."

Abby kissed her back. "Thanks, Grandma. That means a lot."

Annabelle pulled Abby into a hug and shot Luke a commanding look over her granddaughter's shoulder. "You deserve the best."

Her comment was clearly meant for him. He nodded to let her know he received the message.

Her lips parted in the tiniest smile, then she squatted until she perched eye level with the car seat then brushed her fingers over Elise's silken cheeks. The baby stirred but did not awaken. "Let's get our baby girl out of her car seat. I haven't held her for over a week."

Abby's grandmother had to be seventy-five, but her exuberance made her sound like a girl of half her age.

Luke set the car seat on the bench, proceeded to unbuckle his daughter, and placed her in her great-grandmother's waiting arms. To his astonishment, she stood on her toes and planted a lipstick kiss on his cheek, effectively allaying much of his anxiety.

"We were all wondering when you would ever get here. Did you have to stop to nurse her?"

Abby laughed. "No, thank goodness. But she'll probably be hungry soon. Is dinner ready? Maybe I can eat before she wakes up."

A heavy hand on Luke's shoulder made him blank out on the rest of the conversation between Abby and her grandmother. He watched them head toward the backdoor and the expansive yard and gardens to greet their waiting guests.

Determined to make the best day possible for Abby, Luke pivoted and came face to face with her grandfather. *Here it comes, the well-deserved lecture, maybe even an ultimatum.*

The inscrutable expression in the man's gray-blue eyes gave no clue to his thoughts, and Luke's old craving reared its evil head. He stomped it down with a single-word prayer, *Jesus,* and felt his muscles relax. The coin resting in the bottom of his pocket reminded him that with faith and courage miracles happen one day at time. "Hello, Mr. Collins."

"It's good to see you, son." Ethan smiled.

Luke smiled back. He wanted to thank the man for letting him back in his home, but he couldn't get those words out. "Good to see you, too, sir."

"How's school? Abby tells us you're very busy with your tutoring job."

"I am."

"But you still make time to see her and the baby every night. I'm glad to see that you're getting your priorities straight."

Luke processed the elderly man's words, which contained both a compliment and a warning. "Yes, sir. Abby and the baby come first, and they always will."

The man's gaze held Luke's. "None of us are perfect, Luke. Some of us hide our faults better, but we still have them."

Luke studied Ethan. Was this olive branch his way of extending forgiveness as well? Luke had to know. "Sir, about last Christmas ... can you ever forgive me for stealing those pills?"

Ethan's expression softened. "If my granddaughter can forgive you, so can I." He extended his hand.

Luke stared in disbelief. Could it possibly be that easy?

The man gripped Luke's hand and yanked him into a hug. For a man approaching eighty, Ethan Collins possessed surprising strength.

Uncomfortable with this unexpected display of affection,

Luke clapped the older man's back. "Thank you, sir."

Ethan released his hold and stepped back until several feet separated them. "You're family now. That's what family does. Forgive and forget."

How could any of them forget all he had done to feed his addiction? It didn't seem possible. Impossible for mere human beings, that was certain.

"I can see by the expression on your face, son, *you* don't think we can forget. Am I right?"

"Yes, sir." Defeat weighed those words, and once again, despair knocked at the door of his mind. "Not a day goes by that I don't remember some disgusting, horrible thing I did."

The pained expression on the man's lined face did nothing to alleviate the far-reaching effects of Luke's addiction. Had he been wrong to hope, wrong to let Abby believe they could actually build a life together, in spite of the cataclysmic fallout he had caused?

"Follow me into the kitchen, son. I want to share something with you."

Luke did as the elderly man asked. Without asking, Ethan poured two tall glasses of iced tea, handed one to Luke, and exited the kitchen. He didn't ask where they were headed but was genuinely surprised moments later to find himself in a bookshelf-lined study. Ethan lowered himself onto a dark brown, leather couch and gestured for Luke to join him.

Luke wasn't sure he was ready for this conversation, but avoiding it would only magnify and prolong his anxiety. He sat stiffly at the opposite end of the comfortable couch and waited for Abby's grandfather to begin.

The man lifted a worn Bible from a mahogany end table and opened it to a bookmarked place. He met Luke's gaze with a stern expression. "You need to hear this, Luke."

He had only started studying the Bible eight months ago, during his first days at Ellis Rehab. Was there something important he had missed, something that would silence his doubts and fears once and for all? "Go on, sir. If there's something God wants me to know, I want to hear it."

A frown deepened the lines in the man's weathered face. "Not until you stop calling me sir."

"What do you want me to call you?" Luke resisted the urge to squirm like a third-grader.

"Ethan? Grandpa?"

Luke released a nervous laugh and shook his head. Both seemed altogether too familiar. "Mr. Collins?"

The older man nodded. "I'll settle for that. For now. But after you and my granddaughter get married, you'll have to decide between Grandpa or Ethan."

"Granddad?"

"That'll do." Ethan sipped his tea, his keen eyes studying Luke.

Surprisingly, Luke's anxiety disappeared entirely. Whatever the older man wanted to share would make all of the difference in his world. "So, what do you want to read to me?"

"It's from the third chapter of Philippians, verses thirteen and fourteen. 'Brethren, I count not myself to have apprehended ...' None of us have arrived at the place where God wants us to be, Luke. Not even the people you *think* have it altogether."

Luke opened his mouth to argue.

But the older man held up one hand. "'But this one thing I do, forgetting those things which are behind, and reaching forth unto those things which are before, I press toward the mark of the high calling of God in Christ Jesus.'"

Luke tried to digest the words, to figure out how he could

possibly follow what appeared to be a clear directive, a way to live that would please the Lord.

Ethan shook his head in dismay. "Once more, I can see that either you don't believe this verse applies to you, or you don't think you can do what it's asking. Am I right?"

Crushed by a tsunami of shame-filled memories, Luke bent over, his elbows on his knees and his head in his hands. Tears welled in his eyes and trailed down his hands. He had asked for forgiveness, over and over, so why did he still feel so vile and worthless?

Killing yourself is the only way out.

That's a lie. God has a good plan for me.

Luke's shoulders shook with the struggle and with sobs that racked his soul. *Jesus, help me. Please.*

A hand on his back and whispered words of prayer drew Luke from the precipice of destruction. He raised his face to the older man and saw tender understanding where he most deserved condemnation.

"You've sought God's forgiveness many times, but I suspect you haven't fully accepted His forgiveness."

It was true. Forgiveness was an unwrapped gift with the potential to transform his life, if only Luke had the courage to accept it. Abby's grandfather laid his right hand over Luke's, the weight of it grounding him in this place, in this moment.

"Christ's blood washes you clean. He died in your place. He took your punishment."

The words came like soft rain watering the broken places of Luke's heart with hope.

"It's time you stopped punishing yourself, son. God's love makes you a new person, the person He created you to be before the foundation of the world. God, and God alone, will give you the strength to do what he asks of you, including forgetting every evil thing you've ever done. Especially that. God's strength in you is strongest when you realize how utterly helpless you are."

That Luke understood. "Thank you. Ethan."

"You're welcome." He clapped a hand on Luke's shoulder, closed his eyes, and began to pray that Luke would accept forgiveness and forgetfulness. "And, Father, make us both the men You want us to be, today and every day because the people we love are depending on us."

*

Abby could tell there was something different about Luke the moment she spotted him with her grandfather, the two of them striding in her direction like men on a mission. She was rocking the baby to sleep on the swing several yards away, but she couldn't miss the glow of excitement on his face, an expression she had not seen since his days as Easton High's star quarterback. At first, she couldn't name it for what it was. Then it came to her. Joyous expectation shone from his every feature, like a heavenly glow, almost the way she imagined Moses must have looked after he had been on the mountain with God.

Grandpa pressed a quick, gentle kiss to her forehead. "Congratulations, Abby. Your grandmother and I are so proud of you."

"Thank you, Grandpa."

His fingers brushed Elise's cheek where she lay pressed against Abby's shoulder. The baby sighed in response to the sweet caress. "I'll leave the three of you alone for a few minutes. Grandma probably needs me to do something for her." He shot a wink in Luke's direction.

Momentarily startled, Abby struggled to catch up to whatever had transpired between them. The two men exchanged a conspiratorial glance.

Grandpa grasped Luke's upper arm. "Happy wife, happy life."

Luke nodded then lowered himself gently to sit beside her without awakening Elise. "My plan exactly." The length of his thigh pressed against Abby's, familiar, possessive, welcome.

She giggled. "You'll find out that many decisions are that simple."

Luke smiled and took her hand.

Still feeling mystified by this unexpected ... something— she couldn't quite name it, Abby needed a moment to process this change in Luke. She watched her grandfather walk away. His stride conveyed the eagerness of a young lover. Grandma didn't need his help. He simply wanted to let her know he was available for anything she might need on this busy day. Two servers carrying silver trays of appetizers mingled among the fifty or so guests. Abby smiled as her grandfather came up behind her grandmother and slipped one arm around her waist. The brief kiss her grandparents exchanged made Abby long for a lifetime of loving Luke.

"What are you thinking, babe?" Luke whispered in her ear, his breath tickling her skin.

All of her senses seemed to be heightened. The sweet, clean smell of her baby's satin skin and silky hair, the fragrance of Grandma's English garden in full bloom, the soft whir of humming bird wings feasting from several strategically placed feeders, the accelerating beat of her own heart at Luke's solid presence beside her—he'd bought a new spicy cologne, and its heady scent—all of this awakened her deepest desires. "I want that to be us someday. I want our grandchildren to see us as models of what a good marriage looks like. I want you to come up to me in forty or fifty years and slip your arm around my waist and pull me close like

Grandpa just did Grandma. And I want you to be as crazy in love with me then as you are now."

He grinned, then leaned in to kiss her neck, once, twice, thrice. He met her gaze with a serious one of his own. "That's a tall order."

No doubt, no fear, no dread marred his tone. What exactly *had* transpired between Luke and her grandfather?

"You really believe we could ... we could love each other for forty or fifty years? That we could ..."

He cupped her chin and eased her face toward him until their eyes locked in a mutual promise. "Abigail Marie Collins I promise that with God's help, I will love you as much and more than I do right now, every single day for the rest of our lives. I promise that we will face every trial, every hardship, and every sorrow together. I will never lead you where God would not have us go. I will never give you cause to doubt me or any course of action I might take. I promise you will always be able to trust me, not because I have been strong enough to kick my addiction, but because I am trusting God for everything we need."

Caught up in the wave of his words, Abby blurted, "Then let's get married tomorrow."

He brought her face so close to his that their noses touched. "As much as I would love that, I still need to be able to support you and the baby."

Frustrated, Abby backed away. She wanted to voice her agreement. "We don't need much."

"We need more than you think. I've already worked out a budget. Trust me, babe, I can't support you yet. But I'm getting closer."

She brought her mouth close to his. "Kiss me then, so I'll remember what I have to look forward to."

His eyes darkened, and she felt the color rise to her

cheeks. Flirting would have to be enough for a while longer.

*

Other than brief conversations at the center on Saturdays, and sometimes, the occasional Sunday, when Luke volunteered to share his story with the residents, he and Jake had not had time to catch up. Seated at a wrought iron table outside Panera Bread, Luke forked a mouthful of salad greens, grains, and chicken into his mouth. Silently, he thanked God for all this man had done for him. The sun heated Luke's back, and condensation coated his tall cup of iced coffee. It was a typical western New York day in early July, but poised to make a critical decision, he sensed an updraft of change in the humid air, a change that exhilarated him.

Jake bit into his turkey and avocado sandwich. He studied Luke, and a slow smile spread across his tanned face. "You look good, man."

What he meant, of course, was that Luke no longer had that haggard look of a heroin addict. His skin was clear and his cheeks fleshed out, a physical manifestation of honest work and wholesome R and R, most of which consisted of long walks with Elise, either in her stroller or the baby pack. His daughter liked the baby pack best. He did, too. The pressure of her warm, little body against his chest kept him grounded in a way nothing ever had before. Not even his love for Abby had done that. Pricked by self-rebuke, he resisted the pull of self-flagellation, a dead-end road. He loved both of his girls with all of his heart, and he thanked God for them every day. "I've been clean for six months and eight days."

Jake took another bite of his sandwich. "No slipups?"

Amazingly, no. Not even a close call. He had avoided the places and people that populated that life that was no life at all. "None. Checking back into Ellis after being home less than a month was tough, but it was the right choice."

"Have you been going to NA meetings?"

"Yeah, I got my sixth month coin. I started out going every day, but since Elise was born, I'm down to twice a week. I check in with my sponsor, you know, text, call, at least once a day. Lately, I find my strength on my knees with my Bible open to the Psalms." If he'd been talking to anyone other than Jake, Luke might have feared being judged a fanatic, or he might have felt the need to explain. Instead, he said what he'd come to say. "I don't think I'm meant to be an addiction counselor."

Jake's steady eyes showed no surprise, only acceptance. "What *do* you want to do?"

Luke grinned. "Teach Math."

Jake laughed, spraying coffee across the table. He covered his mouth. "That's not what I expected. High school Math or college level?"

"High school. I've been tutoring at the ECC North campus, mostly freshmen who didn't master the concepts in high school. I meet with a student once or twice, identify the gaps in his understanding, and together we build the foundation needed to finish the course with a decent grade. I didn't let on to the football team, but Algebra was my favorite class in high school."

Memories of his final game swept over Luke. Intense pain struck him as he collided with the damp ground. The agony threatened his mind like a heavy, black curtain shutting out even the merest glimmer of light. Luke drew in a sharp breath and blew it out. Out of the corner of his eye, he glimpsed the brilliant sun reflecting off the restaurant windows, and the memory of that awful day that had destroyed his dreams of playing college football and possibly going on to the pros mercifully faded. Needing a moment to regain his equilibrium, Luke reached for his iced coffee and pulled a long draught through the large straw. His fingers twitched, shook, and the cup wobbled, slipping from his grasp. He set it down with a frown.

Jake was talking. What was he saying?

"Are you all right?" Jake leaned across the table, his gaze concerned.

Luke managed a nod.

"Your face went white as a sheet. For a minute, I thought you might pass out."

Luke used his napkin to wipe the beads of sweat from his brow. His hands stopped shaking. God was in control. Luke no longer defined himself by his past. "I was remembering the day I blew out my knee."

"Oh." Jake drew out the word, increasing its weight, acknowledging the significance of that disastrous event. "That's how you ended up on heroin."

"Yes. And no." He forced himself to meet Jake's eyes. With this man, especially, Luke did not want to hide the truth. "I don't remember how long it was after the surgery, a few weeks maybe, before I didn't need more than ibuprofen for the pain."

Shame washed over him. His cowardice had nearly cost him everything that mattered.

Jake nodded, understanding, encouraging Luke to continue. The man was a good listener.

"Even the physical therapy wasn't as hard as I had feared it would be." He paused, ready at last to share the whole lowdown truth. "I kept taking the oxycodone because I didn't want to think about what I was going to do with the rest of my life. And I refused to talk about it. With anyone."

Not even Abby. Especially not with Abby. Why did I shut her out, Lord?

Jake chewed the last bite of his sandwich. His dark eyes declared he had heard versions of this story countless times. "That's Satan's plan—divide and conquer. An isolated person is easily manipulated." A glint, razor sharp appeared in those usually kind eyes.

Luke had seen that look before. It was a determination to defeat their common enemy. Understanding dawned. Satan had driven a wedge between Luke and his family, between Luke and Abby, between him and anyone who might have helped him, had he only been willing to ask. Was he wrong to give up the idea of counseling altogether? Addicts received the truth best from other addicts, those who had climbed out of the pit of a deadened mind and a dying body. "Maybe, I should reconsider."

Jake bit his chocolate walnut cookie in half. "Reconsider counseling?"

"Yes. You're right about the dangers of isolation. And you and I both know that addicts believe no one understands what they're going through. At first, we have trouble believing that even other addicts get us, unless, of course, someone is offering us another hit of something."

Jake grimaced. "Isn't that the truth?" He finished the other half of his cookie. "So, what do you want to do? Forget about teaching and become a drug counselor after all?"

Luke shook his head. Slowly, definitively. "Why can't I do both?"

Jake frowned. "Get two degrees? That sounds like a lot of work for a guy who wants to get married in four months."

"You're right. Obviously, I can't work two full time jobs, but I'm pretty sure I could continue volunteering at least every other Saturday."

Jake folded his napkin and laid it over his empty plate. "Okay, but if it gets to be too much, let me know."

Luke popped a chocolate-covered macaroon into his mouth. "Will do. I know my stress limit."

Jake nodded. They were both quiet for a few moments as they finished their coffee. Then Jake leaned across the table, his expression bursting with excitement. "I've got some news, too. Leah is going to have a baby."

"That's great, man. I'm so happy for you. How old is your little girl?"

"Seven. Leah was a little concerned about the age difference, but we're both from big families. We always knew we wanted more than one child."

Luke took this all in. When would he and Abby be able to give Elise a little brother or sister? He hoped she would be younger than seven. In his jeans pocket, his phone vibrated against his leg. He pulled it out. Abby.

"Go ahead and take that." Jake gathered up their place settings and garbage then headed over to the trash can.

Luke connected the call. "Hi, babe. What's up?"

"Just checking to make sure you remembered that Elise has her doctor's appointment at three o'clock. You know she handles the vaccinations better if you're holding her."

For a nanosecond, Luke detected Abby's disappointment.

"I can't believe she's already such a daddy's girl," Abby added.

Luke heard her smile. "Yeah, I can't believe how blessed I am."

"Me, too."

"I'm just wrapping up lunch with Jake. I'll pick you two up by two fifteen."

He disconnected the call, overcome with joy for all God had done for him.

Jake stopped behind his chair. "Sounds like you need to get going. I'll call you in the next few days."

Luke rose and pushed in his chair. "Thanks for everything, man." A simple thank you didn't begin to convey how grateful Luke was for all Jake had done. "You're the best."

"Only with God's grace," Jake called out over his shoulder as they headed in separate directions to their cars.

Luke started humming "Amazing Grace" as he unlocked his car. It was a good day. A very good day. And there was only one reason for that. "God is good. All the time."

CHAPTER TWENTY-TWO

Abby smiled as Elise crawled across the living room carpet toward the couch where Luke sat with outstretched arms. Their daughter would soon be pulling herself up. After that, it wouldn't be long before she would be walking. Abby surveyed the room. It was past time for her to baby-proof in here. "I can't believe she's six and a half months old already."

Luke scooped up their baby and held her at arm's length above his head. Elise squirmed and giggled. He brought her face to his and kissed her nose. She giggled and swatted his nose, her bright smile declaring how pleased she was with herself.

Watching them was much more fun than reading her research notes. Reluctantly, Abby returned her attention to her laptop. She needed to finish this paper on the effects of socioeconomic class on student success in school. They had planned their wedding for the Saturday immediately following Thanksgiving because she had always believed that Thanksgiving weekend was the perfect time to get married, but she hadn't factored in the fact that the semester wouldn't be over for two more weeks. "I don't know how you get all of your work done, Luke. No matter how well I plan, it seems like I'm days behind."

He shot her an incredulous look.

"I didn't say I was turning anything in *late*. I plan to get everything done early, in case it takes longer than I thought it would."

Luke did not respond, probably because he was all too familiar with her work ethic. He deposited Elise on her bottom in the middle of a pink quilt on which were scattered several toys. She immediately flopped over and crawled to her favorite noise-maker, a toy with six different colored pop-up doors. She slapped at a green button and was rewarded with a loud squeak. She clapped her hands and smiled up at her daddy.

Luke kissed the top of her head then pushed aside a stack of books and notebooks on the couch to sit beside Abby. "Babe, you're too hard on yourself—"

"But I'm not even working. You work more than thirty hours a week between tutoring and volunteering at Ellis—"

He placed two fingers over her lips. "First of all, I've always managed on less sleep than you need. Second, you're in your first semester and taking all 100-level classes that require a lot of reading, and most important of all, you are taking care of Elise. That's a full-time job in itself."

Tears pricked her eyes, and a sob pushed its way up her throat. "What if I don't get everything done?"

"You will," he said, wiping the wet streaks from her cheeks with his thumbs. "You always do."

His tender touch threatened to make her cry even more. He cupped her face in his strong hands, and she saw herself in his eyes, saw herself as more competent than she felt at this moment. He believed in her when she struggled to believe in herself. Hadn't she done the same thing for him? "You are going to be a good husband, Luke."

"And you are going to be the best wife." He brushed a lock of hair out of her eyes and tucked it behind her ears. She shivered, suddenly aware of his warm thigh pressed against her leg. She moistened her lips, wanting him to kiss her. Their wedding was less than three weeks away. Images of their wedding night brought a hot blush to her cheeks.

Luke grinned, clearly pleased that he could reel her in so easily. Then his smile disappeared.

Was he thinking of those dark days when his addiction had diminished their perfect chemistry?

He brushed a quick kiss over her lips.

She tried to tease his mouth open with her tongue, but before she could wrap her arms around his neck, he stood.

"I'll start dinner while you finish your paper. What's on the menu?"

"There's chicken marinating in a 13 x 9 pan in the fridge. Preheat the oven to 350°. Peel potatoes for mashed potatoes, and steam the carrots, broccoli, and cauliflower. Ask Sam to set the table. Mom and Dad should be here by six."

"Check. Holler for me if you want me to come get Elise."

"You can't cook and watch her, too."

"I can read to her once I get everything started."

Abby smiled. Luke was going to be a very good husband. He was already a great daddy.

*

The following Monday Luke had formulated a plan to surprise Abby. They had not gone out on a date—not a real date—in so long. Between tutoring, school, and volunteering at the rehab center every Saturday morning, his schedule was crammed to bursting. The last time he and Abby had been alone had been the day he proposed. Since Elise's birth, they'd both been so busy. "Too busy," he muttered, disgusted with himself.

He remembered his conversation with his mom. "Do some small thing every day to make Abby feel special," she'd said. "That's what your dad does for me."

Luke had no idea what those things were. He certainly wouldn't describe his father as the romantic, thoughtful type, but apparently he was, because now that his mother had given him her "little talk on the basic requirements for a happy marriage," Luke had begun to notice that his mother often wore the look of a young girl in love. He had not seen that look on Abby's face since before the Homecoming game. Clearly, he had been too self-absorbed in his own pain and too intent on avoiding it any cost to show Abby that he cherished her. Even now he couldn't believe he'd done that to her. Now, he wanted her to glow with happiness.

He'd called his mother to let her know he would be home for lunch and wanted to talk to her alone. He would need Mom's help to pull off his plan. He found her in the kitchen chopping celery and grapes for her famous chicken salad. Sunlight streamed through the bank of windows illuminating two rows of purple, white, and pink violets. Mom was humming. He wasn't sure what the song was, but it had a serene, soothing quality that permeated the room. Luke stood back, leaning against the doorjamb, and watched her obvious joy as she worked to prepare their lunch.

A memory of her swiping tears from her cheeks as she washed dishes careened through his mind. He had caused those tears and so many more. Luke came up behind her, slipped one arm around her shoulders, and kissed her cheek.

She turned to him with a surprised look. "What was that for?"

He met her eyes, his gaze unwavering. He ignored the tidal wave of shame threatening to drown him and the words he needed to say. Again. Because now, he could really see what his addiction had done to her. Becoming a father had altered his perspective, radically changed who he was. It would kill him if Elise ever ... he refused to even imagine it. "Mom, I'm sorry for all that I put you and Dad through. I didn't get it. Not even when I moved back home after rehab, the first time or the second time."

She touched his cheek, her fingertips wet and sticky from the potatoes. "You said you were sorry. You asked for our forgiveness, and we gave it. Why are you bringing this up again?"

He reached for her hand. "Sit with me for a few minutes."

"After I fix our plates." She gave his hand a quick squeeze then tugged hers free. She sliced crescent rolls, made three sandwiches, and put two on a plate for him and one for her. Then she added a scoop of potato salad to each plate and handed them to Luke.

"Do you want coffee?" Without waiting for his reply, she took two mugs from the cupboard and poured the sweet brew. "It's salted caramel, my new favorite."

His mother fancied herself a coffee connoisseur, and he didn't always like her new favorites, but a moment later, he took the mug she held out to him and sat at the kitchen table.

She opened the cookie jar, and peering inside, shook her head. "They're all gone. I just baked those cookies two days ago. I only ate three."

He laughed, glad to release some of the tension squeezing his heart. "That's what you get when you live in a house with three guys."

She smiled, her eyes sparkling with amusement. "I tell all of my friends that's how I stay so slim." She stirred a baby spoonful of sugar into her coffee, held it beneath her nose, and drew in a breath of its sweet scent. "It smells as delicious as it tastes."

He raised his eyebrows.

She shoved the sugar bowl across the table. "Add a little sugar. It brings out the flavor."

He followed her directive, dumping twice as much sugar into his mug. When he tasted it, it was actually good. "You should buy this again."

"I think I will." She sipped her coffee and bit into her sandwich.

Unsure how to begin, he ate one sandwich and half of his potato salad as he watched a cardinal eating seeds at the bird feeder hanging on a pole a few feet beyond the back deck.

They ate quietly, but several times, he caught Mom studying him. Finally, she said, "You didn't answer my question, honey."

"I was remembering all of the times I saw you cry. In the last two years, you were always crying about me, about my addiction. I can't believe I did that to you." He forced himself to look, really look, at his mother. Deep lines furrowed her brow. How long had she had them? Worry over him had aged her. "You were terrified, weren't you?"

A sheen of moisture brightened her brown eyes, and in seconds, two tears trailed down her cheeks and dropped off her jaw. She opened her mouth to speak.

But he held up his hand. "Every day, you must have wondered if ... if I was going to end up dead." He rose from his chair and knelt before his mom. "Please, can you ever forgive for making you live with the worst fear any parent can ... for making your life a living nightmare?" Unable to speak another word, he laid his head on her knees, and wrapped his arms around her legs the way he had as a boy.

"It's okay, Luke. It's over." Her fingers stroked his hair. "I love you. I forgive you."

Tears welled in his own eyes. Determined to put the past behind him, Luke blinked them away. He stood, pulled his mother to her feet, and hugged her. "I love you, Mom. I'll never hurt you like that again. Ever."

She inched away from him to look into his eyes. "I know you won't. I pray for you every day, and you're doing so well. You've rebuilt your life." She smiled. "You're getting married in two weeks. Your father and I are so proud of you."

Proud? They were proud? He had despaired of hearing those words from his mother ever again. God had transformed his life into a walking miracle. In his own strength, Luke had done only two things—cry out for help and accept it, from whomever and whenever it came. "I need your help, Mom."

She frowned, so briefly that he almost missed her concern. "Everything's good." He touched her arm reassuringly. "But I need you to babysit so I can take Abby out on a real date."

His mother smiled. "I was wondering when I was going to have my granddaughter all to myself."

*

Luke parked the car in front of his parents' garage. "I thought we were going to the mall to start our Christmas shopping and get a bite to eat." Abby caught the mischievous twinkle in Luke's eyes.

"We are, but I promised Mom I would bring Elise by for a visit." He averted his face as he shifted the car into park and cut the engine.

What was he up to now? He had been acting strange all day, starting with him insisting she wear a dress to the mall. Her first choice, a dark green sweater dress, which she had put on over plaid Christmas leggings was, in his words, "too casual." Totally ignoring her scowl, he had marched past her into her walk-in closet and emerged a moment later with a silver silk blouse and a navy velvet skirt. She smoothed that skirt down over her tall leather boots. Pleased at the possibility of spending time alone with Luke, Abby said, "Maybe your mother could watch Elise for an hour or so."

Luke grinned. "Great idea." He got out of the car and walked around to open her door.

His Cheshire cat expression suggested he had already planned for his mother to babysit. But why keep it secret? "Luke Bradford, you are up to something, and I'm going to find out what it is."

He raised one eyebrow then shifted to open the back door.

With his attention entirely focused on unbuckling Elise's car seat, Abby couldn't study his face for any clues. "I'm going to ask your mother."

He lifted the car seat out of the car. Somehow, he managed that feat without waking up their daughter. "Be my guest. She doesn't know anything."

Abby punched his left arm, a completely ineffectual gesture given his heavy wool jacket. "I knew it. I knew you were up to something. When you showed up in a tie—"

He planted a kiss on her mouth to silence her.

From behind her came the sound of Christmas music playing. Abby stepped away from Luke and pivoted to see his mother standing in the open doorway. "You're here."

"Hi, Mom." Luke's voice lacked the conspiratorial tone Abby expected. "It's too cold out here for Elise. Let's get inside before she wakes up."

*

"This isn't the way to the mall." Luke hadn't leaked a

single clue in their ten-minute conversation with his mom, and now, Abby *knew* something was up. "Where are we going? Wait a minute. Isn't this the way to your grandparents' house?"

Luke grinned but did not reply. He turned on the radio. "I'll Be Home for Christmas" filled the car.

Flabbergasted, she stared at the tiny twitch of his mouth—his tell that he was keeping something from her. She would have to wait. She glanced at the console. 96.1. That particular station had started playing Christmas songs already, even though Thanksgiving was two weeks away. She didn't that mind at all. She loved everything about Christmas, except last year. If only she could erase that Christmas from not only her memory but her family's, too.

This Christmas will be different. Luke is clean, and you'll be married.

Their wedding was in fourteen short days. She sucked in a breath. In two weeks, she would be Mrs. Luke Bradford. She stole a look at his chiseled profile. He was going to look devastatingly handsome in his tux, and if their engagement pictures were any indication, their wedding photos would be beautiful, too. Every detail—photos, music, flowers, food— had been tended to by their wedding planner, who, by Abby's standards was the most energetic and organized person on the planet. Her grandmother had insisted on hiring a wedding planner so that Abby could focus on taking care of Elise. And then there were her four college courses. Mom had suggested that she wait to begin in January, but Abby had wanted to get started as soon as possible, especially since she needed to take the lightest possible course load that would allow her to still be considered full-time.

Luke patted her knee. "You got pretty quiet all of the sudden."

His concerned tone soothed her nerves, a little. She shouldn't be anxious, but her emotions had been swinging like a pendulum from the moment she had ripped "October" off the kitchen calendar. One minute she'd be excited, completely confident that everything was falling into place, as if God had sent angels to pave their way and eliminate every possible difficulty. The next minute, she was absolutely certain something dreadful would happen to spoil their hard-won happiness. "Luke, why won't you tell me what we're doing today?"

He cast her a sidelong glance, a soft smile revealing his dimples. "Relax, babe. They're playing my favorite Christmas carol."

As Luke sang along, he pulled the car onto a long driveway lined with pine trees flecked with early snow that would be melted by tomorrow when the temperature climbed back into the forties. Abby felt like they were entering a picturesque Christmas card. She leaned forward in her seat to get a better look as the house came into view. His grandparents' three-story home was sided in sage with dark green shutters framing windows with grids in the lower panels. Tiny white lights, together with a single electric candle gave each window a soft glow. A Christmas wreath hung on the front door. Tall oaks shaded both ends of the house. Abby recognized it from a family photo that hung in his parents' dining room.

Luke parked the car, waited for the last notes of "The First Noel," then reached to turn the key to cut the engine.

"'The First Noel' is your favorite Christmas song?" She laid her hand on his thigh. "I never knew that."

He shifted in his seat to look at her.

The intensity in his blue eyes suggested that he had a story to tell her. The muscles in her neck tightened, and she forced herself to relax. This would be a good story, not a painful one. She unbuckled her seat belt and turned her body to face him.

"Last year, on Christmas morning, Jake played "The First Noel" on his guitar while he and his wife, Leah, sang. I'd heard that song hundreds of times. But it was all new. The part about the star giving great light grabbed me, made me believe, really believe, that there was a way out for me."

"Oh, Luke, I—"

"I'd been drowning in a dark pit—no one knows that better than you." Anguish shrunk his pupils to pinpricks, and he closed his eyes as if he couldn't bare her looking at him, seeing him through a lens of shame.

She touched his arm. "We don't have to talk about this anymore, Luke."

He met her gaze again, his expression determined. "When I stole your grandfather's oxies, that's when I knew I could never be the man you deserved. No amount of trying or good intentions was ever going to change that."

She opened her mouth to speak.

But he shook his head. "Everything Jake and Leah did, everything they said, the way they related to each other and to the residents, all of it pointed to God's amazing, forgiving love. It might sound corny, but they were my shining star. Their testimony—their story of all God had done for them, sparked a hope that blazed away the darkness lurking around every corner, waiting to suck me back in if I dropped my guard even for a moment." He stared off, avoiding her eyes.

Abby wanted to hug away all of his pain, but she sat very still and waited, praying in the lengthening silence. Finally, she said, "I can't even imagine how hard it was for you."

"Thousands of heroin addicts had tried to get free and

failed. Who was I to think I could succeed, could stay clean, permanently? That's when I started beginning and ending each day on my knees, Abby, asking God to help me forgive myself and to help me be the man you need and deserve."

He prayed on his knees every day? She prayed every day, too, but her prayers were more like a continual conversation, messages interspersed during her daily activities. Maybe she should set aside specific times to talk things over with God. Maybe she and Luke could pray more together, the way they had in the chapel at Ellis Rehab and that day in the restaurant. Abby wanted to weep for joy. They really were going to be okay. Tears puddled in her eyes and spilled down her cheeks.

"Babe, don't cry."

She brushed the moisture from her face and neck with her gloved hand. "These are happy tears."

He didn't look convinced.

She smiled. "I love you so much, Luke. I was so scared. Scared I was going to lose you forever, that my love and my prayers weren't strong enough to … save you."

Luke took both her hands in his. "Babe, you couldn't save me. That wasn't your job. Jesus is the only one who could save me, the only one who can save any addict."

He was right. She had tried so hard to be everything to him and for him, but that was never God's plan. Instead, He brought other people into Luke's life, people who pointed him to Jesus. She and Luke wouldn't be here at all if his father had not insisted Luke check himself into Ellis Rehab.

And now his grandparents were letting them live here in this amazing house so that she and Luke could get married. Her fears for their future faded, dissipating like the morning fog burned off by the sun. She gave his hands a squeeze then pulled hers free and leaned back against the car door. "I met

Leah that one time, but I'd like to meet Jake, too."

Luke's brows knit together in thought. "Yeah, we could do that. After our honeymoon, we can have them over for dinner. They have a seven-year-old daughter, and Leah's expecting another baby. You'll have a lot to talk about."

Abby smiled. Getting to know another young mother could be good for her. She still kept in touch with Megan and Lisa via text messages and social media, but her best friends were attending Allegheny College, a four-year liberal arts school three hours away in Pennsylvania. Their lives diverged more with each passing week. "I think I could manage dinner. As long as you promise to help."

"Of course. We're a team, babe." He leaned over the console to caress her cheek.

His hand and his words warmed her heart. In spite of her initial reticence when Luke had shared his grandparents' invitation, Abby felt a growing excitement about living in this spacious home. She smiled and opened her door. "I assume we're here so you can give me a tour."

The moment she exited the car, the carefully tended landscaping caught her attention. A curved stone walkway lined with narrow flower beds featuring the bright faces of purple, white, and yellow pansies peeking through the snow led to a beautifully carved oak front door. Some twenty yards to her left, at the end of the driveway, a two-story, four-car garage was sided in the same sage green as the house. She headed in that direction. Beyond the garage, a path led to what Abby assumed was an English garden, complete with stone paths, benches, arbors, and a pond, which she could barely see in the distance. This place really was way too big for two people in their eighties to care for. Abby wasn't surprised that they wanted something smaller. A twinge of discomfort marred her excitement. Living here in his grandparents' home when she and Luke had no way to buy it from them didn't seem fair. "I still can't believe your grandparents agreed to let us stay here, rent free."

Wearing the exultant expression of a kid on Christmas morning, Luke took her hand. "Babe, that's the best part. Grandpa found a tenant for the garage apartment. A couple from Nigeria. The guy's in the UB medical program. He's got another two years, and his wife just arrived in the U.S. with their eighteen-month-old baby."

Abby stared up at the row of three paired windows above the garage. "*That's* big enough for three people?"

"Trust me. It's a lot bigger than it looks. There's two bedrooms, a full bath, a large room across the front that is basically a kitchen, dining area, and living room all in one. And in the back, there's even a small studio that can be used as a study. There's also a full balcony. Grandpa had it built for my great-grandmother. She lived there for five, no six years, until she couldn't handle the stairs anymore and had to move into a first-floor senior condo."

"Okay, so it's probably big enough for a family of three, but I don't see how that helps us. We really should be paying rent."

"My grandparents don't need us to pay rent because we're buying the house from them." Luke's grin deepened his dimples.

She wanted to kiss those dimples.

He took her hand, gently pulling her back toward the house.

"Wait! What did you say? We're *buying* this house? No way. No bank is going to give us a mortgage."

Luke turned the key in the lock. "We don't need a mortgage. We're collecting the rent money from the doctor and his wife and turning that over to my grandparents."

Luke held the door open for her.

Abby walked into the spacious foyer. Trying to take it all in, she sat on an oak bench, and took off her snow-covered boots. "Their rent is enough for a house payment? How can that be?"

"It's not, entirely. Roughly half is their wedding gift to us."

"Roughly half of the value of this, all of this place? They're *giving* it to us?"

"Yes, they are. It's their investment in our future. Grandpa's words, not mine."

Abby let that settle in her heart for a moment. This was more than a wedding gift or an investment in their future. It was forgiveness and confidence and a new start.

CHAPTER TWENTY-THREE

On Thanksgiving morning, Luke woke early. A nightmare gripped his soul. Joe! A scream rose in Luke's throat, threatening to shatter the tranquil pre-dawn hour. Muffling the sound with his fist locked against his half-open mouth, Luke lurched to sitting position then rolled from his bed onto his knees.

"God, it was just a dream. It wasn't real." His desperate words ricocheted from one corner of the room to another. "It can't be real. Joe's too smart for that."

Luke's heart slammed against his chest. He sucked in several deep breaths, forced himself to slow his breathing to normal. The hardwood floor beneath his knees, his shins, and his bare feet grounded him. "God is only a prayer away." Didn't Jake say that every single Saturday?

With his head in his hands, Luke pleaded for protection for his little brother. Only Joe wasn't so little anymore, and thirteen-year-olds had too many opportunities to experiment with drugs, drugs they foolishly believed were fun, but were often deadly.

After all Luke had put his family through, surely Joe would be smarter.

Still, Luke couldn't shake the image of his brother, a rubber strap tied around his upper arm and a needle poised to puncture a bulging vein. A wave of nausea crawled up from Luke's churning gut. He jumped up, flung open his bedroom door, and raced down the hall, but by the time he reached the bathroom, the need to vomit had passed.

He had to get control of himself. He was getting married in two days. His life was on track, God was in control, and no tragedy was threatening God's good plan for Luke and Abby and their baby girl.

It wasn't quite five thirty. Joe was still asleep, safe in his bed, two doors down the hall.

But Luke had to be certain. His sweaty hands turned the bathroom doorknob, and a moment later, he inched his brother's door open. The hall light cast a dim beam across Joe's sleeping form. He was sprawled on his belly, his hands gripping his pillow.

Needle-like tears pricked Luke's eyes as relief flooded his mind. *Thank You, God.*

Luke shut down his next thought before it could fully form. He couldn't go there. Joe was fine. He had learned his lesson by watching the excruciating effects of heroin on his older brother. Joe would be wise. He would know that drugs promised an escape from the pain of the present only to destroy a man's hope for any happiness or peace. Satan's evil design to numb the mind and body cast the soul into a dark abyss. Joe had seen that.

The boy rolled onto his back. His eyes finding Luke's, Joe mumbled, "Morning."

"Not quite, little bro. Go back to sleep."

Joe shielded his eyes from the light. "Why are you up? Is something wrong?"

Shamed by the fear in his brother's words, Luke shook

his head. "Everything's fine. I had a nightmare, that's all."

"Want to talk about it?"

The compassion in Joe's tone seemed older than his years. Luke had done that, too—stolen his brother's childhood. "Maybe later. Go back to sleep."

Joe didn't need to be asked again. Relieved, Luke eased his brother's door closed.

He needed a shower. The hot water pelting his back would drive these crazy fears from his head.

The light overcomes the darkness, Luke. Choose the light, and darkness will flee.

"Thank You, Jesus." Luke worked the shampoo into his hair as steam filled the shower stall. "I need You every minute of every day. Help me remember that You want me to come to You with every worry and every fear."

Please don't ever let my little brother use any drugs. I couldn't stand it ... to see the light go out of his eyes. The way it did with Cole.

Some thoughts shouldn't be put into words.

But the image of Cole dead on his bathroom floor morphed into Dustin.

So, that's the way it was going to be. If Satan wanted to terrorize him, then Luke would take action. After his shower, he would call Dustin and invite him to come over for Thanksgiving dinner. His friend hadn't R.S.V.P.'d to the wedding evite, and Jake hadn't heard from him either. In the four months since Luke started volunteering to sit in on the Saturday morning group sessions, sometimes sharing his story, other times talking to residents one-on-one in informal conversations after the session concluded, Luke had not seen Dustin once. That was good, right? At least, that had been Luke's assumption. Now, he wasn't so sure.

Why had he let so much time go by without checking in

on his friend? Since he'd been released from Ellis in February, Luke hadn't even tried to contact Dustin. Not one time. Why had he been so neglectful? Guilt burst like firecrackers in his brain. He had wanted to put distance between himself and everything to do with rehab. He had been thinking only of himself. How many times since he had committed to helping the residents at Ellis had God prompted Luke to get in touch with Dustin? Five or six times? Ten times? Had he contacted Jake? If Dustin had called, the older man hadn't mentioned it. Luke didn't even know if his friend had the same phone number.

But God knew where Dustin was.

Luke grabbed his cell from where he'd dropped it on top of his pile of clothes before getting in the shower. Then he made the call.

It rang four times before Dustin picked up. "Hey, man."

His friend's thin, faint voice confirmed Luke's concern. "I haven't heard from you. You got my wedding invitation, right?"

"Yeah, meant … to let you know … been … busy."

"Got any plans for Thanksgiving dinner?"

"Nah, no … appetite."

No appetite. That wasn't good. "I'll come pick you up. My mom puts on a spread to rival the best restaurant in town."

"Thanks … for the … invite. I … I think … I might be … sick."

Luke prayed for wisdom. "What's your address? I'll bring you a plate."

"East Ferry. You've been … here before."

He hadn't. Dustin must be confusing Luke with someone else. "Yeah, sure. Give me the house number."

Dustin's mumbled reply was barely audible, but Luke managed to scrawl the number onto the back of an envelope.

"Leave the door unlocked. That way if you're sleeping, I can leave the food in the fridge."

"Sure. See ya, Luke."

Thump. Dustin had dropped his cell.

Luke rushed to his room, hauled on clean clothes, scribbled a note for his parents, sprinted downstairs to the kitchen, dropped the note next to the coffeemaker, grabbed his coat, and headed through the side door into the garage. All in less than three minutes.

He started the engine. It would need a minute or two to warm up. He shoved his hand into his pocket, pulled out his cell, and dialed Jake. "Hey, Jake. It's me, Luke."

"What's up?"

"It's Dustin. He's in trouble." Luke rattled off the address, grateful that he had thought to call Jake. He would have narcan.

"I'll meet you there in five minutes." Jake said something to Leah.

Relieved, Luke disconnected the call. Jake's house was closer. It would take Luke about fifteen minutes to reach Dustin. Luke prayed Jake would get there in time. Leah and Jake would be praying, too. And Abby, if she was up.

Luke keyed in a brief text, his trembling fingers making minor mistakes. Luke breathed deeply, blowing out tension and drawing in strength for whatever they would find, corrected the errors in his message, and sent it to Abby. Then, he sent a second text. "Don't worry about me, babe. I'm fine."

Seconds later, he was speeding down the road, praying for mercy and protection. The nightmare had been a warning and a threat—not against his brother but against Dustin, the man who had first directed Luke to the light of God's unconditional love. His friend needed that love to have skin on. Now.

You call yourself a friend? Friends keep in touch. You abandoned the guy.

Luke blew out a sharp breath. Was that Satan or his own guilt talking? Either way, Luke couldn't change the past nine months. Now was what counted. He eased up on the accelerator. Four miles over the speed limit would be safe. He didn't have time to be stopped for speeding.

*

Elise's soft cry grew to an insistent wail in less than a minute. Abby kicked the blankets off, swung her legs over the edge of the bed, and reached to check the time on her phone. 6:53. She had missed a text from Luke. She would check it as soon as she got the baby settled. The whole house didn't need to be up before seven o'clock on Thanksgiving morning.

She opened the nursery door. Elise's bright blue eyes rested on Abby's face. One crocodile tear rolled down each pink cheek as she raised her pudgy arms to be picked up. "Good morning, sweetheart. You slept late this morning." Abby nuzzled the baby's neck, trailing kisses until Elise giggled.

After a quick diaper change, she carried her daughter back to her bedroom, settled her in to nurse with pillows supporting both their backs, then reached for her phone to check Luke's message. There were two.

The first said, "Heading over to Dustin's. He's in trouble. Pray." The second message eased her mind a bit. "Don't worry about me, babe. I'm fine."

Abby bit her lip. Who was Dustin? They hadn't gone to school with anyone named Dustin. Wait. Luke had introduced her to a guy at the rehab center named Dustin. The guy had a bright smile, but a dimmed expression in his eyes suggested … "Lord, no. Not again."

Elise yanked her mouth from Abby's breast and tugged on her shirt. Abby repositioned her daughter on the other breast.

Should she try to call Luke? Yes, she needed to call right now. She swiped her screen, navigated to her favorite contacts, and tapped Luke's name. The call went straight to voicemail. "Luke, it's me. What's wrong? Why aren't you answering your phone? Call me as soon as you get this message." She disconnected the call, and with lightning speed typed a text. "Call me ASAP." She hit send then typed a second message—"I'm praying."

Panic snaked up her spine. Luke couldn't take finding another friend dead of an overdose.

God, please, let him get there in time.

*

A siren blared in the distance, the sound growing closer, coming for Dustin. Luke parked on the road, leaving the driveway open for the ambulance. He pushed his car door open, hit the lock button, got out, and closed the door. Sprinting down the sidewalk, then the driveway, through the side door, and up the stairs, the film of his life morphed to slow motion. With each step, he repeated the same prayer. *Please, God.*

Halfway down the hall, Luke spotted the tarnished brass plaque—2 B. He opened the apartment door without knocking. Instantly, Jake's steady voice reached his ears. What was he saying? Luke strained to hear Dustin's voice but couldn't.

He bolted through the house, down a narrow hall, led by Jake's reassuring words to an open bedroom door. Dustin was sitting up. Luke stared transfixed, relief flooding through him like rain after a deadly drought. *Thank You,*

Jesus.

Steadying himself, he leaned against the doorframe as the adrenaline rush dissipated.

Propped up in a circle of pillows, Dustin slouched against the headboard. "Hey, man, you came."

Jake turned to look over his shoulder at Luke. Neither spoke. Jake simply nodded. His expression told it all. He had found Dustin unconscious.

His friend lifted one arm then let it drop back on the worn, wool blanket. "Looks like you and Jake saved my life. I was barely breathing when he got here."

Luke couldn't tell if he heard relief or regret in Dustin's words. He wanted to ask what had happened, why Dustin was using again, but those answers didn't matter right now. "I should have kept in touch."

Dustin slowly shook his head. "When you're clean, you stay away from people who are using. And they definitely don't want to see you."

He was right. But it only made Luke feel worse. For a few minutes, he stood stock-still, feeling utterly powerless.

But that was a lie.

From the minute he had sensed that Dustin was in trouble, Luke had sprung into action, praying, calling his friend, and contacting Jake. Dustin was alive because Luke had connected his nightmare to the urgent burden that followed. God's message had been clear. Joe was fine. Dustin was not.

Luke sat on the bed and gripped his friend's hand. A dark shadow clung to Dustin's ashen face. Luke couldn't bear it. He stood, moved to the window, and raised the dusty blinds. Soft light illuminated piles of clothes, shoes, books, dirty dishes, and empty take-out boxes containing scraps of crusty and moldy food. All of it told Luke how his friend had been living. But for how long? Had today been an isolated slip-up? Though Luke tried, he couldn't convince himself of that. Dustin's descent had left him in a pit for a week or more.

"You can always call," Jake was saying. "We can help. You know that."

Dustin tried to smile, but the muscles at the corners of his mouth pulled back into a grimace. "I didn't want help."

The despair in his words, in his tone, but most of all in his eyes, left Luke cold with dread. An addict who doesn't want help is on a one-way trip to death. "You'll start over. Jake and I will help you. I'm at the center every Saturday morning."

Dustin's eyes widened in surprise. He raked his trembling hand through his unwashed hair. "Maybe."

"EMTs!" two men shouted from the front of the apartment.

"Back here," Luke cried. "In the bedroom."

Dustin's gaze rested on Luke. "Thanks for the dinner invitation, but it looks like I've got plans."

"We'll talk next week."

"Oh, yeah, you're marrying your baby mama in two days. Congratulations, man. I'm happy for you. I really am."

Two men in dark uniforms, one carrying a stretcher, the other a medical bag, entered the bedroom. Their calm expressions suggested their vast experience with similar situations.

Jake stood, whispered something to one of the EMTs, probably telling him how much narcan he had administered. "Looks like you guys knew what you were doing. We'll take good care of Dustin from here. You'll be able to get an update from ECMC in an hour or so."

Jake looked to Luke then gave an almost imperceptible

nod toward the door. They stepped out of the room to let the EMTs do their job.

Once they were out of earshot, Luke asked, "What happened?"

Jake shook his head. "Two weeks ago Dustin found his girlfriend dead. She was with another guy. He died, too."

"Both of them overdosed?"

"Yeah. Dustin didn't even have a hint that his girl was seeing someone else."

"Maybe they were just shooting up together."

Jake shook his head. "She was wearing a slinky red nightgown."

Bile churned its way up Luke's throat. What a kick to the gut! Dustin deserved better. Sometimes, life wasn't even close to being fair. If Luke didn't believe that God would work everything together for good, he would give up entirely.

But Dustin had faith. Why hadn't he been able to pray through?

Luke knew the answer to that question. Sometimes, a man needed another man to stand with him. Maybe two. He and Jake would do that for Dustin. Their hands would lift him out of this dark valley until Dustin had the strength to climb back to sobriety again. For the first time, Luke was glad he and Abby had decided to postpone their honeymoon until next spring.

*

Abby smiled at her grinning daughter. Elise smacked her palms against the warm bath water, spraying water and bubbles into her own face and all over Abby's shirt. Who knew a seven month old could have that much strength? Abby dabbed at Elise's face with the corner of a towel. Elise wrinkled her nose then slapped at the bubbles again. Abby blinked droplets of water from her eyes. "Enough, baby girl.

We need to get you washed and dressed."

"Want Grandpa to take over?" Dad asked, resting his hand on Abby's shoulder.

"Sure. Then I can take a couple of pictures for her baby book."

Dad knelt beside the tub, picked up a yellow squeaky duck, and quacked at the baby. Elise burst into musical giggles. He started singing a song he was making up on the spot, something about a princess and a magic duck.

Abby hurried to the nursery, thoughts of taking pictures suddenly eclipsed by her need to check on Luke. She had meant to grab her cell before settling Elise in the bathtub. What was going on? He should have called her by now. The phone was on the changing table right where she'd left it, next to the baby's flower-print onesie and her pink blanket sleeper.

For several seconds, Abby stared at her cell, overcome by suffocating dread. Had Luke left her a text? A voicemail? Would it be bad news?

Fighting fear, she recited a verse from the Psalms that she had memorized last week. "'He shall not be afraid of evil tidings: his heart is fixed, trusting in the LORD.'" She wanted to trust God, but she was scared. What if the worst happened? What if Luke had found Dustin dead? What if...? She clapped her hands over her ears to drown out the voice in her head. The voice of death, destruction, and despair. The voice of Satan tempting her to give up on Luke, to give up on God.

"Jesus, help us." She drew in a deep breath and lowered her voice. The last thing she needed was for Sam to march in, asking questions she didn't have any answers to. "God, I trust You to protect Luke. Everything is going to be okay, no matter what the news is. Help me to believe that."

Her heart still raced, and the tightening in her chest refused to ease up. Saying that everything was going to be okay might strengthen her faith, but would speaking the words make them true? What if God's plan for her was to raise Elise without Luke?

Abigail Marie Collins, get a hold of yourself.

She unlocked her phone, swiped the notification, and read Luke's message. "Made it. Heading to ECMC." Her knees wobbling with relief, Abby sank into the rocking chair. She typed a reply, "Can you talk?"

A few moments passed without a response. Should she try to call him?

"We're all done." Dad held Elise, who wriggled in his arms, dislodging her pink princess towel. "Do you have an outfit picked out for her wear today?"

She shook her head. "You choose."

Dad gave her a knowing look, opened his mouth to ask her what was wrong, then closed it again, biting down on his lower lip. His expression spoke volumes. The last two years had been rough, and her dad would do anything to insulate her from more trouble and pain, but he couldn't protect her, and he knew it. He carried Elise over to her closet. "Let's find you a pretty dress to wear for the Thanksgiving pictures. Maybe two, just in case you have an accident."

Elise giggled as if she understood her grandpa.

Abby laughed, too. "You two crack me up."

Then, her smile disappeared, replaced by nagging anxiety. Luke had stood on the precipice yet again. Had he been tempted by heroin's fleeting fantastical freedom? By the familiar pull of oblivion that inevitably followed? Even if he were tempted, he would never choose nodding off over spending time with her and Elise. Luke had been clean for eleven months.

Determined not worry, Abby grabbed her phone and took a video of Dad struggling to get Elise into the pretty dress with its splash of colorful leaves cascading in a diagonal sweep across the bodice and down the skirt. She watched him clumsily tie a copper-colored ribbon in her daughter's silky hair only to have Elise snatch it out a moment later.

Abby smiled. Today, this Thanksgiving, she had so much to be thankful for. A family who loved her. A beautiful, healthy, baby girl. Luke. Their wedding in two days. An amazing house. She refused to succumb to fear.

But when her cell rang out with the first bars of "O Holy Night," the phone slipped from her hand, landing on the carpeted floor at her feet. She stared at it for several seconds, drawing in a sharp breath, her heart pounding against her ribs.

"Aren't you going to answer that?"

Dad's concerned tone jolted her to action. She grabbed her phone and heading out of the nursery, connected the call. "Luke, what's going on? I—"

"Dustin's okay. He'll be at ECMC for a few days, then he'll go back to Ellis."

Tears pricked her eyes as she tried to muffle her sobs with one hand while holding the phone up to her ear with the other hand. "Luke, oh, Luke."

"Babe, don't cry. I'm all right."

She closed her bedroom door and sank onto her bed. Leaning against the headboard, she hugged her knees to her chest. "I ... I know how hard it was for you when ... when you found Cole. I was so scared, Luke. I didn't want you to go through that again."

"Neither did I. But Dustin's going to be fine. Jake and I are heading to the hospital now. We shouldn't be more than an hour. If I'm going to be longer than that, I'll call you."

"I love you, Luke."

"I love you, too, Abby."

When he disconnected the call without saying goodbye, she shuddered. His tone was comforting, but an undercurrent of something else pierced her heart.

He was hurt.

She had hurt him. The tremble in her voice, even her carefully chosen words, had failed to hide her fear. Why had she burst into tears? He was probably asking himself, why doesn't she trust me? I've been clean for almost a year. What Luke had to do was far more difficult, so why couldn't she do her small part? Why couldn't she be brave?

Her body shook with a grief so dark she could barely breathe. What if Luke didn't want to marry her because he believed she would never fully trust him?

A firm pounding on her door penetrated her panic.

"Abby, breakfast is ready." Sam sounded annoyed, hungry. "Mom said we can't start without you."

Abby sat up and looked at her reflection in the mirror. Red splotches covered her face and her eyes puffed out like the neighbor's Pekingese. "I'm not hungry."

"But Mom said—"

"I have a headache." It wasn't a lie. Her head was throbbing. "I need a nap. If Elise starts to fuss, have Mom bring her to me."

"Whatever. As long as I get to eat now."

Sam's hunger had apparently blocked his usual detective traits. Abby lay back down on the bed, pulled a soft throw over her, and closed her eyes, one prayer on her heart. *Please don't let me ruin everything.*

*

Sometime later, Abby heard her bedroom door creak open. Expecting to see Mom, Dad, or even Sam holding Elise,

Abby swiftly sat up and straightened her hair. Hopefully, her face wasn't covered with red splotches. She did not want to answer any questions.

To her relief, Mom entered and shut the door behind her. "Sam said you have a headache. Are you getting sick?"

Lavender perfume, her mother's signature scent, permeated the room as she situated herself on the foot of Abby's bed.

Flooded with memories of Mom's helpful advice, Abby felt a spark of hope. "I messed up again. With Luke."

Patience softened the lines between her mother's brows. At forty-five, she was still beautiful. Dad gazed at her as if the flowers bloomed just for her. Abby wanted Luke to look at *her* like that, like she was his whole world. Now, she feared he would never be able to look at her at all without wondering if she were doubting him yet again. "I ruined everything. Luke knows ..."

"Knows what, honey?"

"That I don't always trust him. I want to. Most of the time, I do, but when something happens that could drag him back into ..." She exhaled, twisted a corner of the blanket, then watched it uncoil. "I get so scared that I can't think straight. And then I feel so guilty for not trusting him, for not having more faith in him, for not having more faith in God. What is wrong with me?"

Mom shifted closer. She brushed a damp strand of snarled hair from Abby's face, then cupped her cheeks. "Nothing is wrong with you. Ever since you were a little girl, you've tried to carry the weight of the world on your shoulders."

Her mother's tender words soothed Abby's shattered nerves for a moment. If only Mom could tell her what to do. "But you don't know what's happened."

Mom patted Abby's hand. "Luke called."

"He called *you*?"

"About fifteen minutes ago."

"Why didn't he call me?" Abby lurched back and leaped from the bed. She started to pace, then marched to her closet where the vinyl garment bag containing her wedding gown hung, pressed and waiting for her to put it on in just two short days. "I don't think he wants to marry me anymore." She choked out the words then covered her face with her hands.

Mom pulled her hands away, forcing Abby to face her. "What on earth are you talking about? Luke loves you."

Abby pivoted away and reached for the garment bag. She slid the long zipper open and peered at her beautiful ivory gown. She fingered the seed pearls that edged the neckline. She was going to look so beautiful that Luke wouldn't be able to take his eyes off her. Tears spilled from her already puffy eyes. She forced herself to meet her mother's gaze again. "Why would he want to marry me when he knows I still don't trust him, even though he hasn't touched heroin in more than a year?"

"Oh, honey, he hasn't given you any reason not to trust him, has he?"

"No, he hasn't. Not even once. That's what makes me feel so awful."

"Then, where is this all coming from? What did you say to him?"

"Nothing. I didn't have to. Luke knows me. He knows how hard I've tried to put it all behind us. But when I'm scared, I can't hide it. Not from Luke."

"Honey, we're all scared sometimes. It's just human nature. Luke understands that."

A light knock sounded on her door, and Abby's heart

pounded with dread.

Luke entered without waiting to be invited inside. He stood before her, the hurt in his eyes daggers through her heart. How long had he been in the hall? How much had he heard?

Avoiding Abby's eyes, Luke focused his attention on her mom. "Good morning, Stephanie."

"Morning, Luke." Mom glanced at Abby and back at Luke. "I'll head downstairs and make a fresh pot of coffee. There's still French toast casserole warming in the oven, if you're hungry."

"Sure. Later." He smiled politely, but there was no smile in his tone.

After her mother left, Abby and Luke stared at each other for a long moment. She wrapped her arms around her middle, a feeble attempt to protect herself. From what? From the destruction of her dreams?

His eyes softening, Luke came to her, clasped her elbows, and moved into the circle of her arms. He studied her face, searching her eyes for answers. "Do you want to talk about this?"

She did. And she didn't. Because this could be the beginning of the end for them. She could feel it like a sharp and empty pit in her stomach, and she couldn't force a single word past her lips. *God, help us*, she prayed, desperation surging up from the deepest part of her heart.

With one arm around her waist, Luke led her to the window seat. Their knees touched, and she wanted to fall into his arms and pretend nothing was wrong. The sound of Elise crying downstairs reached them, reminding her that whatever they said would affect their daughter's life, maybe forever.

Luke leaned back against the alcove wall, waiting,

watching her, listening for Elise to stop crying. "Grandma has the magic touch."

"Grandpa, too."

"How much time before she needs to nurse?"

"Not for another hour."

"Good." He placed his hand on Abby's knee, drawing circles on her thigh with his index finger. He leaned close, so close their breaths mingled. He was going to kiss her, as if a kiss could fix what was wrong between them.

She placed one finger over his lips and shook her head. "We need to talk."

He caressed her hair, sending shivers through her. "Talking is overrated."

She smiled at his feeble attempt to make her laugh. "I love you, Luke."

"I love you, babe."

"Even when I ... when it seems like I—"

"Like you don't trust me."

Her face flamed, and she lowered her gaze.

He cupped her chin, slowly raising her face until she couldn't look away. "I love you, Abby. I've dragged you through hell, and you still love me. You've never given up on me. Not even when you were terrified that I had given up on us and on our baby."

Sharp tears clogged Abby's throat. She had to ask, or she would always wonder. "Do you really *want* to marry me, even though I don't trust you, not the way you need me to, and certainly not the way you deserve?"

"Abby, babe, don't you get it? I didn't *deserve* a second chance, but God forgave me. How can I not forgive you?" He put his hands on her shoulders. "We're in this together."

His fingers kneaded her tense muscles with a strength that went far beyond the physical. He was no longer the boy she had fallen in love with three years ago. He was a grown man, a man who wanted to build a life with her, in good times and bad times. She touched his face, tears pooling in her eyes and spilling down her cheeks.

"Babe, please don't cry anymore."

"I'm so sorry, Luke. I don't want to ever hurt you."

He brushed her tears away with his thumbs. "We're going to get through this, Abby. And I'm not going to get angry with you if sometimes you don't trust me. That wouldn't be fair. But I promise you this. Every single day, I will do what's best for our family, you, me, and Elise. I'll never make another decision without considering how it will affect you and our family, without talking to you."

She believed he meant what he said, right now, in this moment. Was that enough? Could they build on that fragile trust? She bit her lower lip, praying she would say the right thing, do the right thing, think the right thing.

Luke frowned. "No more worrying. And definitely no more biting on those beautiful lips." He leaned close and covered her mouth with his, teasing her mouth open with his tongue.

She wrapped her arms around his neck and slid onto his lap. He released a low groan. Startled at his swift response, she scrambled to her feet. Passion smoldered in his eyes. She smiled. "Just two more days to wait."

"Two days and six hours until we can sneak away from the reception."

She laughed. "I didn't know you were counting the hours."

"Of course, I'm counting." He reached for her hand, playfully trying to pull her back onto his lap.

But Elise's sharp cry dissolved her romantic mood. "It's time to nurse the baby." Abby stepped back, tugging Luke toward the door.

He shrugged in defeat. "I hope our daughter understands that her daddy needs some alone time with her mommy."

Abby laughed. "I feel exactly the same way. But for now … our daughter comes first."

Almost on cue, the baby's cries reached peak volume.

"I agree, to a point. But my dad told me that the best way for me to make sure my children are happy, is to make their mother happy."

"Hmm. That sounds like something *my* dad would say."

"And they would be right. I might not have their experience, but I do know that a strong family is based on a strong marriage."

"I love you, Luke Bradford."

"And I love you, soon-to-be Mrs. Bradford."

Abby smiled. They would all be okay, in spite of everything they had been through, in spite of whatever they might have to face together. Together, she and Luke would learn to count on each other. And they could do that, not because either one of them would ever be perfect, but because they belonged to God, and He would help them.

CHAPTER TWENTY-FOUR

Abby smiled patiently as her mother fussed over her in these final moments before she would become Mrs. Luke Bradford. Mom made another minor adjustment to Abby's veil, seventy-two inches of bridal allusion, which according to Marie, the owner of the bridal shop, was the perfect tulle for a veil. Held to her chignon with more pins than Abby could count, not even a fifty-mile per hour wind could rip the beautiful veil from her head, though it was far too cold for outdoor shots. Thanks to her grandparents' generosity, Abby's wedding photos would be taken inside at the Buffalo Botanical Gardens. It was really happening. In less than an hour, she would be Luke's wife.

"Abby, you are the most beautiful bride I have ever seen," Mom declared with tremor in her voice. "And I'm not just saying that because you're my daughter."

"You really think so?"

"Absolutely."

"Absolutely perfect," Meg said.

Lisa nodded. "Totally gorgeous."

Abby fingered the tiny seed pearls that edged the embroidered lace border of her veil, pleased with her choice.

Both the delicate lace and the glistening pearls perfectly matched those of her wedding gown. She studied her reflection in the full length mirror, satisfied that she did not look like the exhausted mom of a seven-month-old baby and more than a little surprised at the amazing transformation. The gown and veil made her feel intensely feminine, as lovely as any model in any bridal magazine. Most days, Abby would describe herself as merely pretty, but today she felt breathtaking, beautiful, and unforgettable. She smiled, pivoted, and kissed Mom's cheek.

Violet eyes glistening with tears, Mom tried to smile, but her lower lip twitched then trembled.

"Hey, don't you dare cry," Abby said. "You'll get me crying."

Lisa handed Mom a tissue. "Abby is going to take Luke's breath away. But we don't want to start a tear-fest, or the whole effect will be ruined by red splotches all over Abby's face."

"Absolutely no crying allowed," Megan agreed. "Your wedding pictures are going to be stunning. Luke looks just as amazing as you do."

Abby smiled, her thoughts drifting far into the future. She and Luke were snuggled up on a sage green love seat in their sunroom with their wedding album open in their laps. His hair was white, and his face was lined with wrinkles, but his eyes sparkled with the same vibrant blue she had first fallen for. He clasped her wrinkled hand, his thumb tracing the blue-green veins, and she rested her head against his heart, still beating faithfully for her. He pressed a kiss to her grey head and whispered, "Marrying you was the smartest thing I ever did."

"Abby?" Meg asked. "Are you listening? They're starting the bridesmaid music."

Abby blinked twice, surprised to see Megan, Lisa, and Mom staring at her with concerned expressions. "I was just daydreaming about growing old with Luke."

Megan and Lisa laughed. Even Mindy, Jake and Leah's seven-year-old daughter, let out a musical giggle. "You're not old," she said, wrinkling her pert nose and shaking her head.

"It's a little early to be thinking about getting old." Lisa smoothed her burgundy gown over her flat stomach.

Abby laughed with them. At eighteen, even thirty seemed far off. "Maybe so, but it's a comforting thought, knowing we're meant to be together always, knowing that our marriage was always part of God's plan for us."

Mom dabbed at the moisture clinging to her dark lashes, dropped the tissue in the wastebasket, and brushed a kiss over Abby's cheek. "I need to get into the church. Are you all set, sweetie?" Mom bent down until she was eye level with the flower girl.

Mindy swung her basket of burgundy and cream rose petals. "I'm ready, Mrs. Collins."

Mom took the little girl's free hand. Together, they stepped into the hall, and the low murmur of hushed voices mingled with the bright chamber music, a cheery Classical piece suggested by Abby's soon-to-be mother-in-law.

Lisa and Meg each clasped one of Abby's hands. "We're so happy for you," Lisa said.

Meg kissed her cheek. "You really are the most beautiful bride I have ever seen."

Her two best friends blew her kisses as they glided from the room. Very soon, her dad would come for her. Needing a moment to steady her nerves, Abby walked over to the window. Among the bare branches of a grove of flowering apple trees, tiny snowflakes swirled in delicate curves and waves, forming a lovely picture against the soft light filtering through white clouds. A moment later, a bright red cardinal lighted on a bare branch of a nearby apple tree. In a second, his cream-colored mate flew down to perch beside him, so close their wings touched. Did cardinals mate for life? They sure looked as if nothing but death could ever separate them. As beautiful as any Christmas card, the pair burst into soft trills, creating a harmonious song.

Overcome with emotion, Abby brought her hand to her mouth. "Lord Jesus, thank You. Thank You for the miracle of this day and for every day after. Help me to always be grateful and to trust You, and Luke."

A firm knock sounded on the door, interrupting her prayer. Her dad. Abby blinked back a tear. Today was not a day for weeping but for rejoicing. God would always be with her, to help her conquer her fears, to replace doubts with faith, faith in Him, faith in Luke, and faith in herself.

With one hand on the open door, Dad greeted her with a broad smile. He looked dashing in his tuxedo with its burgundy vest and tie, but his eyes were wistful. "Are you ready, beautiful?" He held his hand out to her. "It's time for me to give my baby girl away."

Abby flew into his arms. "Oh, Dad. I love you so much. I don't know if we would … if Luke and I would even be here if it weren't for you and Mom." She swallowed around the sharp sob forming in her throat. "Thank you for not giving up on Luke."

Dad pressed a kiss to her cheek. "We're proud of you. And of Luke, too. You've both worked hard to get to this day."

Abby stepped back. She didn't want a single ugly shadow from the past to mar her happiness. Today, she and Luke were beginning their new life together, a life that was possible only because of God's great love for them. "God has been so good to us. I'm so thankful. I never imagined I could be this happy, Daddy."

His eye's glistened with restrained emotion. She hadn't called him Daddy in more than five years. "Your mother and I prayed for Luke's recovery every day." He touched her upper arm, then quickly dropped his hand, his expression suggesting he didn't want to wrinkle her sleeve. He took her hand instead, his eyes never leaving her face. "Even at his worst, you loved him, and we chose to love him, too, because you loved him."

"Thank you, Dad." Abby whispered past tears clogging her throat. "But we need to change the subject, or I'm going to cry. And with a splotchy face, I won't take Luke's breath away the way I know Mom did yours."

Dad's smile transformed his face, and his eyes sparkled with joy. Abby knew he was remembering his own wedding day as the first notes of the "Wedding March" drifted from the sanctuary.

"It's time, Abby girl." He clasped her elbow and led her from the room, down the hall, toward her new life.

*

From the other side of Ian, Jake leaned forward to give Luke an encouraging look that he translated as, she'll be here, man. Luke willed his heart to slow to a steady, regular rhythm. He stared at the broad, sanctuary entrance and forced himself to release the breath he'd been holding. *Jesus, thank You for this miracle, for making Abby my wife. Make me the husband she deserves and the father Elise needs.*

Luke drew in another sharp breath. The pianist had started the wedding march several minutes ago, or was it only several seconds? Time seemed transformed into something irregular, unreliable. Had Abby changed her mind? Had she decided she didn't want to marry him after all?

Patience, son.

God's still small voice quieted Luke's nerves and restored his confidence. His heart continued to race with eager anticipation. He had prayed through countless desperate days and nights of withdrawal and temptation for God to set him free and to give him this new life. By God's grace, Luke would never go back to the old one. Faith, like an Artesian well, bubbled from the depths of his heart, and a wave of thanksgiving brought tears to his eyes.

In a moment, his bride would walk down that aisle, and the impossible dream would become real, as real as the solid oak floor beneath his feet. He stared at the doorway, willing her to appear.

And then there she was. His Abby, on her father's arm, moving steadily forward, her eyes never leaving Luke's face. Stunning in a cream-colored gown that hugged her curves, she had never looked more beautiful. Her face radiated pure joy, and for a split second, he remembered the anguish he had put there so many times. So many times, she could have, should have given up on him, but here she was, walking toward him, choosing to unite her life with his, a life in which he would vigilantly guard against even the most minute temptation. A tear slid down his cheek and then another. Abby quickened her steps, and Luke smiled.

When her dad placed her hand in Luke's, he acknowledged the man with a brief nod. Abby leaned close, and before Luke could protest, she kissed the moisture from his face. Then, she stepped back, gave him an encouraging smile, and passed her bouquet to Meg. He and Abby turned as one toward the front of the church, where Pastor Schwartz waited to perform the ceremony that would unite them as husband and wife.

Luke tried to concentrate on the traditional, familiar

words, but the promises in Abby's eyes drew him into an intimate circle that included only the two of them. His heart ached with the force of the love he felt for her, and by the tender, astonished expression in her eyes, he knew she felt it too, this unbreakable bond that God had forged between them. She squeezed his hand, squeezing his heart, too. Wasn't the bride supposed to be the one who cried?

Elise let out an insistent wail, shattering their perfect moment. Abby's expression instantly shifted from alluring wife to concerned mother. The pastor looked to her for a signal to pause or to continue the ceremony. Luke glanced over his shoulder to see his mother carrying Elise from the sanctuary, her whimpers growing faint.

Abby released a breath, and Pastor Schwartz's features relaxed. "The bride and the groom have written their own vows."

Luke took both of Abby's hands in his, praying that neither his memory nor his voice would falter. "Abby, I am honored to become your husband. I don't deserve you, and if it weren't for God delivering me, I wouldn't be standing before you now, the most blessed man on the earth. I promise to never give you cause to doubt me or my commitment to you and to our family. I promise to help make all of your dreams come true. I promise to support you, to comfort you, to laugh with you in happy times, to cry with you in sad times, to work beside you and for you all the days of our lives. I promise to pray with you and to trust God's plan for us. I promise to cherish you as Christ cherishes His church. I promise to lay down my life for you and to love you with all of my strength until my last breath."

Abby's lower lip trembled, and her eyes filled with what he knew were tears of gratitude for God's amazing grace. Luke gave her hands a gentle squeeze of encouragement, and whispered, "Don't cry, babe."

Abby smiled and traced a heart on his left hand. "Luke, I promise to always believe in you. I will honor and respect you. I will never let fear spoil our love. I will never go to sleep angry with you or doubting you. I will never assume I know what you're thinking. I promise to always give you a chance to explain and know you will do the same for me. I will trust that as I bare my heart to you, you will reveal your heart to me, each and every day. With God's help, nothing will ever separate us. I choose you for my husband today and always. I will walk with you through whatever life brings, and I will love you and stay by your side until my last breath."

Luke resisted the urge to lift her into his arms and kiss her.

"Do you have the rings?" Pastor Schwartz asked the best man.

Ian, his best friend and favorite cousin, reached inside his jacket pocket and produced the two platinum bands. He handed them to the minister, who bowed his head to pray. "Heavenly Father, you have brought Luke and Abby through some of the darkest times two people can endure. But we trust from this day forward, as they place their lives in Your perfect care, that you will bless them with a strong and enduring love to sustain their marriage through sickness and health, through good times and bad times. Bless these rings, the symbols of their love and devotion. Amen."

Luke opened his eyes and drank in the sight of his beautiful bride. "With this ring, I thee wed," he said as he slid the slim, platinum band onto her slender finger, overcome again with wonder that so much strength could reside in such a delicate frame. His Abby had tried to be his rock, to save him from himself, and he had nearly broken them both. God helping him, from this moment forward,

Luke vowed to bring her only joy. The dark night of anguish was over. The light of God's love made all things possible. Deliverance, forgiveness, redemption, and a future.

Abby smiled up at Luke. "With this ring, I thee wed," she said, her voice sure and steady as she eased his ring over his knuckle and onto his finger where it would constantly remind him of all he had to be thankful for.

"Before God and these witnesses, I now pronounce you husband and wife. You may kiss your bride."

Luke didn't need to be told twice. He swept Abby up into his arms until her feet dangled against his ankles. He stared down into her sweet face, his Abby, his wife. He covered her mouth with his and drank in the nectar of her love, the precious gift Luke could never have imagined would be his for always.

She giggled against his lips, and he released her, setting her gently beside him. "Let's go greet our guests, Mrs. Bradford."

Abby smiled up at him. "We'd better hurry, Mr. Bradford, before our daughter demands my attention."

He leaned close and planted a kiss on Abby's nose. "I'm okay with sharing you because I know you'll always return to my arms."

With a flirty wink, she tucked her hand in his pocket. "I promise."

He captured her hand, brought it to his mouth, and kissed her palm. "And I promise, to keep all of my promises to you, Abby Bradford. Every single day of this amazing life."

Dear Reader,

When I decided to write a redemption story about recovering from drug addiction, I had no idea my hero would be a heroin addict. Yet, in the midst of the opioid crisis, it seems nearly everyone knows someone affected by this devastating addiction. Perhaps, Abby and Luke's story has spoken to you at the point of your greatest need. Whether it is for yourself or for a loved one, remember that Jesus died to set the captives free. Recovery from addiction may seem nearly impossible, but Matthew 19:26 provides this promise: "With men this is impossible; but with God all things are possible." Absolutely nothing can separate you from God's perfect love. His plan is to give you an abundant life beyond all of your hopes and dreams. Jesus has promised to never leave you nor forsake you. It is my prayer that this story has inspired you to look to God and His unfailing love for yourself and for everyone dear to your heart.

I would be happy to hear from you. Please contact me at authorlaurahervey@gmail.com.

Yours truly,

Laura Hervey

If you enjoyed this book, please consider giving me a review on Amazon, Goodreads, or your favorite book review site.

About Laura Hervey

Laura Hervey writes inspirational romance. Her first novel, *Scarlet Tears,* is a redemption story about a former call girl who rebuilds her life. Laura is also the author of a variety of short works, including articles, opinion pieces, poetry, short stories, and devotionals. *Light in a Dark Place* is her second published novel.

Laura lives in western New York. She attends the Bible Tabernacle, a non-denominational Christian church and is a member of American Christian Fiction Writers. She teaches English Language Arts. When she isn't writing or teaching, she enjoys spending time with her two children and her grandchildren. She shares her home with two dogs, a German shepherd and a miniature Dachshund.

Visit Laura at her author website, www.laurahervey.com, or follow her on Facebook, @AuthorLauraHervey.